Beast

BY

JORDAN MARIE

Cover Art by Letitia Hasser RBA Cover Designs
Models: Connor Smith
Photographer: Reggie Deanching R plus M Photo

WARNING: This book contains sexual situations, violence and other adult themes. Recommended for 18 and above.

I left my past behind me.

I ran.

I didn't slow down, and I *didn't* look back.

I couldn't outrun the memories—*or escape the nightmares.*

I came to North Carolina to die.

Alone.

I want to be left alone.

Which would have been fine, if *she* wasn't here.

Hayden Graham claims to want the same thing I do—to be left alone.

But, she's a thorn in my side.

The woman stumbles into one mess after another.

This time the mess she's in puts her life and her unborn child in danger.

I'm barely existing—rotting from the inside out.

She's a woman in distress, waiting for a Prince to save her.

I'm no Prince. I'm just a wounded animal.

A Beast.

She tastes like Heaven. She only adds to my Hell.

She makes me feel things I don't want to remember…Want things that I can't have.

Hayden just might be the one to finish destroying me.

DEDICATION

Jenny Vaughn Owens, my beautiful new friend, I hope this story lives up to what you wished for Beast. I truly tried my best. Most of all, I hope you have everything good in this world from this day forward. You deserve it.

A special shout out and thank you Liese Haley for letting me use your name, umm…sorry in advance. Also, thank you to Jana Kick for letting me turn you into a sweet nurse who helped our girl Hayden out.

And to the rest of my readers, I hope you love Beast. I tried hard. From the fifty changes on his cover that drove Letitia crazy, to going through a million photos to find the one that was actually Beast to me, and finally to the hours, days and weeks I spent trying to make sure the emotion and pain came through. I worry I failed. I pray I didn't.

Xoxo
#BB4L
J

TABLE OF CONTENTS

Prologue	1
Chapter 1	4
Chapter 2	7
Chapter 3	11
Chapter 4	13
Chapter 5	16
Chapter 6	24
Chapter 7	27
Chapter 8	30
Chapter 9	34
Chapter 10	38
Chapter 11	43
Chapter 12	47
Chapter 13	50
Chapter 14	55
Chapter 15	57
Chapter 16	60
Chapter 17	63
Chapter 18	68
Chapter 19	72
Chapter 20	76
Chapter 21	80
Chapter 22	84
Chapter 23	87
Chapter 24	91
Chapter 25	96
Chapter 26	100
Chapter 27	104
Chapter 28	107
Chapter 29	112
Chapter 30	115
Chapter 31	118
Chapter 32	121

Chapter 33	125
Chapter 34	129
Chapter 35	133
Chapter 36	137
Chapter 37	141
Chapter 38	145
Chapter 39	148
Chapter 40	151
Chapter 41	154
Chapter 42	157
Chapter 43	160
Chapter 44	164
Chapter 45	167
Chapter 46	171
Chapter 47	175
Chapter 48	178
Chapter 49	184
Chapter 50	189
Chapter 51	192
Chapter 52	197
Chapter 53	201
Chapter 54	204
Chapter 55	210
Chapter 56	213
Chapter 57	218
Chapter 58	223
Chapter 59	230
Chapter 60	233
Chapter 61	236
Chapter 62	240
Chapter 63	243
Chapter 64	247
Chapter 65	252
Chapter 66	256
Chapter 67	260
Chapter 68	264
Chapter 69	268
Chapter 70	271
Chapter 71	276
Chapter 72	279
Chapter 73	284

Chapter 74	287
Chapter 75	291
Chapter 76	294
Chapter 77	299
Chapter 78	304
Chapter 79	308
Chapter 80	314
Chapter 81	318
Chapter 82	323
Chapter 83	327
Chapter 84	330
Chapter 85	333
Chapter 86	340
Chapter 87	347
Chapter 88	352
Chapter 89	355
Chapter 90	359
Chapter 91	366
Chapter 92	370
Chapter 93	374
Chapter 94	378
Chapter 95	382
Chapter 96	386
Chapter 97	393
Chapter 98	398
Chapter 99	408
Chapter 100	413
Chapter 101	415
Chapter 102	420
Chapter 103	424
A Note From the Author	427
Other Available Titles by Jordan	428
Links	429

PROLOGUE

Beast

"DADDY, WILL YOU build me a house?"

"If you want me to, Princess. Get your blocks."

She carries a large clear tote bag of blocks. Through the plastic, you can see a vast array of blocks in all the colors of a rainbow. Blocks are her favorite toy and one we've played with for hours upon hours.

"You've been gone, Daddy."

"I had to get some work done."

"You leave me alone a lot. I don't like it," she says, while she pouts her little face, looking up at me with hurt shimmering in those precious blue eyes, hiding the unshed tears I never want to see.

"Daddy has to help Uncle Skull out sometimes. But I always come home to my best girl."

"I get scared when I'm alone, Daddy."

"You have Mommy, Princess."

"Mommy doesn't like me."

"Of course she does, sweetheart. Mommy is just real busy," I tell her, but it's a lie. Jan isn't busy; she's a fucking selfish bitch. I should kick her to the curb, but I don't. I keep her around to help take care of Annabelle. Annie is everything good and right in this world, and I've not seen much of that shit.

"She locked me in my room yesterday when I told her I was scared."

"She did what?"

"There's a monster under my bed, Daddy. A real one. He says I'm going to die. I don't want to die."

"You're not going to die, Princess. Daddy will never let that happen."

"You promise? If I die, who will take care of you?"

"You're not going to die, Princess. Daddy will always protect you. Cross my heart, stick a needle in my eye," I tell her with a grin.

"Ew, Daddy!" she laughs, her nose scrunching. "That's gross! You can't put things in your eye!" she giggles. Her laugh is the single best melody I've heard in my life. It dives down inside me and brings warmth to parts that have been frozen since before I can remember. Sometimes, I think without Annabelle, I wouldn't be here. I was almost a walking shell before she came along. Now my world centers around her. Without her, I don't want to imagine the monster I would become. I'd probably live up to my road name then. The monster who lurks beneath the surface would take over.

Before I can think about the past—the pieces of me that are completely broken, I reach out and tickle Annie. Her giggle deepens, and she lets out a squeal that could shatter glass; it changes into a full-fledged belly laugh. Instantly, it feels as if the sun is shining in the room—which is impossible. There are no windows in her room. I don't want my daughter sleeping where some fuck-wad might break in and take her. I have enemies. There's no way I will let them touch the one person in my life who matters.

I lift Annabelle over my head, rolling on my back. There are little blocks pressing into me, but I ignore the discomfort. Tossing her up in the air and then catching her. It's an old game. *A familiar game*, and her laugh goes on and on, filling me with joy. The only joy I've ever truly known is her beautiful face, laughing and smiling, her eyes shining with love.

This.

This is what life is about. This is why I keep breathing. Annabelle is my air. My reason. My humanity. The one thing that keeps me from truly being....

The Beast.

CHAPTER 1

Beast

I LOOK AT the small, rundown shack and disgust curls in my stomach. The roof is sagging, the clapboard siding is rotting around the footer of the house, the rest is molded green and black from years of weather and neglect. The windows are so old, the wooden frames are decaying around the glass. All the money that Pistol made through the years and this is how his sister lives? When Skull approached me to ask if I would head to North Carolina and check on Pistol's sister, my first instinct was to say no. I was done. I didn't want to have anything to do with my old life. However, when Skull offered me a cabin on Whittler's Mountain in the deal, I finally agreed. A cabin in the mountains away from people sounds like heaven.

I could not care less about Pistol *or* his sister. Pistol is part of the reason my child died. He double-crossed the club I was in and because of that, my daughter was killed. Whatever happens to his sister, I figure she deserves it. I don't give a fuck if she does live in a shack. It's probably *more* than she deserves. Especially if she's anything like her piece of shit brother.

I'm not sure why Skull has gained a conscience about the

woman now. Pistol has been dead for three fucking years. Why give a shit about his sister now? He said he has trouble looking at his daughter and then wondering if Pistol's sister was truly innocent and is paying for the crimes of her brother. Skull took for granted that Pistol's brother, Cade would handle matters with the sister. Apparently, Hayden is only Pistol's half-sister. She's not related to Cade, who didn't even know about her. I guess Skull feels some sense of duty to the bitch. Which means he gave me a mountain—a place to live alone, and all I have to do is check in on the bitch.

What Skull failed to mention was that the barn and converted loft I will be living in is next door to the woman. *The bastard.* It's on my mind to get back on my bike and leave. The problem is, I have nowhere else to go. I sure as hell am not going back to *Kentucky.* My hands are tied, but it takes more energy than I can muster to care. I'll make it clear to the woman I want to be left alone; that will be the last and only time I deal with her. Then, I'll text Skull and tell him the chick is living in a hell-hole…*maybe.*

Walking back to my bike, I veer off at the last minute to take a leak. I've got my pants unzipped and my dick out when all of the sudden I feel something jab me in the back. Looking over my shoulder, I see the long end of a shotgun barrel pointed at me. I follow the length of it until my eyes land on a woman holding the gun. She's five foot nine, maybe ten. Dark bronze hair falls down in dull waves almost to her elbows. There's a beat-up looking brown hat on her head and the clothes she has on are butt-ugly. Maybe she could be decent, but it'd take some damn work. She's skinny—*maybe a little too skinny.* I can see breasts, but they are hard to make out the size of through that huge sweatshirt she's wearing. This woman appears willowy like a strong gust of wind would blow her over, except for one thing.

Her stomach is jutting out, immediately drawing my eye. She's obviously pregnant.

My dick drained, I shake off the excess, slide him back in my pants, and zip up. Then, I turn around to face her.

"You always take a wiz on other people's private property?"

"Only when my dick demands it. You want to lower your gun?"

"Not especially, since you're trespassing. Who are you?"

"I'm going to be your neighbor. Just bought Whittler's Mountain," I tell her, conveniently leaving out the fact that I'll be living next door.

"You look like a mountain man. I didn't know they were selling." She appears confused.

I grunt, walking around her to go back to my bike. "You should leave the gun-handling up to your man. It's dangerous to pull a weapon on a stranger; it could get you killed. You need to think about your baby."

Her eyes darken. "I don't have a man."

"That cantaloupe in your stomach would seem to argue that point," I tell her, my voice straining. I don't talk that much, and I hate the hoarse sound that comes out of my throat sometimes when I speak. It's a reminder of what was taken from me, and I don't need any fucking reminders. I carry that shit with me every second. I look over at the woman one last time. Her gun is down and she's rubbing her hand over her stomach. When she looks back up at me, there's a sadness in her eyes that grabs a hold of my attention.

"Looks can be deceiving," she says.

I shrug and start up my bike. She spares me one last glance, then takes off walking. I watch her almost against my will as she heads back to the old shack I had just been looking at. I guess I just met Hayden Graham…*Pistol's sister.*

CHAPTER 2

Hayden

I WATCH FROM the safety of my front porch as the man on the bike disappears up the hill. I'm not sure how I feel about having someone this close. There was something about him. I can't put my finger on it. I should steer away from him completely. He towers over me, and that's not something that happens much, considering I'm 5'9. His dark hair was pulled back at his neck but a lot was pulled loose from riding on his bike, and it kept his face hid. Yet, even that combined with the large beard he was sporting, didn't hide the scars. They cover parts of his face, especially around one eye. Those are light though, especially pale compared to the ones that run up his hands and disappear under the long sleeved leather coat he's wearing. I've seen enough scars to know those were from a serious fire. I don't know what happened to the man, but I can only imagine the pain he endured.

Still, it isn't that which makes me feel like I need to definitely stay away from him. He's got the appearance of a hardened biker. He reminds me of *them*. That's not the kind of trouble I need. That's how I ended up in the mess I'm in. Not that I think of my daughter as a mess. I rub my stomach in reflex. She'll be everything good—despite how she came to be. That's not her fault. I'll make sure she knows she's loved. That's all I want her to know. *Love.* I don't want the ugliness of this world to touch Maggie…*not like it did me.*

Pushing my thoughts aside, I walk into the house. I'm not actually sure you can call it a house, but it's more of one than I've ever had, and I'll make sure my daughter is happy here. *My daughter.* I'm naming her Maggie. It's not terribly original. It happens to come from my favorite Rod Stewart song, *Maggie May.*

My tiny house does need work though, and sadly it's work that I'm not capable of doing. It's winter, and January at that. The next few months will be the coldest we've had. The roof might hold for a bit longer, though the leaks are getting worse. The cold air coming through the windows and poorly insulated walls freeze me as it is, let alone a few months down the road, when Maggie arrives. I can't let that happen. My only source of heat is a fireplace and some electric heaters I picked up at a secondhand store. I need to find something safer for when the baby is with me. That problem, coupled with the fact that I don't really know anyone who does that kind of work, is summed up in one word—*money.* Working as a waitress in town, I don't get paid minimum wage. I get paid much, much less because I'm allowed to keep my tips. Tips that most people in town rarely leave, besides the odd dollar here and there. That means money is almost nonexistent. I don't have a lot of skills. I didn't get to finish high school; I've never had any kind of training. I am basically good at two things in my life…waiting on people and baking. So, I'm a waitress who has started a side job baking cakes, pies, cookies, and anything else I can think of that might sell. Several local businesses offer my items for sale now. The church and my boss being the main two, and because of them, I've managed to make quite a bit extra. Still, money is tight, and I have a long way to go before I can afford to hire a handyman. The other main problem with that is I have no idea how I can handle having someone in my house. I figure I'll have to cross that bridge when I come to it.

That thought is somewhat depressing as I walk into the kitchen, standing by the sink. I try to shake myself from my thoughts on things that aren't changing anytime soon. Instead, I concentrate on everything I need to accomplish today. Pastor Sturgill will be by later, and when he comes, he will expect no less than three pies and five dozen cookies. I don't have time to worry or daydream.

The sound of a motorcycle jars me, causing my head to jerk up, looking out the window over the kitchen sink. I see the man coming back off the hill. Instead of turning left to cut back on the main highway that leads into town and away from our adjoined driveways, he turns right. Something about that causes my heart to kick up in speed. I watch as he drives straight to the old barn.

I move quickly to the window by my kitchen table. It has a perfect view of the barn and fear begins to form in the pit of my stomach, making me feel nauseous, while I continue watching the stranger. He pulls his bike into the covered parking area that connects to the barn, shuts it off, and he sits there for a minute. Just that simple motion causes my breathing to increase. There's only one reason he would pull into the old barn. *Only one*, and it's not a reason I like. It's a reason that *terrifies* me.

I watch as he gets off the bike, walking to the small door under the shed that has remained locked by an old rusty padlock. I have a bad feeling about this—*a very bad feeling*. Then I watch as he reaches in his pocket. *No. He can't be doing that. There's no way...right? RIGHT?*

My hopes are dashed as the chain and lock fall to the ground.

I have a new neighbor...only he won't be on top of the hill away from me. He's going to live across from me in the old barn.

What will happen now? I try to swallow down my panic and my fear. I try, but I don't think I fully succeed. Surely God can't be this cruel. Haven't I been through enough? Will I have to move now? How can I live this close to him...a man who reminds me of *them?* For all I know, he *could be* one of them. That knowledge sinks into the pit of my stomach and it's all I can do not to throw-up.

I can feel the nerves and panic clawing at me, but I do my best to beat those feelings back down. I can't let the anxiety get to me. Not today. I had been doing so much better. I can't go backwards. I have to be strong.

I have to think of Maggie.

CHAPTER 3

Beast

I CAN FEEL eyes on me. Too many years being across the sea and on enemy land has ingrained that feeling inside me. Since there is only one house around and no one else is here, I know who is watching me. I don't turn around to look at her. There's no point. She's already stopped existing for me. As far as I'm concerned, I will never talk to her again, and I'll be just as happy if I never see her again.

I take the key Skull gave me and turn the old lock. It doesn't turn smooth, what has to be years of rust hinders it. I get it to break free with a quick yank, then the lock and the chain fall to the floor. I open the door and instantly, a musty odor assaults me. This place hasn't been opened up in years. Maybe since Pistol himself came here. That turns my stomach. Somehow, the idea of sleeping in a bed Pistol has been in sickens me. I wonder if there's a cleaning service in town?

I go up the narrow stairway, not bothering to use the light switch. I'll need to go into town if I want lights. I make it into the loft, which has been converted to a very small studio type apartment. There's a kitchen in the corner that consists of an apartment size stove, a small single bowl sink, and an old fridge that I am at least three feet taller than. They don't really match either. The fridge is silver, obviously, a bit newer than the other appliances. The stove is a putrid green and probably was on this Earth before I was born. The sink is white enamel, all one piece, that has cabinets underneath it. There are no other cabinets in the place at all. There's a small table that is only large enough for one chair to be pushed under it. Across from that area lies the living room; which consists of a couch. The couch is old, but probably not as old as the stove. It's covered in a brown and beige fabric that has horrible pictures of a tree stump pattern that repeats over and over. I'm not sure who ever thought that would be a good design, but I hope the designer found something else in life to do, because designing furniture wasn't their calling. In a far corner, there's an old metal bed with a mattress so swayed and lumpy you can physically see it. Beside the bed sits a tub and a toilet. I shake my head, it's all out in the open. None of this shit matters to me though. I can crash here and be alone. That's all I care about.

As rough as my new surroundings are…as *barebones* as it all is, not once do I regret my decision to come here. *Not once.* I don't miss my club. I don't miss my brothers. I don't miss my room there. But most of all, I don't miss the noise.

Right now, all around me is *nothing.* Not a word, not a whisper, there is absolutely nothing in this room but the silence I seek.

This is what I want.

This is what I need.

To be surrounded by…nothing. For a minute, I just stand here and let it envelop me.

I hope the silence suffocates me.

CHAPTER 4

Hayden

"I WILL BE *better today. I will be stronger. I will be better today. I will be stronger,"* I whisper the same two sentences over and over. I whisper them as I make my way through the house. I whisper them as I take my shower. The words stumble, getting lodged in my throat as the soap glides across the scars along my ribs, and even more so as I touch the jagged skin that wraps around my back. *Still,* I get those words out. I count the victory and keep repeating the mantra as I shower and dress.

I'm still saying the words softly, to break up the quiet in the house, as I wash the few dishes that were left from the night before. I'm gazing out the window in my kitchen, when I see the man walk out of the barn. He goes to his bike and appears to be looking for something in the saddlebags. My hand shakes, but I don't let that deter me, because today's goal is simple: *do not panic.*

I watch for a few more minutes until he disappears back into the barn. I'm being stupid, allowing who this man is, or at least who he appears to be, to drag me back down. I put that behind me. That is over. It's buried. *It's dead.* This man is *not* those people. He is not my brother. *That man is nothing to me.*

It doesn't matter if he lives this close. He doesn't know me. I don't know him. He's not here to get to know me. The mere fact he's moving next door is nothing more than rotten luck, and God knows I have had more than my fair share of that.

My hand goes to my stomach in reflex, and I rub the small bump that has now formed on my stomach, when I feel Maggie move and shift. I'm a couple of months behind on my doctor's visits. I hate myself for that. I have insurance, but the local doctor in town knows my history; *knows it and clearly does not approve.* He's always billing me, and I'm beginning to think it's not what I would truly owe after insurance. I think the charges are only what he wants to add to the bill—because he can. If there was another obstetrician in this small town I would go there. But there's not, so I put up with his leering looks and the hateful attitude of his staff, because I don't have a real choice. I let them treat me like crap, which is weak, and I hate being weak. *Today I will be stronger.* The thought pops in my mind, mocking me.

I turn away from the window. I need to get busy packing up everything I made yesterday. Pastor Sturgill will be here any moment, and I don't want to keep him waiting on me. The church's business means a lot to me. The Pastor has helped get my baked goods out there and not only that, he gave me open access to their secondhand shop. I've been able to pick up a baby crib, a dresser, and even a bassinet. They weren't the best thing out there, but they were in decent shape, and with my next check I will be able to purchase a new mattress. I will make sure Maggie has *everything* she needs.

I'm so engrossed in my thoughts and boxing things up that I'm completely caught off guard when there's a tapping noise on the back door.

I wrap my arms around myself until my heart rate begins to calm.

Today I will be stronger…

Maybe not so much.

CHAPTER 5

Beast

I KNOW SHE'S in there. I watched her through the window. On my third round of knocking, I've about had enough. I walk to the small kitchen window and bang on the glass with the flat of my hand. I don't knock on it easy, though not quite as hard as I would like to since the glass is cracked, and the window itself looks older than I am. Hell, it might even be older than that damn stove in the rat-hole I slept in last night. She walks to the window as though she's in a trance, her eyes widen, staring back at me like a deer caught in the headlights of a speeding car.

I didn't think she was much to look at yesterday. She appears marginally better today; her hair doesn't seem as dark. It's almost strawberry color in places, before slowly fading into darker hues. It's long. I don't think I appreciated how long, which is weird because it was worn down yesterday. Today, it's pulled to the top of her head and laying in a crazy mess, that somehow looks natural. What I am noticing more today, are her eyes. They're as large as saucers right now, as she gapes at me. I can see fear and the disgust flickering in them. Do my scars bother her? Yesterday, it had been cloudy and close to dark, maybe she missed them. Just like I didn't notice that her eyes are a strange shade of blue—especially the right one which is a little darker in color. They could almost be called a steely gray.

She moves quickly from the window, and I cuss under my breath. *What the fuck is her problem?* Without a thought, I make it back to the door. I yank hard on the handle at the same exact time she's on the other side opening it.

I let out a grunt when the woman stumbles into me. I catch her easily. My hands grabbing on each side of her, my thumbs and fingers are pressing against breasts that I could have sworn I thought were small yesterday. I hold her still. She doesn't speak, and I'm not sure if it's that fact or the feel of a woman in my arms after all this time that pisses me off more.

I steady her away from me, letting her go, and taking her in. She's wearing another loose sweater that is about three sizes too big, though her stomach is definitely protruding from it. The only difference in this one and the one from yesterday is that this one is a pale yellow and looks better on her.

I know fuck-all about pregnant women. I've done everything I could to stay away from them and Jan…Fuck, I didn't even know she was pregnant for most of the pregnancy. But this one appears exhausted. *Not my problem.* Where in the hell is her man? Obviously, she can't even walk on her own. There's no way she should have a baby on her own. I wouldn't even trust her to hold a child.

A wave of memories crashes down on me. All these thoughts about Jan, of her pregnancy, of Annabelle…*these thoughts are not welcome*. They aren't wanted—*at all.* The fact that the woman standing in front of me caused them to attack me makes me snarl. I watch as the sound I make causes her to jump back like a frightened rabbit.

"Wha…" she starts but stops to take in a shaky breath.

"What are you doing here?" she finally gets out.

I clear my throat. If I could go the rest of my life not speaking, I'd be okay with that. The sound of my voice has been altered from the accident and it serves as one more reminder. *A reminder I don't need.* I clear my throat and rub my hand across my beard, scratching under my chin, subconsciously touching one of the scars I hide behind the hair.

"I need to plug in my phone."

"What?"

"I don't have power. I need my phone charged."

"You don't have power," she mimics, as if she's in a trance. Her eyes are still holding mine captive, and I have to wonder if she's mentally disabled or some shit.

"I just said that," I tell her, getting irritated.

"You want me to charge your phone? *In my house*?" she questions, her eyes widen even further, and she takes two steps back. I nod yes, instead of speaking. "I can't do that," she says, shaking her head back and forth for emphasis.

"Why the hell not?"

"I don't know you."

"I'm not asking you to suck my dick, just charge my phone."

Her head whips back. I shouldn't have said that. She's not the kind of woman I'm used to dealing with. I see the moment my words hit her, there is not a blush like I would expect to see from a woman hearing something so vulgar. No. She's completely different. Her face goes deathly white. She's so pale it wouldn't surprise me if she passes out.

Instead, her head goes down, and I hear a faint mumble come from her, that I have to strain to hear. "I have to go," she says.

I reach out to grab her hand; I'm not even sure why at this point. She tries to push away from me, and I really should let her go, but the woman is annoying me. I mean, *Jesus*, I only want to charge my damn phone. I'd charge it on my bike, but I don't have the right cord. I hold onto her tighter, stopping her from walking away. For a second my eyes go to our joined hands. Hers are small, tiny, and pale compared to mine. The scars marring my hand look even more grotesque with the way the skin stretches just to capture her hand...*It looks wrong.*

Skull and the others tried to convince me once that life didn't have to change. I wanted to believe them. Memories of the day we had a family picnic come to mind. I can hear Lucy and those girls laughing in the back of my mind. My brothers thought I was sweet on the girl. Maybe I was at one time, who knows. At the very least I enjoyed the hero worship she showed me. I would have never acted on it. She was too young for me, and I had been burned so hard when it came to women.

Jan was a fucking cunt. I was trapped with her. I would have made a bed with the devil himself to keep my daughter with me, however. The idea of Jan taking her away—not seeing Annabelle and being able to protect her every day...*terrified me.* So, I did my best to swallow down my fucking pride and keep Jan happy for no other reason than to keep my daughter safe with me. In the end, I failed to protect Annabelle...I failed to be the father she needed...

"Is there a problem?" A man asks, walking around the side of the house.

I was so lost in the past I never heard another vehicle pull in the driveway. I didn't even hear him approaching. This is just another reason why it was a good idea to leave the Devil's Blaze. I was going to end up getting one of my brother's killed.

I turn my attention back to the man who just appeared. I'm kind of thankful he pulled me from my thoughts. I already have sweat popping out over my body and my stomach is churning.

Fuck.

I do my best to concentrate on the now. This man is tall, though not my height. He stands over six foot—*easily.* He's also the opposite of me. Clean cut, with a suburb vibe, wearing navy dress slacks and a shirt with a collar in an annoying color of orange.

The woman is whimpering and gasping like I'm inflicting pain on her. Is she sickened by my touch? Does she hate the fact my hands are grotesque and on her body? *Join the fucking club lady.*

I let her go and she immediately flees from me. The man stands on the deck, facing me—as if he's guarding the woman from me. She instantly moves behind him, half hiding, as if for protection. Something about that sits wrong with me, but I ignore it. I don't know what her issues are, but they aren't my concern.

"No problem. I was asking the lady if she could charge my phone so I could check on getting electricity hooked up. I think from what I'm getting, the answer is no," I tell him. Fuck it. I'd rather just go back to the barn and drink in the damn dark.

"Are you okay, Hayden?" the man asks her, and that just pisses me off more.

"Of course, she's alright. All I did was ask if I could plug my phone in," I growl, defensively.

"I'm okay," Hayden whispers, biting her lip, and refusing to look at me. *Jesus. What is her damage?*

"Good. Do you have the baked goods ready?" he asks her.

"Yes. I was just getting them together when…when I had company," she says, and I wonder where the woman from yesterday is. She talked to me without stuttering then. She didn't act like this. It has to be the scars, either that or not having the gun in her hand makes her feel unsafe. I shouldn't be curious, but there's a side of me wanting to hear exactly why she's acting as if I'm about to kill her today compared to yesterday when she was ready to kill *me*.

"Good. We'll get them in a minute," the man says, patting her hand reassuringly. She's definitely not backing away from him. He's probably the baby daddy. It's clear he's nothing like me, maybe that's why she's got her ass in a knot.

My appearance probably offends the bitch. *Too bad for her.* It can't offend her more than it does myself. Hell, I can't think of the last time I looked in a mirror.

"I'm Pastor Sturgill. I run the Little Pines Baptist Church in town," the man informs me, extending his hand.

I look at it for a minute, then shake it, reluctantly. I grunt in response.

When it becomes clear I'm not going to answer, the man prompts me. "And you are?"

My first reaction is to give him my club name. It's the only name I've used for years—more years than I care to remember. The problem with that is, I'm no longer part of the club. Skull may not have accepted my Blaze cut back, but I left it behind anyway. I left it and the club. *I'm no longer that man.*

"Michael," I answer, giving my name for the first time in years.

"Michael, it's good to meet you. Are you new to the area?"

"Yes. I just bought the old barn over there."

"You're living in a barn loft?" the man asks.

"Yeah," I grumble, annoyed.

"Well then, that's all fine and good. I'm sure Hayden will feel more comfortable knowing there's someone close by for her to call if she needs something."

I'm just as sure that's not what's going through her head, but I don't correct him.

"There's an outlet off Hayden's front porch. I'm sure she

wouldn't have an objection to you charging your phone there, would you Hayden?"

"I…I guess not."

"Good. That's settled."

"Fine. Thanks," I tell them and turn away. The thank you sticks in my throat. I don't see what the big damn deal is, but I would rather it be this way. I won't have to deal with anyone.

I go plug my phone in, and I'm stomping back over to my place when the Pastor's voice stops me. "Might I have a word, Michael?"

Christ. Why didn't I just let the phone go? I started to, but years of being conditioned to always keep one active for the club and for Annie…*Fuck.*

"What?" I growl, and because of the memories I've accidentally set off inside of me, it is a growl.

"I was wondering if we might have a word while Hayden is inside."

"What could we possibly have to talk about, Rev?"

"I'm no reverend. God says put no reverence on any man, I'm merely his servant," he replies, and I don't know what the hell I'm supposed to say to that, so I shrug and wait. "Hayden is very sensitive."

"That's one way of putting it. No worries, man. I have no plans on even talking to her again."

"That might be for the best. She's had enough trauma in her life. I won't have her hurt again. It's important that you know she will be watched over."

"Is she yours?"

"Pardon?"

"Is she your woman? That baby she's carrying, you put it there?"

"Of course not."

"Where I'm from a man—*a real man*, takes care of what's his, so if she's yours you are obviously doing a piss-poor job of it."

"I'm her pastor. I assure you there's nothing else, but I do care about her. I need to know she'll be safe here with you so close."

"She'll be as safe as she ever was. I don't intend to look at her again, let alone talk to her," I tell him, and that's the God's honest truth.

Exhausted, I walk away. I've already talked too much. I want to forget the fucking world and crash with a bottle of whiskey and darkness. *Is that so much to ask?* Behind me, I hear the woman tell the man she's ready to go. I don't look back, but for some strange reason I want to. Her voice is softer than it was yesterday, but I can still hear the anxiety in it. That's not why I refuse to turn around. No, it's those pale eyes of hers I want to gaze into. Because in them, I think I see as much pain as I have mirrored in mine. I relish in thinking that someone else has suffered as much as I have. I enjoy the idea so much that I want to see it again—but I deny myself that comfort.

"Let's get going, Hayden. I was just saying goodbye to Michael. You'll like having him as a neighbor. I know you like your solitude, but Michael is the name of God's most trusted archangel. He's the one who leads the battle against evil."

Fuck. It's been awhile, but I feel a rusty laugh pull up from my chest. It ends as more of a cough, but it was there.

"I'm no angel, Rev," I toss out carelessly over my shoulder, as I keep walking away.

CHAPTER 6

Hayden

I'M SO MAD at myself. I acted like an idiot. It was a combination of the way he looked and the blunt way he talked. He left me feeling rattled. The expression on his face didn't help. He looked so…*angry*. His sexual remark slapped me across the face, and since I was already a little panicked…*I became an idiot.*

"You did really good today, Hayden," Pastor Sturgill says, as he pulls into the parking lot of the diner. He's dropping me off. Then a co-worker, Liese, will take me home. I would have driven myself, but the Pastor always insists he takes me to stock my baked goods at the stores. I think he worries about me. He along with my boss, Charlie are the two that helped me four months ago, when I was at my worst. He's appointed himself my caretaker and unofficial counselor. I feel safe around him, so I can't deny his council helps. I take a deep breath before turning to him.

"Not so good around my new neighbor. He's going to think I'm crazy, Pastor Sturgill. Maybe I am."

"You're not. You're rebuilding your life and Michael is…well, let's just say he's bound to remind you of things in your past that you don't want to remember."

"Maybe, but I should be the last person to cast judgment at the way a man dresses or looks. I hate when people treat me like that, just because they think they know my past."

"You're going to be okay, Hayden. You don't see it because you're a little lost right now, but you're a very strong young woman. That baby inside of you is lucky to have you." He smiles, glancing at my stomach.

His words should warm me. My hand goes to my stomach, and instead of warmth, I'm filled with fear. *What if I fail her?* I look out the window, trying to shake off the worries and sadness.

"I hope you're right, Pastor Sturgill." I look at the sky and frown. "It looks like we might be in for some rough weather."

"The weather forecast mentioned some severe storms. You have emergency supplies, right? In case the power goes out?"

"Yeah, I'll be fine. Thank you for your help today. I wish you'd let me pay you for the gas. You can't keep doing this for free."

"I can and I will. It's a blessing to be able to help you. Stop trying to take away my blessing, Hayden."

"Whatever you say. Thank you, again. I really appreciate it." I open the door to get out and I'm outside, almost closing the car door, before he speaks up again with the same question he always asks me.

"You coming to church Sunday? We sure would love to have you."

"Thank you…I might," I tell him the lie, then I close the door before he can give a reply.

I GOT THROUGH my shift at work, because I didn't have a choice. Charlie always takes it easy on me, making sure I have time to catch my breath, and giving me the easier tables; if she didn't I might have already quit. It also helps that the diner is never really busy.

Liese dropped me off ten minutes ago, and I'm standing outside my door like an idiot, holding the one loaf of banana bread that I kept from earlier this morning. The rest of the stuff sold, and I have more money in my wallet than I've had in forever. I'm even hoping to get the mattress for Maggie's crib after work tomorrow.

I look at the banana bread I saved. I didn't really think this through. I wanted to give it to my new neighbor as an apology. I was hoping he would be outside when I made it home. He's not. I can see the chrome shining on his bike, under the shed. I know he's there, but when I look at the large, black barn with the shiny silver tin roof, I know there's no way I have the nerve to take it to him. Oh well, it will keep. Maybe he'll be out tomorrow, and I can give it to him then. I walk into the house with one last look up at the barn. When I lock the door, I repeat the words to myself that I hope will someday be true.

I'll be stronger tomorrow.

CHAPTER 7

Beast

SOME THINGS EVEN alcohol won't kill. It might be rotting my liver, but it sure as hell does nothing to stop the memories. There are days when I wonder why the fuck I don't swallow a bullet and end it all. That seems like a fucked up way to go out. I was hoping the war with the Saints would pan out, and I could have at least gone out in a blaze of glory. Staring at the bottle of Jack I'm holding, I observe that it's only half gone, but I'm losing my taste for it. The liquor isn't doing what it needs to do. *Maybe nothing can.*

They turned the lights on today, but I'm still sitting here in the dark. I like the darkness better. It matches my mood. There's a storm outside. Rain is pounding on the tin roof, and lightning keeps flashing and casting quick bursts of light through the windows. It would be peaceful to me…if I could ever find peace again.

Annabelle used to hate storms. They scared her. She'd get in bed with me, and I'd hold her while telling her stories to ease her fear. Funny how little things like that are what you miss the most. There's so many moments to choose from, but it's the simple times I shared with my baby girl that I miss the most. When I remember them, they feel like they're burning a hole inside of my heart. Rubbing my chest, I close my eyes.

Instantly, Annabelle's face is there. Her beautiful smile and those gorgeous blue eyes. There's so much I miss about her...*so much I hunger for now.* At the top of my list is the way she used to laugh. God, I miss that sound. The way her laugh could light up even the darkest parts of me. She had a beautiful laugh.

The thing that fucks with my head the most is: *I can't hear her laugh now.* I *want* to hear her...just one more time. *I'd give anything for that.* Then, I would commit it to memory, because for the life of me, I can't hear it in my head. It's not there. It's a piece of my daughter that is now just a faint whisper. It's a part of Annabelle that I'm losing, and it's *killing* me. Her sweet melodic laugh is gone forever. *No one cares.* I'm the only one who is torn apart inside, and I can't do a damned thing to change it. It doesn't matter how hard I *crave* it, I can barely hear my own daughter's laughter. I know one day I'll lose her completely. All but one thing. Because the only thing that I can't forget... *are her screams.*

God, her screams haunt me... they're destroying me. A real man...*a real father* would have saved her. He would have found a way. *I failed.* You read all the time how these parents do amazing things to save their children in times of emergency. Some woman lifted a whole fucking car. I read that somewhere. *I was useless.* I couldn't do something as simple as get my daughter out of a car. She was alive. I heard her yelling...I heard her crying for me. I heard her *begging* for me. *"Daddy!"* she cried out in full panic. I tried to get to her. I tried so fucking hard, but it was all for nothing. *I failed her.* I failed my princess. My scars are a permanent reminder. A reminder that I am a failure.

A large crash next door makes me jerk, and I do my best to push the thoughts of Annabelle away. My hands are shaking.

Fuck, I can even feel tears as the wetness pools on my face. This is what I am now…a fucking drunk who cries alone in the dark. I hear another crashing noise, and it's closely followed by a loud scream. I put my whiskey down and stumble to look out the window. A tree has fallen in my neighbor's backyard. It looks like it missed the majority of the house, but clearly part of the tree crashed through one of her back windows. I start to turn away, going back to lay down. That's when I see her come outside in the pouring rain.

What the fuck does she think she can do? Is she going to try and move the whole tree? Doesn't she care that she's carrying a baby?

A better question might be why the hell I care. She's nothing to me. Just another selfish, stupid woman. I walk back to the couch, dismissing her. She's probably just like Jan. Obviously, she doesn't have a maternal bone in her body. I grab the bottle and take another swig. Maybe I can drink until I pass-out. Closing my eyes, allowing the memory of Annabelle to come back to me, I will it to never leave.

"Daddy," her voice calls out to me. She's reaching for me, and I need to touch her. I extend my hand, trying to do just that—take her outstretched hand in mine. I can almost feel her. Then she's gone, her voice… it disappears when the sound of an engine rumbles. I drop the whiskey bottle, not caring that it lands on its side and pours out onto the old wooden floor. I walk to the window, my head swimming, and I'm not sure if that's from the alcohol or from the strength of the memories. Lightning streaks through the sky again, and I see that crazy-ass woman standing in the pouring rain holding what looks and sounds to be a fucking chainsaw.

"Son of a bitch!" I growl out. I should get out there before she gets herself killed. *She's a fucking lunatic.*

CHAPTER 8

Hayden

DAMN IT! *Does God hate me?* How much more does he expect me to take? I stare at the limbs and broken glass that just showered over the baby's bed. One of the branches crashed against the bassinet and crushed in the top. I was going to use that to put her in my room at night… I start to cry. I can't stop my tears, and I hate crying. I've spent so much time crying, and doing so is a big reinforcement that I'm weak. That's not the feeling I want to teach my daughter. It's not a feeling I ever want Maggie to feel.

For her part, Maggie picks this moment to kick me—*hard.* That feels like her telling me enough is enough and really, *it is.* It's more than enough. I will not let some *fucking* tree be what breaks me after all the shit that I've endured up to this point in my life. This tree will not rob my daughter! With that thought and little else, I throw on my hand-me-down yellow raincoat. That was smart, well the smartest thing about this whole endeavor. Then, I push my feet into the nearest available shoes and march to the door with only one thing on my mind. *Revenge.*

My first stop is the old rickety shed at the end of my yard.

The rain is pouring down, and it might have been a little smarter (as if anything about this could be) had I stopped to grab a flashlight. Luckily, (if it doesn't strike me) lightning keeps flashing and helps shine my way through the dark. In the shed, there's an old chainsaw. I found it here along with some other tools after I moved in. I never got rid of any of it, and now I'm glad for that.

I've never started a chainsaw in my life, but it has to be kind of like a lawnmower, right? The task sure seems a lot harder than I imagined. After the sixth time (okay probably closer to ten) of trying to start the damn thing, my arm is tired, and the fire inside of me is starting to subside. I decide to try one more time, and by a miracle of miracles, it actually works. I somehow manage to find the throttle and press the lever. Instantly, the motor cranks up. I keep my finger there, gunning it gently. Then, I walk back towards the house and that damn tree.

The chainsaw is heavier than I planned for and that along with the rain tries to exhaust me, but I must do this. I will not get pushed around anymore. I'm not going to stop until I prove that not only to myself, but my daughter. I bring the bar of the chainsaw down on the tree. Sawdust instantly gets thrown out everywhere. I feel a moment of elation, but in reality, I only manage to get the blade about an inch inside the tree when it stops cutting. I pull it out and start again. Apparently, the chain is so dull that I'm going to have to do this in slow increments. I don't care. I'm doing it and that's all that matters.

It's raining so hard I can't see, even with the lightning. Everything is blurry, because water is pouring down my face, interfering with my vision. The sound of the chainsaw, the pounding of the rain, and the thunder all combine to be so loud I hear nothing. Add all of that to the fact that I'm completely engrossed in what I'm doing, and I don't hear or notice anything around me. So, when this giant bear behind me growls out, I scream like a little girl.

"What the fuck do you think you're doing?" Michael yells through the noise, and I scream. Okay, it isn't a bear. But he's hairy and mean enough to be one.

I jerk around to face him, pulling the heavy chainsaw with me. Only, I forget to let off the throttle, and in my fear actually press harder. I hold the chainsaw in front of me like a weapon, wielding it like I'm Hercules lifting a sword. This probably isn't a smart move, because it's *really* heavy, and my arms are so tired that it begins to tip back towards my chest and face. I lean my body back to get away from the weapon, adrenaline making my body shake. I admit the smarter thing would have been to let off the throttle, or to at least pull my arm forward, but I'm kind of in a panic. I also pee a little on myself, but I'm blaming that on Maggie. She does like to dance on my bladder.

I scream again when the hand I have on the handle of the chainsaw is grabbed…*hard.* My first reaction is to fight for control, which lunges the chainsaw toward Michael. I, stupidly, still don't take my hand off the throttle and instead try to get control of the chainsaw. I don't know why, except it's mine, and he looks mean. I don't think it'd be wise to give it to him.

Okay, maybe that's a good enough reason.

When I don't immediately turn loose, he twists my wrist, and the pain spreads instantly from there and up my arm. I cry out, but lose my hold on the chainsaw. He grabs it and physically throws it away from us. It lands ten feet across from us in a large mud puddle—instantly dying. I stare at it. I glance at him. Next, I glare at the hold he has on my wrist. Then, I look at him again. His long hair is loose now. It's not held back by anything, and the rain has drenched him so that beads of water cling to his face and neck. His long beard reflects the same state and there are droplets of water running from the burly hair.

Lightning chooses this moment to blast through the sky, highlighting his face. I blink against the rain, thinking what I just witnessed can't be true, and jumping as the sound of thunder rolls around us. Mother Nature in her infinite wisdom, chooses this moment to unleash another large flash of lightning. I think Mother Nature might just be a bitch, because now I can see clearly. My captor's face is revealed in the stark light. His dark eyes are looking down at me, and I swear it appears as though liquid hate is rolling off him and pouring into me. The stark scars on his face are menacing with so much anger held on his face, and right before we're plunged back into darkness, an image of Jack Nicholson from the movie, *The Shini*ng comes to mind. I jerk my hand to get it free.

He refuses to let go.

I try again, with the same result.

Finally, after all this, I do what any sane woman would do under similar circumstances.

I faint.

CHAPTER 9

Beast

I'M ABOUT TO light into the crazy fool when she goes slack in my arms. I'm tempted to let her fall in the rain and leave her laying there. With my luck, she'd pick up that fucking chainsaw again and actually succeed in killing herself this time. Instead, I pick her up in my arms and carry her to the door of her house.

She might be pregnant, but she weighs next to nothing. She's obviously not taking care of herself, another mark against her. I shuffle her body around so I can open the door, then I take her inside. The house is cool, *almost cold.* I walk her through the small hallway. I have to walk at an angle to prevent raking her legs or head against the pale blue walls. I get her into the living room. There's a piece of crap couch in there with actual duct tape covering tears in the worn fabric. All the money Pistol made through the years and *this* is the shithole his sister lives in.

My stomach turns, and if the man were alive, I'd be sure to kill him again. Laying her on the couch, I then proceed to the small fireplace. Grabbing a couple pieces of wood that she has placed close by, I put them on the fire while raking through the red embers. It doesn't take long for the popping and crackling sound of wood burning to be heard.

Glancing back at the woman, I see she's still out. I think about taking her coat off, something to help so that she doesn't catch pneumonia from being so wet. In the end, I do none of that. I don't have it in me to touch her, and I don't really want to look at her.

Instead, I walk back through her house, looking for the window that was broken. I find it in a small bedroom in the rear of the house. It's obviously the room she is turning into a nursery. There's wallpaper on the walls that's a pale yellow about half way up the wall that has little stripes on it. The rest of the wall has been painted a creamy white and there are zoo animals hand-painted above the wallpaper. The animals are cartoon like, but expertly drawn. They're all wearing some kind of strange article of clothing in yellow that matches the wallpaper. There's an elephant wearing a yellow beret, a penguin wearing a yellow tie, a hippo wearing a yellow tutu, and I stop looking when I see a lion wearing a yellow hat and matching scarf, because by then, I see the window.

Raking my hand along the side of my face, I scratch my beard, and automatically search for the deep groove of the scar I have there. I shouldn't bother. *This isn't my job.* This woman isn't my concern. Still, I find myself figuring out what I need to board up the window in here. If I don't do it, the crazy woman will be back outside trying to saw the damn tree again. I look at the baby furniture in the room. Clearly secondhand, and though there's nothing wrong with buying used furniture, these pieces are crap. They're completely worn-out, about all they are fit for is a bonfire. Then I notice the crushed bassinet.

Something sifts through my gut that I can't name, and I'm not about to investigate. Whatever the feeling is, however, becomes the deciding factor. I find a flashlight on her kitchen counter. The batteries are weak so the light is pale at best, but it will have to work. I go outside to the small shed by her house I noticed earlier. It doesn't take me long to find the supplies I need.

The first thing I grab is an axe that's hanging on the side of the wall, then take it back to the tree. I cut off enough of the branches so that I can physically push the tree, dislodging it from the house. The rain has slowed, but it hasn't stopped, so that's all I fool with for the night. Then I return to the shed to grab the ratty old piece of plywood and some assorted nails. It's not much, but it will work until she can get someone out here to work on it.

When I go back inside, the woman is standing by the door to the room. She looks pale and there's a tremble in her body that visibly moves through her when she sees me. I ignore it—*and her.* At least she's changed into dry clothing, she must not be a complete idiot. I allow a brief glance. Apparently clothes that are three sizes too big for her are all that she wears. I begin picking up the broken glass and clearing the small room of the debris.

"I can do that," she whispers. I ignore her, grunting as I continue to work. "You really don't need to do all that. You've done enough," she says again.

I grunt, mostly ignoring her, as I take the large pieces of glass and set them inside a bucket I found in her mudroom when I first came through the door.

"Broom," I order.

She jumps, wrapping her arms around herself. "What?" she asks, but I don't repeat, I only sigh in frustration and wait. She swallows nervously, then runs in the direction of the kitchen. She's back with a broom and dustpan. She starts to sweep but I take the broom from her. She freezes and looks up into my eyes. I look at her wrist and I can tell there's a bruise forming. I did that. The sight of it annoys me as much as she does.

"No," I tell her, taking over.

She stands there watching me, but thankfully doesn't offer to talk further. When I get the room reasonably cleaned up and the debris cleared out—even the tree limbs, I decide I've had enough. I pick up the broken bassinet to toss out to burn later when she speaks again.

"Please. Mr. um…well…*Michael.* Don't do that. I want to keep it."

I freeze and look over at her. It's been so long since a woman has said my name, it feels weird to hear it. I'm not sure I like it.

"It's broken," I mumble, telling her something she should already know, and doing it while hating the sound of my own voice.

"I know, but it can still be used. I'll take the top off it and just use the bed part itself. It will be fine."

"It's broken.

"*I know,*" she insists, a little more forcefully, her face flushing into a pale red. "I can still use it to keep the baby in my room," she says, her hand trembling as she moves it across her round stomach. "It will work until I can afford something better," she states, her voice sounds defensive.

Her feelings aren't my concern.

I shrug in response, putting down the bassinet. I walk out of the room and can hear her following me as I reach the small mudroom. I have the door open, intent on doing nothing more than getting back to my space, my quiet…*to be alone.*

"Michael?" her soft voice reaches me, stopping me from leaving the room. Almost against my will, my head raises to look at her. "Thank you," she adds.

I stare at her a moment and leave without a reply.

CHAPTER 10

Hayden

I LOOK UP at the clock for the hundredth time. This day seems like it's never ending. The diner is about dead. We never get a lot of traffic on Mondays, but today is worse than normal. Usually, Charlie sends me home on days like today, but the other girls called in sick so I'm all she has. The end of my shift is only thirty minutes away. *Surely, I can make it thirty minutes?* We only have one customer right now. I guess I should be thankful. It's been so slow, I haven't had to deal with a lot of people. I'm still a mess from the night of the storm, and I'm sure it wouldn't take much to push me into a panic attack.

After the mental pep talk, I start wiping down the bar. Charlie's Diner is a small Main Street café in the center of Whitley City, and calling Whitley a city is silly. I've seen cities, and this definitely is not one. We have one street, (Main) and one flashing caution light, because the road dead ends without warning. That's it. You literally have to pull into a parking lot and turn around to leave the small town. The only thing in town is this diner, the courthouse, a local bank, and an old Five and Dime Store, which is really like a Dollar General store, but they never changed the name with the times. If we want to go grocery shopping, to the movies, or even a chain restaurant, then we have to drive at least two hours away. The only other businesses in town are the clinic where unfortunately I am forced to go to the doctor, and Pastor Sturgill's church.

Maybe that's why I like the place though. I'm never going to be comfortable around people, and though most of the people here don't like me, at least I know what to expect from them. The unknown monsters can be scarier than the monsters you know.

Charlie's looks like a diner on the set of *American Graffiti.* Chrome barstools, and red leather fabric with the booths and bar matching. This diner is far from fancy, and the only thing that probably doesn't belong is the country music that Charlie blasts from an old radio and cassette player she keeps behind the bar. It's obviously a throwback from the eighties when breakdancing and boom boxes were all the rage.

I jerk up out of my thoughts when I hear the bell ring, indicating someone opened the door. I'm hoping it's the waitress who is taking over my shift this evening. The smile I have ready freezes on my face when I see Michael instead. My mouth goes dry, and I bite my lip. I know it's horrible, especially considering all that work he did, even in the pouring rain, but I haven't spoken to him since that night three days ago. I should have gone by and thanked him. I really should have thanked him when he cut the tree up and had it stacked by the house so I could use it as firewood. I didn't. I just keep remembering how he didn't exactly receive my thank you so well the first time around. Okay, mostly I just chicken out, afraid to face him again.

I kept repeating my mantra about being stronger. I kept picking up the leftover banana bread to take to him. I never did. I had to throw out the bread this morning. Where Michael is concerned, I'm definitely *not* growing stronger.

I watch as he scans the room. His eyes flit across me, and I think I see his face tighten in response. He doesn't want to see me either. That causes a curl of sadness to unfold in my stomach. Which is crazy. I mean, it's okay that he doesn't like me. Still, he was nice to me. Other than Charlie and Pastor Sturgill, no one has really been nice to me before—at least not without wanting something.

He sits down at a corner booth, still intimidating me. I'm not sure if it's the fact he's so tall or the way he looks. Even through all the hair, you can tell he has a harsh face, angular in shape. He has scars and although they look painful, they do nothing to take away from the virile face that stares at me. It's his eyes that may scare me the most. So dark and deep, I'm afraid they see through me. He's wearing jeans and a black t-shirt today with writing on it. I'm curious as to what it says, but I can't make myself stare long enough to read it. Inhaling a deep breath, I let it out, grab a menu, and go to take his order.

"Hi, Michael," I greet him, and I know my voice comes out timid and quiet, but at least I used words. In response, he only manages a grunt. I know he can talk; he did at the house, but apparently, I'm not worth the effort today. Getting his order should prove interesting. "Here's the menu. The special today is meatloaf. Do you need time to look at the menu, or do you know what you want?" He looks up at me then, and it must be said, the look he's giving me indicates even louder than before that he really doesn't want me to be here. "Right. I'll just give you a little time. Do you know what you want to drink?"

"Coffee." It's one word, and he didn't even bother to look at me when he gave it. But I guess it's better than a grunt.

Leaving him with his menu, I go to get his coffee, bringing it back to him just as the bell on the door rings again. I look up and my heart stops…freezes mid-beat…then stutters back to life as fear ignites through me. My hand trembles and hot coffee sloshes out on my hand. Even the hot, stinging burn doesn't jar me as the two men come in the door, heading straight for me.

"What the fuck?" Michael's hoarse voice growls, and it breaks through enough of my panic to see he's reaching for the coffee, probably because I've just poured the scalding liquid all over my hand and down on his legs.

"I'm so sorry," I cry, still not really feeling the pain on my hand. It's red. Logically, I know it has to hurt, but there's too much panic and adrenaline running through me. I place the coffee carafe on the table—or rather I try. I might have succeeded if Jack and Dog hadn't sat down. Instead, it misses the table and crashes to the floor in a shattering crash that echoes through the room. I feel like I have a million eyes on me, which isn't rational, but that's how I feel.

Michael jerks his leg, as more of the coffee hits him before making it to the floor. *Shit.*

I'm saved—kind of, when Charlie comes from behind me. She puts her arms on each of my shoulders. I jump, making a bigger mess.

"I'll take care of it honey. Go in the back," Charlie says, her graveled old voice, softening to an almost tender quality. She's holding two towels and wraps one gently around my hands.

"Fucking up as usual, hey Tricks?" The sound of that old nickname forces bile to rise in my throat. I hate them. *God, how I hate them.* What are they doing here? They never come here. I bite my lips, refusing to turn around and look at them.

"Go into the back, honey. Now."

I nod weakly, and I might have been okay, but I look down at Michael. That was a mistake. *A big mistake.* Michael is returning my stare, but I've seen that look before. That look they all have. The look that every man gets when he hears the name the Shadow Dwellers Motorcycle Club gave me. A name I hate. A name I can't stand. A name that has tears threatening to spill from the brims of my eyes now. One lonely tear escapes as I turn away from him, and run away into the kitchen. Today, I can't even pretend I'll be stronger someday.

CHAPTER 11

Beast

"YOU TWO NEED to get out."

"Now, Charlie is that anyway to greet paying customers?" One of the Shadow Dwellers answers. I can't say as I blame her. Jesus, I hate everything about these pricks. I only wanted a simple fucking lunch.

"I wouldn't take your money if I was starving," she mutters. "I want you scum out of my restaurant."

"You're getting too cocky, old woman. We'll leave when our business is over with our friend here," he answers, and that's about all I can handle.

"If that's what's keeping you, then you can just go. I don't have any fucking business with you, and we sure as hell aren't friends," I growl.

"In that case, I'll take your order," the old woman says, her withered face, spreading into what is almost a smile. I order a burger while watching from the corner of my eye as Hayden flees into the kitchen. She's not coming back. I should be glad about that. I shouldn't be worrying about her. I definitely shouldn't be thinking about going after her. *Definitely not.* What the hell would even bring that thought to mind?

I lay the towel over my leg—not really caring that much. Then I look up at the two men who sit down and make themselves at home. I really hate these fuckers. I hate their entire club. The Shadow Dwellers are a bunch of sniveling cowards. They're fucking scum. I don't normally give a fuck about clubs and how they get their money. It's their business. But the Dwellers are notorious for human trafficking. How the fuck did Hayden get mixed up with them?

"A little birdie told us you were in our territory. Blade doesn't like the disrespect you're showing him, brother."

"I'm not your brother," I growl at the little weasel who's speaking. I've dealt with him marginally before. Some club business sent us through the northern part of North Carolina, which is what they claim to run. They're way out of their territory here. This asshole is the Vice President of the Dwellers, and he's a fucking prick. I didn't like him when we dealt with them, and I like him less now. He's tall, skinny, and the ugliest motherfucker I've ever seen. That's ironic coming from me, considering how I look these days, but this fucker…he's ugly all the way through. His pockmarked face and blond, greasy hair is just the beginning.

What was his name? My eyes go to his cut, and I read the name Mad Dog. Oh yeah, that's original.

"Customs are customs," the other one says. This one I've never actually seen, but he's not that different looking. His cut says his name is Big Jack and that makes me want to laugh. I shit bricks bigger than this asshole.

"If I was still in a club, maybe I'd care. But since I'm not…" I shrug, appearing unconcerned and that's easy, because I'm not. I'm through with that life. I'm through with idiots like this, and I'm really through with club politics. "I don't give a fuck," I tell him.

"You're not here on behalf of the Blaze?" Dog asks, and something about his look sends off an alarm bell, but I ignore it. I'm not in this mess anymore.

"There's nothing in this fucking town the Blaze cares about anymore, that includes me," I mutter, just wanting him gone.

"We heard talk you left the Devil's."

"Seems that *little birdie* is quite the talker."

"You know how it is." Dog shrugs.

"Maybe you could tell me how the hell you knew where I was today. You having me followed? Because club or not, I'm not about to take that shit." I study them for a minute, making sure my face shows my boredom in having to deal with them. "Tell me boys, does Cade's uncle know you're in his area?" I ask them. These fuckers want to pull my chain, then they need reminded, I know what the score is. Cade is over the Blaze's Florida chapter. His uncle, however, is thick in the Torasani family. The Torasani's aren't a family you want to mess with. Messing with them has a nasty way of making it so you stop breathing.

"You just said your people didn't give a fuck about this place anymore," Dog growls.

"Blaze may not, but I can't say the same for Torasani. This is their territory."

"Where we go is our business. You talk awful big for a man who doesn't have muscle backing him," Jack says.

I don't say anything for a bit. I watch Dog shift in his seat, and I know my silence is unnerving him. I'm doing it mostly to make sure my voice doesn't crack around him, but let him think what he wants. Finally, I get tired of dealing with them. My face goes ice cold, then I lean up, so he can see how fucking serious I am. "The day I need anyone to back me up when I'm squashing you piss-ants is the day they need to plant me in the ground."

"Be careful what you ask for," Jack says, but he doesn't get what Dog sees. I watch as Dog puts his hand on Jack calling him back. *Weak-ass little punks.*

"Be careful who you fucking follow," I warn.

The waitress brings my food to the table and the look on her face says she doesn't want anything to do with anyone at this table—*including me*. Probably a wise move.

"You two need to get the fuck out of here," she tells the other two men.

"You forget yourself, *old woman*," Dog says.

"You don't run this town. You need to leave," Charlie says, surprising me. I think I might like this woman.

"Listen here, you bitch," Jack says, reaching out to strike Charlie and fuck me, I shouldn't get involved, but for some damned reason I can't stop myself.

I reach up and grab Jack's hand. "Dog, I think you need to take your little puppy and leave. You're ruining my dinner. Your message was delivered. Go back and tell Blade as long as you fucks stay away from me we got no issues. We clear?" Dog looks me over, nods his head slowly.

"Let's go," Dog tells his boy.

Jack makes a growling noise and yanks his hand free. I let him go, not taking my eyes from them. The diner is silent as they leave.

Once they're gone, the woman called Charlie looks at me. She blows a strand of gray hair out of her face and the deep wrinkles on her face only get a little deeper as she studies me.

"You don't keep good company," she says, watching me.

I shrug, and take a bite out of my burger. Then I do what I do best.

I ignore her.

CHAPTER 12

Hayden

"YOU OKAY, CUPCAKE?" Charlie asks, and I fight down my panic.

In all honesty, I'm three steps away from a full-blown panic attack, but I'm doing my best to beat it down.

"What are they doing here? You promised this place was safe. I can't stay here, Charlie. I can't," I tell her, and I'm whispering, but even so she can hear the fear thick in my voice.

"They're gone now, honey. Apparently, they had business with that man you were waiting on."

"He's friends with them?" I cry, panicked. The thought of my neighbor having those men at his house. Of being that close again...*I'll have to move. I can't stay, there's no way.*

"No. I got the distinct impression he didn't like those men at all," Charlie says, scratching the side of her chin. "But they definitely have moved in the same circles, so that's not good."

She's right...it's not good at all. *I'm going to have to move...*

"I'm going to go home, Charlie," I tell her, wondering if I can manage to get out of town on the two hundred and fifty bucks I have saved up. My hand goes to my stomach. Maggie deserves better than this.

"Keep your head up, cupcake. I'll see you Wednesday."

"Maybe," I tell her, weakly.

"Don't do anything rash. I know you're scared, Hayden," Charlie says, putting her hand on my shoulder. I know she's serious when she uses my real name.

"That man lives next door to me," I tell her, wincing at the terror in my voice.

"Look at me," she urges, and I bring my eyes to her. "I got the idea that those yahoos were afraid of that man in there. So maybe having him next door is a good thing."

"I've never known any of the Dwellers to be afraid. They think they own everyone and everything." *I should know.*

"I haven't before either, well besides the Torasani family—which is another reason you should stay here. That plus, I definitely saw fear in Dog's eyes when he was talking to him. So, hold tight for a little while, honey. Maybe this man is what you've been waiting for."

"Doubtful. He didn't like me before, and you didn't see his face when they called me…" I break off. There's no way I can say that name aloud. That's not who I am. *That's never who I was.*

"Maybe, but I have a feeling about him. I don't think he'll stand by and let a woman get hurt. I'm telling you he gives me good vibes. Him being here is a good thing, I feel it in my gut," she says, as her leathery hand comes and strokes against my hair. She lays in the tanning bed way too much—so much her skin is the color of dark chocolate and leathery to the touch. But considering she's almost sixty-nine, she looks amazing and gets around better than some women in their forties.

Charlie has been wonderful to me. I would have given up a long time ago if not for her and Pastor Sturgill.

"You and that gut of yours." I laugh it off, but her words

have helped some of my panic disappear.

“It’s never betrayed me. It didn’t with you, cupcake.”

“His name is Michael,” I tell her.

“Not much of a name,” Charlie says, she shrugs, curling her lips to the side.

“Pastor Sturgill says that’s the name of God’s most feared archangel who fought evil.”

“Not much of a church-goer, but I’d say that’s a good omen.”

“I hope you’re right.” I smile tightly. Unease is still swimming in my stomach.

“You and me both, cupcake. You and me both,” she answers, hugging me close.

CHAPTER 13

I HEAR A car turning into the driveway before I see it. I've been pranking around on my bike. Turns out not getting roaring drunk every fucking night has its drawbacks. Those mainly being I have too much time on my hands. I've been trying to fill my time by tinkering on my bike. I've been kicking around the idea of getting a truck or something. I ride my bike and never really cared about finding a cage to drive around in. I had a vehicle through the club in Kentucky…*once.* I didn't worry about bringing anything here besides my bike, but fuck, Kentucky winters aren't this cold. Today is the first decent day we've had in a week and it's still barely twenty. My eyes stay on the road, waiting to see whose vehicle shows up.

It's been few days—maybe a week since I ran into Dog and his flunky at the diner. I've gone back a couple of times for breakfast. I've seen Hayden there, but that Charlie woman is the one who usually waits on my table. Which is fine. *More than fine.* Hayden has kept to herself. There's been no more midnight chainsaw events, and she hasn't even looked in my direction. That's exactly what I wanted.

I won't pretend I'm not curious to know how Pistol's sister messed around and got herself involved with the Shadow Dwellers. The Dwellers are fucked up assholes. They are still merely existing because of the stronghold they have in a major city. There's not a club around that's not fed up with their shit. No decent club gives them the time of day. Their allies consist of men covered in shit and when I say that, it's not just words. Scum stays with scum. If this Hayden chick messed with them, she should be counting her lucky stars she's not tied to a bed spread eagle somewhere across the border used in ways that most women couldn't imagine—*or worse.*

I watch as that run down little Ford Fiesta that Hayden drives pulls into her driveway, and disappears into her detached, run-down shack of a garage.

How that fucking car is even running is beyond me. It's loud as fuck, and not in a good way; it sounds like it's about to die at any moment. The stench of burned oil is so strong my nose curls as I hear her shut it off. I turn around facing my bike once again, making sure that when she comes out of the garage all she gets sight of is my back. The last thing I want to do is to encourage a conversation with her.

"Uh…Michael?" I hear from behind me a few minutes later, and I hold my head down. Apparently, I haven't made it clear that I don't want to talk to her. I don't turn around. Maybe she'll get tired and leave. "I didn't see you at the diner today," she continues, I can hear fear in her voice, and something else I can't name. It's there in the way her voice falters and trembles. Again, I continue being the bastard I am and don't reply. I expect her to give up and leave.

It's quiet for a couple of minutes, and I hear the sound of walking. I breathe a little easier, knowing she's going to leave. Then she does something few people do—*especially these days.* She comes around to face me. I'm looking down at my bike but she's standing in front of me so in my vision all I see is her protruding stomach, covered in a dark blue, extremely worn jacket that's stretched to zip around her. *She needs a thicker coat.*

"Will you talk to me for a minute? *Please?*" she asks, surprising me further. Picking up a rag I had lying across the seat of my bike, wiping the oil from my hands, I raise my eyes to her and see the paleness of her face. She doesn't look good. I don't mean that in her appearance. She's never going to be a raving beauty. But today, she's pale and her nose is red, like she's sick. Which she probably is considering the crazy bitch has no brain.

"What?" I ask her, my voice rumbling, my tone clipped. She jumps slightly, but does her best to hide it.

"I wanted to explain about the other day."

"No."

"I mean you know, about those men and…"

"No," I tell her again, turning away from her, to go towards the tack room, carrying my tools with me. I've been finished for twenty minutes, and suddenly, I'd rather not be here. The peace from earlier is gone, and there's only one person to blame for that. *Her.*

"What do you mean, no?"

"Exactly what I said," I tell her, and to reemphasize that because apparently, she's simple-minded, I repeat the word, "No."

"But, I wanted you to understand…" she says, her voice going quiet, and with that I've pretty much had enough, which means I'm going to have to talk to this woman, which pretty much pisses me off because of one reason…*I do not like to talk.* I spin around right before I get to the tack room. She stops mid-step, almost colliding into me. I harden my face, which isn't that difficult, because I'm the first to admit I'm not a happy person, and now I'm fucking pissed on top of that, because this *bitch* won't leave me the hell alone.

"Understand what?" I bark.

"How they…I mean *why* they know me. I'm not…it's not what you're thinking," she says. Her face is red with embarrassment, and her body is trembling. She's like a scared mouse, which would be great if she would just fucking leave and run away.

"I'm thinking I don't like you, and I don't want to talk to you," I confide, not hiding the strain in my voice.

"But—"

I cut her off, not letting her respond. "And it's not because of who you are, which would be reason enough. It's not because of who your family is, which trust me would *positively* be more than enough reason. It's not because of what you look like, which ain't that fucking great, and it's *definitely* not because of who you've let between those legs of yours."

She gasps. Her face drains of color and her hand comes up to her face like I hit her. *Not yet, honey, but if you don't get out of here…*

"So, you have nothing to explain. I don't like you. I don't want to talk to you. If that's not plain enough, and you need a fucking reason, how about the fact that you're pregnant. You obviously got that way without either caring about the father or worse, pushing him out of your life. You can't even care for yourself let alone a child. And from what I've seen, you don't give a damn about that baby in your belly. *Those* are more than enough reasons as to why I don't like you. So, get the fuck out of my space and leave me alone!" I growl, my voice cracking, and that just makes me feel worse. I need her gone. I need her to leave before I'm tempted to wrap my hands around her neck and choke the life out of her. She's just like Jan. A selfish whore who should never have children.

"How dare you. You don't know me," she whispers, and it's a whisper so soft I have to strain to hear it. "I love my child," she says, bringing her hands up to hold her stomach. They're trembling and there's a brown paper bag in one of them. I watch as it bounces with each shuddering shake of her hand. There's a thread of hurt in her voice that almost makes me want to believe her, but I don't. Jan would try and be innocent when she wanted to be too. "I would never harm my child. I would protect her with—"

"Were you protecting her when you went out in a lightning storm and almost killed both of us with a fucking chainsaw?" My words hit her straight on. I see it in the way the gray color of her eyes widen and her pupils dilate. I should let it go with that, but I don't. I continue, giving her part of the anger that I've been carrying around for what feels like a lifetime. "I've seen women who care for their children. I *know* women who gave up everything to keep their child safe, lady," I bark at her, my mind going to Beth. Hell, I don't like Beth. I blame her and Skull for the loss of Annabelle, but I can at least admit that she did her best to protect her own child. She has my respect for that, if nothing else. "I've seen women who do that, and *you* are not that woman. You're not even close."

Those words are the ones that deliver a killing blow inside of her. I see it and somewhere under the anger it registers. Tears gather in her eyes, but she doesn't cry. A few tears spill out and run down her face, but she doesn't cry. There's no sound. No heaving, gushing of the tears, no begging for understanding like women so often do when they're called on their shit. No. She looks at me without replying. The bag in her hand drops to her feet and without another word she turns to leave, giving me the silence that I crave. Leaving me alone.

Exactly like I want.

CHAPTER 14

Hayden

IT'S BEEN THREE days since my neighbor decimated me with his words. I can't manage to even be mad. I mean, a lot of it was bullshit, and I'm used to closed minds. But, there was truth there. I can't take care of my child like I want. Michael might be a major asshole, but he wasn't wrong in that at least. And he was right again when he yelled at me for going out into the rain. In truth, I've been sick ever since. Being pregnant, they won't really give me medicine, and even if they did, it wouldn't really help. A cold just needs to work itself out of your system. So, I'm trying to tough it out and drink plenty of orange juice for the vitamin C. *Would he think that's wrong too?*

Luckily, Charlie is understanding and she has made me stay off work for the last three days. I can't really afford it, but since the run in with the jerk next door, I really can't handle being in the public yet. I need time to recover. As a result, my mantra of being stronger tomorrow has been temporarily changed to being stronger next week. I figure that's better than next year, which is what I really want to say at this point. *That or…never.*

Tomorrow, I need to do a lot of baking, but I don't feel well enough tonight to tackle it. Instead, I'm lying on the couch watching horrible, romantic comedies. *Kate and Leopold* is the latest one. Why can't life be like that? Your dream man coming to you from another time. A time when men were not such assholes and actually cared about women. *Why?* I burrow down under the cover. I managed to get a fire roaring in the fireplace, but the house is still cold. I probably have a fever, but I don't have a thermometer. It takes too much energy to worry about it anyway.

I watch the movie, then another. By the next movie, I'm starting to think my plan to sleep it off won't work. I'm feeling worse, and now I'm not cold. I'm burning up. I feel like I'm on fire. I've kicked off the cover, but I only grow hotter. I look around for my phone. I should go to the doctor. My head is spinning and my vision is kind of blurring. I might be panicking. You chill with a fever, right? You don't get hot. I thought that was the way it went. I've not been sick a lot, so I can't be sure. *Crap.*

This is one of those things a mother should know before she has a baby. She should know if her daughter is cold or hot and what that means. *I don't.* I don't know anything. Michael was right. Maggie deserves so much better than me. That's when I start crying. I can't stop, and I don't want to. I continue to allow my misery, my doubts, my fears, and the hurt over Michael's harsh attack wash through me and take over.

CHAPTER 15

Beast

I REFUSE TO label what I'm feeling as guilt. I was a fucking dick, I get that and hell, I own it. But a lot of that was Hayden's fault. She shouldn't have pushed me. Still, I saw pain in her eyes and it's bothering me. Not a lot, but enough that here I am, three days later, showing up at the diner. It would have been easier to go to her house, but I couldn't seem to make myself do that. Not when I picked up the bag of cookies she dropped that day, and not even after eating those cookies. Cookies, which I will admit, were better than anything I've ever tasted. They were peanut butter with chocolate in the center, and they had a salty-sweet taste going on that I had never tasted before. They were fucking good. I get that she was trying to be nice. Maybe she was hoping she could use me for something, I don't know. It's possible…*more than possible.* I'd say definitely. Still, I don't know her, and I should have just walked away.

The diner is mostly empty when I walk in. It's never extremely busy. I'm not sure how the place stays open. There's no sign of Hayden and that's probably for the best. I don't know what to say to her, yet. I just know I don't want to encourage her to talk to me.

There are three other people in here. There's an old man, who is probably in his seventies, and a couple of men my age who are probably on their lunch hour. It's the same three people that have been here each time I come in. *Regulars I guess.*

I sit down and wait for a waitress to come and take my order. I'm here a few minutes and no one seems to be coming over to me. There are two waitresses, one is standing at the table talking to the old man quietly. Every now and then she looks over here at me. I'm used to people staring at me. I don't really care about that. But it's clear that she's not going to come take my order. The other waitress is actually *sitting* at the bar and she's shooting me dirty looks.

Well ain't that just a bucket of fuck. I bet the little bitch went whining to her co-workers. Which just means I shouldn't feel anything, especially guilt. She's conniving, exactly like all the other women I've come in contact with. That woman Charlie comes over, though I can tell she'd rather be anywhere else. It's a feeling I know well.

"Pancake platter," I order. "Coffee for the drink."

Charlie glares at me, following the pointed look with the shaking of her head. "We're out of pancakes." My eyebrows raise at that, but whatever.

"Fine. I'll take the Western Omelet."

"We're out of eggs," Charlie answers just as quickly. There's laughter in the corner where the waitress is standing. I pull my eyes away from her and back to Charlie.

"They're eating eggs," I tell her, motioning toward the men at the other table.

"We just ran out," Charlie says, her face impassive. She hasn't even taken out her ordering pad to pretend she's going to take my order. So, I decide to push her.

"So, no more breakfast today?"

"Exactly," Charlie answers, her arms cross at her chest and a look of victory comes over her face.

"Then I'll order a burger," I tell her.

"We're out."

"You're out of burgers?"

"There's a big cow shortage in the area," Charlie answers, and everyone in the diner laughs at that. Everyone but two people—*me and Charlie.*

"I take it your friend came running to you about the other day."

"She told me."

"Where is she?"

"Don't know. She's been sick and she didn't show today. That girl has fought more battles than any woman should ever have to fight. Maybe you were the one that finally made her leave this town and start over," she says with a shrug of her shoulder. "What you need to understand is that girl is like a daughter to me, and I don't care who the fuck you are or who your friends are. I won't be serving your kind in my diner."

"My kind."

"Pretty much," she says, stalking off.

I feel everyone staring at me. *That little bitch thought she could punish me.* Maybe I didn't make myself clear enough to her. When I demanded that she leave me alone, I fucking meant completely. I stomp out of the diner, letting the door slam behind me. If Hayden Graham didn't get the message before, I'll make damn sure she gets it now.

CHAPTER 16

I POUND ON the door again, when I don't get an answer. I have so much anger inside of me, but no one brings it out like this woman does.

"I said, open up!" I growl, and I'm straining my voice to say it loud enough. The pain feeds through my blood, increasing my anger. If she's going to try and act like a spoiled bitch, then she could at least own up to it. I mean, *what the fuck?* I called her on her shit and put her in her place. There was no reason for her to involve others. Did she think she could manipulate me? What the hell does she want? It makes zero sense, but damn it she must be playing some kind of game.

When I pound the door again and she doesn't answer, I decide to give up. She has to come out sometime. This bitch doesn't know who she's dealing with. I start to walk back to my place, but one last thought has me looking into her kitchen window—*like a fucking peeping tom.*

I expect her to be standing there watching me. I'm surprised when she's not. What I didn't anticipate is that the window has ice frozen on it. It's been cold, sure, but the heat from inside the house should have kept ice from forming. I look through the window and that's when I see her. Hayden is crumpled on the floor. From where I'm standing her face is hidden, but I can see her hand lying against the worn carpet, her body turned at an awkward angle. I can't see a lot, but there's one thing I can confirm…*She's not moving.*

I run back to the front door and try the knob. It's locked. I step back and ram my shoulder into it hard. Pain shoots up my arm, radiating into my neck, but the door gives way. I walk over to the woman. She's extremely pale. It wouldn't surprise me if she is dead, but a quick check tells me she has a pulse. The house is ice cold. There's no fire in the fireplace—not even reddened coals. I place my hand on her head and she's got a fever. This is what going out in a thunderstorm to wave around a chainsaw will get you.

I need to get her to a hospital, but all I have is my damn bike. I take out my cellphone and dial 911. I give them directions to the house and pick her up. As I put her on the sofa, she whimpers, which I guess is a good thing. I find a worn blanket wadded up on the floor. I pull it over her body. The operator said it would be forty minutes before an ambulance will get here, which is crazy. I know this town is in the middle of nowhere, but there should be a damn hospital close by.

Her lips look dried. I go into the kitchen and get a glass of water. I bring it back in, sitting on the edge of the couch cushion. I wrap my arm around her shoulders to pull her up, propping her body up with my hold. Her head lolls to the side, but she slowly starts coming around. I feel like an idiot. I have no idea what I'm doing, but hearing her moan and watching her eyes slowly open, reassures me a little.

"Drink," I order.

"What are…doing…" she doesn't really make a complete

sentence, but I guess it's good she's talking—though her voice sounds like she's swallowed a jar of salt and had zero water. It doesn't even sound like her. It has a hoarse quality that reminds you more of a male's voice.

"Just drink," I tell her. My voice is clipped, probably because I'm trying to figure out how you can worry about someone and have them disgust you at the same time.

CHAPTER 17

Hayden

"I'VE GOT YOUR release papers, Ms. Graham," the nurse says, coming in my room.

I'm sitting in my hospital bed. Dressed in the same clothes I was wearing when they brought me in. It feels good to finally be out of that hospital gown. I've been in here for two days. I'm feeling better. I wish they had let me go home yesterday. I'm lucky, I know. I'm okay and the baby is good. But, at the same time, I've been off work for a week now. I can't afford that. Hopefully, my medical card will pay my bills, but everything else? That's going to take money.

My hand goes to my stomach to rub Maggie as best as I can. There's a flutter of movement and I smile. She can feel me. I pray she understands that I love her and I'm sorry. My fever broke the day they brought me in, but I was severely dehydrated and had a major ear infection. The doctor gave me medicine, I'm not happy about taking it, but he promised that it was safer for the baby than for me to continue being sick. I was worried because my fever had spiked. I'm not sure how high it got, but I know that can be very dangerous for a baby. So far, all the tests and ultrasounds reveal that Maggie is doing great. However, I should start going to the doctor more often now. That part's not going to be fun. I wish I could come here to the doctor, but there's no way my little car would make the two-hour round trip. There are days that just driving into Whitley to go to the diner is more than it can handle. I'm going to have to suck it up, choke on my pride, and go to the local clinic.

"Do you have a ride home?" she asks, looking around the room, and bringing my thoughts to a stop.

I give her a half smile. She can look all she wants, but there's no one here. If a nurse hadn't have looked at my records to discover the *man* that was with me when they brought me in, I never would have known. When she first read me the name Connor Michael Jameson, I had no idea who that was. It took forever for me to connect the name *Michael* to someone in my life…like my asshole neighbor. It shocked me. I'm grateful, as much as I don't want to be. I really thought if he was given the choice he would have left me to die.

"I'm afraid not. I was planning on grabbing a taxi," I half-lie to the nurse. I can't afford a taxi home.

Liese Haley, said she would come and get me and she will. She offered to be here early today, but I felt guilty about making her miss her shift. She lives from check to check much like I do. Charlie would have done it, but she's out of town today. Pastor Sturgill is out of town, so that makes my options limited.

I told her I'd find a McDonalds or something and crash till she got in town. It was the simplest solution. I'll grab a taxi to McDonalds and text Liese and tell her where I am. I have just enough minutes left on my crappy pre-paid cellphone to do that.

"We normally can't release you unless you have a ride home," the nurse says, worry lines appearing and crinkling in the center of her forehead, showing obvious concern.

"I'm afraid I don't really have anyone. It's just me and Maggie," I tell her, rubbing my stomach. "We'll be fine. I *technically* have a ride."

"I'm not sure that's what the hospital guidelines mean," she says, shaking her head. She looks at me and she's about my age. Her name tag says Jana Kick. She's a beautiful woman with mocha skin, dark hair with almost purple highlights and the kind of body men are drawn to. She has a professional job, one that ensures she will always be able to take care of herself and her children.

The last thing she would probably understand is the mess I've made of my life. The bad decisions, the pain, the hurt…all of it. I pray she'll never know it, because I wish I didn't. I've lived through it, and I wouldn't want other people to do the same. Still, I don't want to risk that she won't let me go home. I need out of here. I need to get back to work. I need to get more baked goods out. I was just starting to get my head above water, and I can't lose that now. My hand pats my stomach again on reflex. *Especially now.*

I put my hand on her arm to get her attention. Her soft eyes look at me, and I let my guard down enough so she can see me pleading, and how desperately I need her to agree.

"I'll be fine. I promise." Jana stares at me for a minute and my breath lodges in my chest while I wait to see if she will agree. Then she gives me a tight smile.

"A ride is a ride, right?" she says, and I take a deep breath in relief. She goes over the rules and the follow-up appointment they've made with the local clinic. I'm dreading that, but it definitely needs to be done. She hands me a bunch of papers along with a few prescriptions, and just like that, I'm free.

I always thought hospital policy was wheeling you out in a wheel chair, but I'm not offered one. She walks me down to the elevator. Then we're at the front doors, before she's telling me bye. I'm sure she's skirting one or two rules for me. *Maybe more.* I'm more excited that I won't have to hire a taxi. I have no idea how much it would have cost me to take a taxi to the nearest McDonalds, but any amount right now is more than I can afford.

I step out into the cold air, wishing I had a coat to wear. I'm waiting for a truck to go by so I can cross to the walkway. Instead, the big gray truck pulls up and parks in front of me. It's thrown into park so hard, it jerks causing it to rock on its wheels. I sigh, as I hear the driver getting out. I mean, it's kind of rude, but it is the pick-up and drop-off lane, so not unexpected. Still, the driver had to see me standing here. *Just another reason people are annoying.*

I turn to walk around the truck, dismissing it and the driver. I need to get inside somewhere before I get sick again. I can't afford to, and it wouldn't be good for the baby. I've only taken a few steps when I feel a hand grab my arm. I cry out, looking at my shoulder and seeing a large, tattooed hand wrapped around my upper arm. Fear instantly hits me. My head goes back to see who it is. For a moment, I'm scared to death it's *him.* Then my eyes focus on Michael. The fear dies down, even in the face of his anger.

"What are you doing here?" I ask. He pinches the bridge of his nose and for a second I think he might roll his eyes at me. It's hard to tell he has so much hair, and when he leans his head down it covers his face like a shroud.

"Let's go," he says, not really answering.

I'm in his truck—*I didn't even know he had a truck*, and he has me buckled in before I know what is happening. He closes my door after testing the belt to make sure it's secure. Then he gets in on his side, starts up the vehicle, and we're merging into the traffic on the main road all before I think I can even blink. He also does all of this without one word. Not a grunt, a groan, or even a huff of breath does he offer. But then I don't guess he needs to, because in a way he answered my question. *He's here for me.*

Crap.

CHAPTER 18

Beast

"WHAT ARE YOU doing here? How did you know I was getting out? When did you get a truck? Why are you here? Do you know how to talk? How many tattoos do you have? Did it hurt when you had your fingers inked up? Do you have lips under all that hair?"

That's the questions I find myself ignoring from my chatty passenger. Admittedly, the first part of those questions came pretty quickly into our ride. The last few, are kind of strange and a little funny—or they might be if I still laughed. They came farther into the ride, and in ten to fifteen minute intervals.

I haven't answered any of them. I haven't really looked at her. The last question was about thirty minutes ago. I'm taking that to mean she's given up. Which is good, because I don't plan on answering her. Part of that is because for the fucking life of me, I don't know why I picked her up. I have no idea what I'm doing. All I know is that when I heard Charlie discussing with some other waitress that they would have to wait until evening to get Hayden...I stepped in again to help her. I don't know why, and it has me confused as hell.

Charlie, however, she found it funny. I was also right about her. I like her. Since she heard I rescued Hayden and got her to the hospital, she has let me start eating at the diner again. By that, I mean she brought me breakfast out to my place the next morning and told me she would see me tomorrow at the diner. Charlie is a woman of few words, and that is one characteristic of hers I can definitely appreciate.

She also laughed at my reaction about Hayden not having a way home. I growled. I did this loudly, and since I was staring right at the women, Charlie knew immediately why. The waitress, she called Liese, jumped a good foot in the air, but Charlie just grinned. She knew she had me, and that's when I found myself *really* liking her…even against my will.

Nothing else was said between us—*see a woman of few words.* But, when I went to the counter to pay my bill, she handed me a to-go-bag instead.

"For Hayden," she said. I pinpointed her in my gaze, a look that in all my years as enforcer of the Devil's Blaze never failed me. Fuck, some men started begging when I looked at them like that. Not Charlie. *She laughed*, and went back to the other waitress—completely dismissing me. I growled again, for the good that did, and then I left.

"I like your truck," Hayden says, kind of lost. She brings my attention back around to her, but her words annoy me. I tighten my hand on the steering wheel, as I spare her a quick glance. She's finally eating the food that Charlie sent to her. My nose kind curls at the smell of it. *Fried bananas?* "It's a really nice truck," she says again, right before taking another bite of her sandwich.

It is a nice truck. I rode my bike into the city to get Hayden. Stopped at the first dealership I found and bought it. It's a brand spankin' new Ford F-150 and loaded with all the latest options. I figured if I was going to drive a cage, I'd do it in style. It was kind of cold driving my bike in town, but then I liked the cold getting into my lungs and the feel of the wind. I've lived my life on the back of a bike for a reason and since…*since* losing Annabelle I really didn't care if I got in another car.

That day at Hayden's however, when she needed to get to the hospital and there was no way for me to get her there quicker…it bothered me. It shouldn't have, and I don't like that it did…*but it did.* I'm not about to tell her that. Just like I'm not about to tell her the color of this truck reminded me of the color of her eyes. She'd probably make something out of that, and there's nothing there. Gray is a good strong color. It's not a fucking sissy color either. That's all there is to it. No hidden meanings whatsoever.

"I really appreciate you helping me. Maggie and I are very grateful," she says, and I don't want to, but I can't seem to stop myself.

"Maggie?" I can see out of the corner of my eye how she freezes when I ask my question.

Her lips move into a small smile, right before she pops another fry into her mouth. She had to be starving. *Aren't they supposed to feed you in a hospital?* "My daughter," she says, her hand going to the swell of her stomach. Her head leans down, this time there's a full smile on her lips, and she almost appears happy. "I'm naming her after a Rod Stewart song, *Maggie May.* Maggie will probably never listen to Rod Stewart, but it's a good song and a pretty name. She needs a pretty name." Her rambling words make me feel weird.

There's a slight chance I misjudged her. It appears she might genuinely care about her child, at least enough that she has already given her a name. On the heels of that emotion though is another one. One that is stronger and proves what a fucked-up, twisted asshole I really am. I resent that child in her stomach. A child that is completely innocent, but in this moment, I hate. I hate this faceless, unknown little girl who will be blessed with the name Maggie. I hate her name, and I hate her mother. What right do they have? Why does this woman get a child? *What is so special about this unborn Maggie that she can have a life when my Annabelle can't?* My hands shake as I tighten them on the steering wheel.

Hayden rattles on beside me, but I'm tuning her out. I feel raw inside, and the misery is too close to the surface. I reach over and blast a Metallica song that comes on the radio, drowning Hayden's voice out. Then I go back to concentrating on the road. Hayden gives up talking, sparing me a quick glance. She puts what's left of her food back in the bag, and looks out the passenger window in silence.

Finally.

CHAPTER 19

Hayden

"I GUESS HE doesn't like the name Maggie," I whisper to the door that was just slammed in my face. Michael didn't say another word from the time I told him the name of my daughter, to the time when he dropped me off at my house. By dropping me off, I mean he pulled into my driveway, jumped out, came around before I had a chance to move, undid my seatbelt, then picked me up, and carried me. He did all of this including managing to open my front door while still having me in his arms. A front door, which by the way, is brand new and solid wood. It has an oval, stained glass panel that depicts flowers and birds on it. *It is beautiful.* It also has a heavy-duty lock with a kick-ass handle *and* a deadbolt.

I wanted to ask where the door came from, but two things stopped me. One, I figured Michael wouldn't answer, and two, I figured I already knew—especially since he had the keys. Keys which he dropped into my palm—also without another word, when he set me down in my living room. My legs were weak and only got weaker, when his big hand cupped one of mine, pulled it down between us and deposited the keys inside. I stared at the small silver keys that were united by a small, plain metal key ring. I was just gearing up to question him about it, when he stepped back and slammed the door in my face. *Slammed.* Not lightly, nope. He slammed the door so hard the walls rattled. I jumped, but not that much. I would have thought the windows would break from the force of the door slam. That's when I looked around and noticed that every window had been replaced in the house. *Every window.* When I looked in Maggie's room and saw the new window…I wanted to cry. They're double insulated, with heavy duty locks and the outside is vinyl. I have no idea why he would do such a thing. I shudder to think how much it all cost him. Seeing it all confused me and even embarrassed me a little. Still, I was blown away.

Michael might not like me. I'm thinking that fact is pretty clear. *I've been un-liked a lot in life, but none have made it as apparent as Michael has a knack for—even if he mostly stays silent.* Yet, even if he doesn't like me, he's helped me. I have no idea why he has, but he has. So, one thought has settled into my heart, and this one thought seems to have pushed away the fear and even the hurt I held against my grouchy, next door neighbor.

Even if he doesn't like me, he doesn't want to see me or my daughter hurt.

That one thought is pretty freeing. It's the closest I've come to feeling safe in my entire life. Maybe I felt safe with Maggie's father…at least in the beginning, but that didn't last long, and mostly was there because I was young and stupid. He sure never gave me any reason to feel safe. He definitely would have never put up a new door to keep me safe. Plus, if he found me unconscious on the floor, the only thing he might have done was step on me.

Michael may not know it, but with his actions, he's given me a reason to like and trust him. It's a strange feeling; one that almost feels like a miracle. Maybe Pastor Sturgill is right and my neighbor having the name of God's favored archangel is a good thing. A sign that everything is okay.

I rub my stomach and whisper, "It's going to be okay, Maggie." She kicks against my stomach, and I'm taking that as her agreement.

Looking around the house, I notice the wood container by the fireplace is full. Beside the container sits a plastic bag, and I open it up to discover there are two new lighters along with five of those large fire logs. *The nifty ones you buy and light the package on both ends that burn for hours and make starting a fire so simple.*

It doesn't take a rocket scientist to figure out where all of this came from. That feeling of freedom inside of me blooms a little more. But what really pushes me over the edge to where I think I might even *like* my neighbor is when I open the fridge.

Inside, there are assorted groceries. Milk, lunch meat, eggs, hamburger, chicken, and even orange juice—it's all inside. The fridge was almost bare before I became sick. There was nothing in it but yogurt, an almost empty jar of pickles, and some butter. I don't even see that in here now. There are brand new containers of those things, but the old ones are gone. I close the fridge with my heart hammering against my chest. Then I look around the rest of my kitchen. There's a brand new loaf of bread, a box of cereal on the counter, and some apples, bananas, and oranges are strewn across my kitchen table.

Michael bought groceries and not only a few items, but a lot. I lean against the counter, and I feel tears slide from my eyes again. The windows left me crying and speechless, but this… this seems larger, because Michael had to do it hands on. It wasn't a matter of buying something and having it installed. It was…shopping. It was almost like…*caring*. I don't know how to process all of this. I'll never be able to repay him, and I know in my heart that if I try, he'll just turn mean again. Call me crazy, but that's not something I want to experience again. So, I just stand here, leaning against my old laminate, fake, butcher block counter, and I let the tears go.

Connor Michael Jameson, my hateful, taciturn, grunting neighbor, made me cry…again.

But this time, the tears are good—*definitely good.* These tears wash over me, in a cleansing way. For the first time in my life, I experience true tears of…joy.

CHAPTER 20

Beast

HAYDEN HAS BEEN back home for two weeks. She's not tried talking my ear off—which is good, because after the ride home, I got the distinct impression that she could. She's actually not bothered me at all, except for one small thing. She keeps leaving different things for me outside the door that leads to my loft. Over the past two weeks, every morning when I open the door there's either been pies, cakes, cookies, or candy. Every single morning like clockwork. Well, every morning except this one. Today, there is nothing here. Maybe she's given up. That's for the best. I ignore the disappointed feeling that is resting heavy in my gut. I had gotten used to the treats, but that's all.

I'm about to get on my bike when I notice the garage door she keeps that rolling wreck parked in, is open. Almost against my will, I walk over there. She's not in the garage but I hear her back door open. I turn as she walks towards me.

"Hi, Michael," she says, her voice full of stress. "Did you need something?" she asks, wringing her hands together. I stand there annoyed and a little uncomfortable.

"There was no cookies," I tell her. I watch as her lips form a perfect 'o', then slowly spread into a brief smile.

"I'm sorry. I overslept. I had plans to make you something special today. I was going to do it when I came back home. But since you're here, you just saved me some steps," she says in rapid fire. She takes a minute to get a breath, which I figure might be a good thing, but then she starts in again. "Actually, I was just about to come ask you a question. I'm running late. I can't get my car to start, and I'm supposed to go to the doctor today. I can't miss it. Today is ultrasound day. I can't believe my luck lately," she complains, and she says all of that without stopping. I let the words register for a minute and I frown. *She wants me to take her to the doctor?* Fuck, no. No way. *Not happening.* I open my mouth to tell her that when she carries on some more. "Can I borrow your cellphone?" That wasn't the question I expected from her.

"What?"

"Your cellphone? I want to call Pastor Sturgill to see if he can take me into town. He said anytime I needed him to call, and I've always tried not to unless we were dealing with the baked goods, since his church uses those in their fundraising. But, I don't have any other choice right now. If you could let me borrow it to call him, I'd appreciate it."

I bring my hand up to my face scratching my beard, touching the scars underneath. I should give her the phone and walk away. I've done too much where Hayden is concerned, especially since I'm starting to enjoy seeing signs of her. That's not smart. An old friend's wife, Dani, is the only person I've put myself out there for in forever, and that's only because she had a world of pain in her eyes when I first met her. It was a pain I knew—*a pain I was familiar with.* But, I'm not part of this world anymore. I'm existing in it as some type of cruel joke, but I definitely don't have a place in it. I wanted to. For a while, I let myself believe my brothers were right. That eventually, I would have a home with them again, and I believed that maybe my life would return to *normal.*

Instead, I watched as if I were on the outside looking in. Everyone went on with their lives. Everyone continued living and laughing. They had children, they had husbands and wives, they had *life.* I went through the motions, waiting for that moment when I'd have that again. That moment when the darkness would leave, the pain would stop suffocating me, and the emptiness would stop devouring me. Then maybe, I could breathe the same air as them. It never happened. That moment never came. It's never going to happen—*I know that.* Still, instead of doing the sensible thing and handing her the phone, I do something incredibly stupid.

"I'll take you," I offer before my brain can even register the words.

"I wouldn't ask, but I haven't put minutes back on my phone yet, and I... *What did you say?*"

"I said I'll take you."

Her lips move, opening just slightly. I can see a breath move through her chest. Her gray eyes widen, and I'm instantly regretting my offer. I'm about to just hand her my phone and be done with it, when she does something unexpectedly.

"Thank you, Michael. I'd really appreciate that," she says, calmly.

That's it. No squealing, no hugging me, no acting like I'm doing something fantastic. Nothing, just a simple, *calm,* thank you. I was preparing for her to go crazy, hug me and kiss the side of my face while gushing out her gratefulness. But she only gives me a quiet thank you.

Which means...I don't back out. I don't hand her my phone. I don't tell her I've changed my mind. I go back to my place, get my truck, and I do all of it while wishing she would have at least tried to kiss me.

Fucking hell.

CHAPTER 21

Hayden

I CAN'T BELIEVE Michael offered to take me to the doctor. Actually, I can't believe he spoke enough to even propose he take me to the doctor. I was so surprised and relieved, it's a wonder I didn't squeal. *Or kiss him.* Because I had the insane urge to kiss him—and that should scare me to death. It doesn't though. Maybe it's because I know he doesn't like me. I don't have to worry about Michael in that way. It makes it easier to be around him, if I'm being honest.

Now that we're on the road however, I'm full of stress and worry. I'm wringing my hands together trying to snap myself out of it and squash down the panic. Sadly, nothing is working. We pull into the parking lot of the local clinic, and I am still on the edge of a panic attack. I find it ironic that going to the doctor is the main reason this panic attack is coming on and *not* being alone in a car with a man. Normally, even being around a man would do it—especially if that man was huge, covered in tattoos and mean. I know that's not fair. Michael's been kind to me in a weird, strange way. Though still, he *is* mean. Anger oozes from him. At the same time, I've been in the truck with him twice now, and I've never once been afraid of him either time—*despite the anger.*

"You okay?" he asks. Michael has a good voice. It's deep and gruff, making me wonder if he has a seven pack a day habit. I never smell cigarette smoke on him, so I doubt that's the case. He doesn't talk much, and sometimes when he talks his voice breaks off. I've noticed the scars marking his hands and arms. There are much fainter ones on his face, and there are some along the collar of his shirt that seem to disappear. *By that I mean his beard is so long and bushy it hides them before I can investigate further.* I have to wonder if whatever accident he was in has left some permanent damage to his voice. Maybe talking hurts him and he's silent, not because he just hates being bothered with me, but because it's physically painful. *Not likely, but a girl can dream.*

"Yeah. You can just wait out here for me. I'm never in there for long," I tell him, not really looking at his face. I go to undo my seatbelt and his hand stops me. He puts his much larger, scarred and ink covered hand over mine, swallowing it. I stare at our hands for a minute. I can't help but wonder how much pain a man had to endure to have the kinds of scars he has marring his skin. They're burn scars. I don't have a doubt in that. I had a neighbor once who got trapped in a house fire, and he had scars that were so much like these. I bring over my other hand, moving my finger across his ink. I feel a shift in the mood surrounding us. It's so drastic that it becomes an almost physical thing. I feel his hand tighten on mine underneath. His fingers clamp down tightly until he's holding it to the point of pain. I drag my eyes up to look at him. Can he read my nervousness in my eyes?

"What's wrong?" he asks again, more insistent. I get a little lost in his dark coffee eyes…so dark they're almost liquid black. They're dark, inky and seem to drill deep down inside of me. I swallow, wondering if those dark eyes see all my secrets. They seem like they penetrate so deeply they must know everything. They draw me in so profoundly that I lose track of everything, including the fact I'm letting my thumb move back and forth along one of the grooved indentions on his hand.

"Nothing," I lie. "Thank you for bringing me. I'll try and hurry."

I wait for him to move his hand. When he doesn't, I get this nervous flutter in my stomach that's clearly not the baby. *What is happening to me?*

Michael clears his throat, then increases his already painful pressure on my hand. "I'll go in too," he says, and my breath lodges in my throat.

I don't want that. I really, *really* don't want that. Michael hasn't made a secret of how he feels about me. I pushed it aside, because despite his judgments—and admittedly, some of them were not wrong, he's been really nice to me, and I haven't had that a lot in my life. But, once he sees how the others treat me and feels he has his judgments confirmed, our tenuous friendship will end. I don't want that to happen. I don't want that to happen in a way that means if it does, I will grieve it. Even though all I've done for two weeks is bake desserts and take them to his door, he feels like the first real friend I've ever had. *With the exception of Charlie, but she's also a woman and my boss, so the dynamic is extremely different.*

"No. It's okay. I will—" I don't finish, mostly because he has my seatbelt undone, out of the truck and is standing at my door all before I look up.

Michael actually has my door open and is grunting. *A clear sign for me to get out of the vehicle, I'm sure.* He does all of this before I make a move. And even then, I still don't move. I don't move because I'm staring at my hand. The hand that he had his overtop of. The hand his fingers were pressed into painfully. The hand that felt like electricity has been steadily pounding inside of it. The hand that now feels…*sad. Can hands feel sad?* Mine does. So sad, that it makes the rest of me gloomy. Despondent enough that I'm pretty sure the emotion I'm grappling with is…loneliness.

What is happening to me?

CHAPTER 22

Beast

I'VE FINALLY DONE it. I've slipped off the fucking deep end. That's the only explanation for why I'm escorting a woman, one I barely know, into a doctor's office—for a *prenatal* appointment. Keeping my hand on her back as we walk to the office, I push the door open for her as we get there. She looks up at me then. Her gray eyes are huge, and there's fear in them so thick not only can I see it, I'm pretty sure I can taste it. There's a fine tremble running through her body and so much tension in it, she's stiff. *What the fuck is going on here?* Did the hospital give her bad news? Is she worried about this appointment?

She gives me a tight smile and goes inside. I follow her, my hand still on her back and that's another problem. I need to go back to the doctor myself because my hand is fucked up. Ever since she touched it, it's burning. Not deeply, but enough that I have to wonder if she touches it again if it would stop.

She walks up to the small reception area, and I can't help but notice the tension coming from her is increasing. She signs her name and we find a couple of seats in a nearby corner.

"You don't have to be here, honest. I'll be fine on my own. You could wait in the car. Or you could go home, really. I can walk to the diner and get a ride from Charlie later. There's no point in us both being here," she rattles and the entire time she's talking she's looking around the room as though she's afraid people are staring at us. It hits me then.

Of course. I remember Lucy's words. *"He's repulsive. A woman would have to be drunk to want to be with him, and even that might not be enough."* Women are all the same. Does she think it bothers me? *Fuck, no.* I was only doing her a favor. I won't make that fucking mistake again. *Never again.*

I growl, getting up, and walking off without looking at her. I don't offer her words. I don't need to explain. I stomp out, leaving her behind me. You'd think I'd know by now that you can't let your guard down around women. They're all evil and the only time they can be bothered with you is when they want something. I've been done with them for a long time, this one almost made me forget that.

"Michael," I hear Hayden yell as I open the door to my truck.

I stop walking, even while calling myself every name under the sun as I do it. I turn to see her standing by the front door, confusion on her face, but that's probably just an act too.

"I…uh…well… you're leaving…now?"

Jesus.

"I'm leaving. Don't worry," I rumble, getting in my vehicle and slamming the door. I start the truck, ready to pull out when she pounds on my window. I put it back in park and hit the button to roll the window down.

"Michael…"

"What?" I ask, exasperated and nearing the end of my rope. I make it back to my place I will not give this woman the time of day. She could literally choke and need me to give her CPR and I'd refuse. I will stop giving into my instincts where Hayden is concerned.

"You seem...*upset*...well, more so than usual," she says as if that's an explanation to why she's here, when it's not. It's ridiculous. *This* is why she followed me out there?

"Go back in, Hayden, before someone sees you with the *beast*," I spit out at her, then I throw the truck in reverse, and back out. She jumps back to keep the truck from hitting her. There's no way I would have hit her. I'm not that far gone. *Not yet.*

Lucy was right.

Hell, everyone was right.

I really am an animal.

A *beast*.

CHAPTER 23

Hayden

MICHAEL'S WORDS HIT me like a hard slap to the face. *I'm such a moron.* Does he really think I don't want to be seen with him? That seems unreal to me, but his parting shot at me seems to indicate that.

I walk slowly back to the reception area. My mind keeps going over everything that just happened. *How could Michael think I wouldn't want to be seen with him?* That concept is so foreign to me. I think I'm in shock.

"Miss Graham," the receptionist calls, demanding my attention.

"Yes?" I ask, walking to her.

"I'm afraid we'll have to reschedule."

"What? *Why?*"

"The doctor is booked up and when we called your name you weren't in here. It wouldn't be fair to put everyone in here off while we wait for you now, would it?" I look around the room and there are a few people here, but only like three or four. Besides, I was only outside for five minutes, ten tops.

"I really need to see the doctor. I was only outside for a few minutes. Surely, you can work me in. I am supposed to have my ultrasound today, it's the first time since I got out of the hospital."

"I'm sorry there's nothing I can do," she says and the look on her face says there is, but she's not doing it. It also signifies she's doing this on purpose and hates me.

I hate her too, and I'd like nothing more than to slap the hell out of her. I don't though. I have bit my tongue since moving here and I continue doing it for one reason. I need quiet. I need to be accepted here if only for my daughter's sake. If what Charlie says is true, Whitley is the only place close that I might be safe from the Dwellers. Somehow my useless brother managed to do one thing for me. He somehow gave me a sanctuary. I am grateful for that, even if I hate him for so many other things. I need safety for Maggie. I can't let closed-minded people like this bitch push me away or cause me to react.

Charlie always tells me that stirring shit only spreads the stink around and attracts more flies. She's not wrong, and really, I've had too much shit…*too much.* I don't want more, and I don't want any of it to splatter on my child. If I had the money, I would have moved farther away. I would have moved to a place no one had heard of the Dwellers. I don't have that luxury, and I'm scared I might get in a bigger mess. The Dwellers consider me their property, even now. They have a lot of enemies. That much I know for sure. What happens if I end up among those people who think they can use me to lash out at them? *Or worse use Maggie.*

So, as much as I hate it, I took the small house my brother gave me and the sanctuary I'm told he found me. I still don't know why he did it. Maybe he felt guilty. I don't fucking know or particularly care. He sent me a goodbye letter years ago telling me his sins had finally caught up with him and that he was sorry.

It was too little and way too late for that to mend whatever bridges had been burned between us. I don't know what happened to him. From the hints in the letter, I figured it wasn't good. I hurt over that. *I did.* Yet, and I know it sounds cold, I had washed my hands of my brother. When I needed him the most he betrayed me. He betrayed me in the worst way imaginable. He may have helped me in the end…but by then too much damage had been done. I hope God has mercy for him, I'm not a good person, because I have none.

"When can I reschedule?" I ask the receptionist, feeling deflated. If I had any pride I'd tell her to go fuck herself, and I hate myself that I don't. She gives me a date which is just a couple days away. I look at the card, nod my head in agreement, and leave.

I walk outside feeling completely dejected. I shouldn't have panicked about Michael. I just didn't want him to see the way the girls in the office treated me. I *really* didn't want him to see how the doctor felt about me. I saw the look on Michael's face that day in the diner around the Dwellers. I think if I saw it again—*or something worse*, it would crush me. In a very strange way it feels like I have a friendship with Michael now, and I really want to keep it.

I look down at the appointment card in my hand again. Maybe I can ask Pastor Sturgill if he could start taking me into the city for my appointments? I could trade baked goods for the ride. It's not ideal, but as I'm getting farther along in my pregnancy, I'm starting to worry. If these people hate me this much, what happens if something goes wrong and the baby and I are in danger? If they look at me now like I'm worse than the dirt under their fingernails, how can I trust them to guard my child's life when it counts the most? Of course, the other side of that coin is the fact that the Dwellers are in the city. My sanctuary, such as it is, could be in danger. I'm worrying enough about the actual delivery, but Charlie assures me the Dwellers are terrified of the Torasani family, and those are the people my brother brokered a deal with. I'd feel more secure if it wasn't so confusing and…*unknown.*

With a heavy sigh, I take off walking. I should go to the diner, but I just have too much on my mind right now. I pull my thick blue shawl tighter around me and take off walking the direction of home. It's a nice day for a change and maybe my time alone will help clear my mind.

CHAPTER 24

Beast

I SHOULDN'T HAVE let her get to me. She doesn't mean anything—just another dumb bitch. God, sometimes I get so fucking tired of going. *So fucking tired of breathing.* I've been parked out by a local marina for thirty minutes doing nothing but watching the water. They've let the levels of the lake down for the winter and it looks as sad as I fucking feel. *No.* Sad is not a good word for what I feel. Sad is a luke-warm description. What I feel inside of me, I've never found words to describe. I'm not sure they're invented. All I know is that now I'm broken and I'm pretty sure everything inside of me is … *black.*

I give up trying to figure shit out and start driving home. Fuck it all. I thought leaving the club would make things easier. It has in a way. At least now I'm not faced with happy couples and children playing every damn day. I don't have to see their stares or hear the whispers. I don't even have to talk. Life is better this way. My decision to leave was the right one. I just need to make sure I keep Hayden away from me, because for some reason she's become a weakness.

I get about five minutes out of town when I see her. *Mother-*

fucker. Hayden is walking along the side of the road, wrapped up in that old, worn-out, blue coat she was wearing. Shit, it's not even a coat, more of a worn wrap she puts around herself. It's not as cold today, but it's still too damn cold for her to be walking like this. What the fuck is she doing here anyway? She was supposed to be at the doctor's office. It's only been half an hour since I left her…at least not much over that—*and she's walking.*

I pull up beside her and hit the button to roll down the passenger window. I do it even knowing I shouldn't. I do it even knowing that I had just decided to stay far away from this woman. I do it thinking I have lost my ever-lovin' mind.

"Get in," I bark.

Hayden's big eyes widen in surprise and she jumps. That's not the first thing I notice however. That would be the tears on her face. Still, even though she's been crying, when she sees me she smiles. *She smiles.* She gets in the truck and closes the door quickly.

"Thanks. I swear when I decided to walk home, I really thought it was closer," she murmurs.

"You're crying," I point out. She looks up from where she's trying to latch her seatbelt and sighs. Then she finishes what she was doing, and looks out the window.

"I'm just feeling sorry for myself. I didn't think anyone would catch me," she half-laughs at herself.

"Is…Maggie okay?" I ask, despite not wanting to.

Her face snaps to mine. Her pale, unadorned lips are shaped like an 'o' and her face flushes in pleasure as her eyes heat. *What the hell?*

"You're the first person to call her Maggie with me," she responds, not answering my question, but at least explaining the look on her face.

"Answer me," I grumble; the look on her face does things to me I can't explain, but I'm pretty sure I don't like it. *Maybe.*

"She's fine…or well…I guess. They couldn't see me," she pauses for a second and gets a faraway look in her eye before continuing. "The doctor had an emergency. It's fine though. I'm actually thinking of switching doctors. Maybe I'll start going to one in the city," she says, and the last part her voice lowers as she nervously picks at the frayed end of her coat. For some reason, I get the distinct impression she's lying to me. "Michael? Can I tell you something?" she asks, her voice dropping down and going even softer than before. Her gray eyes are on me. I've turned my attention back to the road, but even turning away from them, I can feel their intensity as it pierces through me. I want to say no, because I've already crossed the line I drew in the sand. I was done with her. It was time to go back to the reason I got here and it doesn't involve bringing more unwanted people into my life. *I ignore all of that.*

"Yes," I tell her, wishing like fuck I could call the words back even as I say them.

"It wasn't you."

I turn into our joined driveways, parking by her back door. I stare straight ahead for a second, not sure where to go with this conversation—*or even if I wanted to.*

"You had it all backwards. In the doctor's office. I wasn't ashamed of you. Why you would even think that I don't understand. I mean, you have looked in the mirror, right? Okay so your beard has gone a little crazy and your hair could use a bit of a trim, still…"

"Stop," I growl, her rattling annoying me, but this subject pissing me off even more.

"Sorry," she says, but she doesn't sound sorry. She proves this when she continues on. "I'm just saying I was embarrassed."

"Get out," I growl, already knowing she was, and I don't want to hear about it or hear her apologies. It's the truth. It is what it is, and I don't really give a fuck—

"It's just I saw the look on your face when those men used the nickname that Bl…" she stops talking. Her hands are shaking…*No. That's not it.* It's not her hands but her entire *body* trembling and the force of that causes her hands to shake. Her face is white and honest to God, she appears to be a step away from passing out. I've seen enough fear in my life to know that's exactly what is coming off her in waves.

"Stop," I tell her, because whatever she wants to say, it's scaring her to talk about it, and I honestly don't really give a fuck.

"But you need to know," she says, looking down at her shaking hands. God, this is a fucking headache. Why did I pick her up? Why do I keep doing this shit? *What the hell is wrong with me?*

"It doesn't matter," I growl. It is a growl and it's full of exasperation because I'm done. I really am one hundred percent *done.*

"It does! It was just pride. I think of you as my friend, and I just…*God,* I'm making a mess of this."

Her friend? Fuck, me. Jesus. I've sworn off women since Jan. I was pretty much done in general. I feel cold inside. I have nothing to offer anyone, especially women. I sure as fuck don't want one as a *friend.* I have no idea what to say to her. I tighten my hands up on the steering wheel and wait for her to get the fuck out of here.

"People don't like me, Michael," she confesses, tearfully. I don't know what the fuck I expected from her. This wasn't it, however. I snap my head around to look at her. "And believe me when I tell you they don't like me in a way that they don't make a secret of it. And…well…I didn't want you to see it. I didn't want things to change between us. Anyways, I just wanted to say…*I'm sorry*."

There's a lot to take in here. I can't even begin to process her confession before she jumps out of the truck, runs to her house and disappears inside. I'm left here staring after her thinking the one sentence that seems to apply with every run-in I have with Hayden.

What the fuck?

CHAPTER 25

Beast

PEOPLE DON'T LIKE *me Michael.*

It's been a long time since I've been haunted by anything but Annabelle's screams. For two days now, the look on Hayden's face and her distraught confession has taken over. It should be a welcomed relief, and maybe it is a little, but after years and years of living like this, the change is too abrupt. I've lost so much of Annabelle. So much of her is *fading*. As much as I hate the nightmares I crave them too. I need them. I need my daughter. Hayden is stealing those memories away from me and it must stop. I should stop her before the dreams never come back.

I've been watching her out the window as she moves around. There's something that is becoming increasingly clear. Hayden Graham is broken too. I get that, and maybe I understand it more than anyone could. *I sympathize with her.* That also needs to stop. She's getting under my skin, and I don't want that. She's trying to slip beneath my guard and again, that too should stop. I can't allow her to get close.

What I need is a plan. That's how I've lived my life. Plans are how I've survived and made sure my club was safe. I like things clear cut. You see what needs to be done, and you do it. *Simple as that.* I need to figure out how to make it clear to Hayden that we aren't friends. That we aren't even neighbors. I'm here to be alone. That's it. Once I set the record straight it will be okay and life can return back to normal.

"Can I come up?" I hear her from the stairway below. *Motherfucker.* The loft apartment has no door. You come through the door in the barn that leads to the stairs and the loft is all open. I like that it's open and normally it helps me feel less caged in. *Until today.* Today, I don't like it at all. Why the fuck didn't I lock the door after I went out to my bike last night? *Maybe because I was shit-faced.* Jesus. I don't want her in here. I. Do. Not. Want. Her. In—

"Hi," she says, taking a deep breath. She's holding her stomach, and smiling at me. She looks so young and innocent.

I want to scream at her to get out. I want to command her to leave. The words freeze, and instead, I grunt my displeasure and just stare at her. I'm sitting on the beat up old sofa and seeing her in my space is making it hard for me to even move. *Leave.* I try and will the word into her brain, even if I'm not saying it aloud. *It doesn't work.*

"Shew! Stairs are rough on a pregnant woman. I hope I'm not bothering you."

You are. For some reason, I don't say that to her either, I just stare at her.

"Wow, this place hasn't changed. My uh…brother used to stay here some. He was an asshole though so I tried to never come over here. I was kind of glad when the front door was chained. I had hoped whoever he rented it from forgot about the place. I mean it's been empty for so long. I liked being alone. Obviously though I mean, it's good you're here. I didn't mean it like how that sounded. Well, not really," she rattles on, with her face getting redder by the second. She's obviously nervous. She keeps grabbing the end of her shirt with her free hand, curling the fabric under her fingers. Embarrassment is so thick on her face she'd glow in the dark. It's kind of pathetic and that's the only reason I don't call her out and make her leave. *The only reason.*

"It's just...I wanted to bring this to you. I've got a doctor's appointment today, and I need to head out. I didn't want to just leave this outside. I thought you might like some of them for breakfast," she continues, walking around the couch to face me. She hands me a white plastic container. I take it from her, opening it, and finding blueberry muffins inside. "I uh...make them from scratch. The store had a sale on fresh blueberries the other day and well, I couldn't resist. Even though muffins aren't in big demand. People would rather have cookies and cakes...pies are big too. But well...I like muffins," she says, her voice breaking off uncomfortably, and she's avoiding my eyes now. The woman seriously talks ninety-miles-an-hour.

I want to throw the muffins back at her. I want to demand she leaves. Instead, I find myself taking a bite of one. *Motherfucker.* At first bite, blueberry flavor hits my tongue; the spongey cake around it is light and moist and better than anything I've ever eaten in my life. She's looking at me expectantly and I open my mouth to once again try to make her go.

"They're really good," I tell her. My brain and mouth are totally going against my command, and that's just fucked up. *What the hell is Hayden doing to me?* Those gray eyes of hers light up, and she stops wringing her hands together. Those pale lips, which I thought were way too thin, bloom out into a full-fledged smile and she looks almost...pretty. *Christ.*

"I'm so glad you like them. I have plenty of time, but I like to drive slow in my car. Better safe than sorry. So, I better get going. Me and Maggie have a date with a sonogram," she laughs holding her stomach. "You have a good day, Michael," she adds, turning to walk back down the stairs.

I manage to bite my tongue and not say anything. She's on the fourth stair before visions of her driving down the road in that death trap come to mind. I can virtually see her pulling out at a stop sign and the piece of shit decides to quit and she gets t-boned. The vision is so clear, I growl and she jumps. Her hand tightens on the wooden rail as she looks over her shoulder at me.

"I'll take you," I mutter. "I have to go into town anyway," I lie. *What the hell is wrong with me?*

"Oh...you don't have to do that. I'll be fine—"

"Let's go," I order, putting the muffins on the table, and grabbing my keys that are lying there. *I'm fucking losing my mind.* I prove that further by grabbing her hand and helping her walk down the stairs so she won't fall.

I'm taking Hayden to the doctor. I didn't yell at her for invading my space. I didn't demand she leave me alone. I haven't done one thing that I needed to do.

It's clear I'm swimming in a bucket of fucking insanity at this point.

CHAPTER 26

Hayden

I THINK I'M getting used to Michael. I might even *like* him. Which shocks me to death. When I...*escaped* the only thing I wanted out of life was to be...*alone.* I sure as hell didn't want to be around another man for the rest of my life. It's different with Michael though. He's not like that. He's never acted in a sexual manner toward me. He's never even acted in a manner that would indicate he even looks at me like a female. It's strange, but in my mind, he's become asexual. *We're friends.* I've never had one except for Charlie—*especially a male one.*

"You really didn't have to do this," I tell Michael again.

In response, he gives me his signature grunt. The man just doesn't speak a lot. It kind of makes me smile. I lean into the door, my head pressed against the window as I watch the rain begin to fall outside. I love the rain. I could watch it for hours upon hours. It feels...*clean*...it even *smells* clean. There are days when I feel like *I'll* never be clean again.

We've pulled into the doctor's office way before I'm ready. I give Michael a tentative smile. He's pulled up to the door so I'm taking that to mean he's not planning on going inside. That's good…I guess. I'm starting to feel better when he's with me. I should worry about that. "Thanks, Michael," I tell him gently. I even find myself patting his hand again, which garners me another grunt, and makes me smile yet again.

The smile soon fades as I enter into the waiting area. I go to the desk and sign in, before taking a seat. I'm the only person in the room, and I figure it shouldn't take long. After thirty minutes, I'm starting to realize I was wrong. I look through the glass, front entrance doors and see Michael out there. The rain has stopped and he's standing beside his truck now, leaning over the side of bed, his head down as his hand rests against the top of the bedside. He's so big and tall, he makes his truck look small. His face is hidden beneath the hair. He hasn't pulled it back and it blends in with his long beard. His long sleeved blue flannel shirt covers every inch of his massive arms and is buttoned even to cover his neck. It looks good on him, but…*wrong*. His jeans are dark wash, with just the faintest hint of distress here and there while the big boots he wears ensures he looks like a man no one would mess with. I think he could even make the Dwellers quake in fear. That thought makes me smile. Michael picks that moment to look up and even through the distance and the glass door separating us, I'm sure he sees me. His eyes bore into me and the anger in that look makes my smile falter. In that moment, I wonder if Pastor Sturgill is right, because he looks like an avenging angel—beautiful but tragically filled with vengeance. My heart hurts for the pain I read clearly on his face.

"Ms. Graham," the receptionist calls, pulling my attention away from Michael. I swallow down my nerves and walk to the front desk.

"I'm here," I smile, my smile is met with a stern face though. Stern isn't exactly the right word. It's more like *resting bitch face*.

"There's a conflict with your appointment. The receptionist shouldn't have scheduled the appointment for today. Wednesdays are days when the doctor is not in the office."

"But you're the one who scheduled—"

"I'm very sorry, there's nothing I can do."

"But I'm scheduled for an ultrasound. They were supposed to check on the baby because I've been sick."

"There's nothing I can do. You do know there's a free clinic to deal with people like you? If it's urgent you should try there."

It's crazy, I know. They've been treating me like crap the entire time I've been coming to the doctor here. Yet, I hadn't realized just how deep their hate went until just now when it slaps me in the face. I've taken *a lot.* I've paid over and over for my supposed crimes. *I think I'm done.* I'm about to tell her that when this large, ink-covered fist comes down against the reception desk.

"The doctor will see her today," Michael growls. His fist hits the counter so hard that the stuff that's on it literally bounces. I wonder for a second if it might crack and break, but miracle of miracles it holds together.

"Sir—"

"I don't like you. I don't like the way you spoke to Hayden. I'm done with you. I want to talk to your boss. *Now.*"

"But—"

"Now!" he growls, and the anger coming off of him is like nothing I've seen before. I'm nervous just witnessing it. His body is seriously vibrating and his voice is dark—*deadly.*

I spare a glance at the receptionist, and notice her face has gone white. She has also backed up a good five steps. If I was her, in the face of Michael's wrath, I'd quickly go into another room. *Maybe another state.*

"Michael..." I whisper, thinking maybe I should talk him

down. I'd hate for him to end up in jail over this.

Michael grunts at me, literally that's all he does. Grunts. Then he turns back to look at the woman again. "You have two minutes and if I don't have someone here, you won't like what happens next," he tells her, and this time his voice is quiet and soft, but somehow, it's even more menacing.

I watch as the receptionist visibly swallows and runs from the room.

Oh boy…

CHAPTER 27

Beast

I RUB MY hand along the back of my neck, the tension is getting to me. I can feel a hell of a headache coming on. I need my fucking head examined. Somehow, I've gone from this morning where I was done with all things Hayden to now, a few short hours later, where I find myself waiting in a dark room while she has a sonogram. *A sonogram of the child she's carrying.* I never thought of myself as a masochist but fuck, maybe I am.

"Let's see what's going on in there," the nurse says, watching me instead of Hayden. I don't respond. This whole place is fucked up. When I heard the way that woman talked to Hayden, I had to put a stop to it. Hayden had been in the hospital. She needed to be monitored closely, and I don't care what the fuck the problem is between her and Hayden, that child is innocent.

That's the only reason I did it, too. It didn't have shit to do with the look of hurt on Hayden's face—*not at all.* Hayden is looking up at me now, and the look on her face bothers me. It's almost like hero worship, and I'm no one's fucking hero. I should tell her flat out! Tell her that I couldn't care less how people treat her. I start to. *I really do.* It's just when the nurse raises her sweater up and reveals her stomach I get sucker-punched.

I've seen her stomach through her clothes. I've never seen it revealed like this. It's smaller than I originally thought, which means Hayden is a fuck of a lot skinnier than I realized. But, her stomach does have a noticeable bump with the skin stretched tight accentuating it. With all the times I've seen her in those oversized clothes, somehow, I expected her stomach to be larger. Right now, it seems so small…delicate…something in need of…*protection.*

I watch as the nurse squeezes out a jelly-like substance on Hayden's stomach and proceeds to spread it around. I watch her move the wand around and adjust buttons on the machine. All at once the noise blasts from the machine. My body stiffens as I hear it. It's been a long time since I've heard that noise. The last time was when Jan was pregnant…*with my daughter.* This isn't my daughter…this is Hayden's…*but still it does something to me.* It's a clear sound, strong, steady; the sound of it hits me. I didn't want to be here. I didn't want to hear it. *This child is nothing to me.* But…hearing the heartbeat causes a warmth to hit me. I want to write it off as nothing, but before I can attack the emotions that are being unleashed Hayden reaches out and grabs my hand. Now it is shock that courses through me.

The other day in the car, Hayden moved her thumb over my scars. I still hadn't processed what her touch did to me. Here she is, reaching out grabbing my hand, holding it tightly in hers, and she's doing it all while her child's heartbeat is echoing around us. I look down at our joined hands. Mine are scarred and inked. Hers are pale, small, with long slender fingers, and the nails trimmed short and unadorned. It looks wrong. It feels wrong. Yet…at the same time it feels…*right.* Fuck.

I should pull my hand away. Yet, for some reason I don't.

Then the nurse turns the screen around. Her words get lost to me. They're drowned out by the beating of the child's heart and the roar in my ears. But my eyes are glued to the screen as she points to different areas on the screen. She shows the head and legs and inside the body you can see it. The small, flickering beat of a tiny heart.

The sight on the screen shouldn't mean anything to me. The child is not mine, but instead, there's this warmth inside of me, spreading through parts that have been cold for far too long. *A purpose.* A sense of duty comes over me. I wasn't able to save Annabelle. *I failed.* This child, I *can* protect her. God knows the woman suddenly clutching my hand right now needs a protector. Which means so does her child. An *innocent* child. In a world of darkness innocence should be protected.

I can do that. It won't set right my failures of the past. Yet, it might help me to breathe without feeling like I shouldn't. Perhaps this is why I was spared. To be here in this exact place for this child.

"It's Maggie," Hayden whispers, and I look down at her. There are tears streaming down her face. Silent tears, but tears of joy. She's a puzzle. I had her pegged to be just like Jan, but there's no doubting that she's happy. There's no doubting she cares for this child. I don't know what to do with these urges to protect them. I don't know what this means. The only thing I can be sure of is that I can take care of Hayden and this child. I can make sure they're safe. That's my reason.

My purpose.

CHAPTER 28

Hayden

"THAT'S THE FIRST time I've seen her. They don't like to do ultrasounds until you get further along. I'm only four months. So, I hadn't been able to see her. Wasn't she the most beautiful baby you ever seen?" I ask Michael as we make it out to the truck.

In response, he gives me his trademark grunt. It makes me grin. *A true grin.* It's one that makes me feel warm and happy. He seems so tough and cold, but I looked at his eyes as he watched the screen. *Maggie got to him too.* That has to mean I was right, and he's one of the good guys. I've seen evil…I've lived with it and that is not who Michael is. I feel safe around him. That couldn't happen if he was like the others. I was right in letting my guard down around him.

"If you hadn't seen her before then how do you know she's a girl?" Michael asks.

The tech didn't reveal the sex of the baby. She said she was being shy.

"I don't know for sure, but I just have a feeling. She's definitely a girl," I tell Michael, and his reply is a grunt, and I can't stop myself from laughing this time.

I pull my eyes away from Michael, and watch as we turn back on the road. I expected him to head us in the direction of the house. Instead, he turns in the direction of town. Before I can question him, he grunts out—a word this time.

"Hungry," he rumbles out, and there's a moment of panic. I might be congratulating myself on letting my guard down and trusting my neighbor, but it's panic just the same. Something about going out in public with him seems…*scary*. That doesn't make sense. I mean we were together at the doctor's office. I held his hand when I looked at my child for the first time. How can sharing a meal with him be scary? It's still there though. That feeling of panic and flushed heat that makes my heart pound against my chest.

As he pulls into the diner, I try to convince myself it's because we're going to eat at the place I work. My co-workers will assume that he and I are dating. *Which we're not.* That would be preposterous. I mean, all you have to do is look at him and you can see that Michael would never pick someone like me to date. We're just friends. I'll make that clear and everything will be okay. It's just a lunch meeting with friends. People have those all the time…*right?*

Well okay, I don't, because I don't really have friends. But I'm sure for *regular* people, a lunch together would be…*normal.* I've always longed for a normal life and maybe that's what is happening. Maybe that's why I'm feeling so panicky. I'm getting a real life, *finally*. One my brother can't ruin, and one *no one* can take away from me. With that thought, I am out of the truck and meeting Michael in front of his truck the minute we park.

Michael gives me a frown, the kind that could make my knees quake—*if we weren't friends*. But since we are, I just grin up at him. This earns me another grunt. He puts his hand on the small of my back and directs me toward the front door. His hand is warm against my back and momentarily flusters me as we go through the doors.

"Hey, Hayden, I didn't know you worked today," Liese calls out. I don't see Charlie anywhere, which is unusual. I smile at Liese, who next to Charlie is probably the only one in town that really cares about me. She might even miss me if something happened to me. I haven't talked to her a lot, but she's been good to me and helped me before when I was in a jam. I've watched her little boy a few times, and I've given her some baked goods from time to time. Until Michael, that's the only friendship I've ever truly worked at keeping. Liese is good people and though she doesn't know my full past, I realize she knows some of it. She knows it, and she doesn't judge me. She doesn't shy away from letting others know that she likes me. That means a lot to me.

"I'm not. Michael brought me into town for my doctor's appointment, and we decided to grab some lunch," I tell her with a smile. I'd stop at the front bar and sit down so I could talk to her, but Michael keeps his pressure on my back. I go with him to the main back table. I usually like to hide against the wall on the few occasions I have ventured out. Michael doesn't give me that option. Instead, he puts me in the chair facing the wall, while he takes the one against the wall across from me.

"What can I get you guys?" Liese asks, almost immediately. Michael looks at me pointedly—with another grunt. I swear I'd almost believe this guy was a caveman that was only recently unthawed from the ice. There was a movie about that. I think I'll make it my mission to make Michael watch that someday…*if I get the chance.*

"I'll have a chocolate milk, peanut butter and banana sandwich with melted cheese, and French fries," I tell her.

"I'll have the cheeseburger box," his dark voice rumbles. "Lemonade for the drink," he adds, and I can't stop the gasp that comes out of my mouth.

Liese grins at me and goes back toward the kitchen.

"What?" he asks, when I don't seem to form words soon enough to suit him.

"I just…it's just that…"

"For a girl that talks so much, you have trouble forming sentences that make sense," he grumbles, his voice cracking as he finishes, causing him to frown.

"It's just you don't look like much of a lemonade drinker, Michael."

"They don't sell whiskey here," he answers, watching me closely.

"Well, no. But I figured you for soda or a beer man maybe."

"What's wrong with lemonade?" He eyes me, confused.

I shrug. "It seems so…cheerful," I tell him, honestly, and for a second, I think he's smiling. The muscles along his jawline moves and it could be entirely possible. It's also impossible to know since he's covered with so much hair.

"What the hell is a peanut butter and banana sandwich?" he asks, turning my question back on me.

"Elvis loved them," I tell him, defensively.

"With cheese?" he asks doubtfully.

"I'm pregnant and apparently, Maggie demands them." I shrug and there it is again. I'm pretty sure he's smiling. I wish I could know for sure. "Can I ask you a question?" I propose, tilting my head a little, wishing I could see his lips. There's a glimpse of them through the dark hair but that's it. He gives me a heavy sigh, but he doesn't say no. I'm going to count that as permission. "Does it hurt you to talk?" Shock comes over his face at my question. He wasn't expecting it and it was probably a very rude question to ask, I couldn't stop myself, however.

Liese brings over our drinks, and he stares down at his lemonade, completely ignoring me. I figure that means he's not going to answer. I'm kind of ashamed that I just asked him that question so bluntly. I shouldn't have pried. I hate it when people do that to me. I don't know what possessed me to be that way with Michael. I, *of all people*, should understand there are just some things that you don't want to talk about. While the question seemed perfectly innocent to me, I know he's covered in burns, and I can tell it had to be horrific just from the scarring. Of course he wouldn't want to talk about it. *I'm an idiot.*

"It doesn't hurt, it's just tight, and I hate hearing…I hate hearing the change in my voice," he tells me, and I know he's giving me absolute honesty. I cherish it, because I'm pretty sure Michael hasn't spoken to people about this before. I don't know why I think that, but I know enough to know he's a solitary person, so I'd lay money on the fact that I'm right.

I decide to change the subject to something *safer.* "The hospital gave me your name when they were going through my papers. Connor Michael Jameson. It's a beautiful name. Is there a reason you go by Michael rather than Connor?"

He grunts. Hmm…I have no idea what that means. I thought talking about his name would be safer than his scars or voice. My new friend is going to be difficult to get to know if this is any indication. I decide to give up and just stare out the window. He wants silence. I can appreciate that. Sometimes holding a conversation takes too much effort.

CHAPTER 29

Beast

"I DON'T GO by either name. Michael is what my bitch of a mother called me," I tell her finally, if for no other reason than to stop her from staring out the window and ignoring me. This might have been a mistake. I should have dropped her off at home, made sure she had food and left. I was just thinking that the child needed food and set about making sure she got it. Protecting this child might come with quite a few complications. *Most notably, her mother.*

The waitress brings our food and for a few minutes Hayden is preoccupied with arranging her plate, drink, and then making sure the cheese is melted correctly on her sandwich. It's very strange watching her. When she reaches for the salt shaker, I take it from her.

"What?" she asks, confused.

"Salt's bad for the baby," I explain, proceeding to use it myself. I practically pour it in my ketchup. I'm not ashamed to admit that if it was possible, I would totally be addicted to salt. That said, I'm adding more than usual, because each second that ticks by Hayden's mouth opens a little more, and her eyes widen with shock.

"I hate to tell you this, but I don't think that much salt is good for anyone," she finally answers. Her voice is a mixture of sarcasm and exasperation. It could almost make me smile…*yet again.* Hayden is a very strange creature.

"Doesn't matter. I'm not carrying Maggie," I tell her, and fuck if I don't let loose a chuckle, when this time she grunts at me.

"If you don't go by Michael or Connor what do people call you?" she asks, taking a bite of her sandwich when she finishes her question.

I think about not answering her, but then she'd probably take to ignoring me again and looking out the window. "My club gave me a road name," I tell her, reluctant to share with her what it is. She looks up at me and a look comes over her face that I don't like. I'm not sure how to describe it, but I know that mixed in with it is fear.

"You…you are in a club? Like…A biker gang?" she says, her face going noticeably pale. She's even pushing her chair back as if she's getting ready to run.

"It's a club—*not* a gang. And I used to be. I'm not anymore," I growl. I never thought she would be so judgmental. She doesn't have a right to judge. Has she looked in the fucking mirror.

"Were you…were you part of the Dwellers?" she asks, and it's then I notice her hands are trembling.

Suddenly, I'm clued into the fact that this is more than my being part of a motorcycle club. No, this has much more to do with the Shadow Dwellers in general. I gathered she used to be a hanger on or a plaything to the Dwellers. They're a twisted fucking bunch that's for sure, and I have to wonder how Hayden didn't wind up one of the girls they sold. Now I'm starting to wonder exactly what Hayden's full story is. I'm going to have to make her tell me. It's not because I want to know more about her. No. I'm being logical. I need to protect the baby. That's the *only reason*, I need to know. That's *all* this is.

"I'd slit my own throat before I'd join any brotherhood with the Dwellers," I tell her with frank honesty.

Her face jerks up and she looks at me, her steely eyes wide. She studies my face for a few minutes before she nods in agreement. Slowly, second by second, her body releases the tension that has gathered into it. She still looks unsure however, and for some reason I find myself wanting to reassure her. Which pisses me off. So, instead I go back to my food—ignoring her.

"Does that mean your…*club* was different than the Dwellers?"

"As night and day," I confirm. I may not be a member of the Blaze anymore, but I don't like my brothers being compared to a bunch of inbred ass-fucks.

"What was your club like?" she asks, and I don't want to answer. If I answer, I have to think about my brothers and the life I had once. I shrug it off instead. Swallowing down my answer, I pretend interest in my food, which has suddenly become dry as sawdust. *They were like a family.* I want to tell her that.

I don't.

CHAPTER 30

Hayden

"I'M SORRY. I get the feeling I offended you, I didn't mean to. My views are jaded when it comes to bikers," I tell him, hating that I caused him to withdraw. For a second, I felt panic threaten to overtake me when he mentioned he was part of a club. It was a crazy reaction considering I had already assumed at least in my head that Michael was a biker. It stands to reason that he belongs to a club...or according to him belonged to a club.

"You were Dwellers' property," he says matter-of-factly. So calm and quiet he says those words. He doesn't have a clue to the misery and pain those simple words hold. He may not know, but they inflict enough pain that I want to get up and run out of the diner. *Run and never turn back.*

"I'm no one's property," I say in a soft whisper that I hate. I'd rather growl out my words with such strength that no one could ever see me as weak again.

I sneak a glance up at Michael to see how he takes my declaration. He's not making fun of me or laughing, which I thought might be a distinct possibility. When I look up at him, he's nodding in agreement. Something about that warms me as nothing else could. It's an agreement, but more than that. It's an agreement from a man I like, and I think...*respect.* Because of that it feels like there's a healing inside of me. A warmth that coats over the jagged hurts that have been inflicted on my soul. He doesn't know that. No, he would probably think I was insane if I told him. It's there just the same.

I take a breath, wanting to push the conversation in a different direction—*needing it to.* "What did they call you?"

He stops mid-bite to look at me.

"Beast," he says, putting his burger back down. I'm frozen for a second. Beast? I mean it could certainly fit. He's so tall sometimes I get a crook in my neck staring up at him, and I'm not exactly short. He's also broad, his body so impressive he could make three of me. He's a beast of a man, so I can see it. Yet, for some reason it shocks me. The more I think about it, however, the more I want to giggle. He looks up at me and studies my face. I'm still unable to hide my amusement. "You find that funny?"

"I'm just wondering how many women volunteered to be Beauty," I tell him, giving up my fight and giggling—especially when the shocked look of surprise covers his normally taciturn face.

"You're a strange woman, Hayden," he answers, shaking his head. This time however, there is no doubt. He's smiling and that makes me feel good.

"I can't call you Beast. I think I'll stick with Michael. Maybe I'll call you Mikey," I tell him, grinning, then sneaking my fry into his mound of salty ketchup.

"You will not call me Mikey. No one has called me Mikey and lived to tell about it," he says sternly, but his eyes are twinkling at me. "And put that fry down. That's too much salt for you and Maggie."

"Can I call you Mikey?" I ask, with a smile.

"Abso-fucking-lutely not," he says—still unyielding, but his eyes are still twinkling in their dark depths.

"Then I'm keeping my fry," I tell him with a shrug, popping it in my mouth. The salt explodes in my mouth. He didn't just over salt the ketchup. No, he has what is equivalent to the largest salt mine in the United States. I cough, even though I try to suppress it. I cough again and again, gagging on the salty taste that overpowers everything. *"How do you eat that?"* I ask, in between coughing and spluttering. I reach for my glass and take a huge drink. It takes two more drinks before I'm able to stop coughing, but it doesn't matter. I barely notice. All I notice in that moment is Michael is laughing. It's not a loud laugh and it didn't last particularly long. But he laughed.

He laughed.

CHAPTER 31

Beast

"HI," HAYDEN CALLS out, drawing the word out as she climbs the stairs. I hold my head down, biting down the urge to tell her to leave.

I haven't talked to her in two days, not since I brought her home after lunch at the diner. It's a fucked-up thing, but I have been avoiding her. Being around her seems to make me feel better, and I don't deserve that. After spending six years in Hell, that feeling could become addicting. The last thing in the world I need is to be addicted to Hayden Graham.

"Are you in here?" she asks, just as she pops up from the stairway. She looks up at me with a large smile. "There you are. I was wondering if you were busy?" I forbid myself to talk to her. I can't encourage this…*I can't.* "Well, I mean, if you are, it's okay. I was making dinner, and I made too much really, and I was going to watch a movie. If you don't have any plans and well, if you want to, you could come over. You don't have to. So, please don't feel like you do. I just thought that you have to eat, and I have to eat and maybe we could eat together. *Maybe? Possibly?* Okay. Well. Um…"

I watch as she rattles on crazily before breaking off to just stare at me. Her cheeks are red with embarrassment, and I should stop being an ass and just tell her I don't want to have dinner with her. I should, and yet *I don't.* I can't seem to get those words out.

"You shouldn't be climbing the stairs."

"What?" she asks, confused.

"You could get hurt. You shouldn't be climbing the stairs on your own."

"I'm pregnant, not disabled," she defends.

"You could fall," I point out what she should already know and ignoring that she's trying to be cute. *She is cute.* That thought settles in my mind. I never thought she was much to look at, but today she's wearing these soft blue leggings with a long ivory like sweater that comes down to her knees. She's got her hair brushed until it shines and it falls softly along her shoulders and back. I wouldn't have thought she was pretty before, but today she looks…almost beautiful. *Maybe it's the pregnancy glow.*

"Do you want to come to dinner with me and Maggie?" she asks, instead of answering.

"What's for dinner?" I ask, instead of telling her no. *I can't believe it.* I've obviously lost my mind.

In response, she grins at me like she just won a war. "I made meatloaf, mashed potatoes, and corn," she says, seeming very happy with herself.

"What if I don't like meatloaf?" I ask her, enjoying our conversation and isn't that just a giant bucket of fuck. I'm getting in over my head here. I know it, but for the life of me I can't seem to stop it.

"You love meatloaf. You order it at the diner all the time, and for dessert, I made apple pie," she adds, and fuck, she's been paying attention to me—more attention than I would have ever dreamed. *How did I miss that?* She's also right. The last woman who cooked meatloaf for me was Annie—*Sabre's old lady*. It was damn good.

"Okay," I tell her before I can talk myself out of it.

"Just like that?" she asks surprised. Her gray eyes widening.

"You didn't want me to agree?"

"I did, I just figured you'd make me work harder for it," she says with complete honesty, and I find myself smiling, yet again. *At her.*

"I thought about it, but then you'd have to walk down the stairs by yourself," I tease her, and I watch as Hayden's mouth opens, closes and then opens again. Then she laughs. It's a nice laugh, and for some reason, hearing it feels good enough to keep the smile stretched on my face.

Fuck.

CHAPTER 32

Hayden

"DO YOU WANT some more pie?" I ask Michael, as he pushes away from the small table, holding his stomach. I must admit that I'm feeling pretty pleased with myself. He had two heaping platefuls of food and two pieces of pie on top of that. I watch as he rubs his stomach, and his dark eyes look up at me ruefully.

"If I eat anymore, I think I might explode. I take it you are not the cook at the diner," he answers.

"Nah, Charlie's sister does all the cooking. She's good and quick."

"You're better. Charlie doesn't know what she's missing," he tells me, and I feel like I just won a medal or something. I'm not used to people praising me.

"Thanks, I'm glad you enjoyed it." I stand there for a minute grinning at him like an idiot. He looks back at me and he almost seems relaxed. Before I can be any more of a goofball, I grab plates and start carrying them over to the sink, trying to find anything to do, because suddenly the atmosphere between us seems uncomfortable, and that's the last thing I want.

"I'll help you wash the dishes," Michael offers, starting to get up from the table.

"Please, don't. There's no need. I washed up the pans and things as I cooked. What's left, I'll just leave in the sink. I'll get them later, or in the morning. I was wondering…I mean I was going to watch a movie. Would you like to watch it with me?"

His eyes harden for a second and his body goes stiff with tension. I've pushed too far. I should have known better than to ask. "Hayden…" he starts, but I cut him off.

"I'm only asking because I like the company. Honestly, I don't have a lot of people in my life. Liese has her baby and she stays busy being a single mom. Charlie is kind of a loner, and I wouldn't want to bother her outside of work. I respect Pastor Sturgill, but I wouldn't want to invite him to dinner alone. He's a Pastor, and well, it wouldn't look right if I kept inviting him to dinner."

"Do you care what people think about you?" he asks, leaning back against his chair and appraising me. Suddenly, I feel like I'm being tested. I have to wonder if I'm going to pass. I take a breath as I think about his words and I want to laugh, but I can't. I smile, though it's more of a resigned, sad smile.

"I think people have pretty much made their minds up about me, Michael. I meant, what they would say about Pastor Sturgill. I wouldn't want to do damage to his reputation or his standing in the community."

"But you don't care about mine?" he asks, and those eyes of his are almost twinkling again. I'm getting the distinct impression he's joking with me. I shake my head at him, wishing I knew exactly what ran through his mind sometimes.

"After the fit you threw at the doctor's office I think people have already made up their minds about you. I'm sorry to tell you this, Michael, but, hanging around with me, taking up for me, is probably not a good thing."

"And why is that?"

"Because people are assholes and the majority of them are mean," I tell him, honestly. Once upon a time, I might have thought differently. Life has shown me the error of my ways, however.

"What movie are we watching?" he asks, surprising me.

"It's a surprise," I announce, grinning. "I think you'll like it. The hero reminds me of you."

"God help me," he jokes, and he really does joke this time.

I laugh, happy he agreed to watch the movie with me and happy in general. I like having a friend—a friend I feel safe with. We move into the living room. Michael sits down on the sofa while I put the DVD in the player and set the volume.

"There we go," I tell him, once it's all set. Then I go sit in the chair across from the sofa.

"You can sit here with me. You can't see the television from over there," Michael says and he's right, but it feels a little strange to sit with him. I don't want to say that to him, however.

"Okay," I agree with him, not wanting to ruin his mood by accidentally offending him. Once I sit down on the opposite end from him, I pull my feet up under me, hugging my legs, and wait for the movie to begin.

"I didn't realize people still used DVD players," he smirks. I look over at him and he's smiling again, even with that mountain of hair on his face I can tell it. He's got his broad arms stretched out, one along the top of my couch and another on the arm of it. He's wearing a long-sleeved thermal top in red and it's stretched across his large muscles. He looks relaxed, almost normal. I find myself smiling back at him as the last of the nervous tension I was holding in fades.

"Well, I'm sorry, I can't afford internet and in truth I probably wouldn't have it if I could."

He scrunches up his face. "You don't like modern conveniences? You'd be the first woman in history."

"I like indoor plumbing. Does that count?" I answer, and he chuckles again.

"That counts," he mutters, turning back around to the television. It doesn't take long. Maybe about five minutes before he finally turns back around and looks at me. "Encino Man? Please tell me Hayden you are not a Pauly Shore fan."

"What's wrong with Pauly Shore? He's probably one of the great actors of our time."

"You can't be serious?" he asks me, looking dumbstruck.

I sift through my brain trying to think of another Pauly Shore movie. "Clearly you have never watched *Son In Law*. His work on that movie was far before its time."

"You're scaring me, right now, Hayden," he says, and I laugh so hard that I snort. I happen to look up as I do and I notice he's smiling so big now there's no way he can hide it. "You're a strange woman," he says again, turning back around to watch the movie.

He keeps repeating that, and for some reason, I'm glad he thinks so.

CHAPTER 33

Beast

"THANK GOD THAT is over," I joke, looking over at Hayden. I don't mean it. This has been one of the best nights I can remember having in forever, even with the awful movie.

"Oh, come on! Admit it. You loved that movie," she defends, her face bright, lit up with laughter. *Did I really think she was homely at one time?*

"There was not one thing *anyone* could love about that movie, Hayden," I tell her, making my face completely serious, which is harder than I thought it would be.

"But you had to like it. It's about your people."

"My people?" I ask her confused, I should have noticed the sneaky look on her face, but for some reason I didn't—*at least not in time.*

"Of course. The caveman has to be like your long lost relative."

"How do you figure that?" I ask, unable to stop myself.

"Oh, come on. You grunt more than you ever talk," she laughs, surprising me. I thought she was going to make a remark about my hair or beard.

In response to her assessment, I grunt, which she finds hilarious and laughs so hard, the legs she has pulled up against her front kick out and she throws her head back in laughter. She laughs so hard she does that cute snorting thing again, taking air in loudly. In this moment, she's everything I wish I was. Happy. Warm. *Free.*

I force myself to pull away from her because I have the strongest urge to take her in my arms and kiss her. I can't help but wonder if I kissed her, would I be able to take some of that warmth inside of me? Could Hayden erase some of the cold blackness that has taken over. It's a fool's dream. Hell, even if it was possible, I don't deserve it.

"Going to the bathroom," I tell her, as I walk away. My voice is gruff, and I notice her laughter stops. I miss it almost instantly. Once I close the door, I lean my head against it and fight against the ache I feel. I haven't touched a woman…haven't even wanted one since before Jan died. The few times Jan and I had sex wasn't worth the time it took. I didn't like her, I never respected her, and if not for Annabelle, I wouldn't have taken her back into my bed. I've thought about women since, but not enough to act on it. Taking a woman into my bed would mean revealing my scars, it would mean putting myself out there in a world I'm no longer part of. In a world I don't deserve to take part of.

I know nothing of Hayden, other than her brother was fucking scum. She has some kind of connection with the Dwellers, and if that isn't enough, she's pregnant. She's the last person in the world I should be thinking about touching.

I stare off to space for a few more minutes, trying to get myself under control, trying to pull those damn walls I have back up around me. Then I get angry with myself for even contemplating this shit. Life is for the living, and I've been dead a fuck of a long time. I need to let Hayden know that, and demand she leave me alone.

I march in the living room to do that very thing, but I freeze when I get back in there. She's lying on the sofa, curled up almost in a ball. Her head is resting on a throw cushion, one hand under her head and another wrapped around the front of her stomach. She's sound asleep, and despite her growing stomach, she looks so innocent I could almost ache. She can't sleep on that couch all night. I'm sure I felt springs poking through when I sat there. I lean down to pick her up. Her scent tingles my senses. She smells like cinnamon and vanilla, reminding me of the apple pie she made tonight. *I'd like to eat her.* Hayden's body instantly curves into mine, and I feel my fucking cock stretch in interest. I've been dead for so long, at first, I'm not even sure what is happening. Then my cock hardens further when Hayden moans slightly before snuggling into me. *Jesus, I have a hard-on.* What makes it even worse is I want more. I want more even as I hate myself for wanting it.

She moans again, and her fingers dig into my shirt, capturing some of my chest hair in her hold. I ignore how good that feels and take her into her bedroom. I take her to the bed, holding her with one arm while bracing her on my knee. It isn't hard because Hayden is way too light. *She needs to eat more.* A strong wind could knock her over. That can't be good for the baby. I use my free hand to pull down her covers and quickly lay her down.

She's still wearing her clothes, but they're loose—she should be fine. I grab the covers and slowly pull them up to her body, stopping once they cover most of her stomach. I rest there, looking at her. Again, completely amazed at how beautiful she truly is. That golden bronze hair shines against her pillow and her face is relaxed in sleep. Right now, I'd be hard pressed to think of anyone prettier.

Then suddenly, my world is rocked even more. I feel movement against my hand that's still gripping the cover at her waist. I move my hand so my palm lies flat against her stomach and after a second I feel the movement again. *The baby.* Moving. Kicking. *Living.* Hayden doesn't stir, she's completely out, but the child doesn't seem to care. I can feel another movement under my hand. It feels as if she's turning against my hand. Warmth fills me as I savor this connection. Again, I remember the feelings I had at the doctor's office. This child…*Maggie.* She will be my purpose. I will be her protector. As if she agrees with me, Maggie kicks again and then goes still. I reluctantly drag my hand away.

The decision has been made.

CHAPTER 34

Hayden

IT DOESN'T MAKE sense but I've been sad all day. I wish I knew a reason why. The truth is I've been tired ever since I woke up in my own bed this morning and Michael was gone. I forgot how great it felt to spend time with another person and not have to worry—*to not be afraid.* I don't have work today, which means I need to be baking. That should be easy, except I burned the last two batches of cookies. At this rate, I'm going to go broke, instead of making money.

I'm peeling apples at the sink, lost in thought when I see the bike pass my house. I can't tell who it is exactly, but I know that it isn't Michael. My heart drums in my ears. I could delude myself into thinking this isn't anything to worry about, but I know better. My hand goes to my stomach. No matter what, I need to protect Maggie. *She's all that matters.* I walk to my utility room, grab the shotgun that I keep there. I make sure both barrels are loaded, and I hurry outside before whoever is outside can get a chance to come in. I learned a long time ago that you stand a better chance of surviving if you don't allow yourself to be trapped. I can run outside. Inside the house, I can be cornered. What's that old saying? *The best defense is offense.*

I have my gun aimed and the trigger ready to pull by the time the rider is off his bike. I breathe marginally better when I notice it's not one of the Dwellers. That's a good thing, but still I don't know who this guy is. He turns to look at me, his eyes go to the gun and then back to my face.

"Hey there, darlin'. I'm looking for a big, beefy idiot covered in hair—goes by the name Beast. Wouldn't happen to know where I can find him, would you?" he questions with an easy smile. He's good looking, you can't deny that with soft brown hair. He's lean, tall, and perfectly groomed. He has on a club cut like Blade and the rest of the Dwellers used to wear. His hair is long too, like Michael's, maybe even longer—but it's *pretty.* On Michael, his hair looks almost animalistic. It's unkempt, and sometimes I even wonder if he brushes it at all. Yet, it still looks good. On this man, you can tell he spends time on his hair. It looks amazing, but for me at least, nowhere near as appealing as Michael's. This guy's hair is prettier than mine.

"Does he know you?" I ask, not ready to tell him where Michael lives. What if this guy is here to cause trouble for him? I admit he looks pretty laid back, but who can tell with a man who pledges his life to a club? Michael says his club was different, but my experiences have jaded me to that possibility.

"He does. You could tell him Diesel is here to see him."

"She doesn't have to tell me anything," Michael grumbles, coming out of the barn. He doesn't look happy to see the man. Of course, I've not seen Michael happy to see anyone. "What are you doing here, fuck-wad?" Michael asks, and with that kind of greeting, I'm keeping my gun pointed at the guy.

"Think you might call off the skirt?" Diesel asks, looking over at me.

"I think I'd rather her shoot you. I thought I told Skull I

didn't want to see anyone. The point of me leaving the club was actually *leaving* the club."

"Last time I checked motherfucker, I wasn't part of *your* club, and I'm not here for them."

"Then why the fuck are you here?" Michael asks.

The man looks back at me, pointedly staring at the gun. Then, his eyes travel back to Michael as he folds his hands at his chest, leans back on his bike and waits.

"Hayden, put the gun down. This asshole isn't worth the lead in the bullet," he says, and I slowly bring the gun down.

"Just as sweet as ever I see," the man jokes and Michael flips him off.

"I don't want company," Michael says again.

"Better get used to it. I'm not alone," he says, Michael gives him a look and the man shrugs.

"Crusher and Dani are with me."

"Motherfucker."

"Does the heart good to feel so wanted," the man says, looking over at me and winking.

I wait for a minute or two to see if Michael invites me to stay around. He doesn't and for some reason that makes me more than a little sad, which is crazy. I don't like being around people, Michael is the rare exception. He makes me smile and feel safe. He's like Liese, Charlie, and to some extent Pastor Sturgill. People I don't feel pressured around. People who I care about and trust. I mean, not that I *care* about Michael—other than as a *friend.* When the two men shake hands, I take that as my cue to leave. I turn and go back to the door. I've almost got it closed when Michael calls out.

"Hayden?" My head jerks up with a smile, and I swear I think I feel excitement. Is he going to invite me to join them? Maybe I could invite the two of them over for coffee. I made some puff pastries and they're pretty good. I could give them some food while they talked. It'd be nice to have company while I worked in the kitchen. "Thanks for looking out for me," Michael adds, dismissing me. I give him another smile, before I close the door. After shutting it, I lay my head against it as that feeling of disappointment hits me again. *What is going on with me?*

CHAPTER 35

Beast

"WANT TO TELL me what you're here for?"

"Can't I just want to see that pretty face of yours?" Diesel asks, when we finally get under the parking area of the barn loft. I haven't invited him up, because I don't really want him in my space. What I really want is for him to turn around, leave, and never come back. However, I don't think I'm going to get my wish.

"You're wasting my time," I warn him, my voice betraying my aggravation. I have things planned for today. Things I don't want Diesel watching. I'm done with the fucking life. I'm done with these people. I know that makes me a dick, but it just is what it is. I don't know how to make it any clearer.

"You're just a cheerful fucking bastard, aren't you? How in Hell did you ever get that pretty little thing next door to care about you?"

"It's not like that, but Hayden is none of your concern."

"Hayden, is it? Pretty name. Unusual. It fits her. I take it that's not your bun occupying her oven," he says, looking between me and the open door with stairs, as if waiting for me to invite him up. He can just keep waiting. That shit is not going to happen.

"Hayden is none of your concern."

"Hey if you're…"

I hold my hand up. "Stop what you're saying," I tell him. Suddenly tired, I rub the back of my neck and let out a sigh, deciding just to give him the truth. "Hayden is Pistol's sister."

"*Fuck*. She's knocked up?" he asks, and I don't bother replying, there's really nothing to say.

"Why are you here?" I ask him again, anxious to get this over with.

Diesel brings his eyes back to me. He seems to study me for a bit, and I know he has something to tell me. I had hoped this was a simple visit, with just some old friends butting in where they were no longer wanted. Suddenly, I got the feeling that this is not what this is. *Not at all*. "Shadow Dwellers have been asking about you. Did you tell these fucks you weren't part of the Blaze anymore?"

"Wasn't trying to keep that shit a secret, Diesel. It's the fucking truth."

"You know as well as I do that the Dwellers aren't the fuckers to admit that shit to. Do you think they wouldn't love to fuck with you—or worse, in an effort to get back at Skull or fuck, even Cade?"

"I have nothing to do with Cade."

"You're part of the same club, even if he is over the Florida chapter. Besides, Cade and the Dwellers fucking hate each other. You know that. You show up here with your history and tell Blade and his crew you're no long part of the club…*Shit*. It's like waving a red flag in front of a fucking bull—and ese' that bull is already charging full steam ahead."

"I told you I couldn't give a fuck. They want to try to tangle with me, I'll deal with it. I'll deal with it alone."

"The fuck you will. Just because you got your head in your ass, doesn't mean the rest of us do. You're a brother and once a brother, always a brother. The. Fucking. *End.*"

"Last time I checked you aren't even part of the Blaze."

"Don't hand me that bullshit. You know my loyalty and my club is always with the Savage crew first, but we stand with the Blaze. You are part of the Blaze. Just because you're being a fucking prick, that doesn't mean that shit stops."

"Beast!" I hear Dani cry, jerking my attention away from Diesel. It's a welcome reprieve. I was just about to lay into the son of a bitch, and I'd rather not. I like Diesel. I respect the motherfucker, but he doesn't have clue one on the shit I'm going through. Dani comes running towards me, and I open my arms instinctively, she runs into them and hugs me tightly, despite her man's growl of dislike.

Crusher seems like a good man. I haven't dealt with him that much. He's a straight shooter I can respect, and he treats Dani good, which makes me half-way like the asshole.

"Hey there, hummingbird," I greet her, talking into her ear, my fingers wrapping into her dark hair as I hold her close.

"Every time you call her that, I have to resist the urge to plant my boot into your fucking balls and grind them into dust," Crusher growls.

I ignore him. Dani and I have a connection that started before the two of them ever got together. She's a good woman. If I were still a whole man, I might have been the one in her life now. But I'm not whole. I'm not even half a man on most days. Dani's had a fucked up past. She understands, and I probably understand her more than anyone else ever will. Seeing her find a point in her life where she's happy? That means a fuck of a lot to me.

"Missed you, you big lug," Dani laughs, giving me one last squeeze before I put her down.

"It's going to rain, I wasn't going to invite these assholes up, but since you're here, let's move this party upstairs," I tell them—mostly to Dani. She stays close to my side. Crusher growls as he looks at us, but Dani being Dani, she sticks her tongue out at him.

"Jesus Christ, how I ever got my balls owned by such a sour woman," he grumbles, but you can see by his eyes, he's completely in love with her.

I know she feels the same. Maybe that ability—the ability to love is what finally healed her. I'm not sure I ever had that ability with anyone except Annabelle, and it surely won't ever happen again.

Diesel takes off up the stairs with the three of us following him. I keep my hand on Dani's shoulders and just before I let her go to walk in front of me, I look over her head in the direction of Hayden's house. I wanted to spend the morning with her, so I could make sure she ate good. Just another reason to be pissed at Diesel.

Crusher takes his moment to get between me and his woman. He puts his hand on her ass and follows her up the stairs. His hold is one of ownership. I could tell him he has nothing to worry about in me, but I know he wouldn't listen.

I follow them all up the stairs, wondering how long it will take me to get rid of them.

CHAPTER 36

Hayden

"WHAT THE FUCK are you doing, Hayden?" I hear Michael growl. My head jerks up to look over the top of my car, the evening sun is starting to set and there's a glare that has me shielding my eyes.

Michael is standing by his barn, talking to his guests. The man with the hair is on his bike now and there's a woman standing by Michael with another man beside her. She's beautiful. Tall, skinny, with dark hair that shines and is silky smooth. She's everything I'm not, and I can tell by the arm that Michael has close to her, she's special to him. The man beside her is pretty spectacular too, his hair dark and cut short, covered in tattoos and definitely territorial about the woman. You can tell that just from his posture. Do they share her? I'm not stupid to the life of a club member. It wouldn't surprise me. For some reason, it does disappoint me.

"What?" I ask, putting one load of my food into the backseat of my car. There's at least three more inside. I'm running late…burning cookies did not figure into my time management plan.

"What are you doing carrying…that shit out by yourself?" he asks, and he has to break about halfway through the sentence to get it all out when his voice cracks—but then, he's *yelling*.

"Um…the same as I always do?" I tell him rhetorically, not sure what he's getting at and shaking my head because he's acting crazily. I turn away from him and his guests to go back in my house, dismissing him from my mind. I'm in the kitchen loading up my second batch when Michael comes storming in with the hair-shampoo-for-men cover model, the other guy, and all of them are followed by the girl—who stands by the door. *I freeze*. My breath stalls in my chest, and I feel the panic literally crawling up my back. My kitchen is small. I'm trapped with three men and only one of those do I partially trust. I don't have my gun and there's someone standing between me and the door.

"Crazy woman. Are you trying to get yourself killed? There's no way you can see those steps with your hands full. What happened to that damned Pastor? I thought he helped you with this shit?" Michael is grumbling under his breath, and he's saying more than he's ever said to me in one long sentence. Which might be good, but I can't concentrate on it.

I feel a cold, clammy sweat pop out covering my body. I hear the blood rushing in my ears. Everything I look at begins dancing, zooming in and out—distorted. I do my best to take air into my lungs, but it doesn't work. The pressure is so intense it feels like there's an elephant sitting on my chest. I can feel my fingers tingle and my knees go weak. I'm breathing raggedly at best, doing everything I can to fight through the fear and snap out of it. It's a losing battle though. This panic attack is coming hard and strong, and I *hate* it. I hate it almost as much as I hate myself.

Michael is gathering the packages I have on the table, I want to find him. Maybe if I could find him it would help to center me and keep me from going under too deep. But I can't, the blinding whiteness in my vision takes over, changing everything to a weird gray hue with no colors. I'm starting to shake uncontrollably, the carefully constructed tower of packages I'm holding, that comes up to just under my neck, begin rattling. Which causes every eye in the room to turn to me.

"Are you okay, honey?" a feminine tone questions, and maybe her voice is kind, I think it is, but I can't be sure over the way the blood is rushing through me and the loud pounding of my heart.

That seems to be all my ears can hear. I start backing away. If I can get through the living room and out the front door, maybe I can get away. Maybe I can get control. It was a mistake letting Michael in. He was nice, but I just can't be around people. Not long-term, even though I'm getting better, I'm just too damaged...*too dirty*. The desserts I'm holding fall to the floor with a crash. I shake my head back and forth, backing up faster. It feels like I might just pass out.

"Hayden?" I hear Michael, his voice laced with concern.

I stumble backwards, closing my eyes for a minute, trying to block everything out. I feel a hand touch me and I scream. It's a scream filled with nothing but complete and utter terror.

"Jesus-fucking-Christ."

"What's wrong with her, Brother?" The men are asking, I don't register it, not really.

In fact, I think I'm still screaming. I've hit the wall in the hallway, and Michael is here in front of me, putting a hand on each of my shoulders.

I stop screaming. Now I yell, "*Don't touch me!*"

"Hayden, sweetheart," Michael says, but even though it's his voice, it's not his face I see. It's someone else's. *Someone else's entirely.*

"Don't touch me!" I scream louder, pushing against the wall, only wanting to get away from the demon I see in front of me. *"Don't you ever touch me again!"*

"What is going on in here?!" I hear just before I hit the ground.

"Oh God, not again. Please God, not again. Please…please…-please…" I cry, rocking back and forth, sobs racking my body as misery fills the very air around me. *"Please…"* I cry brokenly. *"Oh God…please."*

CHAPTER 37

Beast

"BEAST, COME AWAY from her, honey, you're making her worse," Dani says, pulling on my arm. I'm on the floor trying to get Hayden to come into my arms but she just keeps pushing harder against the wall each time I try.

"What the fuck is wrong with her?" Diesel barks.

"Get away from her! Everyone get out of the house," Pastor Sturgill commands, and he's fucking out of his mind if he thinks I'll agree to that.

"What's wrong with her?" I ask this time, directing my words to the Pastor. It's all I can do to keep my words even and quiet. That's the best I can do even if they vibrate with anger. I don't want them to scare Hayden further. *If that's even possible.*

"Having all of you in here must have triggered one of her panic attacks. You all need to leave. It's the only thing that will help her right now," he advises. He's probably right. He apparently has had experience with these episodes before, and I don't like that he's the one that dealt with them. I made up my mind yesterday that Maggie and Hayden were my responsibility. Pastor Sturgill is dreaming if he thinks I'm leaving Hayden in his hands now.

"Everyone leave," I order the same tone of voice.

"Beast, honey," I hear Dani. I pull my eyes away from Hayden and look at her.

"I got this," I tell her. She stares at me a minute then grabs Crusher's arm to leave. I know Pastor Sturgill is there, but I'm not wasting my breath on him. I need to get to Hayden before she hurts herself or Maggie.

Hayden's entire body is shaking, tears are pouring down her body and she's breathing so hard that each new intake of breath is a large heaving shudder. I've had zero experience with this, but I've dealt with men on the battlefield who are shell-shocked. Men who have seen too much—so much it breaks something inside of them. I figure that is part of what's going on with Hayden. So, I go with my instincts.

"You need to leave. I can get her to calm down," the Pastor says, starting to walk around me.

"All due respect, Pastor, but if you get one step closer, I will physically throw you out. Hayden and I have this, don't we, honey?" I both warn and question, directing my words at Hayden and ignoring the annoying preacher. I inch slowly toward her, not much and so slowly and carefully that I couldn't have moved much more than an inch. Hayden doesn't scream, or try to push back into the wall again however, so I'm satisfied. I do it twice more. The last time I see her body jerk, so I stop.

"Give me your hand, Hayden," I tell her gruffly, wishing I had a soft voice that wasn't riddled with darkness. I just hope she feels connected with me enough that it helps. She called me her friend, hopefully that's enough. I reach my hand out, instinctively giving it to her palm down. I can't help the scars or the darkness of my hand, but every time I'm with Hayden and something happens she reaches for my hand. Sure, none of those things have been bad, but I'm hoping it still helps. If ever a woman needed something to hold onto right now, it's Hayden and for some reason I don't want to question, I'd rather it be me than the preacher who is standing by the door, yet still refusing to leave.

"Hayden, come on now. You don't want to scare Maggie, do you? Give me your hand," I tell her, and I'm holding my breath as her body jerks against the wall.

Her eyes, almost glassy, look at my hand. I'm hoping that means she's hearing me. She's crawled into a shell, and I desperately need her to come out of it…*to come to me.* "You hear me, don't you? You don't want Maggie to be scared. Hold onto my hand. I'll protect you, sweetheart. I'll protect both of you," I vow to her. I'd already decided it on my own, but now I give her that promise. I ignore the way the words make my heart rate accelerate. It's only because I'm afraid I can't reach her. *That's all it is.*

I am almost about to let the Pastor try. She's been staring at my hand for what feels like an hour. In reality, it's probably been more like five minutes. That feels like five minutes too long…and then…*something happens.* I watch, almost disbelieving, as she takes a hand that was clenched tightly into her chest and slowly lowers it.

"That's it, sweetheart. Hold onto me. You're not alone now," I reassure her, feeling elation glide through my body as her small, trembling arm drops away from her body centimeter by centimeter, until her hand is close to mine. It's all I can do not to grab it. *I can't.* Hayden has to be in charge.

Whatever has happened to her in the past, it was major and she had no control. It broke her and robbed her of something vital…*something precious.* That's about all I understand right now. *I will know more.* Her hand finally touches mine, trembling so hard it jars my hand. I hold my breath as even slower her fingers fan out to encircle my hand. Then a miracle happens. Hayden's thumb hits the deepest groove on my hand the one that runs from the knuckle to the wrist and begins brushing over it, following the scar one way and then backtracking the other. Over and over she does that—three, four…five times. With each time though, I notice her eyes slowly thaw. Her breathing, though still ragged doesn't wrack her whole body, making it quake.

I inch closer to her, keeping my hand still. "That's it, Beauty. Come back to me," I whisper, my voice cracking, giving her the nickname without realizing it.

"Mi…Mi…Michael?" she stutters, and finally, I breathe normal. *She's back.*

I keep our hands joined. It might be my imagination, but I think the scar pattern on my hand is helping to keep her calm. Yet, as best as I can with one arm. I pull her into my lap, holding her close. She instantly curls into me, trusting me. I keep our joined hands between us and just hold her. I let the fingers on my other hand hold onto her shoulder and rest my chin on top of her head. She's burrowed into my body, but with each passing minute the shudders ease.

"I got you, sweetheart. Nothing will get to you while I'm here. I promise," I tell her, going with my instinct and giving her the words I think will mean the most.

"Don't leave," she whispers, her hand tightening on mine.

"I'm not, Beauty. I'm not going anywhere," I promise her, but I find myself looking over at the Pastor while I say it. Maybe because he tried to get me to leave, I couldn't say. He studies me for a minute, then walks out the door, leaving me alone with Hayden. "I'm not going anywhere," I vow once more, looking down at our joined hands and watching her thumb sweep against my scars. "I'm right here for you," I tell her, "I'm right here."

God help me…Hayden's gotten inside of *me*…

CHAPTER 38

Hayden

I MADE A fool of myself…in front of Michael's friends. I can't think about that right now. I refuse to let myself. I choose to concentrate on the feel of Michael's arms around me. His hand is underneath mine and that's my lifeline. I hold onto his hand tightly, my thumb instinctively finding the deepest scar and brushing against it. He's kissing the top of my head like he would a small child. It's nice. It feels safe and that's a miracle for me. I've never had safe…*never.* Every so often, he gives me those words—promises that he will keep me safe, and for the first time in my life, I believe them. Michael's scent wraps around me, further penetrating the haze of fear I had locked myself inside of. It's a stark combination of musty leather and aftershave mixed in with the smell of pine trees after a rain. My mind automatically breathes it in because I love the way it smells outside after rain. As if everything is clean and ready to begin again. I've always wished I could do that. Let the rain wash away the past and feel…*clean.*

"You better, sweetheart?" he asks, and I should tell him yes, because I am.

I find myself reluctant though, because I don't want him to let me go, and I really don't want to feel the embarrassment of my lost control just yet. So, I don't answer verbally. Instead, I bring his hand to my stomach where Maggie is moving. I hold his hand over my daughter, part in gratitude, and partly because I've never got to share this with anyone else. Maggie pushes against his hand, my stomach hardening with her move. I can't be sure, but I like to think her little butt is moving and pushing against my hand. It's different than a kick. It feels like she's hugging me.

"She's worried about her Momma," Michael says, his voice a little stronger, but it cracks. He clears his throat, and I know my time with him is getting shorter. He'll want to go out to his friends. I can't face them. I can't believe I lost control like that in front of Michael's friends. Yet, instead of getting mad, he's holding me, pledging to keep me safe. *How different would my life have been if I had Michael in my life years ago?*

"Thank you," I tell him, but I stop there, because I'm not sure how to list all the things I'm thankful for. "You should go out where your friends are," I tell him, reluctantly, giving him an opening, but still not letting go of his hand. I'm not sure I can yet.

"You need to rest. You and Maggie," he tells me, and he somehow manages to get up off of the floor, all while holding me. He takes our joined hands and uses them to help hold me, but he doesn't take his hand away, or break the way I'm holding it, and I'm glad.

I let him carry me like a small child into the bedroom and lay me down there, all without saying a word. I don't get scared when he lays down with me, immediately holding my hand again and curving his body so he's spooned into my back, our joined hands falling over my stomach.

"Close your eyes. I'll stay for a little longer and then go talk to everyone. I won't be far away, even then. All you have to do is call for me and I'll be here, Hayden. I promise," he tells me, and it might be weak of me, but for once I don't mind being weak.

I close my eyes and concentrate on the feel of Michael surrounding me, his hand in mine and the sound of his breathing. Then I let myself fall asleep feeling safer than I have *ever* felt in my life.

CHAPTER 39

Beast

I LAY HERE until I'm sure Hayden is sleeping. The temptation to stay with her remains, but I know Dani and the others will still be out there. I force myself to get up and leave Hayden, and I can't even pretend not to miss the way it felt to hold her against my body. I'm fucking up royally here. I just don't know how to stop it. Fuck, I even find myself kissing the top of her head again, before I pull the covers over her body.

Once I get outside, I take a deep breath of air, hoping the clean air will return my rational thinking and somehow detach me from this invisible chain that seems to link me to Hayden. *It doesn't.*

"What the hell was that?" Crusher asks as soon as I get outside. His hand is shaking as he rakes it through his hair. He's holding Dani close, and she's still crying, her head on his chest. She just has silent tears running down her face, but somehow that seems sadder, because they're tears of understanding and knowing Dani's history, the fact that she can feel that kinship with Hayden *terrifies me.*

"That's a panic attack," Dani whispers a little later. "A bad one. The kind that drove me to self-medicate," she continues. "What the hell happened to her, Beast?" she asks, and I don't know what to say to that, because I have no idea. I never even had a clue. If she had this kind of problem, wouldn't I have been able to see it clearer before now? How come she didn't react this violently when I was at her house the other night? I can't answer Dani, because all I seem to have are questions and no fucking answers.

"The best thing we can do for Hayden right now is to leave her alone for a little while."

"The last thing she needs to be is left alone. What if that happens again?" I growl, ready to march back inside already.

"You're wrong. Hayden does much better on her own. She limits her interaction with others. She would probably do better with medication, but—"

"She can't take medication while pregnant," Dani finishes and the Pastor nods his head in agreement.

"What the hell happened to her that she has episodes like that?" Diesel asks, and I want to laugh. That wasn't a fucking episode. Whatever Hayden had in there was pure Hell.

"I don't know for sure. I can only tell you from the shape she was in when we found her, it was bad. She was beaten, and bleeding heavily. They didn't think her or the child were going to make it," the Pastor says, and it feels like a damn hand has a death grip on my heart.

"They beat her while she was pregnant?" Diesel roars, echoing thoughts that I can't verbalize. I'm having trouble just breathing.

"Charlie, from the diner, found her lying in her own blood along the side of the road. Someone had dumped her out like the trash. She managed to get her into her car and took her to the hospital. That's when I first met them both. I was the Chaplin on call there. We tried to find her next of kin. Hayden mentioned a brother. He never showed, but there were some things delivered to the hospital. Including a deed to this place."

"Pistol…" I hear Diesel mutter under his breath.

"I think that Hayden must have been mixed up with a gang in the city, but whoever her brother is he somehow got word out though that she was under his protection. They've left her alone."

"I guess the sorry sack of shit did one thing right before he died."

"He's dead?" the Pastor asks, and I nod my head yes, distractedly. My eyes go back to the house, thinking about the woman inside and wondering what kind of torture she must have lived through.

"Will she be okay?" Crusher asks, and everyone else is talking and the Pastor is answering him, but all I can do is concentrate on the house and picture Hayden scared in her bed alone.

She'll be okay. I'll make sure of it. I won't fail this time.

CHAPTER 40

Hayden

IT'S THAT SICK feeling you get when you have made a fool of yourself. That's what is sitting inside of me. I hear movement in the kitchen. I don't fear it though. I know it's Michael. He said he would be here when I woke up, and I don't doubt his words for a second. With my history you think I would, but I don't. *Not when it comes to Michael.*

I force myself to get up and walk into the kitchen. It's quiet, so I'm praying no one else is with him. If they are, I vow to try and be stronger, even if for a few minutes. I peek around the corner of the doorway and breathe a sigh of relief when Michael is all I see. He's standing over the stove, reading the directions on a can of soup.

"I can cook," I tell him, and wow my voice sounds rough, and feels almost the same. I clear it, self-consciously. Michael turns around to look at me. His dark eyes rake over my body, assessing me.

"Come sit," he orders abruptly, and for some reason, I miss the way he called me *sweetheart.* I was out of it for a little bit, but I remember his softness. I hadn't ever had that before. It was...*nice*.

I walk over and sit at the table, feeling out of place. I'm still raw inside from earlier, and I'm so embarrassed I wish the ground would swallow me up.

Michael brings a bowl of soup over and sits it in front of me with a sleeve of crackers. I watch him as he turns back around and fixes another bowl for himself. He should be awkward in my small kitchen, because Michael is extremely tall. I don't think seven foot would be stretching it at all, and his arms are so broad he's wider than my kitchen sink practically. He's like a giant, though for a bit this morning he seemed like a gentle giant.

I want to smile as I watch the way his head bends down to avoid hitting the upper cabinet. He turns around and catches me staring, in return I get a grunt from him—which is oddly comforting. He brings us back a couple of drinks from the fridge—mine a tea and his is a beer. I look at him strangely for a second.

"I don't remember having beer here," I tell him. He grunts again, but he looks at me again, and I see the sadness on his face. I don't want him to feel pity for me. That would kill me.

"Eat, *sweetheart*," he says gruffly. My heart stutters in my chest at his words. There's the gentle giant again.

Words are lodged in my throat. I want to say something, but I have no idea what, so instead I pretend the chicken soup he made is the best thing since sliced bread and eat.

"Where are your friends?" I finally ask, a few minutes later, becoming bored with nothing but the sound of spoons and bowls clanging.

"They were just stopping by. They had to leave today," he says, not bothering to look up.

I push my bowl away and sigh. "I'm sorry if I embarrassed you, Michael. I'm still...I'm learning to cope."

"Will you tell me what happened?" he asks, leaning back in his chair and watching me.

"I...was attacked," I tell him, giving him the truth but not elaborating.

"Who did it?"

"It's not important. It's in the past," I tell him, getting up, and taking our bowls over to the sink. It's then I notice all the boxes that I haven't loaded and then I see a large box on the counter that contains ruined pies that didn't survive me dropping them. "I'll have to remake these," I say, mostly to myself.

"You don't need to worry about it today," he says, and I rub above my left eyebrow. I'm going to get a headache. I can feel the tension gathering.

"I need to at least deliver what I have, I can't afford to lose my customers, Michael. That's income Maggie and I will depend on. I'll have to call Pastor Sturgill—"

"I'll take you," he grumbles, and I jerk my head up to look at him.

"You don't have to, Michael. You've already done so much."

"I'll go do a few things and get my truck while you clean up," he answers.

I swallow. "If you're sure."

He walks over to me, cups his hand under my chin, and he applies pressure until I'm forced to look up at him. "You'll be okay," he tells me, and when I look into his dark eyes, I want to believe him.

I really do.

CHAPTER 41

Beast

I LOOK AT my cellphone. This is the fifth call today I've had from Skull. I click the off button. I'm not sure why it's so fucking hard for him to get the message, but they all need to. That life is over for me. I'm not the man they knew. I haven't been that man in a long time, they are all just too stubborn to recognize it. I stuff the phone in my back pocket and watch as they finish loading the last box into my truck.

I'm standing out on the Main Street of Whitley waiting outside of a local shop, while men fill my truck with items I purchased this morning. It's been two days since Hayden's episode and I've tried to keep a close eye on her. She seems to be doing fine, but there's a sadness about her now that I don't like. Maybe that's the reason I decided Hayden needed something to cheer her up and remind her that her and Maggie are okay. At least that's what I told myself. The truth is, I couldn't resist buying the nursery furniture. I wanted to be the one to buy it for her. I wanted to give her something to smile over. *Me…not someone else.*

"Here you go, Mr. Jameson! We can't thank you enough for

your business," the sales lady says, handing me three large bags.

"You're sure this will be all she needs to get started?" I ask, still finding it hard to believe that things have changed so much since Annabelle was a baby.

"More than enough. You're very generous to your friend," she says, and it's been a while but she's got a look in her eye that I used to remember and immediately act on.

I'm not interested now. Hell, except for that one moment with Hayden, that I still can't explain—I haven't been interested since the explosion. The hard-on I got around Hayden, didn't last long and it hasn't happened since. Maybe something more than just my skin was damaged from the fire. That would be the easy answer. The more complicated one is that I feel dead on the inside. About the only time I even feel marginally normal is when I'm around Hayden. And even then, I can't manage to talk to her like a normal person. I'm about as fucked up as they come.

The saleswoman lets her hand rest on my shoulder. I look down at it and back at her, before stepping back, letting it fall away.

"Thanks for your help," I tell her, not bothering to look back. She says something else, but I've already tuned her out. I get in my truck to get back to Hayden's. I'm getting in too deep with her. I need to keep my distance, but each time I decide that something else happens with her that lures me in. There was a moment the other day after we ate together that I almost kissed her. That would have landed us both in a huge fucked up mess. Hell, even knowing what a mess it could be, I'm still curious as to what kissing her would be like. Of course, now that I've seen what kind of demons live inside of her, kissing her would be the worst thing I could do.

I'm about ten minutes away when I notice two bikes on my

ass. I look through the side mirror, but I can't tell much about them from this distance. I slow down, waiting for them to go around me. They slow down and my hands tighten up on my steering wheel. I don't have time for this fucking bullshit. I speed back up and watch as they do too. One fucker gets brave and comes around the side of me, he manages to hide in my blind spot. I swerve for the fuck of it, and watch as he speeds up quickly. Now that I can see him in the mirror I try and look to see if I can recognize him. I have a suspicion as to who it is, but I need that shit confirmed. I'm about to lock up my brakes, pull the fucking truck over and show these fucks what happens when you invite road-rage.

I don't get that chance, however, when I hear a noise that reminds me of gravel hitting against my fender. A second later, I'm wrestling with the truck as it tries to fishtail. My back tire is going flat. I get it under control and pull to the side of the road. It's then the bikers drive around the side of me. My hand is going for the gun I keep in my console. I'm looking out the window as I get it. My hand wraps around the handle and I'm pulling it up. When the drivers stop across from me. They have skull masks on, so there's no way I can see their faces. I do notices their cut however. It's a Shadow Dwellers. *Motherfucker.* My eyes go back to them and the one closest to me is holding a gun, it's aimed right at me.

For a moment, I freeze. I've been wanting to die for years. This bullet will finally put me out of my misery. I watch as his finger squeezes against the trigger, and I think *this is it.* Finally, I'll just stop fighting it. I close my eyes, expecting to see Annabelle, but I don't. It's Hayden's face I see. *Hayden crying.*

CHAPTER 42

Beast

MY HEAD JERKS automatically when I see Hayden's face. *What the fuck does that mean?* I don't have time to think about it. I thought the man was going to shoot me. Instead he lowers the gun and shoots my front tire. Then they drive off.

"Fuck," I growl, to no one as I get out and look at my ruined tires. *What the hell was that shit about?* I slam my door, kicking the completely destroyed front tire. "Fuck!" I growl out again, so loud that my voice cuts off, mid-scream. I slam my fist down against the hood of my truck. Pain spreads up my hand and I welcome it. It doesn't help the anger seething through me though, and I slam my fist down again wishing it was the heads of those in-bred-motherfuckers. I'm going to kill those son-of-a-bitches! *What did they think they were accomplishing besides making me a bigger fucking enemy?*

I try to get control of my anger so I can sort through this shit. This is how I did my job for years. Keeping control and sorting through every action and reaction to know why or how to strike. They weren't here to end me so what was it? *A warning?* Devil's Blaze never fooled with that shit. We didn't bother with warnings. If you fucked up, then we shut you down. Warning people got messy and usually you had blowback. If you got rid of the problem from the beginning, then you didn't have to worry about getting a knife in your back. Blade and the Dwellers were never that smart, which is just one of the reasons their club is in the shape it's in. I do have to wonder why he felt the need to deliver this particular message to me.

Is he still pouting like a fucking baby because I didn't tell him I was near his territory? Diesel came with a warning, I thought he was stupid, but apparently, Blade is the stupid one. Does he really think he can mess with me? He wants to test and see if the Blaze will have my back? The day I need anyone but myself to take that ass-wipe down is the day they need to bury me in the fucking ground. I'll be paying Blade a visit soon.

First, I need to get my fucking truck on the road. It takes a little bit of shuffling around in the glovebox to find my insurance information, but I retrieve it and search for the roadside assistance number they gave me. I could fix a flat myself, but with two of them and only one damn spare, that's not going to be possible. Of course, the Dwellers knew that. That was probably part of the fucking fun for them. Which worked because the lady on the phone informs me it will be up to an hour before they get a truck out. I get to work changing the front flat myself. If I'm going to have to wait I might as well do something.

I go through the motions, without actually thinking about them. I have the tire off and the spare ready to go on, and I can't tell you how I did it. My mind is too absorbed in why it was Hayden's face I saw in my head when I thought I was going to die. Hayden's and not Annabelle's. I want to be mad at her, but fuck, I'm not sure I can. I've known for a bit that Hayden was snaking her way under my defenses. I should have shot her down sooner. I should have done something to push her away. I could do it now, but I'll admit—at least to myself, I don't really want to. *Shit*, maybe the reason I saw her face is because I was right. Her and Maggie are the reason I'm supposed to be here. I need to protect them. I had decided to before and this is just more proof. *Protection.*

The word hits inside of me. *Protection.* She has a history with the Dwellers. Those fucks didn't try to kill me or take me out, only slow me down. They did it to keep me from getting home sooner. They headed down the road which could have led them out of town, but it would also lead them to my driveway. The driveway I share with Hayden. *It could have led them to Hayden's.*

My heartbeat starts tripping in my chest and a fine sheen of cold sweat breaks out as chills run through me. Could that be what they are after? Are they here to hurt Hayden? I throw the jack and lug wrench in the back floor board, then jump in the front and start up my truck. I still have a flat on the back, but I need to get to Hayden. It's been awhile since I've tasted it, but I know that bitterness is fear. I put the truck into four-wheel drive, gunning it. I'm going to destroy my rim and who knows what else, but I'm not far from the house. If the Dwellers went there after they played with me…

Fuck! Please, let me get there in time…

CHAPTER 43

Hayden

I HEAR HIM before I see him. Well correction, *I hear his truck*. I didn't know what it was. The sound of metal scraping along the asphalt was loud—so loud it even reverberated in my kitchen. Which isn't easy to do now because those new windows that Michael had installed are amazing at keeping the sound out. I run to grab my gun. I know it's stupid, but having something to protect myself makes me feel…*safer.* I don't like being helpless. I've been that way too much in my life. My heart is pounding hard against my chest, and I'm having trouble catching my breath. I'm doing my best to fight down the panic, the memory of the other day is still really fresh. I make it outside and calm down when I see Michael's truck, fishtailing around the corner. My first thought is that something is horribly wrong, all thought of the sound is blotted out of my mind with that fear. But then I notice his tires. *Surely, he knew riding on his tire rim like that was crazy?* Instead of replacing a tire now he will have to replace a rim too. It makes much more sense just to change the tire.

"Michael?" I ask when he jumps out of the vehicle and begins marching towards me.

"Put the gun down," he growls, and it's then I notice I'm half-way aiming at him.

I lower the gun and lay it securely in an old wooden glider that's sitting close by. By the time I turn back around, Michael is there. He grabs me roughly, his hands biting into the skin on my arms. He almost shakes me, bringing me in close to him.

"Michael?" I ask again, confused. His face is angrier now than I've ever seen it. His eyes bore into me, their dark depths slightly terrifying. There's a dark energy rolling off of him in waves. He's literally vibrating with it.

"Are you okay?" he growls, his eyes raking over me, and I have a feeling they're inventorying everything about me.

"I'm fine. I was just about to take a nap," I tell him, sounding a little bit guilty. I should have gone into work today, but I just couldn't handle the thought of it.

"No one has been here to bother you?" he asks.

"No one has been here. Michael, is something going on?"

"I was run off the road. I just wanted to make sure they didn't come here," he says taking a step back, his arms dropping to his side. He's rubbing the back of his neck, while looking around the house as if he expects someone to jump out at any time.

"You were what? Oh my God! Are you okay?" I ask him, and this time it's me that goes to him. I reach out and touch his face. "You've got so much hair you could be dying under there and I'd never know," I grumble, not realizing I'm saying it aloud. I let my hands move down his neck and shoulders, not finding anything wrong, but panicked at the thought that something could have happened to him.

"I think you'd know if I was wounded," he grumbles from above me, and I stop and look up at him. I realize I said the remark about his hair out loud then. I also notice that Michael looks a little more relaxed.

"You could be hiding a family of squirrels in that hair and I wouldn't know it," I tease him. Almost without thought, I reach up to touch the beard in question. The fine, wiry hair tickles against my fingertips. His hands come up to capture mine, stopping their exploration. His hold is solid, but not painful and he doesn't pull my hands away from him or step back. We stand there. His big hands swallowing mine, his thumbs pressed against the inside of my palms.

"What am I going to do with you?" he asks, and I get this feeling in my stomach—a nervous flutter. I press my lips tightly together and swallow as I try to figure out what is going on here. It feels…*important.* I feel him releasing a breath, then slowly, he drops my hands, and steps away from me. I fight the urge to follow him. He looks away from me—towards his truck.

"We need to call the police," I tell him, my voice sounding strange even to my ears.

"I'll deal with it."

"What? No. You should contact the police. They need to know what happened. Maybe if you give them a description of who did this they can find them."

"I know who did it."

"You can't just let—*What did you say?"*

"I said I know who did it. I'll deal with them," he states, calmly. He could be telling me the forecast has rain in it tonight, he's that calm and looks that bored.

"Who is it?" I demand. If Michael knows who it is, then most likely I do. I've lived here longer. He studies me for a minute and something moves across his face, I'm not sure I like.

"No one you know. I need to call roadside assistance again, and tell them I need them to come to the house with a tow truck. Then I need to get some things out of the back of my truck. Can you hold the door open for me?" he calls over his shoulder, turning away from me.

"How can it be someone I don't know? I've been here longer than you…" I return, confused. It feels like he's dismissing me, and I can't say that I like it very much.

"You don't," he just insists, putting his phone up to his ear. *How would I not know them?*

"Are they from your past?" I ask, suddenly making a connection. He used to belong to a club. These kind of things happened all the time with the Dwellers. Maybe Michael's club isn't that different from them after all. I don't like the way that conclusion makes me feel. I don't like thinking anything bad about Michael. Maybe he needed a fresh start. Maybe that's why he left. I can understand that and if that's it, then I can certainly understand that too.

Michael finishes his phone conversation, while standing at the foot of his truck, leaning into the tailgate. His head his down so I can't see his face. His dark hair has spilled forward, covering him and what it doesn't hide his beard hides the rest. He's dressed all in black. I remember Pastor Sturgill's remark yet again about Michael being an archangel. Right now, he looks like a fallen angel and he shouldn't look as good as he does to me…

But he does.

CHAPTER 44

Beast

I COULDN'T TELL her that this was the work of the Dwellers. I knew that would bring fear in her eyes—maybe even another panic attack. I couldn't do it. I'll deal with this on my own and make sure this doesn't touch her. I was terrified thinking they were using me to get to her. That was one emotion I never thought I'd feel again. I've been so dead inside, I didn't think it was possible. It's further proof that Hayden is getting too close.

I almost kissed her a minute ago. The urge to take her lips was there, and for a second, I leaned into her and almost captured her mouth with mine. I wanted to taste her lips so damn bad. That would have been insanity. I don't know what Hayden has been through, but it's pretty clear it has traumatized her and given who is involved, I'm positive it was bad. Kissing her would have probably sent her running away and screaming.

On top of that…I ruin everything I touch. I've failed at the single most important purpose I had in life. I let the one person in my life who has ever loved me—*who I ever loved*, down. I can't get close to Hayden. I'd end up just destroying her too. Lucy wasn't wrong with her childish words. I am an animal. I've become the monster my brothers always said I looked like when they gave me my road name. *A beast.*

"Michael! What did you do?" Hayden cries as I make it to her, carrying the first box.

"Open the door, Hayden. It's heavy," I tell her, mostly lying. It's heavy, but fuck I bench press double this weight without a sweat. I just don't feel like fending off her questions. She opens the door, and I don't look at her. It's stupid, but I don't want to see her face. I didn't do it for gratitude. I don't want that from Hayden. I'm not sure what I want from Hayden, but that's not it. I didn't do this for her. I did this for Maggie. She's the reason I'm still here. I reasoned all that out. I can't ignore the small voice inside of me that if the Dwellers are making a move then Hayden needs me too. *I can't let myself think about that.*

I lean the box for the crib up against the wall in her nursery. Then I head back outside, all without looking at Hayden. I bring in the changing table, the lady said was a must. I don't get it. I changed Annabelle on the couch just fine, sometimes on the bed, and fuck even the floor. I never had a problem. I didn't even know there was a table. Seems as unhandy as fuck to me. Women like to make everything complicated. I place it against the crib box and go back out. *Still not looking at Hayden.* I'm avoiding looking at her and she's gone completely silent. I don't know if that's a good or bad thing. I make a couple more trips. These pieces are already together and covered in blankets. There's a glider with footstool that's black to match the rest of the furniture. And a dresser that's made to match the crib and table. There's also a small nightstand that goes by the glider. The bassinet was all I meant to buy. It's there. Maggie shouldn't have a broken one. This one is white with yellow ribbon accents. Next is a box of cushions and pads for the changing table, and the glider. All with pale yellow covers to match the design that

Hayden has fixed on the walls. A crib mattress, a lamp with an elephant wearing a yellow tutu that for some fucking reason made me smile, and I had the woman add it to my purchases, different sheets and finally bedding that was as close as I could find to something Hayden would want. Hayden might bitch, but I figure all of those things Maggie needs.

When I get the last box inside, I set it in her living room, because half way into unpacking I discovered there wasn't enough room to move in the nursery or hall until I got things put together and the old furniture gone. Then, left out of excuses or reasons not to, I look at Hayden. What I seen on her face isn't what I expected. There's no gratitude or even coy bullshit women do when they think they have you over a barrel. It's…*anger.*

Fucking women never react like you think they will.

CHAPTER 45

Hayden

HE BRINGS IN box after box of things for Maggie. Each time he does, he doesn't talk or even look at me. Each time he does, my disbelief grows. I run through so many different emotions, I get dizzy. There's too many to grasp all of them, so I hold onto the one that I can identify the easiest.

"You have to take them back," I tell Michael, when he finally looks at me. In response, he gives me a grunt. "I'm serious, Michael. They have to go back. I can't keep them."

"The fuck you can't," he grumbles, turning away from me and going back into the nursery. I watch from the door as he grabs the broken bassinet and begins walking towards me.

"What are you doing now?" I gasp, literally blocking the doorway.

"Making room in here so I can start putting the furniture together, while I'm waiting on the tow truck. Then I'll go do some business, and come back this evening to finish putting everything together," his dark voice rumbles.

"But I'm using that bassinet to put the baby in my room until she gets older!" I cry, feeling completely out of my depth.

Michael makes a noise that is not really his trademark grunt, it starts that way but then spreads into a rumbly growl. He places the basinet back down, and he looks at me. He's standing right in front of me, his head bent down to stare at me. I stretch my neck up, so I can stare right back. I should be scared—especially with my history and the mean look this huge man is giving me. I can't explain why I'm not. I can't even explain how I know in my heart that Michael would never willingly hurt me…*but I do.* Standing here going toe to toe with him seems natural.

"I bought a bassinet," he mutters, in the same deep, husky tone as his growl.

"I can't pay for it! I can't pay for any of this stuff! You have to take it back!"

"I paid for it," he says, leaning further down. Remarkably, I don't back up, I don't even think, I act.

"Then go get your money back," I tell him, pushing my finger into his chest for emphasis.

"No." he breathes an exaggerated sigh, straightening back up and pushing his hair from his face.

"No? You can't say no."

"I just did." he's back to the rumbly growl, his brow crinkled up in clear irritation.

"Michael," I start again, but our attention is diverted when you can hear a large vehicle outside. I can't see it but from the noise, you can tell it's big, because it's loud and there's that large air sound and squeaking like the vehicle has air brakes, like those used on big rigs.

"Hayden if you don't want the fucking furniture then I'll throw it out when I get back and burn it. I'm not asking for my money back. I'll get rid of the shit when I get back," he mutters, his voice cracking, but not as much this time as it usually does. *Maybe because he's talking in a lower tone?*

"You'll *burn* it?"

"If you don't want it, yeah," he says, his eyes going back to the doorway I'm standing in front of, when a horn blows. "Can you move so I can get out the door? That's probably the tow truck out there," he says, rubbing his beard around his chin, his forehead scrunched up.

"You are just going to burn all of it?"

"If you don't want it."

"That makes no sense, Michael. Why would you just burn it?"

"Jesus, Hayden. Let me through. I just wanted Maggie to have the best. She deserves that and with all the work you put in fixing the room, I could tell you wanted it. I'm sorry I bothered now," he growls and this isn't a rumbly growl. It's a growl I'm pretty sure would cause tigers to cower in the corner, afraid to move. Then, he puts his hands on my upper arms and picks me up, effectively moving me out of the doorway. He puts me down, out in the hall and turns to leave. I put my hand out without thinking about it, grabbing his shirt in my fist. I stumble when he moves, but he stops when he feels my weak pull on him. "What now?" he asks and this time, I can tell he's exasperated with me past the point where he's even trying to contain it. Still, for some reason I'm not scared.

"Could you bend down here, please? Just for a second?" He frowns, but does as I ask. Before I can second guess myself, or my need to do it. I reach up on my tip toes, bracing myself on his massive chest and lean up and kiss him on the lips. His beard tickles, and it's just a quick peck. To be honest if I hadn't felt the soft give and tasted the faint minty flavor of toothpaste, I wouldn't have been sure I touched his lips. "Thank you, Michael. I'm sorry I reacted badly. I'm just…I'm not used to someone being so nice. Thank you for caring about Maggie," I tell him.

When he says nothing, I start to feel even more awkward. I look at my hands to realize I'm still bracing myself on his chest. I let go immediately and step away. Michael continues to stare at me for what seems like forever, but in reality, is probably shorter than a minute. The horn outside blares again, and Michael continues to stare. Then he shakes his head, grunts and leaves, slamming the door behind him.

Only when he leaves do I take my hand and rub it against my lips, wondering if maybe, just maybe, I've lost my mind. It was a peck. A thank you, but Michael clearly thought it was weird. Maybe I should have only hugged him? Or even better, maybe shook his hand? I shrug it off and go back into the kitchen. I have work I need to do.

CHAPTER 46

Beast

"I NEED A favor," I tell Skull, when he picks up the phone.

In response, he lets off with a trail of curse words. Most are in Spanish, but I've been around him enough to know what they are. I hold the phone out from my ear until there's nothing but silence.

"Are you finished?

"No. I am not done, you shithead! Why haven't you been picking up your goddamn phone?"

"Because I didn't want to talk."

"You didn't want to talk?" he mutters, and I sigh.

I should have called Diesel. I'm standing by my bike. Trying to figure out for the hundredth time why Hayden…*kissed* me. She kissed me. *What the fuck did she do that for?*

"No quieres hablar," Skull mutters, and I growl.

"Quit busting my fucking balls. Either you will help or you won't. Which is it."

"I've been trying to help you, estúpido. You haven't picked up the fucking phone!" he yells, and I mostly ignore him. Looking out at Hayden's house and seeing her move through the kitchen window. *She kissed me.*

"What are you talking about?"

"Motherfucker, you told Blade that the Devil's Blaze had no interest in Whitley! You told him you weren't under our protection!" Skull yells and fuck, if he doesn't stop yelling he's going to stroke out. He's that worked up.

"It's the truth. Now are you going to help me, or do I need to check with someone else."

"It's not the truth motherfucker. I've had Hayden under our protection. I put a call into Cade and he brokered the deal with the Torasani family. Your little declaration to Blade has fucked shit up."

"Why does Hayden need protection?" I growl.

"Because I found out a little over three months ago they beat the fuck out of her and left her for dead. I may not owe shit to Pistol, but fuck, maybe if I had checked on the bitch earlier—" Skull trails off, but the message is clear. He's feeling guilty, but his words leave me confused.

"The preacher mentioned her being beaten. He acted like her brother fixed her up with this place and shit. Diesel figures Pistol had a will or something," I answer, my eyes glued to the house.

"Fuck, Pistol had nothing. That fucker is the one that sold her out to the Dwellers, then when he decided to change his mind it was too late. They used her as leverage over him."

"The Dwellers?"

"Yeah, just one of the snakes Viper and those fucking Donahues climbed into bed with."

"Motherfucker."

"I put a call out to Cade and he may not be kin to Hayden because she was Pistol's half-sister, but he still agreed to make sure she was protected. He called some markers into the Torasani's. Blade found out she was pregnant, and demanded her back, but he's scared enough of us and the Torasani's he hasn't made a move. You going in like a fucking asshole declaring we have no interest there, causes a bunch of fucking headaches," Skull growls.

I take a deep breath and go over everything Skull just said. Cade is the President of the Florida chapter of the Blaze. He's a good guy even if he shares a mother with Pistol. If Skull says Hayden's not kin to Cade that must mean Hayden's father and Pistol's is the same. He was a slimy motherfucker, maybe even worse than Pistol. It's hard for me to believe Hayden shares their blood at all. Holding my head down, I rub my forehead, feeling a migraine starting to form.

"A couple of Blade's goons ran me off the road today. They had me in their sites, but didn't take me out."

"A message."

"I figure. I want all the intel you can find on the Dwellers Compound. I'm going to pay Blade a visit."

"The fuck you will. You aren't going without backup."

"I don't need backup to deal with these motherfuckers."

"I'll have a meeting set up and you will have some of our men with you. That's non-negotiable."

"No fucking way."

"This ain't for you to decide this time motherfucker. I don't want these assholes getting brave and going after the girl."

"What's she to you?" I ask him, even if I do agree with him.

"Responsibility. I should have sent someone after her when Pistol first told me about her."

I think on all the hell that Hayden undoubtedly went through under the Dwellers. I remember her panic attack and the sadness that I see on her face sometimes, and I have to agree with him. It goes against everything I am to agree to let Skull set up a meeting. If it was just me involved I would fucking shut it down at once. It's not just me. I need to protect Hayden and her daughter.

"Set up the meeting. I want it soon," I growl, finally agreeing.

"I'll be in touch. You just make sure to answer your fucking phone," Skull orders, and I disconnect on a grunt. I put my phone back in my pocket and then I march back over to Hayden's. I need to know what the hell she was thinking. *She kissed me.*

CHAPTER 47

Hayden

"YOU KISSED ME," Michael says, and I turn around from the stove. I place the hot cookie sheet full of my peanut butter kisses on the stove top and turn to look at him.

"What?" I ask, confused.

"You kissed me," he repeats, standing there, his face unreadable, his hands at his side.

"It was just a friendly kiss," I answer him, confused. He's been in the baby's room for the last hour working. I tried to help at first and talk to him, but I got tired of being ignored and not even getting a grunt, so I came out here to bake and fix dinner. "Dinner is ready if you're hungry," I tell him, shaking my head and turning back around. "It's nothing special. I just threw together a quick chicken casserole, but if you're hung—" I stop on a gasp as he spins me around. "What's wrong?"

"*Why* did you kiss me?"

"Michael, seriously. Do you have some aversion to being touched? I won't do it again. You were just being sweet, and I had made a mess of everything, and I was grateful. We're friends. I thought it was okay. It won't happen again."

"So, you kiss all your friends?" he asks, his tone disbelieving, his arms folded against each other at his chest. His eyes clearly say I'm crazy, but I'm starting to think he's the crazy one here.

"I've kissed Charlie, yeah, though I guess not on the lips. Yet, in my defense Michael, you're really…" I trail off not sure how to finish that won't make him feel insulted.

"Really what?" he prods, sitting down at the table.

The change in his position gives me something to do, while I try to figure out how not to hurt the big guy's feelings. I move to the stove, taking a plate from the cabinet and dish him some of the casserole. I take it to his plate and then pour him a glass of the homemade lemonade I made earlier. I *still* think it's a strange drink for him, but whatever.

"Really what?" he prompts me, again.

I sigh as I fix my own plate, grab a bottle of water, and sit down across from him. I'm not hungry, but I like having someone to sit at the table and eat with me. I've never had that.

"Hayden," he mutters warningly, when I still remain quiet.

I move my fork around the casserole and when nothing comes to mind on how to be more delicate, I give up.

"You're really, *hairy*." Michael stops with his fork almost to his mouth to look at me. I was afraid I insulted him, but when he looks at me, he looks more stunned. I think I shocked him. Though, I have no idea how. It can't have escaped his notice that he's hairy. If he was a girl I'd call him Rapunzel even…well except for the beard…though I guess some women do have beards. I've seen a few. I don't get it. I'd wax, shave, pluck—*whatever I had to do.*

"You kissed me because I'm…hairy?"

"Well, I mean, I kiss Charlie on the cheek. To do that with you I'd have had to kiss mounds of hair and still not be sure I was in the right spot. As it was, I had to guess where your lips are."

"Do you always kiss your male friends?" he asks, and I frown at him.

"I don't really have any. You know what? With you it's either feast or famine."

"I have no idea what you're talking about."

"You either grunt and don't talk, or you talk about a subject until you're beating a dead horse."

"Beating a dead horse?"

"Exactly."

"This is good," he says, using his fork to point at his food. He's evidently decided that we have played *beat-the-dead-horse* long enough.

"Thanks," I tell him, hoping for some reason that he goes back to grunting.

My head jerks up when he stands. I watch him take out a glass and open the fridge. He gets a glass of milk, and I shrug. Guess he didn't like the lemonade. I think it's better than the store bought, but I don't guess you can please everyone. I jump when he puts the milk beside me.

"What—"

"You need to drink milk. It will help Maggie grow," he mutters and sits back down to eat again.

"You're a strange man Michael." I sigh, but I take a drink of my milk.

In response, he grunts and I can't stop the smile that forms on my face.

CHAPTER 48

Beast

"MICHAEL...THEY'RE SO BEAUTIFUL," Hayden says from the corner, her hand brushing over the comforter and things she just put in the new crib. It's no different from the six times she's said it before. I watch her from my peripheral vision as she moves to the table that has the matching lamp on it. She brushes her hand over it gently, as if she was afraid just one touch would cause it to break. I finish tightening the last screw on the ottoman that goes with the glider.

"Finished," I tell her. I expected her to turn around and look at the chair, but she doesn't. She just keeps staring at the lamp. "Hayden?" I question after a couple of minutes. Finally, she turns around, and I'm surprised when I see a trail of tears that slide down her cheeks.

"I saw this lamp in the window in town a couple of weeks after I got out of the hospital. I wanted it for her, but I knew there was no way I could buy it for her. I told myself that it didn't matter. I kept saying that I could paint her walls pretty and as long as I managed to get her a comfortable place to sleep it would be okay, you know?"

"Hayden…"

"You couldn't have known, but I saw this lamp, and I wanted Maggie to have it, Michael. I wanted her to have all of this."

She just stands there looking more than a little lost. She's crying, and I hate the sight of her tears. Knowing what I do of her past, I have a feeling that she's had way too many tears. I'm not equipped to deal with a woman and obvious pregnancy hormones. I walk over to her, I place my hand against her neck, tilting her so she looks up at me.

"Stop crying," I order her, desperate to stop her tears.

"They're happy tears," she says, as if that makes them better.

"I don't like them. It was just a gift."

"It's an amazing gift," she corrects me, and the look on her face makes me feel…*strange.*

"You're going to kiss me again, aren't you?" I mumble, half wishing she would and half praying she doesn't.

In response, Hayden laughs through her tears. "Considering how much it seems to bother you, no," she exclaims. That shouldn't disappoint me, but I know that's what I'm feeling. "I don't know how to thank you for all of this. I really appreciate it, Michael," she tells me and I shrug it off, I didn't do it for her gratitude. "I need to go work in the kitchen. I have to work tomorrow, but Pastor Sturgill needed his orders early so he's coming by in the morning to pick up some cookies and pies for the Church's widow's dinner. You going back to your place or you want to stick around? You could watch television. Isn't there like a ballgame on or something?"

"You cook for the church?" I ask, following her into the kitchen. Until I find out what the fuck is up with the Dwellers, I don't see me letting her out of my sight. I don't want to tell her that yet, because I don't want her to panic. I'll hang around here as late as possible and then I will make sure I always have my eyes on her place—and her. That's the best I can do.

I lean with my back against the counter, angling so I can watch Hayden as she stands at the stove and begins wrapping cookies.

"Yeah, they're one of my best customers, besides the diner and the Stop-N-Shop in town."

"Why would a church buy baked goods?"

"Well this is for a dinner, but they buy them to sell at their consignment shop, and they buy them for bake sales. That kind of thing," she says, while continuing wrapping the cookies. I reach over and grab one when I notice it's the peanut butter ones like she made me a week or so ago. I take a bite, stopping mid-bite when she stares at me. I figured she would scold me, but she only laughs. "Good thing I made extra." I give her the grunt she seems to appreciate so much, and sure enough, the minute I do it, she laughs.

"How do they make money if they have to buy the things they sell?" I ask her, once I finish the cookie.

"They price them for more money than they pay. I give the church a discount."

"I just figured the members would make what they sell." I shrug, that makes more sense to me and if I'm going to be completely honest, I don't like her doing things for the preacher. I'm not sure why. I just don't like the way he looks.

"They do some things," she says, turning back around to wrap some more cookies. "Actually, I figure Pastor Sturgill buys more than they need, just to help me. I'm grateful. He's been a good friend," she says and something about that *really* bothers me.

My hand comes up to the side of my face and my fingers push into the beard on my chin, as I move them over the indentions I find there. I trace the scars through my beard and think on what Hayden said, and the longer I do, the more I don't like it.

"Do you kiss him?" I ask her, and my question comes out harsher than I intended. Hayden turns around to look at me and her steely eyes grow large as she looks at me in complete shock.

"What?" she gasps, surprise etched on her face—so much of it I want to smile. Still, I want to hear her deny it. I need her to confirm my thoughts. I'm not questioning myself as to why. I have a feeling that I don't want to know.

"Do you kiss him?"

"*Are you crazy?* Why would I?"

"You said you kiss your friends when they do something nice for you," I remind her, and I enjoy the way the heat moves into her face causing her to blush.

She's got her hair up in a crazy contraption on the top of her head again. Wispy strands are going every which way. She's wearing a red, long-sleeved t-shirt, and jogging pants. Her stomach is silhouetted softly in the shirt and she looks beautiful. Young, sweet, and untouched, which seems in direct contrast to her pregnancy. In this moment, I'm not sure I've seen a prettier woman. *How did I ever think she was homely?*

"Pastor Sturgill isn't like you… well…I mean he's a *Pastor*! I couldn't kiss him. I wouldn't want to. Wouldn't God get mad or something?"

I smirk at her answer, while she's busying herself with putting the now empty cookie sheet in the sink and washing it off. I know however, she's just avoiding looking at me.

"I'm pretty sure you're thinking of a priest."

"What? Oh…Well, regardless. I wouldn't even dream of doing that with Pastor Sturgill. He's been good to me, but we're not…*friends*. He's not like you."

"Like me?" I ask, suddenly more interested than I should be.

"Yeah. You know you're different. You're like Charlie," she says, transferring the cookies into a cardboard box.

"Charlie's a woman. A very *old* woman. I'm a man," I remind her, suddenly feeling annoyed. This makes Hayden turn to look at me. Somehow, she's managed to get a little dusting of flour on her cheek.

"Of course she's a woman. But well, you're not a man to me," she says shaking her head, and she says the words like she's trying to explain something simple to a child. *And now I know I'm annoyed.*

"I'm not a man?" I growl.

"No. Well, I mean, obviously, you're a man, but not to me. To me you're…kind of…asexual."

"Asexual?" I roar. Definitely roar. Fuck, I may have given up on my dick for longer than I care to think about, but I am definitely not ready for a woman to think of me as…*Fuck. She thinks of me like a fucking old woman!*

"What's wrong with you?" Hayden asks, and I swear the woman is clueless, which just makes this worse.

"Maybe I'm upset because a woman is standing here telling me she doesn't see me as a man!" I grumble. I didn't think I had pride anymore. Apparently, I was wrong.

"Michael—"

"Don't say it," I warn her.

"Say what?" She stops, looking at me with her face a mixture of confusion and annoyance. *She thinks she's annoyed?*

"Whatever you have cooked up in that silly noggin' of yours."

"Noggin'? Michael, seriously I think—"

"I assure you, Hayden, I am definitely a man."

"Well of course you are. But not with me. With me you're a friend. Like Charlie is my friend. And—"

"I warned you not to say that," I mutter, turning to face her.

"What's got into you?" she asks. "You're acting crazy."

"Men get that way when a woman doesn't notice that they are, in actuality, a *man.*"

"Michael, you're acting nuts. I just don't see you like that. Just like you don't see me as a woman. We're friends," she says again, and Jesus, can she be that clueless.

"Maybe it's time I did something about it then."

"About what?"

"Maybe it's time I showed you that I am a man," I gripe.

"Michael—" I don't let her finish. I don't let her finish because I know she's going to end up saying something else to piss me off. So, I grab her and pull her into me. "Michael, please. I think—" Before she can finish I capture her words with my mouth.

I may regret this. *Fuck.* I know I'm gonna regret it, but I also know I'm going to kiss the hell out of Hayden Graham. *She'll never doubt I'm a man again.*

CHAPTER 49

Hayden

IT'S LIKE I'VE been transported into some Twilight Zone episode. That's what this entire conversation with Michael has been like. I've never dealt with men much. I've had one steady boyfriend and then…Blade. I think it's safe to say my experience in dealing with the opposite sex is limited and not good. The last thing I expect though is for Michael to kiss me.

At first, I'm too shocked to do anything. His beard scratches against my skin and tickles my nose. I hold myself still, it's not that great of a feat, because I'm shell-shocked. My eyes are wide open and they must be huge with surprise. Michael's arm is tight around me. His palm is spread out on my back, and I can feel each finger pressing into me with a bruising force. I'm thinking any minute he'll back away and this will be over. We can awkwardly laugh it off and go to our respective corners. I'm waiting for that to happen. Any minute now…any second—

And then it happens.

I feel Michael's tongue sweep against my lips, seeking entry. I don't let him, of course. That would be insanity. This needs to have never happened. *It can't happen!* Then, his free hand moves to my breast. There has been one side effect with pregnancy that has driven me insane. I want sex. I want sex all the time. Even with the early morning sickness, and my stomach starting to pooch out, I still craved sex. I've went through packages and packages of batteries for my vibrator, because after my experience with Blade there was no way I wanted another man around me. My brain is screaming that now. The traitorous lower half of my body is screaming that Michael isn't just another man. *He's Michael. I like him.*

Nerves assault me. *Fear* hits me. Before they completely take hold his thumb brushes across my nipple. A surge of heat pulses through me. Familiar, yet shockingly different. I've felt excitement for a man before. I've felt what I thought was desire, but this…*this* is different. It's sharper, it's more intense. I tighten my body up, and my hands brace against him to push away.

"No," I whisper, and he pulls back. His eyes rake over me and I hate it, because I know he can read the fear there. The fear that I can't push away. "We shouldn't do this. I don't want this," I tell him, wondering if he will believe me, because I'm not sure I do.

"I think you do," he says, and his voice is different…it's gruffer, but it seems to vibrate—*through me.*

"Michael, I can't do this," I whisper guiltily.

"You're scared," he says, and I can't even deny it. "Keep your eyes open, so you know it's me," he demands and his words confuse me. *How could I not know it was him?*

"Michael—"

"Trust me, Beauty," he whispers, his voice dipping down, and my stomach feels like a thousand butterflies pick that moment to take flight. I gasp when I feel his palm slide against my neck. His skin is rough and callused yet gentle. His thumb strokes against the pulse point in my neck and when his lips brush against mine, I don't think of denying him this time. I've never kissed a man with a beard before, it adds a new sensation, but more than that, Michael's lips are full, soft, and completely at odds with the surly exterior and personality he usually displays.

He doesn't even kiss me like I expected. Instead, it's a soft touch, a smooth, sweet glide of our lips. It's merely a teasing touch and then he pulls away, a mere breath, before coming back. He does this a few times, and it's almost as if he's hypnotizing me with his movements, luring me with them, because each time he breaks away, I find myself following him.

Then it happens. This time as his lips tenderly touch mine, his tongue sneaks into my mouth. It doesn't go far, it's not even assertive. It slides in and teases against the inside of my lip, moves against my cheek, before going back out. I miss its presence immediately.

I could taste him.

Minty, fresh, musky and...*naughty.*

That feeling that you're doing something you shouldn't, but it's so good you can't stop.

Seductive.

I lose myself in his taste, and when his tongue comes back for a second round, I seek it. Our tongues wrap around each other, carefully at first as if neither of us are sure what we're doing, and then again, with more intensity. I think I moan, maybe it was him, because all at once the kiss changes from a shy, gentle exchange into something else. Something different from anything I've ever experienced before.

My hands bite into his shirt, and I hold on for dear life, because I can feel the heat surround us.

Passion.

I've been so stupid. My whole life I've been stupid, because it's suddenly crystal clear that until this moment, I've never truly felt real desire. As many times as I've kissed and been kissed, I've never felt like this before. I might have thought I had good kisses before. I might have even thought I had a connection with the person I was kissing. *I was wrong.* I've never been kissed this way before, until him.

Michael owns my mouth, but with that same thought, I'm pretty sure I own his. It's as if we're fighting a war to see who can claim victory. When he lets out a half-muted growl and I swallow it down, I feel like I am the clear winner. I feel as if I'm in control.

As if that's the signal they needed, my fingers move up to tangle into his thick hair. Michael's hands move down to my ass, biting into the flesh as he pulls me up his body. I break away from his mouth, as my feet leave the floor. When he pulls me up to him, he claims my mouth again, and he kisses me deeper. I wrap my legs around his waist, our tongues continuing their war with one another, my fingers fisting tightly in his hair, holding him to me.

I can feel desire course through my body. I'm not acting on anything but need and instinct, lost completely in the taste and feel of Michael. He pulls me even tighter into him, and the heat from his body is so hot, it feels as if it could burn me. I'm wet with desire. I feel it pooling against my panties, and coating along the inside of my thighs. I want more…*I want more of Michael.* I'm lost in a fantasy where I can be a woman who doesn't have baggage, who doesn't have scars. A woman who can just enjoy the moment. And then it happens.

Maggie picks that moment to push out hard. Her kick pushes against Michael. I pull away from his mouth immediately—*it's that strong.* She kicks again, and this time, Michael must feel it because he pulls on my ass, giving us a little distance between each other. I hold my head down, afraid to look at him and feeling helplessly embarrassed. Then I remember, I'm pregnant, and he's holding me up in the air.

I immediately unlock my legs, and he lowers me to the ground. I don't know what to say to him. I've never experienced a kiss like that before in my life. I can still taste him. I'm already missing him and the connection we had forged. He moves his hand back to my neck and forces me to look up at him.

"That shouldn't have happened," I croak, my voice sounding as if I haven't had anything to drink in weeks.

"You're right," he says, and disappointment blankets over me like a thick fog. Before I can even process that, he's places a kiss on my forehead and turns to leave.

I'm so confused and my hormones are raging. I don't know up from down right now, and the fact that he's leaving only adds to that. I don't try to stop him, though. It's best he leaves. It's best I get control of myself—*alone*.

"It definitely shouldn't have happened," he says again, as he opens the door. My fingers are touching my lips. I can still feel his pressed against mine. My body still feels like sparks of electricity is arcing through it. "It's probably going to happen again, though," he growls as he leaves, closing the door behind him.

I just stand there. I couldn't tell you for how long. A few minutes, maybe longer, I keep standing there, touching my lips and staring at a closed door. All the time, in my head, I'm trying to figure out how I feel about Michael's declaration, because only one thing is sure about all of it. *Michael didn't sound happy about it at all.*

CHAPTER 50

Beast

W*HAT THE FUCK was I thinking?* Kissing Hayden was the single most, stupidest thing I've ever done in my life. That's saying a lot considering I let Jan lead me around by the nose for fucking years. I'd like to say it happened because she said she didn't see me as a man, but the truth is I've been thinking about kissing Hayden for days. I never should have done it though, because I can still taste her.

It's the next day, I've barely slept. I didn't even drink. Instead, I walked the perimeter of Hayden's house. When I wasn't doing that, I sat in the dark remembering the feel of her ass in my hands and her legs wrapped around me. Her taste is haunting me. A mixture of sex and honey, more addicting than anything I've ever encountered in my life. I'm only sure of two things at this point. I'm in deep shit when it comes to Hayden Graham. I need to stay away from her, because she deserves much better than me. Maggie deserves better than me. Hell, if I could figure out a way to protect them both without getting close to them at this point…*I would.*

The other thing I'm sure of is that my dick is most assuredly not dead. I've been hard since Hayden wrapped her legs around me. I've been hard all night, remembering the feel of her body and the taste of her lips. It's the next day and my cock is still demanding attention. *Attention he is not getting.*

I down the last of my coffee, draining my cup. Hayden left for work two hours ago. I know because I watched her out the window like a fucking pervert. She didn't even look towards the barn. Is she running scared after the kiss? Fuck, why wouldn't she? Why I had to force the issue, I don't fucking know. She probably won't let me back in her house—not that I would blame her. Hell, it wasn't that long ago she suffered a panic attack that scared the shit out of me. There's no way I should have touched her, pulled her body against my hard cock so I could press against the heat of her, kneaded her ass with my fingers, and drank from her mouth like a fucking man dying of thirst. Thinking about it now sends a shudder of need through my body.

I reach down to adjust my cock, which is throbbing. If I was another man I would have pushed Hayden up against the wall and fucked the hell out of her. Fucked her so hard she would have felt me for days. Fucked…Hayden…a *pregnant* and obviously emotionally scarred, Hayden. *Jesus.*

I've got to get a handle on shit. I need to be clear headed to deal with the threat of the Dwellers. I don't know what's going on, but I can't let my guard down when it comes to Hayden and Maggie. I need them safe. That's the reason I ended up jumping in my truck as Hayden disappeared down the road this morning. I followed her, staying far enough behind, she wouldn't have an easy time of detecting me. When I was satisfied that she made it to work safely, I came back home. Yet, I've been worrying nonstop since I got back. I would have done better to just campout in the diner today.

Frustrated with myself, I pick up my phone to call Skull. I let it ring until it turns over to voicemail. If I didn't know better, I'd say the fucker was giving me payback for ignoring his calls. Can't say as I blame him. I need to spend the day doing something that will exhaust me. Working until the last thing I can think about is fucking Hayden. *Fucking anyone.* It might not be that it's just Hayden, maybe it's because I've been so long without sex. Even as I think it, I *know* I'm lying. It's Hayden I want. It's just as I feared, she has snuck under my defenses somehow. I should figure out how to stop it before it gets worse.

Maybe I could fix Hayden's front porch. The damn floor is swaying. It'd be dangerous if she walks on it; it could collapse. If she fell, it could hurt the baby. I'll need to run into town and get some wood and work on the supports underneath the porch first. I haven't really eaten yet either. Maybe I could swing by the diner for food...

Motherfucker.

CHAPTER 51

Hayden

CHARLIE IS GIVING me funny looks. I know it can't be my imagination. I feel like I have a giant sticker across my forehead that reads: *"I kissed a boy, and I think I liked it."* It's crazy. There's no way she could know. Her look probably has more to do with the fact that I have bags the size of suitcases under my eyes because I didn't sleep at all last night. I tossed and turned thinking about Michael, thinking about him kissing me, wondering if he liked it, wondering why I liked it so much, wishing he wouldn't have stopped, glad that he did…*the list kept going.*

Charlie might also be giving me those looks because I'm clumsy as can be today. I've broke two plates, I've dropped silverware, and I accidentally dropped a piece of pie in old man Gilbert's lap. Luckily, he just laughed about it. I might be getting those looks from her because every time the bell rings to signal the door is being opened, I jerk around to see who is walking in. I'm alternating between dreading and wishing Michael would come in. That's why when it rings and I look up to see him walk in, I freeze. Which might have been okay. It might have totally gone unnoticed, if not for the fact that even though my body locked up and I couldn't seem to move, I was refilling a glass for poor Mr. Gilbert—a glass of very cold ice water.

"Tarnation, Hayden! What's going on with you today!" Mr. Gilbert yells, jumping up just as three blocks of ice drop from the pitcher onto his lap. *Shit.*

"Oh no. Mr. Gilbert, I'm so sorry. Let me get some towels!" I run to the counter, my face so hot that I know I have to be glowing in the dark. I can see Michael from the corner of my eye as he walks past me and goes to sit down in a corner booth. "I really am sorry, Mr. Gilbert. I'll pay for your lunch. I'm such a klutz today. Please, forgive me."

"Girl, you froze my damn balls!" he yells, loudly, which does nothing to keep me from being further embarrassed.

"My girl's good at that, aren't you, Hayden?" A male voice says at the door.

A minute ago, I could feel the heat on my face. A minute ago, my biggest problem was getting Mr. Gilbert to calm down and figure out what to say to Michael. Now, my problems are much bigger. Any embarrassment I feel, any heat from a blush on my face is gone now. In its place is white, because all color has drained from me, and in the place of the heat is a cold dread that seeps into my system and causes my body to break out in a sweat. I slowly, agonizingly slow, lift my head to see Blade standing in front of me. He's alone, though beyond him I see at least three of his men.

I jerk my head back to the monster at the door. I don't want to see if I know the men with him. Chances are I do. Chances are those memories will do nothing to help me beat down the panic I'm feeling inside right now. *And I'm definitely feeling the panic.*

Blade hasn't changed in the months since I've seen him. I look at him now and wonder how I ever could have thought he was good looking. He's tall. Though not as tall as Michael. I'd say around 6'4" or so. He looks a lot like Pastor Sturgill. His sandy-blonde hair is longer though, and falls to his shoulders. It has a natural wave to it, and there's one curl that no matter what he does refuses to go back with the rest of his hair. It falls over his forehead and gets in his eye. I used to think that was sweet. *I find nothing about Blade sweet now.*

I used to love the blue of his eyes. Now the blue seems lifeless, dull. There's nothing warm in them. I know, because I've seen the demon that lurks under the skin of this man. He's got a tattoo of a snake that is coiled around his neck. That's new. He didn't have that before. Too bad, if he had that, I wouldn't have been attracted to him at all. I can't help but think how fitting it is on him now. He's wearing his club-cut, with a plain black t-shirt underneath. His arms are covered in ink. I used to find that sexy. Michael has tattoos, but his are mostly military, they don't seem…*sinister.* Blade's entire body is covered in ink, but they don't interest me anymore. They make my skin crawl.

"Your kind ain't welcome here," Charlie growls.

"Hush, old woman. I'm here to see *my* woman. Hayden, you haven't spoke to me. Is that any way to greet *your* man?" he asks, and his words punch me as hard as his hand once slapped me.

I can feel the panic edge up. I fight to beat it down. I don't want to give into it. I did the other day when Michael's friends all crowded in my kitchen. The men were standing by the doors and they were wearing their club gear. Memories from the past hit me all at once, and I couldn't fight it down. I will be *stronger* than that today. I was strong last night. I kissed Michael. That has to mean something. *Right?* I tighten my hand into a fist, afraid I'm not going to be able to pull this off, and that's when I feel Michael come to stand beside me. Instantly, I feel calmer. The fear is still there, but I can manage. *I can manage.*

"I'm not your woman. Or did you forget how that ended? Because I haven't. I have scars to prove it," I tell him, and though my voice is not as loud as I would have liked, I congratulate myself because it's not trembling. *I don't sound weak.*

"That's what happens when you're a lying bitch. But you were also keeping secrets from me weren't you, Hayden?"

"I wasn't the only one," I remind him, and that's when the demon comes close to the surface. I see him, just for a second. My body tightens as I wait for him to strike out. I can feel that fear wash through me again, but with one touch it's gone. I look down at my hand which is held in a tight fist. Michael is carefully unlocking my fingers. One by one he peels them back, and I stop and watch him, my hand going slack in his. Once he's uncoiled my fingers and brushed his thumb over the indentions my nails made when they bit into my skin, he takes his hand in mine. *Just like that.* Michael holds my hand. *In front of everyone...proudly.*

"Beast. They told me you were in these parts."

"I told your boys the other day to give you a message. I wasn't trying to hide," Michael says. I can feel the tension radiating through his hand, but his words seem laid back. He seems and sounds perfectly at ease. The only way I know for sure that's a lie is the way the muscles in his hand are stiff and pulsing against my skin.

I take my thumb and brush against the large scar that runs from the knuckle on up to his wrist. I rake the pad of my thumb back and forth. I can't say if it is to calm me or Michael, but it seems to work for both.

"They told me. Did you get my message?" he asks, and I look at Michael in surprise. Had he been talking with Blade's men again? I hadn't seen them around the house. *I don't want them around the house.*

"I figure you know I did," Beast says. "When's our meeting?"

"I don't like the way you're touching my woman. A man could take offense to that," Blade says, and I instantly want to throw up. I have to forcibly swallow down the bile that rises up at his words.

"He might, if he was a real man," Michael says, and my heart speeds up, because Blade isn't one to let something like that pass.

"You filthy motherfucker! I think it's time I teach you about respect," Blade snarls, and he takes a step toward Michael.

"Get behind me, Hayden," he directs me, letting go of my hand, and widening his stance as if he's preparing for battle.

"How sweet that you want to protect my left-overs. Didn't think the Blaze wanted to live off my table scraps. It's okay. You're welcome to the *cunt*. Just as soon as I get that split-tail she's carrying," Blade hurls, and I cry out at the thought of him ever getting near my daughter.

I step behind Michael, my hands going around my waist. I'm having trouble keeping a different kind of panic at bay now. *Why would Blade want my daughter?* He's not the fatherly type, he doesn't care about anyone, and I know that better than most. Why would he do this? I jerk when I feel arms go around me. Old man Gilbert is there pulling me away from Michael.

"Let's get you safe girl. That man doesn't need you distracting him," he says, and I walk backwards with him, but I keep my eyes trained on Michael.

CHAPTER 52

Beast

I'VE MADE A life of being an enforcer for one of the most feared clubs around. You don't do that by losing your cool. I've always locked myself down. I attack and in battle I'm deadly cold. Hearing Blade talk about Hayden as his, brings those emotions to a boil, but I have a handle on it. *I do.* I've got it contained, and I won't let him get me rattled. Until he has the balls to refer to Maggie as a *"split-tail."* I know the saying. It's something used often back home. An offensive term to call a girl, as if they are somehow below a man. I've never had respect for the fuck in front of me, but if that's how he can even think about his own daughter, he deserves to die and it's in that moment I lose sight of being level-headed in battle. All I can think about is ripping out his tongue and letting Hayden feed it to him. I want to end the son of a bitch so he never gets his hands on Hayden or Maggie. This fuck doesn't deserve them. *He never did.*

I charge at Blade with a growl, and I guess that was the last thing he was expecting, because the motherfucker's eyes go round, and he stops advancing towards me. It doesn't matter,

I've had it with him. He scrambles to throw a punch, but he wasn't prepared soon enough. My hand goes around his neck, and I squeeze the shit out of it, picking him up off the ground with just my hold. I push forward, despite him clawing at my hand and kicking me. I stop only when I've slammed him against the wall.

He's clawing harder at my hands, but I'm bigger, and I can't remember a time when I've had this much anger coursing through me. It's beating inside of me like a living thing. When I tried to save Annabelle the largest emotion I could grasp was fear. It consumed me, roared through me and fucking suffocated me from the inside out. Anger is much more preferable, so I let it have free reign.

"You don't touch them," I growl, my voice sounding otherworldly, like a demon possessed and maybe I am. I've lived in Hell so long, it would make sense. *"You don't lay one fucking finger on them."*

"They're mine," he manages to gurgle out, and I tighten my hold on him even more, satisfied when his face starts losing color, only to slowly be replaced by a darkening hue. I want the asshole blue. I want his last breath finished. *I couldn't save Annabelle, but I can make sure this fucker never touches Hayden or Maggie ever again.*

"That's where you're wrong asshole. Hayden and Maggie are under the protection of the Devil's Blaze, but more importantly they're under *my* protection. They're my *property,* and no one touches what's mine and gets to breathe air."

I increase the pressure on my hand. The fucker is getting zero air now and that's what he deserves. I can feel his tendons curved against my hand, the solidness of the bone. It will be easy to snap his neck and that's my goal. Even when I hear the door to the diner open and the sound of boots on the tiled floor. I know Blade's men are there to have his back, and I've made the mistake of leaving mine unprotected. It doesn't matter. I don't give two shits that I'm about to die. I've been wanting death for as long as I care to remember, the only difference is that now, before I go, I can make sure I take Blade with me.

My body jerks as the retort of a shotgun blast rings out. Leave it to these motherfuckers to bring a fucking shotgun to the party. I wait for the white-hot, searing pain of a gunshot to rip through me. I'm surprised when it doesn't, but I don't take my eyes off of Blade. I take pleasure in the fact that I can see a blood vessel pick that exact moment to burst in his eye. *Any second now…*

"I won't have you damn cockroaches in my diner. You don't move," Charlie cries out, and they must have not listened because she shoots again. "The next one won't be a warning shot. You'll lose your nuts and berries if you take one more step," she tells them, and I can hear Blade's men in the background, but I don't give a fuck. *Blade's going to die here.* "Michael, let the asshole go," I hear Charlie tell me, and I can't believe it. I don't respond but I give her a grunt. "I mean it, Michael. Let him go and let them leave. Hayden doesn't need more violence, and you're worth more to her here, than on the inside of a jail cell. She's in bad shape right now," she says, and her words kind of reach me, but I'm lost in a thirst for blood.

I want him dead. This should be the one thing I can do. You don't leave the head on a wounded snake. That just gives him more time to strike.

"Michael. Hayden needs you. *Now.*" Charlie yells, and I concentrate on those words and turn to find Hayden.

She's standing in the corner with an old man standing beside her, but she doesn't see him. Her body is shaking and though it doesn't look as severe as the other day, I know she's lost in another attack. I know she's back inside of her own hell, and I can't leave her there. I take my hand from Blade and back away from him a couple of steps. He immediately drops to his knees, starts coughing and gasping for breath. The disappointment I feel is immense, as the color starts slowly leeching back into his face.

"This…ain't…over," Blade gasps, his voice is so hoarse it's hard to make out. "I'll end you," he vows, as he makes toward the door. His men have to help him to stand and at least that gives me satisfaction.

"Bring it motherfucker. I've taken worse than you down without blinking," I tell him truthfully, already turning away and walking to Hayden. I have to get her out of her head. *I have to bring her back to me.*

"You'll pay for interfering, old woman," one of the men growls from behind me, and I hear another gunshot go off and the cry of a man. *I hope she killed him*, I think, only to feel disappointment when I hear Charlie.

"Drag his ass out of here and get him patched up while he's still breathing. Any of you set foot in my place again, I won't be as forgiving, and you can bet that Victor Torasani will hear about the shit you pulled today," Charlie warns them.

I file away the knowledge that she seems to know the head of the Torasani family as I finally make it to Hayden.

CHAPTER 53

Hayden

I CAN FEEL Michael's arms go around me. Slowly the heat of his body surrounds me. I've panicked again, though at least it's not as deep as I normally go. I feel Michael stroking my hair, his rough fingers somehow gently wrapped around the ponytail. His other hand has captured one of mine and his thumb is brushing back and forth across the top of my wrist. I concentrate on that as I let the shudders slowly leave my body and try to control my breathing.

"Come back to me, *Beauty*. Don't let them drag you back there. You're safe. I'm keeping you safe. Nothing will touch you and Maggie again," I hear Michael whispering in my ear. He keeps repeating the same things over and over, so softly I have to strain to hear them over the way my pulse is pounding in my ears. But, I concentrate on the words. I take them in. I hear his conviction, and I know he means them.

Maybe it's weak to look to someone to save me, but right now it feels like a miracle. I let the tension leave my body as I collapse against him with a sob. I wrap my arms around him.

"That's it, come back to me," he whispers, his voice hoarse

and cracking.

I don't tell him, because saying the words out loud would terrify me, but I'm pretty sure as long as he wanted me to, I'd always come back to him.

I feel him lift me up in his arms and he walks me to a chair and sits down. I go to move off him, but he doesn't let me. I don't fight him too hard. I feel safest when he's around.

"I'm okay," I tell him, or maybe even myself. I can't be sure.

"I know you are, *sweetheart*," he whispers, and I can't decide which is better. The sound of his heart beating when I'm pressed against his chest, or his voice talking to me so tenderly.

I've never had that. Nothing has ever been sweet in my life. Michael gives me glimpses of sweet and I can't help but want more.

"Did they leave?"

"Yeah, they headed out. Fools. I don't know what's got them acting so damned brave all at once. Victor has been letting too much slip by. I'll call him tonight," Charlie answers.

"You need to make sure you keep that gun close," Michael warns her. "Do you have law here you can trust?"

"I've got it taken care of," she says cryptically. "You just need to take care of our girl here. How are you doing, cupcake?"

"I'm sorry, Charlie," I tell her, feeling like an idiot and hating myself for bringing all of this to her doorstep.

"Nothing to be sorry for, sweet girl. That bunch is a plague. They're nothing but cockroaches. Unfortunately, cockroaches seem to survive no matter what you do to kill them."

"That's what you think," Michael growls.

"Michael, you can't go up against Blade and his men," I tell him, fear laced in my words.

"Why in the fuck not?"

"I don't want you to get hurt—especially not because of

me," I tell him, pulling back enough so that I can look into his eyes. Curving my hand along the side of his face, low around his chin and jawbone, I allow my fingers to slightly curl into his beard. "I couldn't handle it if they hurt you."

"Fuck," he growls and my forehead scrunches up in confusion. Before I can talk to him further, he stands up. I move my hands around his neck to hold on, since it becomes clear, even when I try, that he's not letting me down. "Charlie, make sure you stay safe," he warns. "They may try to come back."

"You do the same and keep our girl safe," she orders back, as we go out the door.

"I've got her," Michael grumbles, though not to Charlie because we're outside.

I have questions in my head, but I don't know what I want to ask, so I remain silent as he puts me in his truck and buckles me in. Even when he leans up from connecting my seatbelt and stops to look me in the eyes, I remain silent. When his ink-covered, scarred hand comes up to my face and this thumb brushes against my temple, I'm still silent. When his lips briefly touch my forehead, I keep quiet. Mostly, I don't know what to say. Yet, there's a part of me wondering why he kissed my forehead and not my lips.

I really wish he'd kissed my lips.

CHAPTER 54

Beast

THE ROAD TO Hell is paved with good intentions. I needed to keep Hayden at arm's length. I failed. I wanted to protect her and her child and somehow, I've let Hayden get to me. I can admit it, what I can't figure out is how to stop it. Being around Hayden is like standing in quicksand, and I'm slowly sinking, the more I struggle the deeper I get pulled in.

I look down at her sleeping form and barely restrain a growl. Today was messed up. I can't believe those fuckers thought it was okay to come at Hayden like that. Not if they'd been leaving her alone all this time. It has to be more than me showing up in the town. I've called Skull and Diesel and swallowed my pride enough to have them looking into it. Skull mentioned sending some men down as back-up. I don't want that, but if this shit keeps up, I may not have a choice. I had Skull send a shout out to Cade and one to the Torasani clan. Maybe if I can talk to both of them, I might get better protection for Hayden and Maggie. It's old school but nothing rings quite as true as the old adage, *"The enemy of my enemy is my friend."* I definitely need some friends in this damn town if I'm going to make sure Hayden is safe. I shouldn't do it, but I find myself crawling on the bed behind her. Wrapping my arm around her stomach, spooning her, and pulling her into me. I bury my face into the back of her neck breathing in the strawberry scent of her shampoo.

"You're still here," she whispers.

I have the room dark, shades pulled on the window, but it's barely dusk outside. The street light out front has just started buzzing, I can hear it through the window.

"I told you I wouldn't leave."

"It might be better if you did Michael. I'm trouble. I thought Blade had given up, but he won't stop. I know that now."

"Why do you say that?" I ask her, but I'm sure she's right. The Blade I saw today had blood in his eyes. He wants to punish Hayden. I could see it. She's going to have to tell me more about their past. I'll talk with her about it soon, but not right now. She's definitely had enough today.

"He said that horrible word…about Maggie. He referred to her as…"

"Don't say it," I growl, still hating that word that is only used by sad-sacks with shit for brains.

"But how would he know she's a girl? I mean even the doctor hasn't confirmed it. Why would he refer to her as a girl at all?" she whispers, her voice wobbling. She may have beat the panic attack, but the fear is still there. I want to be the one to get rid of that for her. *Ain't that just another bucket of fuck.* She's smart—even in fear. I didn't catch that. Very few people would know Hayden has proclaimed Maggie a girl. That means Blade has been watching her constantly. He has someone on the inside getting him the information, *he has to.*

"Who have you mentioned Maggie too?"

"I don't talk to hardly anyone, though I guess anyone coming in to eat at the diner might have heard me. I can't trust anyone now, can I?" she whispers, and I can hear the pain inside of her at the thought. Her body tightens, and I kiss her shoulder in response.

"You can trust me."

"Michael…"

"I've got this, Hayden. I won't fail again. You don't need to worry," I tell her, without thinking, only wanting her to stop worrying.

Nothing else is said for a bit. Her breathing has evened out, and I think maybe she has fallen asleep. I should get up from here, though the temptation to stay with her is strong. That's when I feel her fingers wrap around mine and she pulls our joined hands tighter so they rest above her stomach, just under the curve of her breast. I look up at the ceiling, trying to beat down the urge to rub my arm against the underswell. I can feel my dick—the dick I thought was mostly dead, begin to lengthen. *Shit.* I feel her fingers from her other hand dance across my skin. I used to hate being touched. It's the one thing I forbid after I got out of the hospital, even after the burns healed leaving scars in their wake. Hayden's touch I could easily begin to crave. It's a soft whisper, gentle and sweet, which is seductive and yet somehow clean and natural. *God what I wouldn't give to feel clean. To feel…normal.*

"You have so many tattoos," she whispers, changing the subject and surprising me completely. I thought she would talk about my scars. My ink was the last thing I thought she would notice. She brings her fingers against my upper arm, right before you get to the elbow. The room is dark, but there's a faint light shining from the adjoining bathroom. It's enough that I'm sure she can see…*and read.* She rolls over on her back. I have the strongest urge to pull my hand away. *I don't know why I don't.* For some reason, I stay right there—like an idiot. "Who is Annabelle?" she asks, and I don't want to talk about it. I'm not sure I can.

"Someone I lost," I tell her, and even I can hear the sadness that permeates every syllable of my answer.

"Why did you put stars by her name?" I shouldn't answer. Hayden is doing it again. She's getting inside of my head. Getting me to feel…and getting way too close to me. But like a fool, I find myself telling her.

"She used to curl up in my lap at night. We'd look up at the sky and count the stars and she'd find the one she thought was the prettiest to wish upon."

"What did she wish for?"

"Most times she wouldn't tell me, because—"

"Then it wouldn't come true," Hayden finishes, and if my heart didn't feel like it was being squeezed in half, I'd smile, because that's just what Annabelle would say.

"Yeah," I tell Hayden, clearing my throat which is so tight with emotion I feel like I'm choking. "Sometimes she would tell me she wanted a white horse with wings so she could ride into the stars and touch them," I tell her, my eyes closing tight at the memory of my sweet baby girl. *Her blonde hair brushed until it shines, it falls back across my arm, as she looks up at me. Her beautiful blue eyes wide with happiness, and her voice full of excitement and love. Annabelle was always so full of love.* "I don't have much stock in God. He and I have pretty much parted ways, but I hope he's letting my Annabelle touch the stars now," I murmur, not really to Hayden. No. Now, I'm lost in the memories. I feel like I'm bleeding from a wound I can never find and one that never heals. I can't let them all out. Not now. Especially not in front of Hayden. Annabelle is a part of me that no one will see. I fight to keep away from the pain, from the memories that want to engulf me.

"Maybe she's the one who decides just where the stars go now," Hayden whispers, and she pulls my hand up and kisses it. "I know God is watching out for her."

"How do you know," I have to stop to catch my breath. "How do you know that?" I ask, and I hear the desperation in my voice. I need her to tell me my daughter is okay now. *I need her to make me believe that she lives on…*somewhere…*anywhere.*

"Someone that special? God would have to make sure she is always happy."

"Special?" I ask, because I know. God! *I know* my Annabelle was special. But, I need to know why Hayden believes it. Through all of this I've received pity…pats on the back from people who were supposed to be my family, but they don't understand. Their lives went on. They have their kids, their wives, and their life. They're not lost in the darkness. They aren't drowning in memories so filled with pain that they consume you. Memories that rot you on the inside, making it hurt to fucking move. They don't even remember Annabelle unless I come around and only then they do, but only because they see what her loss has done to me.

I *need* Hayden to believe in Annabelle. Not because she wants me to feel better, but because in her heart she believes what she's telling me. I need *someone* to tell me without a doubt that Annabelle lives on…*happily.*

I feel silent tears falling from my eyes, escaping even though I'm closing my eyes tight, and tighter still as Annabelle's face floats across my mind. Her bright, laughing voice yelling out, *"Daddy!"* as I tickle her. Her sweet voice, so distant…I want to grasp it and hold onto it, but I can't seem to.

"She had to be special to have someone like you love her so deeply. She was a lucky woman," Hayden says, her small fingers curling back into mine. She gives up on my tattoo, and holds my hand. She lays there, not having any idea that she just ripped my heart open.

She just lays there leaving me hoping with everything left inside of me that she's right, and my Annabelle is playing with the stars…

CHAPTER 55

Hayden

I COME AWAKE slowly, with the sound of rain hitting against the window pane. I'm warm. *So warm.* I move to stretch and it's then I notice that my hand is wrapped around something—or rather someone else's hand. *Michael.* It's then I become more alert. I'm not sure how I missed it before. The reason I am so warm is because Michael's body is pressed against me, his legs are wrapped in mine, and his arm is lying over my stomach, our hands intertwined; he's pulled me up far enough that his face is buried into the back of my neck. I know, because I can feel his breath against my skin.

For a minute, I just keep my eyes closed and take this in. This feeling of joy, of contentment, floods through me and with it is a feeling I've never experienced at any point in my life. *Safety.* Even after yesterday, right now in this moment I feel nothing but safe. I drink it in, and without realizing it my thumb has started moving back and forth along the largest scar on Michael's hand. It's the strangest thing to try and describe, but somehow brushing against that scar, brings me…*peace.* It's a symbol that this man has endured some of his own nightmares and yet here he is, strong, giving, and dependable. He goes against everything I've encountered in my life.

"Morning," he says, his voice gruff enough that it does something to me and little shivers seem to vibrate through my body like sparks. He pulls away, and like a fool, I try to hold his hand as he rolls over onto his back. I let go reluctantly and ignore the heat I can feel spreading across my face.

I move my tongue over my lips as I move to my back too. My mouth suddenly feels dry and nerves begin to attack me. Then a horrible thought comes to mind. *Morning breath.* I sit up, turning to get off the bed. Michael's hand lands on my shoulder and I can't stop myself from jumping slightly.

"Where you going?" he asks, and it's hard to concentrate on his words when the heat from his hand feels as if it's going under my skin and maybe even warming parts of me I didn't know were cold.

"I uh…thought I should clean up…and maybe fix breakfast and…"

"Are you nervous, Hayden?" he asks, and I'm not looking at him, but I think I can hear laughter in his voice. If I turned around to see him, would he be smiling? I sigh loudly.

"Yes." The strangest thing happens when I admit it to him. Michael laughs. It's rusty, and I can barely hear it. He kind of coughs and laughs, but still…it is a quiet laugh and it shocks me so much that I turn a little so I can look at him over my shoulder.

He removes his hand from my shoulder, and I instantly miss it. "Why are you nervous?"

"Because you're…"

"What?" he asks, his forehead crinkling so that deep lines appear. I can see them peeking through his hair.

On instinct, I reach up to brush hair out of the way.

"Well...*you*," I answer him, enjoying the feel of his hair between my fingers before I let go and watch the stubborn, wavy tendrils fall back. "You have too much hair. I can't see your face," I tell him without thinking, and when I see the look that comes over him, I'm sorry I mentioned it. "I'll just go clean up," I tell him, nervously.

In response, he grunts.

I'm acting too strange around him. Ever since that kiss, I have no idea how to act or be around Michael. He asked if I was nervous? *He has no freaking clue.*

I get the distinct impression that I've managed to offend him talking about his hair, and I have this huge urge to beg him to forgive me. The only thing that stops me is I'm pretty sure I'd make a bigger fool of myself. I go into the bathroom and close the door, wondering if I'll ever be normal.

CHAPTER 56

Beast

F*UCKING HELL*. IT should not be this hard to be around a woman. Before...*before* I had women falling at my feet. I barely had to talk to one. Now I don't know what to say to one when she makes a comment about not being able to see my face. I'm pretty sure I hurt her feelings and that's the last thing I wanted. *Shit.* Why not just call a spade a spade? The truth is that for the first time in years I want to stick my dick in a woman. I don't know why it's happening and more importantly, I *resent* that it's happening.

Of all the women in the world my dick had to come back to life for, it had to be Hayden. A pregnant woman with a world of trouble and eyes that beg for forever should not be where I plant my dick. But, I'm drawn to her in ways I can't explain. I want her as I've never wanted another woman, and apparently, she's going to be the only woman to get a rise out of my dick right now. I thought after Jan, I would have fucking wised up when it came to women. Apparently, I thought wrong. I've been hard all fucking night. Having Hayden's ass pressed against me, even wearing sweatpants has been pleasure and hell. I should have left. Hell, I should leave now. Instead, I'm walking towards the bathroom where Hayden ran to. I'm doing it while knowing it's a mistake, *even knowing I shouldn't.*

"Hayden, I..." whatever I was going to say flees from my mind. I'm struck dumb by what I see when I open the door. Hayden is standing by the shower, the water running in the background, in nothing but a red bra and this lace covered cloth that I guess is what women call panties. I've never been one to pay much attention to what women wear. The goal was always to get them naked quickly and have my fun. Right now, I think I might have missed out, because seeing what is on Hayden is hot. It's like Christmas wrapping on the biggest gift under the tree. The fabric is shaped like shorts, hugging her hips, stretching over her fucking ass like a second skin, and leaving the cheeks to curve out and taunt me. The hard-on I've had all night, feels like a fucking hammer slamming against concrete now. Physically painful, throbbing, and in need of relief that nothing short of slamming into Hayden over and over, *and over* will alleviate it. The one hope I have is when she turns around to face me. That should help. That will instantly cool down this raging wildfire she's started raging inside of me. It has to, because it will remind me that she's pregnant, that she's not mine, and that she's more trouble than she's worth.

Only that's not what happens. It's not even close. Hayden turns around, and I can see her rounded stomach that begins in a slight curve under her bra and bows out, over the delicate lace material that hides her from me. Her pregnancy does nothing to freeze my balls and shrink my cock back to normal, so I can manage to walk out of here.

Hayden's frightened gasp doesn't stop the need that's boiling inside of me either. My eyes are glued to her stomach. I don't see how she's carrying a baby in there. There doesn't seem like there would be enough room for a child to be resting inside of her. I should turn around and leave. I should stop tormenting myself, and yet, *I can't.* I'm in deep shit here and the time for running and taking cover is gone. My resistance is gone. Hayden is *beautiful* and seeing her standing in front of me, it doesn't bother me she's pregnant. Fuck, I'm thinking that makes her even more beautiful and that *scares* the shit out of me.

"Michael!" she cries, and it brings me out of the stupor I seem to have put myself in.

I drag my eyes from her stomach and the swell of her breasts—and how they lean heavily out of the confines of her bra, demanding to be set free. She pulls a towel down from a shelf and covers her body as best she can. I tighten my hands into fists to keep from yanking it away.

"We need to talk," I tell her, which is stupid. Talking is the last thing I want to do. *What the fuck happened to my balls? When did I turn into this man who didn't just take what he wanted?*

Maybe it's because of Hayden's past. I don't know what it is, but I know it has to be traumatic. I thought it was because she is pregnant, but considering looking at her stomach has pre-cum sliding down the shaft of my cock, I'm pretty sure that's not it. Pushing my hand through my hair, pulling it away from my face, I'm frustrated, angry, confused, and *horny.* I'm so fucking horny I can't think; it's not possible because all the blood is surging into my dick.

"Then go back into the bedroom. I'll meet you in there," she orders, her cheeks blushed a bright red, her gray-blue eyes shining with embarrassment.

I suddenly crave to see them shine with something different. How would they look deep tinted in desire…*for me*?

"I want to kiss you." *Shit.* That's not what I meant to say. It's not even all that I want to do, but at least I had enough brain cells left not to blurt out that I wanted to fuck her like a wild animal.

"I need to... *What?*" she gasps and call me crazy, but it fucks with your mind when a woman looks at you like you're insane when you tell her you want to kiss her. "I don't think that would be a good idea, Michael. I don't think it would be good at all," she says, standing up and looking around like she needs a place to run. I'm not sure why that should make my dick jerk against the confines of my pants, but it does.

"We've kissed before," I remind her, and I can actually see the panic flare in her eyes as they widen in surprise.

"And that was a mistake. It's made our friendship weird."

"Funny, I was thinking the fact we both have more baggage than the JFK Airport has done that."

"When you decide to talk, you just go all out don't you?" she sighs. She puffs air through her lips and it causes her bangs to blow away from her face, before slowly fluttering back down. "I'm the one with the baggage and my baggage is dangerous. Too dangerous for you to be around me, Michael. You've already put a target on your back after yesterday."

"It's not the first time, and it probably won't be the last. None of that has anything to do with the fact that I want to kiss you right now, Hayden."

"It's not a good idea."

"You've said that. I just don't happen to agree," I tell her, walking towards her. I watch as her body tenses up and she stares at me, then at the door, already bringing her eyes back to me, as if sizing up if she could make it to the door before I stop her. She can't, and remarkably I find myself smiling at the thought.

"Michael—"

"It's just a kiss, Hayden. What's the harm in a kiss?" I tell her, my voice dropping down to just above a whisper when I'm standing in front of her. My hand curves against her neck, my thumb brushes against her jawline, and my fingers tangle into her hair as I press them against the back of her neck. I can feel her body shudder against me, see her lips slowly part, and her eyelids begin to close. She may be protesting, but Hayden wants this kiss too. She craves *my* kiss.

That's my last thought before our lips touch. When she lets out a small whimper right before her tongue pushes into my mouth and seeks out mine, a feeling of victory erupts inside of me.

Fuck everything else. This right here is the first thing that has felt good to me in so long that I don't give a shit about anything else right now. I'm just taking this while it's here.

CHAPTER 57

Hayden

WHERE IS THE panic and fear I feel around people—*around men?* Why don't I feel that with Michael? Why don't I feel it right now when he's standing in front of me with his face bending down to kiss me? Why, when I'm standing in front of him half-naked, am I not screaming for the door? Why am I not only looking forward to his kiss, but *craving* it?

I do nothing but sigh with relief when Michael's lips finally touch mine. If I want to be completely honest with myself, I'm ridiculously eager for his kiss. I think it's my tongue who seeks his out first. If I want to get even more brutally honest, since the first kiss we shared I've wanted more. The moment our lips touch, our tongues tangle, a spark of electricity goes off, and heat spreads through my body. In its wake, there is nothing but *need.* A desperate need to be closer to him. My hands go up to tangle into his long hair, pulling his mouth tighter against mine, afraid he will pull away. I think of nothing else other than losing myself in the nearness and warmth of Michael while drowning in the taste of him. I don't even notice when the towel I was hiding my body behind, falls to the ground.

I feel Michael's arms wrap around me. I don't have a lot of experience with men. The two that I've trusted, their touch has been extremely different from Michael's. Their skin was soft, and felt good against mine…*I guess.* I never really thought about it. It never failed though, their touch always turned rough, demanding even, and I never liked it once that happened. Michael is completely different. His touch is rough, and almost scratchy, like a loofah against my skin. Yet his hold is gentle, almost what I'd imagine caring felt like. Even when his kiss gets demanding, never—*not once*, does that translate into him hurting me. He makes me feel…*precious.* That's somehow just as addictive as his kiss.

We break apart, both of us breathing roughly. I worry about what I will see in his eyes. Disappointment? Anger? *Regret?* Any of those are possible. Slowly, I open my eyes, hating that I am trying to be a coward. Michael's dark, almost obsidian eyes are staring down at me, but the only thing I can see in them is the same thing that is raging through my body. *Hunger.* He wants me. The knowledge lands inside of me and it should repulse me. What it shouldn't do is make me so wet that I can feel my desire painted against the inside of my thighs. I need to be the voice of reason here. *I have to be.*

"I love your lips, Hayden," he says in his voice that I've come to liken to a mixture of whiskey and cigarettes. It's nothing sweet; it's wicked, dirty, and completely masculine.

I don't know if anyone has ever told me that they love anything about me, especially my lips. I like that Michael does. *I like it a lot.* I take a half-step away from him, that's as much room as he's given me. My fingers come up to touch my lips as I look up at this giant of a man who wreaks havoc on my body and my emotions.

"I like yours too, even though I shouldn't," I tell him, not recognizing my own voice.

"Why shouldn't you," he asks, and I try to concentrate on his words, but his hands have moved down to my hips and his thumb is brushing back and forth on my hipbone. I can feel my eyelids get heavy as I enjoy the sensation. I have to shake myself to pay attention to him.

"I told you, I'm trouble. I don't want you to get hurt because of me."

"You want to protect me?" he asks softly, and when his voice drops down this quiet, it calls to every feminine thing inside of me, sending a million butterfly wings fluttering in my stomach.

"Michael," I sigh, not sure how to continue, or even why.

"Answer me, Beauty," he says in that same tone, but the added nickname makes my heart stutter with happiness while the rest of me drowns in sadness. *I can't have Michael.* Yesterday made it abundantly clear that my past will prevent me from having anything or anyone. Somewhere in the back of my mind, I've even begun making a contingency plan that chills me to the bone. It will destroy me, but it will be what is best for Maggie and that's all that matters.

"I need to protect you and Maggie…or at least try," I tell him honestly, hating the distress I hear in my voice.

"Sweet Hayden, you are a mystery," he says, confusing me further. I have no idea what he means and I'm too confused to try and sort it out. He takes one of his hands and moves it up my stomach. That should bother me. It doesn't, and instead, I look down and watch as he stretches his hand out so the palm is flat as he caresses my stomach.

For some reason, I can feel moisture gather in my eyes. The sight of this scarred hand with ink covering it completely, gently moving against my stomach so tenderly, triggers every emotion I have inside me. I'd like to say it was sexual, that would be easier to dismiss, but it's not true. Right now, as I watch the way his hand is gently moving, and feel Maggie moving inside of me against it…It feels almost like he's loving on her. Like he's showing her that somewhere out in this cold world there's another person besides her mother that cares for her, that could love her.

Oh God! Just the thought of that makes me feel raw inside. I don't know how to deal with it. I look back to his face, needing to break the spell, needing to not read too much into his touch, and most of all, needing to get back into reality. The only problem is that when I look in his eyes, that doesn't happen. Because, before he even speaks, *I see it.* I see it as clearly as if he spoke it aloud.

When he opens his mouth, I push my fingers against those tempting lips to stop the words. I need to stop them, because this man may just be the one person in the world who can completely destroy me. Others have tried it, and though they've made me damaged, they haven't been able to break me. Michael could do it easily, and that knowledge is chilling. I press my fingers harder against his lips, his beard tickling against the skin goes unnoticed.

"It's not your job to protect me, sweet Hayden. It's mine to protect you and Maggie, and I will. I'll always protect you," he vows.

It is a vow. A vow that kills me, because I can't let him take on that responsibility. A vow that destroys me, because I wish I could turn back time and fix my past so that Michael could be my future. I wish I could go back and give Maggie this man as a father. *This is the kind of man she should know exists in the world.* I can't do any of that. I've made so many mistakes, and I thought I had paid enough for them, but it's clear that I haven't, because right now, I'm caught in Hell on earth. I am a woman who has everything she has always wanted standing in front of her, and I can't keep it. With that thought, I can feel the salty wetness hit my lips as the tears run from my eyes.

CHAPTER 58

Beast

I LOOK AT Hayden and the sadness I see on her face hurts me. I move my fingers over her cheeks, trying to wipe the tears and stop them from falling.

"Don't cry, Beauty," I softly tell her, bending down to kiss the tears away.

"Michael, you need to leave me alone," she responds.

"Do you like my touch, Hayden? Do you like my kisses?" I question, needing to hear her admit it. I've not let my guard down around a woman since the explosion. Hayden makes me want to, and I'm tired of fighting her pull. What's the harm in enjoying her? Maybe she can stop some of this loneliness inside of me that seems to torment me with every breath. Some days I fear it might completely take me over. I wanted it to until Hayden tempted me. Until she gave me purpose.

"Too much, but I shouldn't," she answers, her eyes still closed.

"I like that you want my touch," I assure her. I don't add that she doesn't seem to let the scars bother her either. Of course, she hasn't really seen them; not fully. She's seen glimpses of the ones on my neck and arms. I couldn't keep the ones on my face and hands from her, but they don't seem to disturb her.

"You need to leave," she says, weakly pushing me away. She doesn't want me to go. Everything about her in this moment tells me she wants more of what I'm giving her. *Is it fear?* Is she afraid of what will happen if she lets herself go with me?

"Turn around and look in the mirror," I order her, already moving her body so she does that exact thing. I move my hand over the condensation on the mirror, revealing us together. It's a full-length mirror, but I only clear off the top half. Wanting her to see her face and mine together. *We look wrong.*

Her light to my dark.

My ink to her soft flesh.

My scars to her almost virginal appearance.

She might be pregnant, but it doesn't take a rocket scientist to realize she's not the normal type of girl I've dealt with. Everything about her, other than Blade having touched her, screams differently.

"I shouldn't touch you. You should be scared of me," I say the words aloud, though they're more just my thoughts at the moment. I drop a kiss on her shoulder, the part where it meets the bend of her neck. It calls to me and I can't stop my tongue from running over it. I feel the shudder that rocks her body as I look up to watch her eyes. They're glued to mine through the mirror. The gray color in them is almost silver in this light and desire shines in them.

"I'm not scared of you," she whispers, a pale pink blush spreading over her face.

"You should be. There's a reason they call me Beast," I warn her, as my hand moves to her breast, palming her tit, squeezing it gently. "A reason they compare me to an animal," I continue, regretfully letting go of her breast to let my fingers trail along her sides. I kiss against the inside of her neck, tasting her skin. My cock is pulsating like a beating drum. I can feel my balls tighten with cum. I want inside her more than I can remember ever wanting in a woman before. I could scream, because I know that's not happening right now. I need to make Hayden comfortable with losing herself with me—which should be what I concentrate on, instead of warning her away. How the hell I've developed a conscious with the one woman I've wanted in years, is beyond me.

"I've known animals, Michael. You're not even close," she answers, her hands moving to mine on each of her hips. I love the feel of her hands enclosing around mine. Does she think to stop me from moving lower? *Probably, but I won't.*

"But you don't know me, Hayden. Not really," I caution her yet again, my hand pushing from hers and curving behind to her ass, loving how the cheeks overfill my hands. I want to groan at the feel of them. I can't stop myself from pushing into her and letting the hard ridge of my cock press against her. "Fuck, you feel amazing," I grunt, thrusting against her while I hold her in place.

"Michael," she whimpers, and the sound of her voice makes me search out her face in the mirror again, and that's when I see it. I knew it was there, that's what I need to get rid of...*fear.*

"Shh..." I try and calm her.

"I don't think I'm ready to—"

"We're not going to... *do* anything," I tell her, barely stopping myself from saying fuck. Hayden deserves the girly words that women love. I just don't have them to give. I did warn her I'm an animal. "I'm just going to give you a small ride. I want to make you feel good," I reassure her, thinking I may need a medal for denying myself.

"But the baby, I don't know," she stops talking, but I understand what she's saying.

"I will never do anything to put Maggie in danger, Hayden. Trust me," I tell her, my eyes glued to the mirror, never leaving her reflection. I stop all movement holding my finger along the elastic of her panties, that's risen just above the swell of her ass—*waiting.*

"I do," she answers, and those two words are exactly what I needed to hear.

I pull the elastic tighter, knowing it will cause friction against the most sensitive part of her. Her gasp in surprise makes me smile. I let my fingers reach under her, following the path of the red lace until my fingers touch her pussy. I bring my other hand back to her breast, squeezing it, and this time it is my body that shudders with need. Her pussy is so hot and wet it could bring a man to his knees. I could sink balls deep inside of her in one slow easy glide.

"Oh God," she pants, the second I touch her.

"Reach up behind you and put your hands up around my neck," I order her, wanting her hands on me at least—*anyway I can get them.* She brings them up and another tremor of need runs through me just by feeling her fingers touch the side of my neck. It's not a normal touch, her fingers curl in the hair of my beard, then move down to my neck, and stroke against it. I wasn't expecting that. I thought she would hold her hands behind my neck, interlocking them. Not actually caress my skin. The same skin that's scarred. She doesn't seem repulsed. If the way her eye lids are half closed and the sound of her erratic breathing are any indication, she's moments from coming. *Coming by my hand.* Suddenly, I need that. I want to give her pure bliss. I want to tease her body until she loses herself in the pleasure I create.

I push her panties to the side so that the fabric doesn't block her soaked little cunt from me. At first, I do nothing more than hold my hand against her warm heat. A firm hold, one of ownership and God help us both, I want to own her body. *I will own it.*

"So wet for me," I murmur, against her shoulder. "My Beauty needs me to make her come."

"Michael," she cries quietly, but it's a cry full of need, with just a mixture of fear blended in.

I let my fingers slide between the swollen lips of her pussy. The feel of her heated flesh against my fingers is like liquid torment. I should take this slow, but I wish with everything inside of me that it was my face between her legs right now, eating her out until she couldn't recall her own name. *Soon.* Soon it will happen. I make that promise to myself even as I let my fingers move against her pussy and seek out the swollen nub which literally drums against my fingers. Her clit is swollen and thumping against my touch. I push against it, applying harsh pressure. It gives in as her body jumps at the sensation. At the same time, my other hand has pushed her bra up, releasing her breasts to me. I squeeze her bare tit in my hand, kneading it over and over slowly. My other fingers move around her clit in a tantalizing circle. I don't go fast, I don't want to speed this up. This, with Hayden, this moment needs to be prolonged—savored.

"You feel so good, Hayden. So hot, sticky, and sweet against my fingers," I murmur, nibbling against the inside of her neck, then moving down to place tender bites on her shoulder. My teeth rake against the skin at the same time I capture her nipple between my thumb and forefinger, pinching and pulling the hardening bud.

Her cry is like music to my ears, and in reward I increase the friction I'm giving her sweet clit, rubbing across it and then back again, faster, though still not fast enough.

"You're so wet you're drowning my fingers. It feels so fucking good I wish it was my face. Someday soon, sweet Beauty, you are going to ride my face, and I'm going to drink up every last drop of you," I promise her.

"Michael…I'm…Oh God, I think I'm close," she sobs, her hips undulating, her ass pushing against me.

I could come in my pants like this. *I could come like a fucking school boy.* My hold on her breast tightens, as I torture her nipple. My persistent fingers move on her clit faster, their pressure increasing as she tightens her thighs on my hand, trying to ride it. Her ass punishes my cock, those plush, ripe cheeks pushing, grinding against it, while her head falls back against my chest and her fingers bite into my neck.

"I'm going to…Oh fuck! I'm going to come, baby," she cries. She goes completely still for half a second, and then her climax rakes through her body like the force of a hurricane. Her cry rings out, her body shakes, her nails biting into me as her legs threaten to give out. I hold her and continue to manipulate her pussy, gradually slowing down until she rides out the orgasm.

Her head is still thrown back, but eventually her breathing calms and she stops trembling. I haven't pulled my hand away. Jesus, if I could keep my fingers in her pussy all the time I would. *It's that fucking good.* Her nails have sunk into the skin on my neck.

When I look into the mirror I'm not surprised to see a small trace of blood mar what little skin is exposed. Her hold has little shards of pain hitting me and I love it. I watch the mirror as bit by bit her eyes open revealing their silver color dilated and beautiful. It's only then I can make myself take my fingers from her pussy. She gasps and pulls up straighter to look at me, and I can see embarrassment start to cool her desire. I bring the fingers to my mouth, and I hold her stare as I lick them clean. I lick them with the sound of her calling me *baby* still ringing in my ears. Her taste is indescribable, but one taste and I'm addicted. One taste, and I know I'm going to need more of it.

One taste and I know it will be something I crave until my last breath.

CHAPTER 59

Hayden

W*HAT DID I just do?* That's the question that keeps echoing through my mind. I can't believe I let Michael do that…I can't even describe what that is, because the memory serves to make me wetter. Even after a mind blowing orgasm, where Michael only touched me with his fingers, I'm still wet. I'm so wet it's embarrassing.

"Stop it," his rough voice demands, and I jerk my head back up to look at him. He turns me around and I let him, because quite honestly, I can't control my own legs at this point.

"What?" I ask him, trying to escape his eyes. That doesn't work when his hand comes up against the side of my neck and he angles me to look up at him, refusing to let me avoid him.

"Do not overthink what we just did," Michael says, and I take a deep steadying breath.

"My past—"

"We'll talk about it, and you'll tell me. But I could give a flying fuck about Blade and his damn trained monkeys."

"But—"

"No buts, I'm a grown man. I do whatever the fuck I want,

and trust me when I tell you, Hayden, that right now. I. Want. You."

"I'm pregnant," I remind him, as if he could have forgotten.

In response, his hand comes to mine and he grabs it, pulling it to the soft cotton material of his sweats. He presses our hands against the obvious outline of his cock.

"Does it feel like that bothers me at all, Hayden?" he asks, and the intense desire apparent on his face and the vibrating of his voice combine to rock my body with need. My nipples harden, and I wish I had done more than just put my bra back in place earlier. His dark gaze drops down, and I know he can see the evidence of my excitement. I'm pretty sure he's got a smile hiding behind that beard.

"We really need to trim that jungle you've got going on."

"You keep bringing that up," he mumbles, raking his hands through his hair and reaching over to finally turn off the shower I had left running. It's probably completely cold now. I was hoping for a hot shower.

"I like seeing your face," I tell him and even to my own ears I sound defensive.

"You've seen some of the scars," he growls, and he turns away from me to walk to the door. I shouldn't have pushed him. I regret it, but something about what he says bothers me.

"Do scars bother you?"

"Scars are nothing," he says and his voice is monotone. His back is to me, so I can't tell, but I get the impression that he's lost in his own thoughts.

"It was only a suggestion. I just find myself wishing I could see your lips easier and maybe…"

"Maybe?" he asks, finally looking over his shoulder at me.

"It'd be nice to see more of your face. To be able to touch it," she shrugs. "Scars don't bother me, Michael. I'd be the last person to ever be bothered by someone's scars."

"Are you hungry?" he asks, and I'm definitely taking that to mean he's done with this conversation.

"I could eat. I should definitely try to make sure Maggie gets some breakfast," I try to joke, though it feels a little weird talking about her, considering I'm half-naked.

"Then finish cleaning up, and I'll meet you in the kitchen," Michael says, and he turns to grab my upper arms. Then, he brings his head down and puts a kiss on the top of my head before walking out of the room.

I sit down on the toilet, ignoring the way the cold porcelain feels, and bow my head, letting it fall down on my arms, as I think about everything that has happened since I got out of bed. I'm thinking I could be in deep trouble here.

I just have no idea what to do about it.

CHAPTER 60

Hayden

"WHAT'S THAT SMELL?" I ask, curling my nose when I stop by the kitchen door. It reminds me of burnt plastic. Michael turns around and looks at me, his eyes rake over me and cause a shiver to run through me. I can't be sure, but the heated look on his face tells me he likes what he sees. I've *never* felt *beautiful* in my life. *Not once,* but Michael could make me believe it when he stares at me like that. How can he look at me like he could eat me alive? I'm not beautiful. I've never been. I'm plain…*and I'm pregnant.* How could he ever want me? It's unreal. Yet, he did want me. What he did to me…the feel of him…his reactions…those were real…*Weren't they?*

"I'm scrambling eggs," he says, and I can tell by the way his skin wrinkles around his nose that he's smiling.

"You don't cook much, do you?" I ask him, walking over to the stove. The aroma from the eggs is worse close up. I look down at the skillet.

"I made soup for you," he says, stirring the wooden spoon through the *eggs* again.

"Michael, I don't think eggs are supposed to be brown," I

tell him. They're like a brown congealed mess, and I know I see a couple shells mixed in there. "Go sit down, and I'll make breakfast," I tell him, reaching for the spoon.

"Anyone can make eggs," he grumbles.

"Those shells and that smell seems to argue with that. Now hand over the spoon. Our stomachs demand it." Michael looks at me and heat coming from him makes my stomach twist in knots, and I can feel tingles of electricity shoot through my body. My thighs grow sticky wet, and I feel my body throb with need—*all with just one look*. Without warning he bends down and gives me a kiss. It's over before I can really respond, but I find my body leaning towards him as he pulls away. "What was that for?"

"I wanted to cook for you. You wouldn't let me, so I found something else I wanted and took it," he says with a shrug, handing the spoon over.

"Do I get to take what I want next?" I ask him bravely. Shock reads on his face for a minute, his eyes go heated.

"What do you want?"

"Let me trim your hair and beard," I tell him without even blinking.

He rakes his hand through his hair and down his neck, his eyes never leaving mine.

"I want to see your face…I want…"

"What?" he asks, when I break off because I feel the embarrassing heat creep up my face.

"I want to be able to touch your lips and…"

"And?"

"Kiss them without having to search for them," I finish lamely, staring at his hand instead of his face.

Which is apparently what he *doesn't* want, because he puts his fingers under my chin and pulls my face up to look at him. "You can kiss me now," he tells me, and the vibration in his voice feels like it slides against my bare skin.

"I want to see more of you, to touch more of you." I see the indecision on his face. I know I'm pushing it, and I couldn't explain why—not really. It feels like he uses it to hide from me, though and I don't want that. I want…to see him as he doesn't allow others to.

"After breakfast," he says, and pleasure hits me like an explosion.

"You mean it?"

"Just a trim," he grumbles, moving to the table and sitting down. "That's all," he warns, grumpily.

"I'll take it," I tell him, feeling like dancing and giggling.

In response, Michael shakes his head like I've lost my mind. *Maybe I have—but it feels good.*

CHAPTER 61

Beast

SHE'S UNDER MY skin. I can feel her latched on in a way that I know it's going to be hell to get her out. *And what do I do?* Like a fool, I let her sink deeper. I let her cook breakfast, I listen to her laugh, I watch her blush, and I find any excuse under the sun to touch her. Most recently, I pretended there was a crumb on her lip.

"Michael?" she questions.

I reach up to wipe the non-existent crumble away, letting my finger press against the corner of her mouth and watching as her lips break apart to allow a shudder of breath pass through. I put a little weight on my finger, and just like that the tip is in her mouth. Almost instantly her tongue brushes against the tip of my finger. I release a sound which is guttural. I have to fight to escape the image of my cock sliding into her mouth and disappearing inch by aching inch.

Almost seven motherfucking years without thinking of sex, without even wanting it, and now it's all I can think about. My cock feels like concrete. Getting Hayden off was almost innocent, and yet it is the most erotic thing I've ever done with a woman. It wasn't about what we did, it had everything to do with the fact it was Hayden and what she's doing to me. We share some kind of fucking connection I've never experienced before. I should be discouraging her, and instead, I agreed to let her cut my damned hair. I'm swimming in stupidity. You would think I would have wised up after years of dealing with Jan. Suddenly mad at myself, I move my finger and steadfastly ignore the confusion that clouds her eyes.

"You had something on your lip," I lie, clearing my voice and refusing to look at her. "You sure you even know how to cut hair?"

"Will you quit worrying?" she responds, draping a towel over the front of me.

"What's this for?" I ask her, grabbing it. I'm sitting in a chair she pulled away from the table. She's got a comb and some scissors on the table while she's standing above me, hovering nervously, looking down at me with those large gray eyes. Sad fuck that I am, I wasn't able to resist looking at them for long.

"So the hair I cut off doesn't get on your shirt and drive you crazy," she says, looking as if it should be self-explanatory.

"You're not cutting that much off," I warn. God's truth, I am having trouble figuring out why I agreed to let her do this in the first place.

"I won't. Though to be fair, you have so much hair, we should shave you bald and donate it for wigs," she responds, her fingers, combing through my hair, pulling it away from my head. I can't see her face because she's standing above me, but suddenly I wish I could. Her rounded stomach is right in front of me. The pajama top she's wearing keeps rising up when she moves her arms, revealing glimpses of the peach skin beneath it. It should remind me that she's pregnant with another man's baby. A man I despise. It doesn't.

Hell, my cock is rock hard and has been since the moment I stole a kiss before breakfast. I pull the towel away, putting it on the table. "Michael, honestly if you don't—" I stop her by pulling my shirt up and over my head. I can hear her breathy rasp and she's stepped away from me now so I can see her eyes. The desire inside of them leaps out at me. It's there for me to read. No coyness, no disguises, nothing premeditated about it.

How different would my life have been if I had met Hayden earlier. If she had been Annabelle's mother, Annabelle would still be here. There's a lot about Hayden that is a mystery, but I don't doubt for one second that she would lay her life down to protect her child. Thinking of my daughter makes that familiar pang in my chest hurt. I reach up and rub it unconsciously. Even that doesn't dim my hard-on, however, and I feel guilty for having it. I came here to get away from everyone, to retire from the world. Hayden is making me live again. I feel torn and out of control.

"I don't think I've ever given a haircut to someone without a shirt on," she says, and despite my earlier thoughts, I find myself smiling again.

"I'm the one without the shirt," I tell her, choosing to interpret her words differently than she obviously meant them. "But I do like your idea," I agree, and I grab her pajama top and even sitting down and at this angle, it's ridiculously easy to lift it up. Hayden tightens up and her hands try to stop me but I ignore them and don't stop until her shirt is gone and she's standing in front of me in her pajama shorts and bra. I eye her bra. I want it gone. Hayden must read my mind, because she's shaking her head.

"The bra stays on. In fact, I'm putting the shirt back on," she grumbles, reaching for it. My hand lays over top of hers as her fingers curl into the fabric.

"The shirt stays off," I tell her, leaving no room for argument.

She sighs, and I fully expect her to argue.

"You do realize I'm pregnant, right? That I have scars…stretch marks?"

"You're beautiful," I answer, letting my hand move over her stomach. Maybe I shouldn't find her sexy, because Maggie is not my child, and Hayden is definitely not my woman, not to keep. I can't have that. I don't deserve that…*but I want it.* I close my eyes as the truth of that delves a little deeper in. I push it aside, not prepared to think about it, or the repercussions right now.

Hayden's hand captures mine before I can push her shorts down and see even more of her.

"If I have to cut your hair without a shirt, then I should get to trim that beard up… *a lot.*"

"No," I tell her, not wanting her to see the scars. I don't know why she ignores the ones she can clearly see now, but there's no point in—

"Please?" she asks. "I'll owe you one," she adds, and the idea of Hayden owing me anything sends my blood pressure skyrocketing.

Fuck. I nod, *yes* without even thinking. I'm on the verge of telling her that I wasn't serious, but the look of pleasure and victory on her face stops the words. She's too happy.

And I'm fucking screwed.

CHAPTER 62

Hayden

"YOU HAVE BEAUTIFUL hair," I tell Michael as I run my comb through it. I can't help but let my fingers follow. It's so soft it's like silk, but it feels warm and comfortable like cotton.... *like something you want pressed against your skin forever.*

Michael doesn't appreciate me telling him that his hair is beautiful. I can tell by the way he grunts. I've wanted to trim his hair and beard forever, selfishly wanting to see more of his face and those lips of his that feel so amazing when he kisses me. I want to be able to see if he smiles, if he frowns, or if he bites his lip. I've even dreamed of it, not that I would tell him that.

I'm trying to concentrate on cutting his hair and not how incredibly awkward it feels to be in nothing but shorts and a bra, with my pregnant stomach in front of his face. I've already trimmed his hair a lot, although if I'm honest I hurt every time, just because with hair this beautiful it seems like a sin to watch it fall away. The upside is I can see more of his face. I thought he was handsome before. I was wrong. He's beautiful. Completely and utterly beautiful.

He has these strong angles on his face that are completely

masculine and even a little harsh. His forehead is wide, manly, and there's this little scar on it the size of a pea. Along the left side of his face the scars clearly cover a larger area than I suspected, because of the way he always had his hair covering that side. They're grim against his soft skin. On one end, they disappear into his beard, and the other they rise above his cheeks and then fade into the hair at his temple. I feel his tension increase as I softly touch them, following their lines.

For once, I don't have to guess at his thoughts. I know because I've experienced them. I keep my scars hidden, at least the outside ones. Is that why he kept his hair so long? His beard unkempt? Does he think they are as ghastly as I think mine are? Mine are nothing in comparison to his, but the ugliness behind mine taints everything. I can feel his body grow tighter just from the soft glide of my finger against his face. Before he can pull away completely, I find myself bending down to place a kiss along the scar, right at the top. His hands come up and grasp my hips. Their hold is painful from his fingers biting into my flesh.

Before I can question myself, I leave another kiss, followed by another one. Kissing along the jagged line they trail. I feel his body shudder and instead of pushing me away he pulls me. I quickly adjust so that I'm straddling his lap when he sits me down. His forehead presses against mine and I can't stop my eyes from closing.

"You're killing me," he says, in that gruff voice that vibrates so deep I can feel it in my center.

If I wasn't already wet, that would more than do it. As it is, my breaths are labored as if I've been walking for miles, not merely being held by Michael. The scissors fall to the ground. I hear them drop against the old plank flooring. I'm glad because now I can bury my fingers in his hair. I feel his hands shove up my legs, underneath the fabric of my shorts. I have panties on, but he has to feel the way his touch makes me quake, and God I'm so hot. When he touches me, I feel like I'm on fire.

"Michael," I whimper, not sure what to do.

Michael doesn't have that problem. He reaches up and pushes my bra out of the way. Freeing only one of my breasts, the other remaining in the twisted fabric. Cool air hits my nipple, and I moan as a second later his mouth captures it, greedily sucking it into his mouth. He keeps his mouth there, sucking and pressing the nipple to the roof of his mouth, then teasing it with his tongue. At the same time his hand comes back down. He moves to my hips where he pulls me in closer and grinds me against his hard erection.

Sometime last night he changed from his jeans into cotton jogging pants. I liked them. I appreciated them. They hung low on his hips and he totally rocked them. He was mouthwatering and very warm when he snuggled against me. Right now, I appreciate them for a completely different reason. They're soft and stretchy over the rigid outline of his hard cock, allowing it to press against my center at just the right angle. It pushes against my pussy hitting my clit when he pulls me down. My body trembles as desire shoots through me.

"Ride me, Hayden. Ride me," he urges around my breast, before his hands palm my ass and his fingers bite into my skin. *"Fuck baby, ride me."*

CHAPTER 63

Beast

I LOOK UP and watch Hayden's face as she curled over the top of me. Her head is thrown back, her eyes are closed and her body is alive with pleasure. Pleasure I'm giving her. Pleasure she's getting just from riding against the hard ridge of my cock. I should stop this. It's madness for a lot of reasons, most importantly, if it keeps up I'm going to come in my damn pants like a horny kid watching his first porno. The problem is, this isn't some damn movie. This is Hayden and she's beautiful. Even through our clothes I can feel the heat of her pussy, I feel the way she greedily moves so my cock pushes against her in all the right places, and I don't want her to stop. I want her to come. *Just. Like. This.* Using me to get what she wants. I want to give her exactly what her sweet pussy wants—pleasure. Pleasure only I can give her.

"Michael," she gasps, sounding desperate.

"I'm right here," I growl, feeling heat run up my back. It's been so long I've almost forgotten the feeling, but I know I'm getting ready to come. *Fuck.*

"I need," she cries brokenly, her body riding me harder and

faster, but I can tell she's not there. Her body is searching too desperately for something…

"Tell me what you need, Beauty. Tell me and I'll give it to you," I vow, knowing in this moment I'd move heaven or earth to give her whatever she asks for.

"More," she sobs, frantically. "I can't get…Michael," she ends in a whimper, sounding unsure. I'm torn listening to her. I know what she needs-what we both do. I don't know why I'm denying myself really. I want inside of her so much I can taste it. I've resisted because I don't know what her history is, but there's something there. I thought she might have been abused. The panic attacks indicate that, and yet her response to me is completely different. It's a riddle wrapped in a mystery. The mystery being why, when nothing else has for seven years, Hayden makes me…*want*. "Michael," she calls again, bringing my attention back to her. I react on instinct.

I wrap my hand into her long hair and pull her head down to me. My hold is tight, and I know it brings a slice of pain to her from the way she cries. I should be gentle with her, but I'm not gentle. I've never been that way much, and I really don't have it in me now. I bring my hand to the breast I've uncovered, capturing the swollen nipple and pinching it with my fingers. She jerks, but the grip I have on her hair keeps her from moving too far.

"You're going to come for me, Beauty," I growl into her ear, letting my teeth clamp down on the lobe, and my tongue slip along the shell. "You're going to ride my cock and make us both come."

"Oh God, Michael…"

"I'm so close, Hayden. You have my cock so hard right now with the way you're riding me. You're going to make me fucking come all over myself," I whisper to her, my tongue pushing in her ear, to tease her along with my words. Her body quakes on top of me and she grinds against me. "You like that don't you, sweetheart. You like the idea that you could make my cock explode and leave him covered in his own come just by moving your sweet little body back and forth. You like knowing you have my body at your mercy. Don't you?"

"Yes!" she cries loudly, her nails are biting into my shoulders so hard, she's drawing blood. And I like it. I like everything that's fucking happening right now.

"Are you coming for me, Beauty. Is that sweet little pussy coming all for me?" I growl, yanking a little harder on her hair, bending her head back to expose her neck. I run my tongue along her neck. I can feel her pulse beating hard. I bite the skin, too far gone to know if I'm bruising her skin, and mostly hoping like hell I am. The idea fires up inside of me, and I bite into the base of her shoulder and neck *harder*. I know beyond a shadow of a doubt that I'm being too rough now. The bite is going to mark her, and I want it to. I want everyone to see it.

Hayden cries out my name, her body undulating on top of me, stops all at once. I look up and that's when I see it. The exact moment her orgasm hits and then takes over. I push on her head to bring her face down. Her eyes are wide, the silver-gray color deep and glistening. Those thick lips are open. Her breath is ragged and comes out in small puffs. And then her body lurches, her cry is torn from her, not a word, just a cry of release before she quakes with her climax.

My hands release her from the hold I have, only to grab her ass and glide her against my cock, thrusting against her as I forget everything, but the need to come with her. I explode, my cum jetting out in the first release that I've had in years. I come so hard that it's physically painful and my cry mingles with hers. Eventually my body stops jerking, and I wrap my arms around her, pulling her into me. My head rests against the swollen mound of her stomach and that's when it hits me.

Instant regret.

CHAPTER 64

Hayden

I BURY MY head in Michael's shoulder. My body is still vibrating with pleasure. I can't believe I allowed this to happen, *again*. What makes it worse is that I already want more. It might not be smart, nor even particularly safe, but Michael is different from any other man who has been in my life. He's taken care of me, he's gentle with me, and he makes me feel *beautiful*. He even seems to *want* me…even if I am pregnant. That's weird to me, but I'm tired of second guessing and questioning everything. What we just shared, that was good—*more than good*. It was *special*.

Michael's seen my weaknesses and he doesn't mock them. He doesn't use them against me. Again, it boils down to darkness. I've seen darkness inside of men, I've experienced it and Michael isn't tainted with that. So, I lean into him and cherish being held by him, letting a few of the guards I keep up, slip. Which sucks because it leaves me totally unprepared for Michael's next words.

"That shouldn't have happened." My body goes completely solid and tense when I hear him.

Those words aren't what I expected. *Nowhere close.* I don't know how to react to them, except that straddling his lap with my face buried in his neck, breathing in his scent definitely seems wrong now. I go to move off him, but he doesn't let me. He keeps his hold on my body tight, not even letting me pull away. "That's got to quit happening, Hayden," he says, and his words wound me and piss me off at the same time.

I concentrate on the anger, that's a better emotion to embrace than the hurt. I jerk, trying to pull away but again, he doesn't let me.

"Let me up," I tell him, pushing on his shoulders to get space between us.

"I'm not ready to let you go yet," he tells me, and I hate that my body reacts to that sentence. I hate that his graveled voice rakes along every exposed nerve point I have, which is already raw from my climax. I hate it even while I can't hide the way my body hums with the pleasure. The deep tone of his voice should be classified as a sexual weapon. It's that potent. *Damn him.*

"I *want* up," I insist, kind of lying, but mostly not.

"Why?" he asks, and he has the gall to sound confused.

"You just said you didn't want what we did to happen again. Those aren't words that makes me want to stay straddled on your lap."

"I…"

"And honestly, it pisses me off, because you started it!"

"I started it?" he asks, and I can hear the shock in his voice.

"Yes! So, you don't get to act all…" I can't think of the words, so instead I snarl unintelligibly at him, pushing hard against his body, because I definitely want up now.

He lets me up, and I need something to do, so I grab a broom and start sweeping up the hair that I cut. When the broom finds the scissors and comb that I must have dropped when I kissed him, I really want to kick myself. I bend down to pick them up and in my anger, move too quickly and the room starts spinning. I nearly topple over, but Michael grabs me and keeps it from happening.

"Will you be careful!?" he growls, picking me up in his arms.

I drop the broom in surprise. I don't respond, because I'm busy fighting a wave of nausea. *Probably from being picked up like a sack of potatoes.*

"This is what I'm talking about. You're pregnant. We have no business doing what we're doing. You've got to have more control!"

I've got to have more control?

"Me?" I screech. "You were the one who…who…"

"Who what?" he asks, finally lowering me onto the bed. I get up immediately, the room only marginally sways, so I brace myself by holding onto the headboard. Michael must see me stagger a little cause he growls, making a sound like a bear and adds, "I told you to be careful!"

"I'm fine, just mad! And you know what you did. You touched me…*there,*" I accuse him, sounding like I might be three.

"You liked it when I touched you *there.* I should get a medal for touching you *there* and not fucking you like I wanted!" he growls back and his words take my breath away. They do it for several reasons, but the only one my brain wants to focus on is that he wanted to sleep with me…okay no. He wanted to fuck me, which in my limited experience isn't that special for a man, but the fact that he wanted to, and yet *didn't…*

"Why didn't you?" I ask, and even as I ask, I know that somewhere in the back of my mind I'm worried he didn't because I wasn't good enough.

"You should…*why?*" he asks, and his face shows clear shock, as if I should already know the answer.

"Never mind. We can just call it a day. You can go back to your place and..."

"You're pregnant," he interrupts me, and I feel myself blush.

I can feel the heat rise, and I kind of wish the floor would swallow me up. My hand goes to my stomach. I might be embarrassed, but I don't regret Maggie. Even with everything that has happened, I've never once blamed Maggie. She didn't ask to be brought into this world and she can't help that her father is the spawn of Satan. I pray she'll never know exactly who or what he is. I pray for that every day. *Every. Day.*

"It's not like I've hidden that, Michael. I wouldn't try, even if I could. I even reminded you of that when *you* took *my* shirt off. I really think it might be best if you just leave. I'm suddenly really tired."

"Why would I want you to hide that you're pregnant?"

"It obviously bothers you," I tell him, needing out of the bedroom. I go to walk around him to go back to the kitchen when he grabs me by the upper arm. His touch is warm and feels so good. I ignore that feeling. I need him to leave—I need to get some distance here.

"Did it seem like it bothered me when you were riding my cock?"

"It's obviously bothering you now," I tell him, avoiding his eyes and wishing I could call him a liar.

"The hell it is. I think it's fucking hot."

"*You think it's hot I'm pregnant?*" I ask, my body filled with heat and I don't know if it's from mortification, desire, or fear...*It could be all three.*

"Fuck, yes. You're beautiful pregnant. I told you that already. Your breasts are full, the curve of your stomach, the softness you get in your eyes when you think of your daughter, and the way you hold your stomach without even realizing you're doing it. It's a fucking turn on," Michael answers, and I'm at a loss on how to respond to that.

"Then why did you say we had to stop?" I ask, totally ignoring the fact that he thinks I'm hot because I'm pregnant. I'll have to think about that later.

"I don't know what's gone on with you Hayden, but I know something has. I know the Dweller's enough to know that whatever it is, has to be bad, and I've seen your damn panic attacks. The last thing you need is me making demands of you that you aren't ready for."

There's a lot I should say—a lot I could say to him. Not to mention the fact that bringing up the Dwellers should jerk me back to reality enough that I do not say what I'm thinking. It should stop me cold. *It doesn't.*

"What demands?" I ask, unable to stop myself, wondering why it feels like I'm on the edge of a cliff getting ready to jump.

CHAPTER 65

Beast

WILL HAYDEN EVER do what I expect of her? I'm starting to think the answer to that is definitely no. Because whatever I expected from her just now it wasn't her standing in front of me asking what demands, sounding interested, sounding *anxious,* with her eyes wide with shock, and her fucking nipples hard. She fixed her bra before when I let her go, but I'm sure she's forgotten that she's doesn't have a top on. The last thing I want to do is remind her, but there's only so much torture a man can take.

"Put a shirt on," I grumble, adjusting my fucking cock through my sweatpants. This woman is driving me nuts. I just came and I'm already hard again. Hard and in need of a damned shower, because she made me fucking come in my pants.

I watch as her blush deepens. She walks carefully over to her dresser and pulls out a gray t-shirt, pulling it over her head and hiding her body from me. I'm grateful, but hate it at the same time. *The woman is driving me crazy mad.*

"Your hot and cold makes me dizzy," she grumbles under her breath, but I can hear her plainly. If she wasn't pregnant, I'd be tempted to show her what happens when you back talk a real man. "Better?" she huffs, turning around to look at me. Her hair is rumpled from the way I held it earlier and from her putting on a shirt. Her face is blushed with a pink hue and her eyes are still glittering with emotion.

I want her naked. Naked, laid out in front of me, and I want to use her fucking body until I stop aching, until the rage inside of me lessens and most of all until my damned cock is limp.

"Not by a long shot," I answer, instead of giving her the full truth. It's time I steer this conversation in a different direction, before my handprint is on her ass, and I forget I need to handle her with care. "How are you like this with me?" I ask instead.

"Like this?"

"Mouthy, full of fire, there's no way you can tell me that you're afraid right now. How can you be like that alone with me, but have the panic attacks that I've seen you have around others?"

She studies me and the mood in the room changes. I sit on the bed and wait, sensing this conversation may take a while.

"Are you going to tell me how you got your scars?" she asks, and it's then I realize that with my shirt off, I'm hiding nothing from her. It didn't even cross my mind earlier. I was worried about her uncovering my face. *Why the fuck didn't I stop to think before I took my shirt off?*

"No."

"You expect me to answer your questions and give you my secrets, but you're going to tell me nothing about what happened to you?" In response, I nod my head yes. Her mouth opens, shock clear on her face. "Do you think that's fair?"

"No."

"Then you agree you should tell me more about your scars. It's only fair."

"No," I tell her again, starting to enjoy this damned conversation, or maybe just the frustration that is coming off her in waves.

"You're unbelievable," she sulks.

I reach out to grab her and pull her to me, before I can think twice about it. I see the fear in her eyes. She might be hiding behind being pissed at me, but I see the fear.

"I don't want in your lap again," she complains, but I gently maneuver her so that she's sitting cross-ways on my lap. It feels good. It feels right having her in my arms, and that's something that should make me panic, but for some unknown reason, it doesn't.

"Talk to me, Beauty," I urge her, the nickname yet again, rolling off my tongue with ease. I feel her body shudder and a second later, she relaxes against me.

"I'm not afraid of you," she tells me, and those words soothe me. I don't want her to fear me. *Ever.* "I like…I mean…Well…It's different with you…" she rattles, and I can feel the tension starting to return in her body and that's the last thing I want. I squeeze her encouragingly, even kissing the top of her head. "I like when you touch me, Michael. I like when you are around," she finally whispers.

My heart literally stutter-steps in my chest. I lean down and take her lips gently; this kiss has nothing to do with sex and more to do with gratitude. Whatever she's been through, it wasn't pretty and yet, she trusts me enough to let her guard down. It's misplaced. I don't deserve anyone's trust—least of all hers, but I like that she is giving it to me. I break away from her lips slowly, savoring her taste on mine.

"You're killing me, Michael," she whispers with a half-smile, using my own words against me. That earns her another squeeze.

"Tell me about Blade."

"I'd rather not."

"I get that, but I need to know."

"Why? He doesn't have anything to do with whatever is going on between us," she argues, and I hate that I can hear the panic in her voice. The secrets that she's hiding may be worse than I've been preparing for. I had made up my mind to end Blade before. I have a feeling that waiting to end him might be even harder after Hayden tells me what happened.

"He showed up where you worked. He has me in his sights. I need to know, Hayden."

"What do you mean he has you in his sights?" she asks, and I hate the terror I hear in her voice now. I never told her what really happened to my truck. I'm not going to. She doesn't need to know.

"You're under my protection, Hayden. And for some reason, Blade has been watching you. He's made a move toward you. It's time you tell me what's going on."

"Michael…"

"If that's not enough reason, Hayden, then the fact that whatever is going on between us personally makes it necessary for me to know."

"It doesn't…not really. Whatever is between us, it's just us."

"You know better. Tell me what happened, Hayden. Help me understand."

I see her getting ready to argue. Then all at once, I see it. *Defeat.* She's going to tell me, which pleases me, but it hurts me at the same time. I don't want this to be another thing she loses.

Fuck.

CHAPTER 66

Hayden

"I DON'T GET why this is so important," I mumble, but I'm deluding myself if I think he's going to change his mind. I even understand why he wants to know. He stuck his neck out for me, going against Blade. He's entitled to know what happened. The problem is talking about it, reliving any of it, scares me. That's what it boils down to. I don't want to relive it. I don't want to remember how stupid, how weak I was. Those memories torment me enough and do it when I am not expecting it, at times when I have no control. My mantra, '*today I will be stronger*,' is just a joke. I'm not stronger today. I am wondering if I ever will be strong. The shame of that fills me.

"Hayden?" Michael prompts me, and I pull myself out of my head with a sigh.

"I have, or I guess had, a half-brother."

"Had?" Michael asks, and his voice sounds off.

"The last note I had from him pretty much said that he had finally fucked over the wrong people. I haven't heard anything else, so I figured it all finally caught up with him."

"You don't sound particularly broken up about it," Michael

says. I should be annoyed at him, but he doesn't sound like he's passing judgment. There's something in his tone, but it's not judgment. I look up to find him studying me. "I take it you two weren't close?"

"I wanted to be...once I thought we were. I was horribly wrong," I answer, my head down as the memories from the past begin circling around me.

"Tell me," he asks, when I don't say anything further.

"I didn't have a particularly great life growing up. Mom was...in and out of rehab. Dad stuck around, probably longer than most men would have. He had a boy who was about ten years older than me. I'd like to say he stuck around because he knocked my mom up and cared what happened to me. I think though he stuck around so mom could help him raise his son. Not that she was capable of that. But my father didn't really like kids. He wanted Jack because he wanted a boy to carry on the family name. He didn't have any use for a girl. So when mom became too much to handle, he split—taking Jack with him."

"Your father was an asshole."

"Yeah, I think I have a knack for collecting them." I look up when Michael grunts, and I even find a way to smile at the offended look he's wearing. I reach up and touch his face gently. "Present company excluded," I tell him, and I actually mean it.

Michael bends down and kisses me. It's a brief kiss, but it somehow warms me. When it's done, he links our hands together. He squeezes my hand tight for a minute, then his thumb softly brushes against my knuckles as he waits for me to continue. Before Michael, I'm not sure I ever held hands with any man. Now, it's something I crave. With a sigh, I try to concentrate on what I was telling him.

It's not easy.

The story, my story is ugly.

It makes me feel ugly.

"What happened when your father and brother left?"

"Not a lot. Mom stayed high, sometimes she'd disappear for days. I was sixteen by then, and I pretty much raised myself."

"Fuck," Michael mutters, squeezing my hand tighter.

"To be honest, I preferred it that way. Living on my own, was easier. I had a job at a small diner, and I stretched what I made pretty far. Every now and then, my mom would make an appearance, but usually she was only after money. At first, I resisted, eventually it was easier to just give her some money to get rid of her."

"Jesus, Beauty," he says, kissing my forehead. It's a stupid nickname, but for some reason whenever he uses it, I actually feel *beautiful.*

"That was one of my first major mistakes though. Because all I did was train mom to come to me when she was in trouble. Sadly, trouble for junkies is really *big* trouble sometimes."

"What does that mean?" Michael asks, and his body is tense now. I wish I could reassure him, but there's no reassurance to be found in my life—especially when it comes to my family.

"Mom had a supplier after her. She owed him a bunch of money. He thought he would collect it…from me."

Michael doesn't say anything but the intense vibe in the room lets me know he understands what I'm saying. His grip on my hand is almost painful, but I like it. It grounds me to the here and now and keeps me from getting lost in my past.

"When I wouldn't agree to that, he demanded money. Money I didn't have."

"What…what did you do?" he asks, clearing his throat before finishing the sentence. I don't dare look at him. If I do that, I'll never get this story out, and Michael's not going to let me stop until he hears it.

"I made the second major mistake. I reached out to my brother. Jack and I had kept in touch here and there. Enough that I knew how to get him a message. I swallowed my pride and told him what was going on, and I asked if he could help get me away from my mother and her pimp…because that's what her supplier truly was, and he didn't like that I wouldn't agree to join his stable."

"Is your mom still alive?"

"No. She overdosed years ago."

"Good," he says, and that word sounds extremely cold, but I can't find it inside me to correct him. I take a shuddering breath and try to figure out how to finish the story, keeping the details to a minimum.

"Jack offered to get me out of there, and at the time, I was desperate. I didn't realize he had his own agenda."

"What was that?" Michael asks, and I have to fight with myself to give him the answer.

What will he think of me?

CHAPTER 67

Beast

I'M DOING MY best to keep my anger hidden. I'm not fully succeeding, but Hayden doesn't need to know just how much fury I have bottled up inside of me now. Pistol, or Jack as she calls him, was a fucking waste of air. We should have killed him sooner. What kind of asshole would let his sister live like she did and use her on top of all that? *Christ.* I never liked the asshole, but even I was clueless when it came to how pathetic he truly was.

"He brought me out here. I knew he was in a motorcycle club, he talked about his brothers. I assumed that's where I was going, but when I got here, he had arranged it so I was living with the Shadow Dwellers…and he wasn't there. He wasn't even a member. It hit me as strange, you know?" she asks, but I don't answer.

I don't particularly know what to say. Hayden is embarrassed. I can tell by the way she's refusing to look at me.

She sighs and begins talking again, "I didn't know how these things worked. He said they were his friends—allies who promised to help take care of me. He mentioned something about being involved with some heavy shit, and he didn't want me to get caught in the crossfire. He said the Dwellers would protect me."

"Protect you from who?" I ask. Now it's all I can do not to fucking throw something across the room. He was cutting our throats and selling his sister to get allies to hide from us. Jesus, I wish he was still alive so I could kill him all over again.

"He just said his own club was getting involved in something illegal, and he was going to make sure he didn't go down with them. He didn't want me to be used against him—at least that's what he said," she explains. The tone of her voice leads me to believe, she knows better now. Did she find out the hard way what a twisted bastard he was?

"So, he just left you with those assholes and you stayed?" I growl, without thinking. My frustration and my anger both getting the better of me. I know the instant I say it, that it's a mistake. Her body goes completely solid. She pulls away from me, and for once I let her go. She stands up, looking down at me, and I see the pain in her eyes, but it's the hurt that is shining inside them that bothers me more.

"Don't you judge me, Michael. I see what an idiot I was now, but back then…Back then Blade was the first person who seemed like he ever gave a damn about me. I was young and stupid, sure. But, he made me feel like someone cared. I'd never had that and I wanted it. *I needed it.*"

"He's a fucking monster," I growl, more upset that she cared for the idiot at all. Somewhere in my head, I was convinced that he had raped her. That he had hurt her. There was no way someone like Hayden could care about that fucking piece of shit. I don't like knowing that she did. *I hate it.*

Hayden looks at me and holds her hand over her stomach. "I know that now, but for a while…he wasn't. For a while…he was good to me, Michael."

"And when did he stop being...*good* to you?"

"Do you have to be an asshole?"

"It's a simple question." I shrug, knowing my tone made it anything but simple. I'm being stupid, but I can't get over the fact that she once cared for that fuckwad.

"I don't want to talk about this anymore with you," she says, walking away. I watch her leave, but follow quickly. I stop her in the kitchen, spinning her around to face me.

"We need to talk about *this*," I growl. I'm mad, but I honestly don't know if it's at her, or myself.

"No, we don't. You're being a dick, and I don't have any idea why!"

"I don't like the idea of you caring for that asshole," I admit, before I can stop myself.

"I'm pregnant! Did you think I just got that way magically? Of course, I cared for him. If I hadn't, I would have never slept with him! How did you think this happened?" she asks, exasperated, indicating to her stomach with a nod of her head.

"I thought he forced himself on you," I growl.

She takes a step back, her face going white. "You thought I was raped?"

"It made sense. You have these panic attacks out of nowhere. You live like a hermit and you're afraid of your shadow. What the fuck-else was I supposed to think?"

"Wow. You've really thought about this," she whispers, keeping her face down so I can't see what she's thinking.

"Of course I have. Why the hell else do you think I've been afraid to fuck you?" I growl. "I didn't want to scare you."

"Afraid to fuck me?" she asks, and I scowl.

"Damn it, Hayden," I mutter, rubbing my hand across my beard. I'm not handling this well. Fucking shit, I'm not handling any of this like I should.

"You need to go."

"I'm not leaving," I tell her stubbornly. "I can't leave you alone until we get your *ex-boyfriend* and his crew contained." I tell her that coldly. I know the words wound. They were meant to because I'm an asshole. They were meant to, because I'm feeling jealousy over Hayden, and I don't like it. Her head jerks up as I deliver my verbal slap.

"Fine. Then I'll leave," she says, and the tears shining in her eyes makes my stomach turn. Her hurt takes my breath away, and I feel like I've been sucker punched.

Before I can react, she's out the door. I shake my head thinking she's bluffing and just throwing a fit. She can't go anywhere. So, I cross my arms and wait for her to come back in. A few minutes later, she still hasn't walked through the door. I step outside, intent on dragging her back inside, but when I open the door, her little tinker-toy of a car is backing out of the driveway. *How the fuck did she get the keys to that piece of shit?*

Motherfucker.

CHAPTER 68

Hayden

I SHUT MY car off on a sigh filled with disappointment. I'm not sure if the disappointment is directed at myself, Michael, or maybe a little bit of both of us. I'm sitting outside of Charlie's. I know I'm not being reasonable. I just couldn't stand the look in Michael's eyes or the condemnation in his voice. Being with Blade was a huge mistake, an epically huge one, and it was stupid in every sense of the word. I was an idiot. Still, having Michael look at me and talk to me the way he did? *It hurt.*

I needed to get away from him. If I'm honest, I'm surprised he didn't follow me. If I'm extremely honest, I wanted him to follow me and stop me. I wanted him to put his arms around me and just...*accept me.* Which makes no sense, but that's exactly how I feel.

My mind and my thoughts are way too chaotic. I need time to myself. That's all. Charlie is always inviting me over. I'll crash here tonight and try to get control of myself. This relationship...or whatever is happening between Michael and myself, I think maybe it's too much. The last thing I need is to open myself up to *another* man. Although deep down I know that

Michael isn't any other man, despite how much he hurt me back there. My track record with men, as short as it is, is horrible.

I have too much going on, and the renewed threat from Blade and his club, is all I have time to worry about. Maggie needs to be my top priority. I should be packing up and getting as far away from Blade and the rest of his club, as quickly as possible. I should *not* be dreaming of Michael and…

God, we haven't even had sex, but he's still all I can think of. Every time he touches me, I lose complete control. I don't understand why I'm not afraid of him, why he seems to calm me and make me feel safe when all other men scare the hell out of me. It defies explanation, I only know I want more of him. *Which is bad.* I can't have him. I can't let him get close to me—if for no other purpose than the fact that him being close to me is bad for him and me. For some reason, I feel like Michael is the motivation behind Blade coming to the diner. Blade never liked it when someone else got near what he deemed as his property. He told me that himself, those weeks when he was…*teaching me a lesson.* I thought I proved him wrong. I got away. I got free…maybe I was just fooling myself.

Charlie's seems empty. Maybe she's asleep? I should probably leave, but I really can't face Michael right now.

I walk to the front door and knock. There's no answer. I try to look inside through the glass panel on the door, but there's no sign of her. All signs are pointing to her being gone. Her truck isn't here, but her car is in the driveway and that's the one she drives most of the time. Besides, Charlie's always home and when she's not…she drives her car. She hates driving the truck because it's standard shift. She also never lets anyone else drive. She's always going on how people drive like maniacs and she doesn't trust anyone behind the wheel but herself.

It might be nothing, but something feels off. I have to fight through the urge to run and get the hell out of here. Charlie could have fallen or she might be sick. I wish I had brought my cellphone. Being in something other than sleep shorts and a gray t-shirt and flip flops might have been smarter too. I walk around the back of the house. I had to feed her cat once when she went out of town to visit her sister, and she kept one of those keys-hid-in-a-fake-rock things. I nearly shout *'eureka'* when I find it. Sure enough, the key is tucked inside.

I carefully unlock the door. I'm starting to second guess myself, but my head is filled with visions of Charlie burning up with a fever like I had been, or she could have fallen down her stairs and broke her leg. Heck she has high blood pressure and could have easily had a heart attack.

"Charlie?" I call out, and I do it quietly. Which is stupid, because if she were upstairs or the back part of the hallway, she'd never hear me. "Charlie," I call out a little louder.

"Hayden, what are you doing here?" I hear behind me, and I can't stop the small scream from escaping. I turn around, my hand pressed against my chest and look up at Pastor Sturgill.

"I'm looking for Charlie. What are *you* doing here?" I cry, my heart still hammering against my chest.

"You haven't heard," he says.

"Heard what?"

"Charlie's in the hospital. There was an accident."

"Oh God! Is she okay? When did it happen? Why didn't someone call me?" I bombard him with questions, one right after another. My body starts shaking and tears are falling before he even answers one. The tears only fall harder when he finally answers.

"She's in a coma, Hayden. It doesn't look good."

"I have to go to her. I have to go to the hospital," I tell him, nodding my head yes, in answer to my own statements. "I can't believe this," I tell him still crying and trying to take breath into my lungs at the same time. "Will she be okay? Please tell me she's going to be okay," I beg him. Charlie's the only person I have in the world. I can't imagine a world in it without her.

"It doesn't look good, Hayden," he says and that's all it takes for me to completely fall apart. He holds onto my shoulders, awkwardly, trying to reassure me.

"What the fuck is going on?" Michael growls from the door, and I don't even question my actions as I turn to him and practically leap the three steps to him. His arms enclose around me and I hold him close, letting my tears take over.

Michael will fix it. He'll take care of everything, I think stupidly. Logically I know there are things even Michael can't do, but in my heart, I know if anyone can…*it's him.*

CHAPTER 69

Beast

I KNEW WHERE Hayden would go. She doesn't have many friends. It was either Charlie's or that other waitress. What I didn't expect was to walk in and find the preacher holding onto Hayden's arms. For a second, jealousy had me ready to tear his throat out with my bare hands. Then she throws herself into my arms and something clicks into place, I wrap her up, holding her to me and when her tears register, I'm ready to kill again.

"Why is she crying?" I growl at the preacher, wrapping my hand in her hair, needing to feel it's texture, needing to know she's close. "What did you do?" I question him, and my voice drops down with that, sounding like the animal I've been called. The one that lurks underneath, raw and hurting...bleeding and waiting for revenge.

"Charlie was in an accident!" Hayden cries, her voice muffled and broken from her crying.

I look over at the preacher who is watching the two of us closely. Good. Let the asshole look. Let him understand. She's mine, and he better keep his fucking hands off of her. *Shit. What am I talking about? She can't be mine and even if she was, he doesn't think of her like a man would a woman he wants. I can tell that, just by the way he interacts with her. Fuck. I'm losing it.*

"What happened?" I ask the asshole while trying my best to quiet Hayden. Before I can question myself however, I take my jacket off and pull it over her shoulders, knowing it's big enough that it will fall below the bottom of her shorts and cover more of her up. He might not look at her like a man looks at a woman, but he's only fucking human, and he doesn't need to see what he's missing. Hayden accepts my jacket over her easily and curls into me still crying softly.

"Someone ran her off the road last night. She went over a cliff. She was thrown out of the car, but she's in a coma. The doctor says there's some swelling and bleeding on her brain…" he breaks off at Hayden's anguished cry, before finishing lamely, "it doesn't look good."

"What are you doing here?" I ask him, not liking the fact that he was here alone with Hayden. *Why would he be here if he knew Charlie was in the hospital?*

"I was just getting in from the hospital. My church is just up the road from here. I was going to check in. I saw Hayden's car and wanted to stop and check on her. I know her and Charlie are close. I didn't realize that she didn't know," he finishes and I frown. *Fuck*, I'm seeing ghosts where there are none.

"I need to go see her, Michael. I want to see her," Hayden pleads. I flex my hand in her hair, before placing a kiss on her forehead.

"Okay, Beauty. I'll take you to see her. First you're going home—"

"I don't want to wait, Michael. Something could happen. I need to be with her…"

"You need to go home and get dressed," I tell her, gently but stern enough that she knows that this is the way it's going down, regardless of her arguments.

She looks down at herself, and I see the bright pink blush that steals over her. It's clear that until this moment she didn't remember she was half-naked.

"Okay," she whispers, looking shyly over her shoulder. "Sorry, Pastor Sturgill, I uh…didn't realize."

"You're upset. I can take you to get changed and on to the hospital if you'd like?" he offers and fucking hell, maybe I've misread him. He's crazy if he thinks he's getting her away from me.

"I've got her," I growl, before Hayden can respond. "You lock up," I mumble, intent on getting Hayden away from him. I take her to my truck and help her inside. I'm buckling her in before she says anything.

"What about my car?"

"We'll get it later," I tell her, but I wouldn't mind leaving it here permanently. I don't like the idea of her and Maggie traveling in that piece of shit. I may have to see about finding her something else to drive. Something more dependable and with a good safety rating…

CHAPTER 70

Hayden

"SHE'S NOT GOING to make it, is she, Michael?" I whisper the words, full of sorrow. I feel shame even saying the words aloud. I need him to tell me I'm wrong, but one look at his face and I know that's not what I'm going to hear. To his credit, he doesn't say anything. Instead, he wraps me in his arms and holds me. For a minute, I rest against him, letting my head fall against his chest and take the strength he gives me. Before Michael came into my life, I had a mantra that I would be stronger…with Michael I'm doing that less and less. I know it's because when he's with me, I feel safer. I don't know if that's healthy. I suspect it's not, but I'm not sure I care. I feel his fingers comb gently through my hair, and I close my eyes, enjoying the sensation for a minute before I pull away.

"We need to talk, Beauty," he says, his grumbly voice vibrating inside of me. How I can be at one of the lowest points in my life and he still manages to make me react to him the way he does is a mystery. Still, the things he wants to talk about don't seem as significant anymore. Not right now. Not with my friend in the next room, hooked up to machines that are breathing for her, because she can't do it herself.

"I need a break right now, Michael," I tell him, resenting it a little that I have to say it. Resenting that he's pushing anything right now, other than Charlie and what she's going through and how that makes me feel.

"Hayden—"

"I'm just going to the restroom, Michael," I tell him, pulling away. I hear his sigh behind me, but he lets me go. Probably because his cellphone rings.

"Just the restroom. I'll be right here," he warns me, which pisses me off. I look over my shoulder and his eyes are trained on me as I push through the door. I lock it behind me and think about just hiding in here. It wouldn't work. Michael would just break in. I splash water on my face and try to get control of my emotions. Charlie looked so…*vacant.* That's what she looked like. Her body was almost lifeless. I couldn't sense her there. There was no emotion on her face, none of her warmth radiating. Her color was gone. Her skin felt cold…it feels like I've already lost her. The thought brings the tears back, and I do my best to brush them away and try to stop, before I give into the need to cry. I know once I let the tears freely flow, I may cry for days. I need air. Air that doesn't include Michael hounding me about my past and how stupid I was. Air that doesn't feel stale and wrong, reminding me that probably the only friend I have in the world is slipping away from me.

I open the door just a crack. I expect Michael to be standing there. I'm a little shocked he's not. I look across the open room of the I.C.U. lobby and he's standing by the window, his back to me, still talking on his phone. I slide out of the door, carefully closing it behind me. My eyes still staying on Michael's back. Then before he can turn, and I chicken out, I move down the hall toward the elevators. I just want to go outside. There's a sitting area out there, off from the cafeteria. Maybe if I can sit out there and breathe for a little bit, I'll feel better. My heart hurts. I'm not ready to say goodbye to Charlie. I don't know how to let her go. She didn't have brain activity though. The nurse told me that. They're waiting on Charlie's emergency contact to come in and then decisions will be made. Decisions I'm not ready to hear, and decisions I have no control over.

Once outside, I zero in on the round, stone picnic table and benches. There are a few of them placed along a patio area that's been made with white gravel and red stone pavers. They're nestled on each side by flowering pear trees and in between a couple of the trees there's a small pond which has a fountain connected to it. I sit facing it, watching the sun reflect off the water and the change people have been throwing into it…making wishes I suppose. I fish into my pocket and find a penny. I hold it firmly, close my eyes, and wish for a miracle that would bring my friend back to me. I toss it in, watching it slowly sink into the water. It does nothing to make me feel better. In fact, all it does is let the tears come again.

"You always did cry so easily."

Cold chills rise up my back at the voice. It's the last voice I expected to hear, the last one I wanted to hear. I finish wiping the tears away, my body tight. Then I manage to look straight into the eyes of the devil…Blade.

"You always had a knack for making me cry," I tell him, proud of myself for not letting too much of my fear bleed through into my voice. I am scared, but I need to be smart. I can't let the panic take control. Michael is here. He's not that far away, and the minute he discovers I'm gone, he'll come find me. I just need to hold tight. In my pocket is the small canister of pepper spray that I keep with me. It doesn't make me feel as secure as my gun, and definitely not as secure as Michael, but at least I'm not completely helpless.

"You've caused me a lot of problems, Hay. I don't like problems. You know that."

"I don't see how. I've done my best to stay as far away from you as I can. You made it clear that I meant nothing to you," I respond, doing my best to swallow down the bile that rises in my throat. Maggie can feel my tension, I know because she lets out a small kick. I place my hand on my stomach, hoping to reassure her, even when I'm terrified.

Blade's sandy-blonde hair ruffles with the cool wind that blows through. God he's so ugly. How did I fail to see that? I really was stupid. He might have pleasing features, but the coldness in his face and eyes, the darkness that hovers around him—*how did I miss that*?

"That whelp you're carrying is mine. You didn't tell me you were pregnant, Hay. You had to know I wouldn't let you take my child away."

"I didn't know I was pregnant until you had your men teach me your…*lesson* and leave me for dead," I tell him and some of the bitterness and pain is taking over and I'm glad. It's hiding the fear that is very real and rising inside of me.

"You betrayed me. You didn't think you could get away with that, now did you?"

"I didn't betray you."

"Oh, come on, Hay. You were pissed because you found out I was fucking other women and decided to snoop into my life. You should have known better."

"You need to leave."

"I will, but you will be going with me," he says so casually and laid back that it only deepens the fear I feel.

"I'm not going anywhere with you, ever again. You'd have to kill me first," I tell him, hating that there's a tremble in my voice now. I stand slowly, so I can put my hand in my pants pocket without making it too obvious. My hand wraps around the small canister tightly. *I can do this. I have to do this. I have to protect Maggie. Michael is close. He won't let anything happen to me, I just need to hold on and…face the devil…*

CHAPTER 71

Hayden

"I'M AFRAID YOU'LL be coming with me alive. At least until you give birth. Then..." he shrugs, as if he doesn't really care. I should be worrying about dying I suppose, but the main fear stifling me right now is the idea of this monster getting his hands on Maggie.

"Why do you even want Maggie? You're already calling her vile names. Just leave us alone. We're nothing to you," I plead with him, and I hate that I even have to talk with him about Maggie at all. I need to get out of here. If he had any of his men with him, I'd already be in a situation I couldn't escape from. Waiting around is the last thing I should be doing.

"I'll admit, I'm upset that you even fucked this up, Hay. In my world girls are usually only good for one thing. But, she'll be my blood. She could come in handy. You shouldn't have tried to keep her away from me. I own her and you. I always will, your fate was sealed the moment your brother sold you to me. I told you that. Your only escape is death and you're the one who refused to let that happen," he says and he's smiling as he says it. *Smiling.*

"I hate you," I tell him, feeling hopeless. "I did nothing but try to love you, and all you ever wanted to do is hurt me."

"Love," he snorts. "You were always so stupid, Hayden. You were payment for a debt. That's all easy pussy like you will always be." He takes a few steps to me now.

My heartbeat was already out of control, but now it practically pummels itself against my chest. I can feel the beat even in my throat. I yank my hand out containing the small container of pepper spray and hold it between us like a weapon.

"Stop. If you get near me, I'll use this I swear," I cry and I know it's pitiful. Even as I say it, I'm thinking the smarter course of action would have been trying to run back inside. I need somehow to delay him though, because I know if I just take off running he'll catch me easily.

"Are you really this fucking stupid you think that can stop me?" he jeers, and he's laughing at me, his eyes cruel and the sun reflects on his neck making the snake tattoo seem more real…*more terrifying*. Before I can second guess myself further, I aim the canister and spray it. It's military grade, that I special ordered, but it's small and in my haste, I spray his nose and jaw first, I adjust quickly and hit his eyes. He puts his hand up to try and stop most of it, and probably succeeds. His other hand grabs mine roughly. I fight the hold long enough to spray again, before he lashes out and slams the bottle to the ground.

"You fucking cunt!" he growls, his eyes watering and blood red. I might not have got him as well as I wanted, but I did do some damage. He backhands me hard along the side of my face, causing my head to jerk back in pain, stretching my neck with the force of the hit. He tries to rub his face, while holding onto me at the same time.

I know this is my last opportunity to get away and I take my free hand do my best to hit him in the nuts. It's a weak hit, and I know it doesn't do much damage. It shocks him enough his hold loosens on me however, and I'm able to break free. I take off running for the hospital entrance, hoping he won't follow because there will be people around. I make it almost to the doors when the Pastor comes through them.

"Help me!" I cry, running to him. I make it to his side and he pulls me into him, as if to guard me.

"What is going on here?" he asks, looking down at me then back at Blade.

"We have to get inside," I cry, knowing there's no way the Pastor can handle Blade on his own. I have to get to Michael.

I have to.

CHAPTER 72

Beast

"YEAH, SPEAK FAST," I growl into the phone, annoyed. I need to get Hayden home safe. There's not a doubt in my mind that Charlie's accident has everything to do with Blade and his motherfucking club. I've been taking my time, waiting for Skull to meet with his contacts, but I'm done. I have to contain this shit before it touches Hayden.

"Victor Torasani is heading your way brother. Word came down about an hour ago."

"What's changed?" I ask Skull. Alarm bells are going off. The Torasani are settled in New York. They are notoriously private, but Victor has been labeled as a recluse. He's rarely seen. For him to be coming here…

"Haven't found out. Still researching, just wanted to give you a heads up. You're too far away for me to get men to you quickly, so Diesel is stepping in. You should have some backup within a few hours. I can have people at your side tomorrow afternoon, but you're just a few hours from Diesel. His men are already cutting through Cherokee. They'll be there before the Torasani's touch down."

"Get word to have them meet me at my woman's."

"Your woman?" he asks, shock thick in his voice, but maybe not as much shock as I'm feeling right now. *Fuck.*

"I…Fuck…"

"Beast, brother, what's going on?" Skull prompts.

I rub the back of my neck in frustration. Shit. Am I claiming Hayden? Why the fuck would she even want to saddle herself with me? She just ran away from me earlier. Hell, she's hiding in the restroom from me now.

"It's complicated," I hedge.

"Christo," Skull mutters. "Pistol's hermana." His comment annoys the fuck out of me.

"She's a good woman, Skull. She's…*special*," I mutter.

"Is she yours?" he asks, and just the thought of it makes my heart stall. *Mine?*

"She doesn't need to be saddled with someone like me," I growl, looking over my shoulder at the bathroom door.

Skull lets out with a stream of Spanish. I don't know what all of it means, but the majority of it is cursing and it's all directed at me. I start to respond, but there's a woman that comes into my line of sight. She turns the knob to the bathroom door and it opens… *What the fuck?* I thought Hayden was in there.

"I got to go, brother. Just get a hold of Diesel's men and tell them where I'll be," I tell Skull, hanging up before he can respond. I store my phone back in my pocket and go to the bathroom. I try the door, but it's locked. I pound on it. "Hayden! Hayden! Open this fucking door!"

"There's no Hayden in here," comes the scared voice through the door.

Motherfucker. I stomp off. Where did she go? *How fucking long has she been gone?* Fear is grabbing a hold of me and I don't know what to do with it. I can't calm myself and think methodically like I need to. All I can grasp is that Hayden is missing, and I have to find her. *I have to.*

PANIC MAKES IT hard to think logically. I've tried to think of where Hayden might have disappeared to. Women shop, so I figured the gift shop. She's not there. I even made myself go to the chapel, because I thought she might be there praying for Charlie. She wasn't and stepping in there wasn't the best feeling I ever had. The last time I stepped foot in a chapel it was to pray that God somehow turn back time and bring my daughter back to me. They say that he can do miracles—that he can bring the dead back to life. If he could do that, then why couldn't he have saved Annabelle? She was innocent. She deserved to live. Dani tried to tell me that God has a plan that we can't understand. Some mumbo-jumbo about how for her it was so her and Crusher could rescue their son.

I like her, so I didn't tell her she's full of shit. There's no plan. There's no rhyme and definitely no fucking reason. If God exists, he's a twisted motherfucker who is getting his kicks out of destroying me. Maybe I deserve that. Annabelle didn't. Hayden and Maggie don't, and I'm not waiting for God to destroy who I care about, *this time.*

The cafeteria is my next stop. It's completely empty, and by this time, I'm ready to fucking scream. I look around the room feeling helpless and one step away from throwing something through the damn window. That's when I see her. She's outside by the door, but within sight of the window. She's standing with the preacher, holding onto him for dear life. At first, I can feel nothing but jealousy. I'm ready to march out there and rip her away from him. Then I look beyond them to see Blade standing there. He's bent over, screaming at Hayden and way too close to her. I let out a roar that echoes through the hospital. It sounds as if it is ripped out from the pits of Hell and maybe it is. I've spent enough time there. It's time to end this motherfucker. It's time to make sure Hayden and Maggie are safe.

I don't remember walking from the cafeteria to the door. I don't remember taking my eyes off Hayden. But one minute, I'm standing, looking through the window, and the next, I'm outside.

"What's going on here?" I hear the preacher ask.

I make sure I answer for him. "I'm going to kill you, motherfucker," I bellow.

Blade's face jerks up, and I can see his eyes are swollen, before I reach him however, he pulls out a gun. There's screams from the people around us that had been sitting at the tables. My first instinct is to ignore the gun and charge. I may die, but I'd end Blade first. Then the fucker does something that I don't expect. He turns the gun on Hayden.

"Take another step, and I'll end the bitch and just be done with it," Blade warns. There's that fucking fear taking over yet again. I'm starting to resent Hayden for bringing this feeling back into my life. I stop, holding my hands up, like a fucking pussy.

"You try it and you're a dead man," I tell him, which is a ridiculous threat. The truth is he's a dead man walking right now. The minute I get the opportunity, he is done.

"You've become attached to my leftovers. You ain't going to do shit, if you think it will hurt her. Maybe I should just shoot the fucking cunt now so you can watch her bleed out," Blade sneers, and I do my best to keep the image he describes from forming in my head. *It doesn't work*. "The Blaze is just like everyone rumored, little boys who get led around by their dicks by a bunch of pussies. Pathetic really."

"Not as pathetic as a man who gets his dick hard by hurting innocent women."

"There's nothing innocent about Hayden. She was innocent when she came to my bed, but so fucking eager. I'm sure you've enjoyed that by now, though. Hayden always was quick to spread her legs. Hell, Beast, ol' buddy, I bought her one day and had my dick in her a week later."

He's taunting me, his barbs are hitting me right where he wants them to. I do my best not to let it show that they hit. I think I manage to keep my face stoic—*barely*. I hear Hayden's hurt-filled gasp from behind me, and I ignore it too. I keep my eyes trained on the shit-sack in front of me, and I focus my mind on envisioning me choking the life from him with my hands.

"I'm going to enjoy killing you," I tell him, truthfully. Then the strangest look comes on his face. He's looking over my shoulder through the glass behind me. I try to look too, but I'm afraid to take my eyes off the gun.

"Not today, Beast. But soon, I'll show you exactly who will survive our showdown. Enjoy my scraps while you can. Soon, every hole she has will be used by my men, and some she doesn't even have yet. Maybe I'll let you live long enough to see just how much she likes it," he taunts, backing away.

I yell out a war cry at him, and charge. Common sense is gone. I've had it with this fucker. He fires his gun and for a second I lose my breath, thinking he shot Hayden. Then I feel the bullet hit my leg and it buckle under me. I hear Hayden scream. My eyes go to her, and I see the Pastor trying to hold her away from me. My face jerks back around to Blade who is laughing before he runs, getting away from me.

He won't be able to hide though. There won't be a rock he can crawl under.

He's a dead man.

CHAPTER 73

Hayden

WATCHING MICHAEL GET shot is the single, most terrifying thing I've ever endured. I try to run to him but Pastor Sturgill grabs my arm and keeps me from moving. I watch in horror as Michael goes down, and I can't stop the scream that feels like it is ripped from my soul. My hands wrap around the Pastor's arm, and I dig my nails into him, scratching hard. I know I will bring blood, but I don't care at this moment. All I want is to get to Michael. When his hold loosens, I tear free and get to Michael.

"Oh God, oh God, oh God…." I repeat over and over, moving my hands down to his leg. There's a darkened spot on the faded denim of his jeans. "Someone get a doctor! Get help!" I scream.

Michael grunts.

"I'm okay, Hayden. It's a clean shot. It just grazed," he mutters, and he's trying to get up—*like a crazy man*!

"You were shot!" I practically shriek. "There's nothing okay about that!"

"Let me up, woman," he grumbles, and I shift my weight as

much as I can to hold him down.

"No! You aren't moving until the doctor's come and get you. You could bleed out!"

"Damn it, Hayden! Let me up, you're letting that fucker get away!"

"Who cares! I need you to be safe. I need you to be okay, Michael," I tell him, and I realize I'm pleading. The gravity of Michael being shot because of me hits me head on. It robs me of breath and it makes me hurt…everywhere. *He could have died…because of me.*

"I'm fine," he rumbles again, and this time, he manages to get up, but I see the pain on his face. I can only imagine the blood standing up will cause him to lose. The man is insane. *He has to be.* I stand, trying to block him from leaving. He puts his hands on my shoulder to move me. I know, because I can see the intent in his eyes.

"Please, don't leave, Michael. Please. Just let them check you out."

"Damn it, Hayden. I'm trying to protect you. I need to stop that prick from getting away," he growls, full of frustration.

I'm giving up hope of trying to be able to keep him with me when another man comes out the door. He's older. If I had to guess I'd say he might be late fifties, early sixties. He's got dark hair, but there's more than an abundance of gray sprinkled in. It's groomed impeccably, a close cut that you can tell is done by more than just a normal barber. His suit is gray and reeks of money. It's so perfectly cut and tailored your eyes are drawn to it. He's got a lone ring on one finger, a large insignia ring with the letter T, surrounded by a red ruby backdrop.

"He won't be getting far," the man says, his voice coming out sweet and thick like honey. Almost too sweet.

Something about it sets off alarm bells, and I find myself

getting closer to Michael. He must sense it too, because his arms come around me. For a second, I forget that Michael has been shot and is standing up like a crazy man, probably losing more blood with every second that passes.

Then the staff comes out with a gurney. I hear Michael growl and the next few minutes are a blur of activity. The man in the suit, leaves without further word. Michael tries to follow him, or at least talk to him, only to be waylaid by the hospital staff. Cops begin to swarm the area, along with hospital security. They're all asking me questions, and I leave it to Pastor Sturgill to answer, as I stick like glue to Michael's side. Michael refuses to get on a gurney and finally an orderly convinces him to sit in a wheelchair. I'm beside him as they wheel him through the hospital. I'm wondering if life will ever get back under control.

I'm scared it won't.

CHAPTER 74

Beast

"I CAN'T BELIEVE you didn't stay in the hospital," Hayden says for like the hundredth time.

In answer, I grunt, which makes her roll her eyes at me and huff. It's cute and for some fucking reason despite all the shit going down, I want to laugh.

"Get in bed. You're giving me a headache," I tell her. She's pacing back and forth in front of the bedroom door while I'm lying on the bed. Her arms are hugged tight against her chest and she just keeps pacing. It'd be annoying as fuck, if she wasn't so cute.

"I can't get in bed with you, Michael."

"Why in the hell, not?"

"There's men in my living room! Men I don't know! What would they think if I slept in here with you?"

"I doubt they give a damn. But, if they think about it at all, they probably think we're sleeping. Which I might be doing if you'd get in bed."

"Michael!"

"Just do it, Hayden. You need rest. The baby needs rest and

it's not going to get better around here anytime soon." She studies me for a minute, then mimics one of my grunts, and gets in bed. Once she does, I pull her to me, instantly relaxing.

"Be careful of your leg," she chastises.

"My leg is fine."

"That's why they wanted to keep you in the hospital, I'm sure," she sasses, but settles her head against my shoulder.

My fingers dive into her hair without me realizing it. The feel of the soft tresses against my fingers calm me. Having Hayden next to me does that even more.

She's silent for a few minutes, but I can literally feel some of the tension leaving her body. "I can't believe I got you shot," she whispers as if confessing she murdered someone. Her voice is full of shame and sorrow...*over me.* That does something to me, I don't know how to explain it, or what it does exactly, but there's something there. Something elemental that shifts in my thinking of her.

I practically claimed Hayden to Skull today. I've already taken on the role to protect her and Maggie, and even if I keep going back and forth on the issue, I know that I'm taking her body. *What would be the harm in keeping her? If she's not put off by my scars, then why can't I keep her? If she's stupid enough to want me, then why can't I claim her? She may deserve better, but fuck...I have to be better than Blade. I could make sure her and Maggie are taken care of, are happy enough. Why can't I keep, Hayden?*

"You didn't get me shot," I mutter, my thoughts are full of images of tying Hayden to me. Can I trust myself to keep her and Maggie safe...*permanently?* "You just kept me from ending that fucker's life. Though, I'll still get him, I just wish I already had."

"Do you think Victor has already?" Hayden asks, referring to Victor Torasani, who was the man who showed up at the hospital today. I had a meeting scheduled with them tomorrow at Charlie's diner. Of all the connections I thought that Charlie might have had with the Torasani clan, I would have never guessed that she was Victor's ex-wife. How the fuck does that happen? He's vowed revenge on the Dwellers and he'll really get it. I could sit back, but that's not who I am, and I owe the fucker my own retribution, so I'm not going to stop.

"I don't know," I tell her, but I'm doubtful. If the Torasani's already had Blade in their grasp we would know. "I guess I'll find out tomorrow."

"I don't want you to go face them alone. They're dangerous."

"I'm not exactly a pushover, Hayden," I grumble, feeling a little slighted. No man wants to think a woman feels he's not capable. *Me especially.*

"I didn't say you were, but you are just one man," she sighs in answer.

"I'll have some of Diesel's men with me. I'll be leaving a couple here with you."

"I have to go stock shelves at the church and the supermarket and places. I'm already late. I don't want them to stop selling my products, Michael."

"That preacher will take you, and Ace will be riding with you. I want men with you at all times. I'd rather send Ace with you alone—"

"No," she whispers, and I can hear the fear. I need to rid her of that someday soon.

"I get you don't know him and he might scare you," I start to try and set her at ease.

"It's not that I'm scared, it's just—"

"It's okay, Hayden. That's why Pastor Sturgill will be there. You know him. He'll be there too."

"Are you ashamed of me?" she asks a few minutes later.

"Why would I be ashamed?" I ask, truly surprised and confused. Who knows what women get in their heads.

"Because I'm weak. I try to stop it. I swear I do. I know I need to be stronger, for Maggie," she continues to whisper.

"Hayden…"

"I really do try, Michael. I don't like being weak."

I kiss her forehead. "You are getting stronger."

"I'm not. Not really."

"You are. You didn't have a panic attack today, did you?" I prompt her and she's silent for a minute and I hope she's thinking things over.

"No, but that…that was because I knew you were close by. You would find me," she says and my hand searches hers. Linking our fingers, I stare at our joined hands. It's a simple connection; it has been from the beginning. Yet with Hayden, the simplicity of holding hands means so much more than it ordinarily does.

"I'll always find you, Hayden. I promise you that. You don't have to be afraid or worry about telling me anything. You're safe with me," I tell her, and I'm serious, even if there's this huge fear inside of me that I'll somehow fail her, like I did Annabelle.

Hayden leans up on her elbow and looks down at me. "I know that. I wish…I wish I had met you a year ago…or even longer. If I knew men like you existed…" she stops talking, her eyes are shining in the semi-darkness of the room.

"Scarred and twisted?" I try and joke, suddenly uncomfortable with the emotion surrounding us.

That's when Hayden shocks me for the millionth time. She brings her lips to mine without warning and kisses me. Her sweet taste explodes on my lips and it's that moment that's my doom. That moment when I surrender everything that I am to her.

CHAPTER 75

Hayden

I HATE WHEN he refers to his scars. I've seen the look on his face when I touch them. I know they bother him, and even if he doesn't want to admit it, they make him feel less somehow. I hate that for him, because if there's one thing I know, it's that I've met men who are "less" of everything and Michael could never be one of them—not inside where it counts the most, not in the very make-up of being a man and definitely not in the way that he looks. Michael is physically beautiful, the scars do nothing to distract from that, at least not in my eyes. The only one that I wish would disappear is the long one on the right side of his face. Not because it hurts me to look at it, but because I know that it hurt him. It left its mark so deeply on him that he grew his hair long, his beard longer still, all with the hope of hiding its viciousness.

"I think you're beautiful," I tell him honestly when we break apart. My eyes are trapped by his, nervousness bubbles up in my stomach, and I let my hand hold his tight, keeping us joined, because his strength gives me courage.

"Hayden—"

"And inside, Michael," I interrupt him, letting my free hand move down his neck to his chest, keeping it over his heart. I can feel the steady beat thumping under my hand. *Strong. Brave. Trustworthy.* "Inside, you're the kind of man they write fairytales about." Even as I'm saying the words, I know I shouldn't. I feel his body tense underneath me, and I can feel the change in his attitude.

"I'm no Prince Charming, Hayden. I'm no *hero* to save the day. I'm not capable of that, trust me. *Fuck*, even now I'm in your bed instead of trying to make sure you're okay because of the day you've had. Instead of trying to help you grieve over what Charlie is going through…all I'm thinking about is spreading your legs and fucking you so hard we both *forget everything*. Fucking you so hard our brains stop working and the only thoughts either of us have is how *deep* my dick can get inside of you."

"There's…I mean those men outside—"

"I don't even give a fuck about them. I hope they hear us. Christ, Hayden I'm already hard thinking about burying myself between your legs and the idea of them hearing you scream for my dick, just makes me harder. Do you get that? Do you get that I'm not some knight in shining armor? I'm a fucking scarred animal who wants to fuck you raw and hard while wanting everyone to hear it. I want them to know that you let the *monster* between your thighs and that you're fucking enjoying it."

"Michael—" I start, his words shocking me. Yet, as I hear them and look in his face as he says them I'd be lying if I didn't admit they turn me on. *A lot.* His words are carnal, dirty, wicked, and filled with desire. His desire for me is there, easy to read on his face. He wants me and he doesn't care about my past, or anything…he just wants…*me.* I don't understand it. I've never been the kind of woman to elicit that reaction from a man. *Never.*

"You don't care that they would know you're with

me…Michael I'm preg—"

"And I don't even fucking care about that, Hayden. I still want to take you like a fucking animal. I want to roll you over, pull you up on your hands and knees, and thrust inside of you with my hands full of your ass. There's nothing *sweet* about me. I'm nothing you should ever want in your bed, Hayden. You'd do better to stay the fuck away from me."

There's so many emotions swirling through Michael right now. The force of them is so strong they are almost physical. I can't sort through them, and I'm not sure how each would make me feel right now. What I do know is what his words are doing to me and how the thought of him *wanting me* makes me feel. Maybe the smart thing would be to back away and leave. No one has accused me of being smart in life. Right now, however, what I'm about to do seems like the smartest thing I've ever done in my life.

I stand up and I'm pretty sure that Michael thinks I'm going to leave. It's then I realize that he was trying to scare me away. I nervously slide my fingers around the waist band of my pajamas, hooking my panties too. Then, I push them down my legs. I'm blushing. I can't watch Michael as I do it. I leave my shirt on. It's long enough to hide my own scars. I know I'll have to eventually tell him about them, and maybe soon if he doesn't back out from this. Still, right now, the only thing I want to concentrate on is being with Michael…on feeling like a woman…a beautiful woman…*Michael's woman.*

I hear the mattress squeak as he shifts, however. Involuntarily, I peek up at him and he's sitting in the bed. I see shock on his face, but it's overshadowed by the hunger there. *Hunger for me.* A quiver of want runs through my body, leaving me achy and greedy in its wake.

Leaving me wet…

CHAPTER 76

Beast

I WAS PUSHING. I was trying to push her away. Does she really see me as some kind of hero in her mind? Fuck. I can't even begin to tell her how wrong that is. So, I pushed. Only Hayden surprised me, yet again.

She didn't run.

She didn't back away.

As I watch those pants slide off her unbelievably long legs, I sit up in the bed. Christ, this woman's legs are a work of art that lead all the way to heaven. She's gorgeous, and it's hard for me to believe there was a time when I thought differently. She peeks up at me, her face blushing a bright red. I love that she has this shyness. I don't give a fuck what went down in her past. Hayden is special, I may not like that she was once Blade's, but she's not now…*she's mine.* I let that cement a little deeper inside me. I don't deserve to claim a woman. I especially don't deserve Hayden, but fuck, I've tried to warn her, and I can't fight anymore. I'm taking her, and whatever happens, happens. There's only so much a man can take, and I've reached my limit.

"Hayden, you need to…" I trail off as she finally looks at

me.

"Like this, Michael?" she asks, shyly. She slides on the bed, inching up slowly, and braces herself on her hands and knees. She lays her head to the side and looks at me…like a fucking trained submissive waiting to be conquered, and it's too much for my poor cock to handle. He was hard before, but now it's fucking physically painful to breathe.

I stand without answering, I think words are beyond me right now. I think I grunt at her in reply, but I'm not sure. I'm too busy pulling off my sweats and getting into position behind her.

I move my hand over her ass, loving the way the plush mound of flesh moves under my fingers. I pull the cheeks apart, admiring how the small opening to her ass moves. "You sure this is what you want, Hayden? Do you want me—*like this*?" I question her, giving her one last chance to escape. Leaning down, I place a kiss against the base of her spine, letting my tongue drift against it, tasting the salty, heated skin. Following an imaginary line that trails over her ass, I allow my teeth gently to nibble her flesh. My fingers slide slow between the lips of her pussy, finding the hot, wet center of her.

"*Fu…ck,*" I growl the word out without thought as her arousal slides against my fingers. She's so wet. I've barely done or said anything and she's soaked. A jolt of need fires through my body, sending electricity and heat through me. It's so intense my hand on her ass convulses. I dig my fingers harder into her ass in reaction, at the same time my teeth literally bite her. She jerks from the sting of pain, but she doesn't pull away. Her body pushes back into me and she tries to ride my hand. So fucking responsive…*so fucking perfect.*

"I'm sure, Michael," she says. Her voice is laced thick with desire while her head is bent down as her body gently rocks against me. "I'm sure."

Grabbing my cock, I push the head through the lips of her pussy, letting her juices coat me, and loving how she cries out at the intrusive first touch. The head of my shaft slides against her throbbing clit. I feel her body jerk like it's been touched by a live wire. "You're perfect," I tell her, and for the first time in my life, I really mean that when talking to a woman. The only thing not perfect about her right now is that she left her shirt on. I have it pushed up, but I want it gone. The problem is I can't wait that long. *Next time.*

"Please, Michael. I want to feel you. I want you inside—" her words end with a cry as I drag my cock against her clit one last time, then I find her warm, wet entrance and slide inside of her. I hold myself back. I want nothing more than to thrust into her hard and fast, but I don't want to risk hurting her child. I'm a bastard for touching her, but I could never harm her or Maggie. After the head of my cock slides in, I push in, slowly. I go deeper inch by inch, stopping when I feel her body tighten and convulse around me. It's sweet agony.

"Are you okay, Beauty?" I ask, needing to reassure myself and her before continuing. She doesn't answer, instead she pushes back against me, taking my cock deeper inside. "Easy," I caution her. "I don't want to hurt you. We'll do this nice and easy," I tell her, needing to slow her down and remind myself. The urge to fuck her hard is *screaming* at me. The sweetest torture.

"You feel so good, Michael," she says, moving away from me and then pushing back against me, fucking herself with my cock, taking what she wants. *Fucking hell, this is the hottest thing I can remember experiencing.* "I don't want nice and easy…I need you," she cries out, and the sincerity in those words shine, warming something inside of me I thought was gone forever.

Me. She needs…*me*. She's not pulling away from me. She's not scared of me. She's not disgusted by the burns covering my body. She wants me. She's begging…*for me*. I push inside of her, deeper, trying to be gentle and trusting her to tell me if I go too far. I bend over her body, my hands wrapping around her hips holding her to me. The fingers on my right hand caress against the hardened, rough texture of her skin. I know the feeling…scars. They feel intense. Something happened to her and it had to be painful. I make a mental note to find them later and kiss them. The thought flashes through my mind and then leaves as I lose myself in just how good it feels to be inside of Hayden. I lean over her, loving that I can. I've always been so large, towering over most everyone. Hayden is the first person to make me appreciate that, because I stretch over her and kiss her shoulder. Taste her skin that is a mixture of perspiration and sex.

"You've got me, Beauty. I'm not going anywhere," I growl in her ear, biting down on the lobe. Her body quivers under me with the bite, her pussy tightens around my cock, squeezing it so tight that I barely remember to breathe. "Does it feel good, Hayden? Don't let me hurt you," I plead with her, my sanity almost completely gone. I keep one hand on her scars and let the other move across her stomach to her breast, kneading it gently, and worrying the swollen nipple.

"Good. So good, Michael," she whimpers. "I'm going to come," she admits, but I already know. I feel the exact moment her climax hits. Her body tightens beneath me as she moves faster against my cock, squeezing me so tightly that my balls constrict, nearly taking me with her.

Leaning down further, I let her back rake against my chest as she works my dick. My hand moves from her hip to her hand. She's supporting herself with her arms, so she can't move it, but I just place my hand over hers, not stopping until my fingers slide under to connect with her palm. There…that feels *right.* It's with my hand on hers that I finally take over. Thrusting in and out of her, letting her ride out her orgasm while chasing my own.

I feel my cum gathering before it boils over, erupting from my cock inside of her tight little pussy, and I roar just one word. Just one, but it's the only thing left in this world that I care about.

"Hayden!"

CHAPTER 77

Hayden

I FEEL HIM gently wrap his arms around me and pull me to my side and into his body. I rest my head against his chest, and circle his massive body with my arms. Michael feels so good, so warm and solid next to me. *So safe.* I place a kiss against his chest where his heart is beating.

"If you tell me that this shouldn't have happened, I might hurt you," I joke, my voice sleepy and full of satisfaction.

Michael grunts in return, making me giggle. He kisses the top of my head and his fingers softly brush through the ends of my hair. The soft touch feels so good, I kiss his chest again, then move to his shoulder, before finally burrowing into his neck and placing kisses against his pulse there. I bring my hand slowly to his stomach and back to his chest, letting his chest hair brush against my hand, loving the feel of it…*of him.*

"You keep that up and I'll end up taking you again, and we shouldn't," he mumbles in his deep voice. I tense, then pull away slightly before taking my hand and making a fist and half-heartedly hitting him in the stomach. "Umpf!" he groans, making the noise as air leaves his body. "What did you do that for?"

"I told you not to say we shouldn't have had sex!" I growl back, upset that he would mess up this moment. For a second, it felt like perfection, exactly how I always envisioned being intimate with someone would be—*but never was.*

"I didn't. I just meant, your body needs to rest, Hayden. You've been through a lot today, and you are delicate right now, because of Maggie. I just want us to be safe."

"Oh…well, that's better, I guess," I mumble, slightly embarrassed. "You should have said that," I scold him.

He grunts in reply, and pulls me back into him.

"I should get up. I need to take a shower," I tell him, yawning.

"What for? It's late, Beauty. Go to sleep," he says, sounding as if he's almost there himself.

"But…" he sighs in frustration, and I feel guilty because I like that he was so relaxed. I've not seen him like that.

"But what?"

"I…well…I mean…"

"Jesus, Hayden, spit it out," he mutters and that annoys me.

"I'm messy!" I mutter at him, pushing away and getting off the bed. Men are such idiots, apparently even good ones. I've never been with one before, but even upset, I can admit that Michael is *definitely* a good man—the kind I wish I could have given Maggie for a father. *Shit.* I can't think like that. I can't wish for the impossible and that's totally impossible. Michael will leave soon. He probably hasn't left me yet because he wants to make sure Maggie and I are safe. Still, he won't stick around. There's no way he would want me permanently. There's no way *I* should want a man permanently. Michael's just messing with my mind, making me believe in dreams I thought had died when I was a child. He's making me wish for fairytales; which is nuts.

There are no fairytales—for me, *there never has been.*

"What do you mean you're messy?" Michael asks, grabbing my arm when I go to walk away. He moves fast for a big man. He's standing up now too, and I look down to see his body, and I really mean *see him.*

"Michael, you're naked," I squeak.

"What are you talking about?"

"You're naked!" I repeat, louder, and yet somehow, I still manage to squeak the words.

"Hayden, I know! We just had sex. Now why are you getting out of bed," he huffs, and I look at his face and the frustration is vibrating off of him, which should annoy me. It does, but he just looks so beautiful standing there. His newly trimmed hair and beard. His dark eyes, the lean cut of his large body, the ink covering him in different designs, patterns, and words, not to mention the freaking twelve pack of abs he sports—not really. But my mind blurs when I try to count each delicious indention, all of him is fantastic…*even the scars.* They mar his perfect skin, and some of them are truly horrific in nature, but they are still beautiful, because they are part of him. Unlike my scars which are much smaller and just contained in one spot, his cover him. I don't know how he got them, but I instinctively know he got them being a man. *A good man.* He has a military tattoo, so he was probably wounded overseas. His scars aren't like mine. His are honorable. His are…special. They make him more…*not less.*

"I told you. I'm messy. Your…well… I mean…You're kind of dripping out of me…"

"I'm…dripping…out of you?"

"Your cum," I tell him, and I'm glad the room is kind of dark, because I don't want him to see how embarrassed I get at admitting that.

"You're getting out of bed to wash me away?" he roars, and

he really is roaring. I'd almost lay odds that they could hear him a few counties over.

"Well, yeah," I whisper, still not able to look at him, but that's because my eyes are glued to one *certain part* of him. "You're really big, Michael."

"Damn it, Hayden. What are you talking about?" he asks, and he sounds confused, but I'm not really paying attention. His dick is hard again and it's pointing up at me, bouncing and teasing me. It's almost as if it's saying, *'Do you want more of me?'*

I do…I really do.

I smile. "You're like really, really big." I catch myself almost moving my hands for emphasis.

"Hayden?" he asks again, and his voice has changed. I force myself to look up at him. His eyes are focused on me. I expected to see his irritation and maybe even anger. I don't. What I see is shock. I don't answer his earlier question. I ask the only thing on my mind at the moment.

"How did you fit inside of me?"

He snorts…*literally snorts* with laughter at my question, then he picks me up in his arms, as if I wasn't pregnant and outgrowing my clothes. He picks me up as if I was light as a feather.

I hold onto him with a startled gasp. "Michael! Your leg! What the heck are you doing?" I ask when he starts walking away from the bed.

"My leg is fine. It was just a graze and it's the last thing you need to worry about."

"But—"

"I'm going to take you into the shower and wash my cum from your body. Then I'm going to show you exactly how I fit inside of you."

"Oh," I whisper softly, the images sliding through my mind like a movie—a very erotic and explicit movie, causing my entire body to flush hot.

"And then I'm going to fill you so full of cum it's *leaking* down your legs, and that's exactly how you will sleep, Hayden."

"I will?" I ask him, my body trembling in his arms as we make it into the bathroom.

"You will. You'll sleep with your body completely full of my cum and your pussy and legs covered in it."

I swallow, my eyes closing, envisioning exactly what he said.

"Nothing to say to that, Beauty?" he asks, after standing me on my feet and reaching over to turn on the shower. My eyes pop open, sensing his fiery gaze on me. His eyes are appraising me, and I lick my lips, my body feeling like the slightest touch might send me over the edge.

"Umm... just one thing," I tell him, through a whole body tremble as he takes his cock in his hand and strokes it once.

"What's that?" he asks, but I've stopped watching him. My eyes are glued back to his massive cock, and I watch as a bead of pre-cum appears on the head.

I want to lick it. I want to taste him on my tongue. I almost fall to my knees on instinct, but he's so damn big I need him inside me again.

"Hurry, Michael," I answer honestly. "*Please*, hurry."

CHAPTER 78

Beast

I RUB THE back of my neck in irritation. I don't like being away from Hayden. Shit. The truth is it almost killed me to leave her today to meet with Victor Torasani. I came close to taking her with me. Diesel had sent some of his men to help out. The truth is, I don't know a fucking one of them, definitely not enough to trust them with Hayden. Then Crusher and Dani walked in. I've never been so glad to see two people before. I left him in charge of keeping them safe and told Dani to behave—which will be hard for her. Damn woman is a spitfire.

Still, here I am, waiting in a damn hotel suite, wishing I was back at Hayden's. I look around the room. One night in this fucker probably costs more than I've spent on hotels my entire life. Leather high backed couch, with matching chairs, plush carpeting with mahogany furniture, and crystal lamps and accents. I may have money—more than most would think from looking at me, but I'm not comfortable with this shit. I would rather be in Hayden's rundown house. I've been thinking on her house. It's not a bad place, with some work it has possibilities. I've been working on her porch, but I think it really needs an extension. If I add on to the back of the house, I can enlarge the bedroom and put a door in it that could lead to an outside patio. Hayden would like to sit out there and watch the sunrise…*or the stars.*

"I'm sorry to keep you waiting. I'm afraid I will have to keep our meeting short. I need to get back to the hospital. We've decided to terminate the machines today," Victor says, coming into the room. He sits down across from me as I digest his words.

"Hayden will want to be there."

"Is she yours?"

"She is."

"My wife, she thought a lot of her. Enough to ask me for a favor, when she vowed to never speak to me again," Victor says, and for a moment, he seems like he's lost in thought. I think he might be unaware he even spoke the words aloud.

I want to question him further about Charlie, but I don't. That's his business. I just need to make sure that Hayden is protected and Blade stops breathing air.

"Bring her to the hospital around five. I'll give her a few moments alone with Charlotte. I'm sure you understand I want to be the only one with my wife in the end."

I nod my head, yes, but I don't understand much of anything. Then again, it doesn't matter.

"About the Dwellers—" I start, only to have Victor interrupt me.

"I've neutralized their club. Unfortunately, I've been unable to find the waste of space called Blade. I did get a confession from one of his men that confirms he was the one that ran my wife off the road and shot her. His time is short."

"He can't be left unfound. He's a threat to Hayden."

"I'll deal with it."

"No offense, but my men tell me he's still on the loose this morning. I'm not waiting."

"He may be a threat to your woman, but he took Charlotte. His life is mine."

"Is Charlie...Charlotte the real reason you had protection over this town?"

"It is. My wife couldn't handle the...shall we say, the *business* side of my life. She put up with it, but she never fully understood. I did something she found unforgivable, and then I compounded my mistake and let her leave. I was a fool," he says and the weight of the guilt in his words reaches me.

I understand guilt and failure. Those are emotions that I'm old friends with. I probably understand Victor more than anyone. Still, it's not changing my stance.

"Blade is after Hayden. He's hurt her. He's left her afraid. I'm not sitting around and waiting for you, if I get my hands on him," I tell Victor, looking him straight in the eye. I need this ended now.

"I want to be the one to end him," Victor says, his voice hard. His hand even slightly shakes with his anger. It's probably the most emotion I've seen from the man since I met him.

"So do I."

"You still have your woman. This filth took mine. It is my right. Anything less would make me appear weak, and a man does not live to be my age by being weak, Mr. Jameson."

I cringe at the use of my surname. It doesn't surprise me he knows it, I just don't particularly like it. I'm having a hard enough time getting used to being Michael after all this time. I scratch my beard, letting my thumb seek out the indention of the scar underneath.

"If I get him, I'll end him. It's simple as that. I can't allow a threat to Hayden to live, even if you have certain rights."

"Your...Hayden. She's pregnant, correct? My men tell me the child is this Blade's."

"Hayden and the child are innocent. You will not use them to lure the man to you. I will kill you first," I growl, everything inside of me going cold at his words. I'll rip him apart limb by limb if I have to. No one will hurt Hayden or Maggie. If I have to take on the Torasani syndicate, I will.

"Calm down, Michael. May I call you Michael?" he asks, and I grunt in reply. He apparently takes that as acceptance. "I would not harm Hayden or her child. Charlie's last words to me were that she'd do anything to keep them safe. I will make sure they are. All I meant was that I don't think you want to be the man to put a bullet and end the life of the child's father. I don't think that's a burden you need to carry, nor something you want the child to find out later in life. Because trust me, our sins always find the light of day."

I go over what he said in my mind. I don't like it. I hate it. The truth of what he said is presently sitting in my gut like lead weight and it's burning. Only, it has nothing to do with the fact that he's trying to deny me the pleasure of ending Blade's life. It's more elemental than that. I don't like that he referred to Maggie as Blade's child. *Fucking hell.*

"If I find him and you're not available, he's not polluting the air a second longer," I growl, giving in, but not sure why.

"Fair enough."

It takes me a few minutes to get out of there. My mind is racing. I need time to think. I need to figure out what's happening here. I need to get...control.

Fuck.

CHAPTER 79

Hayden

"So…"

"Yeah?" I look over at the stick-thin, just walked off a fashion show, runway model staring at me across my old kitchen table. I want to like her. I don't think I do. She's loud, but that's not why. She's beautiful, and even though that's intimidating, that's not even why. The reason is simple. I heard Michael call her Hummingbird and I watched him hug her—*affectionately*. Now I'm trying really hard not to hate her.

"You and Beast do the mattress mambo yet?" she asks, with a grin on her face that I find myself wanting to slap off there. Her husband, a man Michael introduced as Crusher spits out his coffee.

"Hellcat, behave," he chastises. His face taking on a warning look. He's good looking, though definitely not in the same zip code as Michael. He's got dark hair, and his skin is a golden tan, but you can tell it's been warmed by hours in the sun. He's got weathered lines on his face that crinkle with a peace, even happiness when he looks at his wife. I wish for a moment that I could elicit the same kind of response from Michael.

"What, Zander? It was a simple question."

"One you don't have a right to ask."

"Beast is my friend. I have every right," she dismisses her husband's concerns.

"Is that all you are?" I find myself asking, and I can admit that jealousy is eating me alive.

"What are you asking?"

"Ladies, I think now would be a good time to—"

"Stay out of this, Zander. She's got questions, I think the least I can do is answer them."

"Jesus, Hellcat, quit stirring up drama. Don't you think Hayden has been through enough."

"I think Beast has been through enough. He needs a woman who is strong, who can help him heal."

"I don't need sympathy," I tell him at the same time Dani answers. Her answer makes me stop though. "You think I'm weak?"

"I think you're broken," she says with a frank honesty that I could almost admire.

"So? I'm still here," I tell her totally bluffing. I hate that she sees me as weak. I hate it because that's exactly how I see myself.

"But why I wonder? Are you here because you care about Beast or because you need someone to save you?" I can see it in her eyes that she genuinely cares for Michael, but that doesn't stop my jealousy.

"I didn't ask Michael or anyone to save me," I tell her, and I swear I think I grunt at the end which sounds a lot like Michael. I fold my arms over my stomach.

"Michael…" she says sounding confused and her face goes pale. "Beast's name is…*Michael?*" she gasps.

Her man curses under his breath and puts his arm around her, pulling her into his body. I don't understand what's going on. I think I should probably feel pity for Dani, because she looks like someone just killed her puppy or something. Instead, I'm mentally high-fiving myself because she didn't know Michael's name. It's a small victory, but still a victory.

"I guess you don't know everything about him," I mutter, unable to stop myself.

"I know if you hurt him, I'll make you sorry," Dani snaps back.

"I think that's about enough. Come on, Hellcat, I know you want to protect your friend, but Hayden is not the enemy," he says, leaning back in his chair.

"Thank you," I huff, wondering if he would still take up for me if I scratch his wife's eyes out.

"No problem. I mean, I think it's amazing you're willing to saddle yourself to an overgrown, hairy giant, who looks like he fell out of an ugly tree and hit every damn branch on the way down." He smirks, appearing so satisfied with his assessment of Michael.

Oh my god! Did he just say that? Suddenly my anger is turned from his wife to Crusher himself. Are these two on crack? I can't believe Michael took all the others with him, but decided these were the two he should leave me with. He obviously doesn't know how crazy they are. Maybe they're on drugs. That's the only explanation.

"Zander, I can't believe you said that," Dani says shaking her head. She has more color now too. Which is unfortunate, because she looks pretty again. I'd rather she be pale and at least not model-of-the-month pretty when Michael comes back.

"I can't either. There's nothing ugly about Michael," I bark, getting up to put my dishes in the sink. I don't think I want to sit and pretend to be friendly to his friends anymore. I'm pretty much thinking they're not his friends. No wonder all he does is grunt. *Who would waste time talking if these were the kind of people you had around you?*

"Come on now girls, he's so freaking big. Hell, he practically has to bend down and walk sideways to get through a damn door."

"You're exaggerating now. What are you up to?" Dani asks watching her husband and she's almost smiling. I decide to ignore her, I'm too upset over the way this man—who is supposed to be someone Michael trusts, is talking about him.

"He's not too tall. He's just right," I mutter. "I like that he's so tall. It makes me feel small and…safe," I continue, not realizing I've said that last part out loud.

"Well, okay, but you can't deny he's hairy. That man has so much hair he—"

"I like his hair too. And he let me trim it and you can definitely see his eyes now and how they twinkle when he laughs. Besides he's got beautiful hair," I lament remembering Michael's laugh, as I rinse my dishes in the sink.

"You make him laugh?" that comes from Dani, and I like that she sounds surprised.

Score! Another point for me.

"Well, I guess keeping his hair long is good. I mean it covers all those scars. Those can't be easy for a woman to look at all day," Crusher says and that's enough.

I'm holding my cup in my hand and I'm fed up. I spin around and throw it at him, wishing it was one of the heavier ones instead of being lightweight and some useless metal. "I think that's enough. Michael is supposed to be your friend. He's been nothing but nice to both of you, and I won't allow anyone in *our* home talking badly about him."

"*Our* home?" he asks, holding the cup—which unfortunately he caught. He's also got this look on his face that says he may laugh at any moment, and he and Dani are both smiling.

I think I hate them. I want them out of here. Michael doesn't need people like this in his life. No wonder he's so closed off at times. "Exactly and you will not talk about him like you have been. Michael is beautiful, he's kind, caring and he's a real man."

"A real man?" Crusher asks, and this time, he does laugh—*the asshole.*

"Yes! He doesn't need to belittle someone about the way they look, so he can feel better about himself," I growl, and this time, Dani laughs.

"She's got you there, Cowboy," she giggles. *Giggles!*

"I wasn't belittling him, whatever the hell that is. I was just simply stating facts. He *is* covered in scars," he returns, and now I get the feeling he's watching me closely. *Good.* Let him, because once I tell him off, I want him out the door. I won't have Michael hurt by his stupidity.

"I like his scars."

"You—"

I cut the man off before he can continue. "I like his scars. They're a part of him. They show that he endured something horrific, but he is still alive. They show he's strong, and tested by the world. They show he is a survivor. He's someone you should admire and be glad to call a friend, not put down. He's more man than you'll ever hope to be."

"Damn," Crusher says, and when I force myself to look up at him, I'm surprised. I see his face is in shock, but more than that, I see…respect.

"I guess she told you, Cowboy. I like you, Hayden. I think you'll be perfect for Beast," she says, surprising me.

"Gee thanks. I don't think I like you," I mutter, annoyed that she still looks beautiful. About the only mark she has against her is her attitude—which sucks, and part of her finger is missing on one hand, and I kind of feel like a bitch for thinking that makes her less beautiful. Great. *She's probably a better person than I am too.* "I'm going to go outside and check the laundry on the line," I huff, disgusted with myself and them too. I need fresh air—*away from them.*

"I'll come with you," Dani offers.

"I think I'd rather be alone," I tell her, honestly. I don't know what I expected, but her laughing wasn't exactly it.

"Then I'll stay here and help Zander find his balls," she snorts.

I pick up the old laundry basket by the pantry shelf and head toward the door.

"I'm all the man you need, Hellcat," he tells her, and even I can admit his voice sounds kind of sexy—*for an idiot.*

"For once, I can't argue with you, Cowboy. You're one hell of a man," she says, and I can hear them kiss as the door slams behind me.

They both need medication.

CHAPTER 80

Hayden

"MORNING, HAYDEN" I look up from pinning Michael's shirt on the clothesline to see Pastor Sturgill standing there smiling.

"Good morning, Pastor. You're early, I didn't expect to see you until later this evening," I tell him with a smile. I finish pinning the shirt to the line, and dry my hands on the sides of my pants.

"I came by to collect the baked goods you made for the yard sale," he says.

"I have them ready, Pastor. I thought that Michael and I were bringing them by this evening," I tell him, and I take the time to really look at him. He looks like he hasn't slept, his hair—which is always well-groomed even looks unkempt. Then again, he was friends with Charlie, all of this must be affecting him too.

"I did too," he says with a shrug. "But Michael called me at the church and asked me to swing by and pick them up. He said the two of you had plans for this evening," he answers, and I'm glad I turned around to go back inside while he was talking.

His words are completely innocent, but I can't help but blush. I remember what Michael and I did together last night. I really want more of that. *Is that why Michael called him?* The thought makes me smile as I make it to the steps.

"Well, I want to see Charlie later, once evening visiting hours begin, so maybe he is just planning ahead," I tell him.

"Probably. I'm sorry that you had to worry about fixing items for the church. I probably should have canceled the sale, but so many depend on the good that the church does. It wouldn't be possible without our fundraisers."

"It's no problem, Pastor. I promise," I tell him, turning around. I don't want him to feel guilty. I'm glad he depends on me for help. I owe him and Charlie a lot for saving me. "Besides, I was nervous and upset. Baking helps me. Do you know if there has been an update on Charlie?"

"Not that I've heard. I actually was just about to drive by there and check on her. Would you like to go with me?"

"I don't think that's a good idea," Crusher interjects, standing on the top step by the door. Dani is behind him, standing at the screen door. I had almost forgotten how annoying they can be.

"Actually, I really would like to go. Are you sure I wouldn't be in the way, Pastor?" I interject, mostly irritated.

"Of course not. You know I always love our rides together, Hayden," he admonishes.

"Beast said you leave this house with no one but him, or without his orders. That means you stay right here, Hayden," Crusher adds, and really, I get that Michael wants to protect me, but this man is just an asshole. Would Michael have left me with him if he knew how much he enjoyed putting Michael down? I'd prefer to be around the Pastor.

"I'm sure he didn't mean Pastor Sturgill. He's a friend. I

travel with him all the time," I argue, unable to keep my aggravation out of my voice.

"I'm just as positive that it includes the Pastor," Crusher maintains, crossing his arms against his chest, like his words are final.

"Whatever," I mutter. "If you give me just a minute, Pastor, I'll get the baked goods." I walk up the steps, giving Crusher a mean look. "Do you mind?" I ask him, when it doesn't seem like he's going to let me by. Then he does, and I huff past his wife to go to the fridge. I take the container out. It's kind of huge, because I did get carried away baking. I wasn't kidding when I told the Pastor that baking helps me when I'm upset. When I turn around Crusher and Dani are standing between me and the Pastor as if they are protecting me. These two are so weird. I do my best to plaster on a smile, then I take the food to him. "Here you go, Pastor."

"You baked so much, Hayden, there's no way the church paid you enough this time," he says, peering through the plastic cover to look upon all the goods inside.

"You're always more than generous," I tell him. "The church is lucky to have you."

"I've only been with the church for about five months now, but I'm starting to find my footing," he answers with a smile.

That surprises me. I assumed he had been here much longer. I guess we must have gotten into town about the same time.

"If you will carry these, I'll just get the box of cookies I have on the freezer and follow you out," I tell him. Before I can get the cookies, Crusher walks in front of me and does it.

"I'll take them out. You stay in here, with Dani," Crusher says. His face is tight and he looks nothing like the lunatic who was laughing and annoying me about Michael. In truth, he's got a very serious vibe about him right now. I look over at Dani and

I can even see tension there. Does he sense danger? I'm not sure what's going on, but my gut tells me to hang back.

"Fine. I'll see you this afternoon, Pastor."

"This afternoon?" he asks, and he looks rattled. Of course, why wouldn't he with the way Crusher is acting. I really need to talk to Michael about him.

"I'm sure you'll be at the hospital when we come by," I remind him, and he nods his head.

"Oh. Yeah, I'll probably be there," he says, and he looks upset. Before I can question him about it, he and Crusher leave the kitchen. The screen door slams behind them, leaving me alone with the beauty queen, Dani.

Just great.

CHAPTER 81

Hayden

"THEY SURE GROW tall preachers in this town," Dani mutters. Crusher followed the Pastor outside and I'm stuck in the kitchen with her.

"He's not real tall," I argue, but he is. He's shorter than Beast, but then most people are.

"He is. He's taller than Zander, though not by much. He just doesn't seem like the preacher type."

"Do preachers have a type?" I ask her, at least glad she's not talking about Michael anymore.

"He just seems too laid back and he struts. I think I could see him in a bar, drinking a beer and shooting pool."

"I don't think the Pastor drinks. I think that goes against his beliefs. I've never seen him drink."

"I'm just saying, he gives off that vibe. You don't see it?" Her eyes crinkle at the corners while she waits for me to argue.

I shrug, put off by her assessment of Pastor Sturgill. "I've never really thought about it. He's been nice to me." He has been so good about helping me. Buying my baked goods, giving me rides. He's been good to me.

"Hmm..." she muses.

"Whatever. Shouldn't it be about time for Michael to come back?" I try changing the subject. I don't like the bad feelings she is putting in my head about the Pastor, he's my friend.

"Are you wanting to get rid of me and Zander?"

"Whatever gave you that idea?" I respond, and I can't keep the sarcastic tone out of my voice. Dani has to have heard it, but instead of getting mad she laughs.

"Okay, okay, your claws can go back in. I admit that I'm a bitch."

"At least you own up to it," I mutter.

"I do. It's just Beast was really decent to me at a time when I was hurting. He's a special person and he's been through so much pain. I wanted to make sure whoever he finally chose to take a chance on...realized they were getting a great man."

My eyes soften on her. "You think he wants to take a chance...on *me*?"

"I absolutely do. I don't think he'd be here if he didn't. I know he wouldn't be so protective of you," she says, and I search her face, wanting desperately to believe her.

"He's just trying to protect the baby. Michael is a good person. He just wants Maggie safe."

"Maybe, but he also wants Maggie's mother," she grins.

"I don't think—"

"His eyes follow you, constantly. You said you made him laugh. Beast doesn't laugh. I've known him for years now, and I've never heard him laugh, Hayden."

"Years?" I ask shocked. The thought of Michael never knowing joy, of having been without happiness for years hurts my heart.

"Years," she confirms and it's probably pregnancy hormones, but I feel the tears gathering in my eyes.

"He loved Annabelle so much," I whisper, feeling a tear fall.

"He told you about Annabelle?" Dani asks, her voice sharper than before.

"Not a lot, but from what he said, I knew he loved her completely."

"Well of course he would."

"Yeah—"

"Hayden, I'll need you to come with me," the Pastor interrupts, pushing through the door so loudly that I jump when it slams against the wall on the inward swing.

"Pastor Sturgill? Is something wrong?" I ask alarmed, wondering what on earth is happening.

He's got the strangest look on his face. It's full of anger...and maybe fear. Sweat is beading across his forehead.

"Where's Zander?" Dani yells, moving back away from the Pastor and taking me with her.

"He's fine. He's just outside. I need you to come with me, Hayden. We must hurry now," he urges.

"Why?" I question him, once more.

"Why didn't Zander come back in with you?" Dani asks too, and I'm getting a really bad feeling about all of this—about him.

"Let's go, Hayden," the Pastor says again, and his voice goes harder.

"She's not going anywhere with you!" Dani reiterates, her voice going high.

"She is," the Pastor says, and he takes the few steps toward us and reaches out to grab my hand.

Dani moves really fast and barrels into the Pastor, knocking him down.

"Run, Hayden!" she cries, but if she thinks I'm going to leave her alone, she's crazy.

Ignoring her plea, I instead try and pull her with me. The

Pastor was momentarily stunned by Dani's surprise attack, but he recovers quickly. He grabs her by the hair and throws her away from him. She lands hard, crashing against the sink. Shit. Shit. *Shit.*

I grab Dani, who seems dazed from the hit she took, pulling her with me, even as the Pastor advances on us. I need to quit calling him Pastor…I have a very bad feeling that he's not a pastor at all. I don't know who he is, but I'm thinking he's not good—and I mean *really* not good. He grabs me by the hair, yanking my head back and pulling me away from Dani.

"Run Dani!" I urge her, "Go find help!" the (fake) Pastor, tightens his hold. I cry out from the pain.

Dani has grabbed a skillet that Michael used this morning to fry bacon in, and charges at him. I let my body go slack so that when he yanks at me, I fall back against him, surprising him. Dani connects with the skillet at almost the same time I bring my hand back and connect with his balls. He lets out a guttural yell but he goes down. He hasn't let go of my hair though and no matter how hard I try I can't get away from him. I fall backwards into him.

"You fucking bitch!" he cries out.

"Does that sound like something a preacher should be saying?" Dani yells and she comes at him again with the skillet.

I shuffle to get up now that he's let go of me. I stand up, and I might accidently on purpose be pushing my knee into his manly area as I get up. He shoves me hard, to move me out of the way. I land on my side, with my hands wrapped around my stomach, right as Dani slams him again with the skillet.

Pastor Sturgill—or whoever the hell he is, goes out this time, falling against the floor, unconscious.

"Take that fucking-mother-fucker!" Dani exclaims out and spits on him for good measure. She's not looking so much like a beauty queen now, more like a wrestler from a Wrestle Mania cage fight.

The door slams open again, and I prepare for another battle, thinking I hope I get the skillet this time. When I look and see that it's Michael who comes through the door, I don't stop to think, I simply run to him. The minute I hit him, his arms go around me and his head burrows into the side of my neck.

Nothing has ever felt so good.

CHAPTER 82

Beast

IT'S THAT FEELING you get in the pit of your stomach and that burning at the back of your neck that makes you feel like something is wrong. The nervous jitters you get when you feel like time isn't on your side. It's all of those combined that tells you something is fucking wrong. That's the way I feel during the drive back to Hayden's. I find myself breaking the speed limit and racing to get to her. I'm so much on edge that I feel like I can't breathe. I knew I shouldn't have left her. I should have taken her with me to meet with Victor. If anything is actually wrong, I may kill Crusher.

I pull into the driveway and that feeling I have, only intensifies when I see the preacher's car in the driveway. I told him not to come around, that I was putting the house on lockdown. He kept whining about picking up some baked goods that Hayden baked for the church, and I even made it clear that I would drop them off this evening at the church—*myself.* Something about that asshole rubs me the wrong way and him being here is setting off a lot of internal alarms. I grab the gun I keep in the console, jumping out of the truck the minute I throw it into park. It rocks from the sudden stop, as I slam the truck door. I've only taken a couple of steps when I hear Hayden crying out as if in pain. I pick up my pace, running to the door. Out of the corner of my eye I see Crusher lying on the ground. *Fuck*. I grip the gun tighter, throw open the kitchen door, prepared to end that fucking preacher's life.

What I see throws me completely. There's Dani standing over the preacher, wielding a deadly looking…*skillet*. My eyes zero in on Hayden. I expect to find her in the corner, scared and maybe in the midst of a panic attack. Instead, she's standing there looking at me. Then she takes off towards me, literally jumping into my arms. The minute my arms wrap around her, the fear eases. I hold her close, burrowing my head into the side of her neck, taking in her scent, feeling her close to me. It calms me.

"What's going on, Beauty? Are you okay?" I ask her softly, still drinking her in.

Dani comes out of her trance though and drops the skillet with a large clang, as it lands on the wood floor.

"Where's Zander?" she sobs, and I remember I seen him laying outside.

"Fuck," I growl, letting go of Hayden—mostly. I'm still holding her hand. One more quick glance at the preacher tells me he's out. "He's outside," I tell her, and we walk out there to find him. "Stay right here," I order Hayden when we make it outside, insisting she stay at my side. If there are any further surprises in store, I want her at arm's length. I squat down and check Crusher for injuries. There's no obvious wound. But I can see a swelling on the side of his head. My best guess would be he was knocked out with something.

"Zander, honey," Dani says, touching his face and lifting him up. "Cowboy, are you okay?" she questions. Putting his face in her lap as she manages to slide under him.

"Let's get him loaded in my truck and take him to the hospital," I tell her.

"We should call an ambulance," Dani argues.

"As slow as they are, Michael could have him at the hospital sooner," Hayden says, mirroring my thoughts. I stand up, getting ready to bend down and pick Crusher up when he moans.

"Thank God," Dani whispers, her tears dropping down on Crusher's face almost as fast as she tries to wipe them off it.

"Quit crying, Hellcat, it takes something harder than a fucking rock to bust my head open," he mutters, sitting up and holding his head. "Tell me you put a bullet in that sack of shit."

"Not yet," I tell him. "Your girl knocked him on his ass."

"That's my woman," Crusher says proudly, even while in pain.

"I had help. Hayden wouldn't run even when I told her to," Dani says, going into Crusher's hold, hugging his side.

I look over at Hayden and I might be glad she didn't give into a panic attack, but right now I'm pissed.

"You should have run."

"What? I couldn't leave Dani alone to face him, Michael," she says, her eyes wide with surprise.

"You could and you should have. You needed to take care of Maggie."

"I do take care of Maggie, but I wasn't leaving Dani alone," she says stubbornly.

I grunt, because there's not much I can say to that.

I sigh, changing the subject. "We need to figure out what to do with the preacher."

"I don't think he's a preacher, Michael," Hayden whispers, and Crusher almost laughs, but his pain makes the sound into something else.

"What are we going to do with him?" Dani asks, moving her hand delicately over Crusher's wound.

"I'll call Victor. I got a feeling he'll lead us to Blade."

"He's how Blade knew about Maggie and why I called her a girl…" Hayden says, quietly, more to herself than to the rest of us.

I don't answer, instead helping Crusher get to his feet. Then I capture Hayden's hand. There's really nothing to say in response, because I'd lay odds that she's right. There's a connection between the *would be* preacher and Blade.

I feel it.

CHAPTER 83

Hayden

"I OWE CHARLIE so much, Michael. What if she doesn't know how much I loved her? I thanked her, and she knew I cared about her, but I can't remember ever telling her I loved her. I should have done that. I should have," I whisper against his skin.

It's late. Probably close to midnight. Michael and I are lying in bed after an exhausting—both physically *and* emotionally—day. All the lights are out in the house and the moon shining through the bedroom window is the only light visible. The house is quiet. Dani and Crusher are spending the night in Michael's barn, but there's two other men in the house. Michael said they were part of Diesel's crew. They seem nice enough. It's still hard for me at times to get used to having other people in my home. Tonight, after we came back from the hospital—the hospital where I had to say goodbye to Charlie, there was a point I had to fight down a panic attack. We picked up a bucket of chicken and sides from town and my small kitchen with Michael and two other men in it, seemed to get smaller. They were talking and laughing with each other, and I was busy trying not to freak out and embarrass Michael. I tried to hide it, but Michael was watching me like a hawk. He didn't say anything, but I know he saw. He grabbed our plates and ordered me to follow him into the bedroom where we ate on the floor in silence. I hate that I can't be stronger for him. I really am trying. I'm getting better…*most days.*

"She knew, Beauty. She never told you either, but you knew, right?" he whispers back. He's got my hand in his, and his thumb is brushing back and forth against the inside of my palm.

"I knew," I tell him, closing my eyes and letting a few silent tears escape. I've cried so much tonight. I don't want to give into another crying jag. Poor Michael has had to endure my tears most of the evening.

Michael turns onto his side and pulls me even closer into him. He kisses my forehead, while wrapping his hand in my hair, letting my head rest on his shoulder. "Come on, Beauty. She wouldn't want you hurting like this. She wanted you happy. She made Victor promise to protect you from the moment she first met you. You need to make sure you honor that and actually *be* happy," he says.

I think over his words, and I know he's right, but there's just not a lot to be happy about tonight. "Do you think she blames me, Michael?"

"Blames you?"

"If it wasn't for me, she'd still be alive," I tell him, my confession is quiet, shaky and full of guilt.

"That's bullshit. You are not to blame for that," he rumbles, his voice vibrating in the darkness full of emotion. "That son of a bitch Blade is the only person to blame for this. He's the one person who needs to feel the guilt. He needs to choke on it, right before he takes his last breath," he adds, and his words are harsh and full of anger. They could almost scare me.

"Michael, you don't—"

"He's going to die, Hayden. His fate is sealed. If I don't do it, Victor will. It's just a matter of time."

I don't know what to say in response to that, not really. Anything I could say would make me a hypocrite, or make me sound like a horrible human being. So, I don't respond, at least not for a few minutes. I think back over the night and the pain that I saw etched on Victor Torasani's face. He loved Charlie. She always spoke of her ex and how she missed him, I mostly assumed he had died, so meeting Victor was a shock.

"It's sad really, if you think about it," I say mostly to myself, as visions of the way Victor held Charlie's hand when I left the room come back to mind.

"What's that, Beauty?"

"He was in love with her. What would it be like to have someone that meant the world to you, that you loved even into your old age, and yet not be able to make it work?"

"I'm not the person to ask about that," he answers, cryptically.

"Why? You don't believe in love?"

"No. I know love is real. It's just people always manage to fuck it up…*to fail*."

"I know I did," I confess.

"What do you mean?"

"Michael, you can't fail any more than I already have with Maggie."

He reaches over and turns the bedside light on. Then, pushing his pillows against his back, he sits up, leaning against the headboard and looks at me. He does all this while I'm blinking, still trying to adjust to the light.

"Explain what you mean with that shit, Hayden," he demands, and the anger in his voice can't be mistaken, but this time I think it might be directed at me.

Oh boy.

CHAPTER 84

Beast

"I THINK IT'S pretty self-explanatory," Hayden says with a wistful breath, looking up at the ceiling.

It's been a fucking exhausting day. From the shit with the fucking preacher, to watching Hayden grieve over Charlie, all of it has just made this day get worse and worse… and it's not finished.

After Hayden goes to sleep, I still need to meet Victor at what's left of Blade's club. That's where he had the preacher taken to, and I'm supposed to help interrogate him. Who knows what fucked-up shit I will learn there. Jesus, and to think I came to North Carolina for quiet. Hell, I came to North Carolina to die. It took one woman to fuck all that up. *One beautiful, amazing, very pregnant woman.*

"Not to me."

"Look at me, Michael. I'm a mess. I go into full meltdown mode without warning. I got someone I cared about killed—"

"That wasn't you, Hayden."

"It was *because of me*, and no matter how much you deny that, it won't change the truth. Even you, Michael. You came here and you don't have to be real smart to figure out you wanted to be left alone, and look what I've dragged you into? What kind of mess will I be bringing Maggie into? How am I supposed to protect her, when I can't protect anyone else I care about?"

"Does that mean you care about me?" I ask her, like a stupid fool, grabbing hold of the only thing that matters to me in all of what she said.

"Really?" she asks, her head jerking up to look at me. "You're going to ask me that?"

"I want to know," I tell her, avoiding her eyes. It would make me look like a sad-fuck who was addicted to her pussy if she knew how important her answer is to me. *Shit, that's exactly what I am.* I should be helping her grieve the loss of her friend, holding her until she sleeps, and instead, I'm lying here with my dick half hard, wondering if I could get away with burying my head between her legs.

"Of course, I care about you. I slept with you, Michael."

"That's not exactly a requirement for most people, Hayden."

"It is for me."

"You slept with Blade," I remind her, the words out of my mouth before I can stop them. When her body tenses against mine, I realize it's a mistake I'm going to regret even more.

"I told you, I cared about Blade at first. I never would have slept with him if I hadn't. I was… young and stupid."

"Apparently," I breathe out, tired of hearing how she cared about this asshole. He's a waste of space, a sorry excuse for air, and I cannot for the life of me figure out how she ever gave him the time of day. Hayden is so much better than him. *Jesus*, she's so much better than *me*.

Hayden gets out of bed and looks at me. She's wearing one of my shirts and this one comes down past her knees. The short sleeves fall half-way down on her arm. Her hair is ruffled and flowing around her face and down past her shoulders. It's probably the wrong time to admire how truly beautiful she is.

"What is it you want to hear from me, Michael? Do you want to hear the whole sordid story? Will that somehow make you understand? Because I warn you, Michael, it's not pretty and I'm not even sure I understand, and I *lived* the whole damn story. *I lived it,* and it sure as hell doesn't make it better for me." I really should stop her.

It shouldn't matter, and mostly it doesn't. But, I'm a bastard and I find I have to know. So, even knowing I may regret pushing her further, I don't stop. "Tell me."

CHAPTER 85

Hayden

"I COULD HATE you right now," I whisper, turning away from him. If I'm going to tell this story, I can't do it looking at him. I don't have that much courage. Will it change how he sees me? Will he leave? When he finds out how stupid I am…*was*…*how stupid I was*—will he want nothing more to do with me? *With Maggie?*

I walk to the window. I stare up at the moon and use the next few minutes to try and bring order to my chaotic thoughts. I close my eyes and try to breathe, knowing this will hurt. For so long, I've dealt with memories and nightmares, but I beat them down. I didn't want to remember. I didn't want to relive that time. I ran from Blade and the Dwellers, but I also ran from the person I was. Can I make Michael understand that? It's so important I reach him. He didn't know I cared about him? *I care too much.*

"Hayden?" Michael asks, his voice softer, and I think I hear a trace of regret.

I want to beg him to just let it go, but I don't. I need to get this out, if only to know for sure if Michael isn't the man I hope he is.

"At first, when I learned that my brother had sold me to the Dwellers, I didn't understand. This is America, right? These things don't happen. We have laws. I have rights. It didn't take long before I realized that I had nothing. My brother used me to try and save his own skin. I was a payment—nothing more, nothing less."

"Hayden, it's okay you don't—"

"You wanted to know, might as well hear the whole story now, Michael," I answer, not taking the easy way out. "When you're sold into a club you have limited choices…mostly you have *no* choices. I was there to be a toy for the club. *A whore.* I was twenty-one, I had a total of one boyfriend in my past. Besides some limited making out, I'd never…I'd never been with a man. With the life I lived and what I saw with my mom, sex wasn't something I wanted. I never wanted to be…*her.* Which was kind of ironic, because that's exactly what the Dwellers wanted me to be—what they *made* me be."

"Damn it, Hayden!" Beast growls, but now I'm too deep into the memories to stop.

"I was terrified. They made no secret about what was going to happen. They took pleasure in delaying it. They put me in a metal cage in the middle of their bar, like I was some kind of animal. They made me watch what their whores would do, they wanted me to know what I was going to be doing. They tortured me with it."

"Fuck…" he rumbles, and I take a deep breath and continue on, hating the way my voice trembles.

"One night, some of the boys decided they had waited long enough. They pulled me out of the cage by the hair on my head. I fought. I kicked, slapped, punched, and scratched, but one small girl against three men, that's never going to be a fair fight.

They pulled me out and held me down, and I really thought that was it, I was out of options…Until I caught the eye of the man in charge," I tell Michael, and by now, I'm talking so quietly I'm not sure he can hear me. I can't bring myself to talk louder, however. "Blade ordered them to stop. He had me sent to his room and had some of the girls clean me up. They left me alone, and I tried to escape, I really did, Michael, but the door was locked and the window had bars on it. There was no escape. Blade came in a few hours later, and I didn't know what to expect—I was prepared for the worst, but he was…*nice*. We sat on the bed and talked. He told me his name and that he was the president of the club. I had no idea what that meant. I was so green." I breathe against the window and watch as the condensation forms, fogging up the glass. I let my finger trail through it as I relive the memories.

"He was blunt, telling me exactly what my brother did and how he couldn't pay his debts so offered me up in trade. He said that Jack—though he kept referring to him as Pistol, had got into some trouble and was trying to find protection to save him from a crime syndicate, though I don't think that's the words he used. I guess it doesn't matter. Bottom line, he sold me, and I was now Dweller's property. Normally, I'd be a club whore automatically, but he said that he liked me. He told me that he thought I was *special*," I confess with a small laugh full of bitterness.

"It was flattering. I've never been that type. The type to catch a man's eye from across the room, I mean. I thought it was a good thing, maybe it was. It kept me from being gang-raped by monsters." I sigh, take a deep breath, and decide to dive into the part that hurts the most. The part that shows clearly how stupid I am. "He told me I was beautiful. Something to be treasured, but his club would view him as weak if he didn't do something with me—he explained that's how his world worked. When he first told me that he wanted me to be a dancer, I didn't believe him. I didn't have the big breasts, the body that those type of women had."

"You're perfect, Beauty," I hear him say gruffly.

I don't turn around to look at him. To do so would mean I'd lose my nerve. "Turns out I had a knack for dancing. I was good at it, but then why wouldn't I be? I was my mother's daughter," I add, hatefully.

"Hayden—"

"I took what came natural, watched the other women, and I learned. At first, it was for survival, but then I noticed I was making Blade proud. He liked how the other men looked at me. He liked them getting turned on by me. It is kind of an aphrodisiac having men looking at you and thinking you're sexy and hot. I can't lie. Especially when it makes the one guy you like out of the whole place want you more. The more Blade seemed to like me, the more I wanted to learn. I needed to be the best dancer, to tease the others. Pathetic, right?" I ask him, risking a look in his direction.

His face is hard, it makes nervous butterflies take flight in my stomach, and not the good kind.

My body shudders as I take a quick breath. I turn away from Michael to look out the window once again. "The game went on for the first seven months or so. The other men didn't bother me. I wondered why, and when I asked Blade, he told me it was because he had claimed me as his property. At that point, we had kissed, but not much more. Yet, I was so glad to be called his, I stupidly asked him if I was. The club had given me a nickname by then, because of the way I could work the stripper's pole. *Tricks.* The whole club watched as Blade carried me to the bedroom and from that night on, the nickname took new meaning. Blade told them all the next morning I was officially his old lady and that my new name, Tricks was even more true in the bedroom. I was embarrassed, but I let it slide. Blade changed some after that, but he was always sweet to me and there were parts of being his old lady that I loved. I liked riding on the back of his bike, I liked how wearing his jacket made me feel and the respect it gave me. All of that was like a drug to a young girl who had been thrown down and forgotten about all her life. Looking back, there were always warning signs, that I didn't know the real man. I'd push those thoughts away though. I ignored them. *How could I be with someone for so long and not see the real person?* But I didn't. Not really. I began to think of it like he was two people. The man he showed his club, and the man who shared my bed every night. I told Blade that once, and maybe that was just another mistake, because he played into that. He told me what he did outside our room, in front of his club was all just for show, all to keep up his image that the club respected. He promised I was the only one he loved, the only one he shared his body with, the only one who saw the *real him*."

"Yeah, right." Michael snorts, and I can feel the shame surge through me.

"I warned you. I was stupid—I was naïve. I was also the laughingstock of the club, and I didn't even know it. What's worse is that whenever I would question it, Blade would carry me away from the club, fix me a drink and show me all the reasons I shouldn't worry. I thought we were perfect together, I didn't even realize he was drugging me." I can hear Michael's growl behind me and the bed move, but I ignore it. "I didn't catch on for a year… until I started realizing I was losing time. I couldn't remember the simplest of things I did the day before."

"Motherfucker. Damn it, Hayden…"

"It's not easy stopping drugs cold-turkey. It's even harder

trying to hide that you're doing it. I managed to though, and what I began to see scared me. It scared me so much that I began planning on how I could escape."

"That's enough, Hayden."

I ignore him yet again, continuing on…just wanting the story finished. "But even while planning on leaving, I didn't stop sleeping with Blade, Michael," I tell him and it's then that the tears start to fall. Maybe they were falling before, but I don't think so. Memories wash over me and that feeling that always comes with it…that feeling of being…*less*…of being *dirty* hits me. "I was scared of what would happen if I refused him. *Terrified.* Do you see, Michael? Do you see how truly weak I am? I let him crawl into bed with me, even knowing what kind of man he was. I let him touch me, I let him *inside* my body. It wasn't rape. I *let* him. I did everything he asked in the bedroom, just to keep him happy—all while trying to find a way to leave."

Memories hit me. Memories of Blade kissing me, of his hands moving over my body. The remembrances of the smell of alcohol on his breath and the horrible things he'd say to me, while he thrust inside of me.

"I let him have my body," I gasp, the tears falling harder. "Out of fear," I whisper, feeling broken. I let my head fall against the window. "He wasn't concerned that I was crying, didn't notice that I wasn't aroused…*he simply didn't care.*" My hand moves to my neck. I'm completely lost in the memories now. "I can still feel the way he would hold me, tightening his hand tighter and tighter, until I couldn't breathe. His laughter would get louder every time the panic took over and, I would dig my nails into his back, drawing blood. I can still remember how he would roll off me, light up a cigarette, pull up his pants and walk back out, never looking back. He'd laugh and tell the boys I was feeling extra wild tonight, and I'd lay in bed feeling used and dirty…." I drift off, for the moment I'm not able to speak, to give voice to the darkness inside of me.

"Shh…Hayden, no more," Michael says into my neck, as he comes up behind me, putting a hand on each of my arms. "That's enough, Beauty," he whispers gruffly, kissing the pulse that's pounding in my throat. *It's not enough, though.* I have to finish the whole story, because I never want him to ask me again.

Never again….

CHAPTER 86

Beast

I'M A FUCKING idiot. *A motherfucking idiot.* I never should have insisted Hayden tell me this shit. It doesn't matter. It wouldn't have mattered if she told me she was married to the asshole. I still would have claimed her as mine. There's no going back, there never was. Before Hayden, I was ready to die. Fuck, I wanted to die. I'm being a complete selfish prick, but Hayden makes life bearable. I'm keeping her. The only thing her telling me has done is ensure Blade's fate is a hell of a lot more painful.

"Michael," she cries, when I reach under the back of her legs and lift her up into my arms. "What are you doing?"

"I want you in our bed, with my arms around you," I scowl, my voice sounds angry, and I know she thinks it's directed at her. It's not, I'm angry at myself—not Hayden. I put her through hell, I should have left it alone. I lie down on the bed, taking her with me and settling her beside me. I hold her close and gently brush her tears away. I hate them, because they're my fault. She shouldn't have had to shed more tears, not after losing her friend tonight. She should never shed more tears because of that fucking prick Blade. Killing him will be a damn pleasure.

"I'm sorry, Beauty. Quit crying. It's over now. You'll never have to deal with him again. I promise you."

"You can't promise me that, Michael. He won't stop. Charlie is dead because of him and he'll keep trying until he succeeds. He warned me of that once. I should have listened," she whispers, her eyes downcast, refusing to look at me.

I put my hand under her chin and pull her face up, so that she doesn't have a choice but to look at me. "I can promise that. I'm going to kill him, Hayden. I'm going to make sure he never breathes the same air as you again. The only question left is how painful I make it."

"I don't want you to do that."

"Do you care what happens to him?" I ask, in disbelief.

"He's dangerous, Michael."

"He's a nuisance, a boy trying to prove he's a threat. He's nothing, Hayden. I promise you. Whatever you think he is, I'm capable of much worse."

"You're not. You could never be like him, not even at your worst. That's not who you are," she denies, vehemently. She shakes her head slightly to add weight to her claim. She doesn't really know me at all. Not the animal inside.

I should feel guilt, because I'm the man who helped bury her brother six feet under. Now, I only wish I was the one who killed him to begin with.

"I can be worse," I warn her, because she doesn't need to see me falsely. I want her to know the truth about me, I don't want to hide my past. It's me, even if I plan on never going back to it.

"Don't say that," she cries, and her body tenses up against me. I twist so my upper body is over hers, with about four inches of space between us. She reaches her hands up to hit my chest. "You are not like him. The man I've been sleeping with, the man who bought furniture for my daughter and has protected me, he is not evil."

"Hayden—"

Before I can try and calm her down, she reaches down and hooks my shirt she's wearing and whisks it over her head.

For a minute, I stare down at her confused, not sure what she's getting at. There's a vibe coming off of her that I don't like. It's a mixture of fear, hurt and anger.

"You wouldn't force a woman to stay with you. You wouldn't do that when she tried to leave because you promised her to your buddies!"

"Hayden, wouldn't do what? Promised you to…What are you talking about, Beauty?"

"The last three months at the Dwellers' clubhouse, Blade had been visiting my bed at night less and less. I wasn't being watched as closely. He was getting tired of me. I was planning my escape, I was taking my time, because I knew I'd only get one shot and if I failed, I would die. But, I heard him," she says, her body is shuddering underneath me, it's not because she's cold though. She's not in a panic attack, but the emotions are similar.

"Hayden, sweetheart, it doesn't matter anymore. It's over, I told you, you never have to go back there."

"He was in his office one night, bragging to his buddies about how he was going to take a new old lady. This one was supposed to be connected with some crime group he was getting involved with the Donnely's, or Donahues, something like that. According to him, she was everything I wasn't, and she would make him powerful. The men started joking, asking him what he was going to do about me."

"What did he tell them?" I ask, but then I already know. Blade's death is going to be so fucking painful it follows him into his next life.

"He gave me to them. Like I was a piece of meat. *She's still high from the drug I put in her drink. You boys can go have your fun now. She'll love anything you do to her. Hell, I might even join you. The more the merrier,*" she says, imitating his voice, or at least the ugliness behind it.

"What did you do, Beauty?"

"He thinks I didn't know, but I did, Michael. I knew I was pregnant and despite who Maggie's father was, I wanted my child. I've *always* wanted my child. I couldn't stay any longer. I had to risk it. So, I ran."

"But you didn't make it."

"I got outside. I made it to a small toolshed. My plan was to stay there, until they left to try and find me or to go into town. I had been watching and no one really used the building. There was a small room in the back and…I really thought I'd be safe in the closet. I thought I could hide there," she whispers. She's crying again, I pull her trembling body into me, situating her head on my chest. I hold her tightly, my hand clenching in her hair. I'll let her cry over this bastard one more time, but I swear this will be the last time.

"Finish the story, Hayden and then, it's gone. It ceases to exist for you, because he will cease to exist."

"Michael—"

"Finish the story, Beauty," I tell her quietly, as tenderly as I can, because I'm not a tender man. I don't have that left inside me.

She takes a deep breath, and lets it out slowly. "I heard the front door open. I couldn't see them from my hiding spot, but I heard them coming. I tried not to breathe, not to move. I prayed and prayed that they would give up."

"But they didn't," I finish for her, that one lone sentence so full of regret. If only Skull had sent me earlier. If only I had gotten to her before Blade had a chance to hurt her. *If only.*

"I was so frantic to get to safety, I didn't notice the mud on my shoes, or the tracks that I made…"

"That led them straight to you," I finish resignedly.

"There were three of them, so big in that small room, all towering over me. All laughing at me. I was defenseless."

"That's why you had the panic attack that day in your kitchen."

"That's why I have all my panic attacks, Michael…"

"Keep going. Telling me will help and then you will forget it."

"I'll never forget, Michael. It's always there."

I pull her head up to me and hold her so that she's looking straight into my eyes. I extend my thumb to swipe at the one lone tear that's making its way down her cheek. "You will forget, Beauty. I promise you that. It will be my mission in life to give you so many good memories, that the bad ones have no room to stay. I promise you. Do you hear me? I. Promise. You."

"Michael—"

"Shh…Tell me the rest. Finish the story so we can start putting it behind you," I urge her, wanting this done. She needs better memories. Happy ones. *Her and Maggie deserve happy memories.*

"Blade grabbed my leg and pulled me out of the closet. I tried to fight him, but I lost my balance. I fell back on the floor when he jerked extra hard. It was concrete and it left me dazed. Dog…he held my hands above my head. The other two held my legs and body still. Then Blade stood up. He was like someone else. I mean, logically I knew he wasn't the man I cared about in the beginning. I knew he was evil, but I had never seen this evil close up, not until that moment. He looked possessed, towering over me, hate pouring out of him, as his boot came down and landed against my side. He did it over and over. My legs, my back, my side, my head, anywhere he could find a good angle, he'd kick. I did my best to curl away from him or use my arms to cover my stomach. I really did, but I started to get dizzy and my vision blurred and everything was this weird gray hue. I knew I was going to die. I accepted it. I hurt for my baby, but there was nothing I could do. If I had told him about her, it would have been like delivering her to the Devil himself. I couldn't do that."

"What happened next?" I ask, when she goes quiet.

She reaches over, grabs my hand, and pulls it down to her hip bone. Slowly, she spreads my fingers out against the fine, spider-web like scars there. I had felt them before. Now, I could see them, though not perfectly with the pale light of the lamp, but I see enough of them to know that getting them would have been painful. A few of the ones have raised edges, showing they went deeper than the others. It's a miracle either her or Maggie survived.

"He took out his knife. At first, he pushed it into my neck, and I thought he was going to kill me. I mentally prepared myself for it when he pushed his knife just deep enough to make the blood flow. He laughed as I cried out in pain, and I hated myself for giving him that. He spat on me, sneering how only he could decide when he was done with his property. I told him I wasn't his property anymore, that he lost that when he decided to drug me. I told him I'd rather be dead than to spend one more night breathing the same air as him," she murmurs. "Which probably wasn't that smart to tell him, but it was honest, and by that time, I really just wanted it all over. I was barely conscious. I knew all hope was gone. I was just so tired…"

"Finish it," I urge her again, but God help me, I'm just one step away from leaving to hunt down that fucking sack of shit, and tear his skin from his body, one piece at a time.

"He began sliding the knife into me, not very deep at first, but over and over in the same spots and getting a little deeper each time. I began fading in and out. Before I went out completely, I heard him tell Dog to kill me and make a lesson of me for everyone to see. Then, he wanted them to leave me where my body would be found."

"I'm going to kill him slowly—one piece at a time," I growl, my insides feeling raw, and my hands shaking with fury.

"No. You can't."

"Why?" I all but howl. It doesn't matter what she says. I'm doing it. There's nothing she can say that will change my mind.

"I don't want you to be the one to kill Maggie's father. I never want her to look at you and see the man who ended the life of the father she never met. Even if he's a horrible man, Maggie might always wonder. I don't want her to look at you and resent you…"

There's a lot to take in there. Most notably that whether she realizes it or not, Hayden sees me in her future. But, on the heels of that discovery—which I like more than I should, there's another. And this one makes me want to scream. This one burns inside of me and I need to obliterate it.

"He is not Maggie's father," I tell her, sliding down on the bed.

"I may not like it, but—"

"He's not her father, Hayden," I interrupt her and I've had enough of hearing about Blade and enough of hearing about Hayden's past.

I've had enough talking.

CHAPTER 87

Beast

"MICHAEL," HAYDEN GASPS, as I shoulder between her legs. "I don't think now is the time for—" her protest dies mid-sentence when I place my lips against the small, raised edge of her biggest scar. I let my tongue run against it, as my hands brush against her warm skin, almost petting her thighs, before sliding my hands under her ass and kneading the flesh there, pulling her body closer.

"Always so fucking soft and receptive. You always want my touch, Hayden," I whisper, not bragging in the least. The fact that she wants me is always a surprise, a miracle. Something unexpected that I never thought I would find. Not something I've felt deserving of, but something I will take anyway. Something I will cherish.

"Michael. Oh God, what are you doing?" she asks, and my lips move into a smile against her thigh. I'm sliding my finger against her ass, pushing against it, though not going inside. Hayden is too green to understand it, but she loves having her ass played with. When I finally take her there, she will detonate into a million pieces.

"Making you feel good, Beauty," I murmur, kissing a path down to her center. "Always making you feel good," I add, without realizing it, intoxicated by the scent of her excitement. I pull the lips of her pussy apart and for a minute simply look at the treasure beneath. Her clit has already swollen, and it flutters with need, visibly pulsating. I run my tongue over it, dragging it through her sweet juices. Maybe it's the pregnancy, but Hayden is always so ready for me. Jesus, she's one step away from the edge now. I could make her come so easily. That's not what this is about though.

Her fingers tangle into my hair and she pulls my face into her hot little pussy. Her legs widen as she grinds up against me. In reward, I push a finger inside of her, sliding it in along with my tongue. Her body trembles as the heels of her feet push against my back. I angle my finger so I can put my thumb against her clit, rubbing it roughly. She's so wet she's drowning me in her cum. The harder I flick my tongue inside her tight cunt, the more that sweet juice flows. I feel her jerking against me, and her cries are getting louder. Her hands in my hair are so fucking wild it's almost painful. She's close to going over the edge. I pull away, despite the way she yanks on my head trying to pull me back—which makes me grin. Hayden completely loses herself in passion. *I fucking love it.* I'm so hard though, I need inside of her. I want to make a few things clear to her. I *need* to make them clear. I can't resist sucking her clit into my mouth and playfully biting it, which causes her to scream out my name.

"Michael! Oh God, please! Baby, don't stop!" she cries. "It feels so good." I let her clit go with a soft *plopping* noise. "Michael," she whimpers again when I leave her.

I shift my body, sliding my sweats off my hips. I don't take the time to undress completely, because as much as she needs me, I think I need inside her more.

I position myself at her entrance, holding my dick so only the tip is pushed against her opening. I slide in slightly. Her walls raking against the head of my cock is enough to make me want to thrust all the way in, but I don't. I hold myself back, even though it's killing me.

"Hayden," I growl, because I'm on a razor's edge here, and I'm not sure how much I can hold back. Her head is rocking back and forth, as she does her best to push against my cock, urging me inside of her. "Look at me, Beauty," I command, making my voice even harsher than normal, because I need her to hear me.

"Michael," she all but whimpers, but her eyes find mine.

"We do this, Beauty and that baby inside of you is *mine*," I tell her, not wavering, not blinking. If I claim her body, I'm damn well claiming this child. I will not hear another person refer to fucking Blade as the father again. It will be me from this moment on. Hayden and Maggie...they will both be *mine*.

"Michael," she whispers, her eyes dilating more, her breath coming out choppy, and her body jerks with my demand.

"This doesn't go further until you agree, Hayden. I want you and Maggie. You're mine from this moment on." I feel like I'm standing on the edge of a cliff, waiting for her decision. Maybe I shouldn't give her the ultimatum, but it feels right. I need this from her.

Her eyes soften and her hand gently moves over my stomach. I'm prepared for her denial. I'm not sure what my next move will be, but I'm mentally preparing. That's when her hand reaches out to me. Her fingers wrap around mine tightly, as she links our hands. "Are you sure?" she whispers, but I see the hope in her eyes. It's shining like a beacon—like a fucking lighthouse showing me the way home after being lost at sea for a lifetime.

In this moment, I've never been surer.

I thrust inside her, slow and carefully. I bring my other hand to hers, stretching it out so the palm is flat. She leisurely does the same, her small, delicate hand flat against my much larger, scarred one. It looks wrong, but at the same time right. *Completely right.* Her fingers push between mine as I begin riding her body, keeping both our hands joined. My cock stretches her walls, raking against them, and the fit is tight even as wet as she is. *It feels like heaven.* I rock her slow and easy. This isn't about sex. Everything about this moment is *different* from anything I have ever shared with a woman. The world has ceased to exist outside of this room.

"I've never been more positive of anything in my life than I am of this, Beauty," I whisper, soothing away her concerns, pushing aside guilt that is trying to make its way to the surface. This moment isn't about the past, or me. This is about Hayden and Maggie, and what I want with them.

"Then, from this moment on," Hayden gasps, her body thrusting up to meet me, causing me to sink deeper inside of her than I've ever been. I want to stop, afraid I will hurt her, but she won't let me. She works her body with my cock, taking what she needs. It's beautiful. "You're Maggie's father. You. Are. *Mine*," she gasps, drawing out the last word as she climaxes. I feel her detonate, her pussy spasms against my shaft, taking me with her. My balls heat, going so impossibly tight that I groan, and then I come. Jet after jet of cum funnels inside her body, bathing her womb.

"Mine, Beauty. Feel me inside of you, painting you in my cum. You're mine," I tell her, claiming her lips, our tongues tangling in a kiss almost as intimate as our bodies. "Maggie is ours, now. Ours," I growl when we break apart for oxygen, and I empty myself completely inside her. I look into her eyes; they don't leave me. Tears are pooled in the corners and I watch as they slide down her cheeks.

"Ours," she agrees. "Maggie is *ours*, Michael."

CHAPTER 88

Beast

I LISTEN AS Hayden's breathing evens out, and I know she's asleep. The last thing I want to do is get out of this bed right now. I'd rather stay here, hold her and forget the outside world. However, I know that's not an option. Hayden hasn't asked about the preacher, which surprises me a little. Maybe her time with the Dwellers taught her it's better not to know. Shit, maybe she'd just rather *not* know what is going to happen. Either way, it works good for me, because it's not something I want to discuss with her. I can't help but find it ironic that the harder I run from my old life, the faster it seems to find me.

Slowly, I stand, getting dressed as quietly as I can. Looking down at Hayden, her hair is messy and ruffled around her head and shoulders, the moon is shining through the window and it highlights the different shades and colors in her hair—strawberry, caramel, and dark blonde…all combining to be beautiful. Her face is delicate and soft in sleep, and her lips are swollen from earlier. I can't resist bending down to place a kiss on her forehead.

She makes a sound somewhere between a sigh and a moan,

stretches, and then she whispers, "Michael." My name on her lips, while she is asleep. That does something strange to me. *Hell*, a woman like Hayden whispering your name while she's sleeping? That would do something to any man with a pulse. It's not *any* man though. *It's me.*

With a sigh, I leave her. I know the sooner I leave the sooner I will return. I don't like leaving her alone—not with Blade still on the loose somewhere. Victor might have neutralized the Dwellers, but he left one snake alive in the nest. I want him dead. There is only one way to kill a snake—you cut off the head. I walk into the living room, shoving my arms through the sleeves of my jacket.

"You don't let anyone in here except Crusher and Dani. I don't care if they say they are the damn Pope," I order them. Most of Diesel's men have gone back. Crusher and Dani are at the barn, and Crusher chose two of what he says are his best men to stay in the house with me and Hayden—Devil and Ice. There's one other man watching the outside of the house.

"Got it. Shoot first, ask questions never," Ice says with a shrug.

"Exactly. I'm headed to meet up with Torasani." I turn around, thinking just to be safe I'll wake Crusher up and send him over here. I'd feel better if he stayed close to Hayden—even if the fucker managed to get himself knocked unconscious last time.

"Don't you think it'd be better if you had someone with you? Someone to help watch your back?" Ice adds.

"Just keep Hayden safe. That's all that matters," I tell him, not bothering to look back, dismissing both of them from thought, my mind already on what is ahead.

"No offense, but if you head out alone and end up buzzard bait, you won't do that girl in there a bit of good," Devil says.

I turn around to look at him.

Actually, out of all of Diesel's men I have to say these two are good. They're no nonsense, and no drama. They look completely opposite of one another. Both are probably in their early thirties, but that is where the similarities end. Ice is blonde with bright blue eyes. He's bulked up and ripped as hell, but he's probably five foot ten, maybe eleven. He looks like he'd be more at home in a suit than leather. He's almost too pretty, if I hadn't been watching him closely the last twenty-four hours, I'd say he's just playing biker to piss off his rich father.

Devil, on the other hand, probably stands around six foot three or four. He's got green eyes and dark brown hair, cut short on his head, with a beard that looks more like he's forgotten to shave for a few days. He's tall and lean, but something about the way he carries himself tells me he could take almost anyone in a fight. He looks like he was born into this life—*much like me.* I wonder if it will chew him up and spit him out, because that's sure sums up what I feel like these days.

"I don't need a babysitter," I mumble, annoyed.

"Maybe not, but Devil has a point. Besides, I got Trace outside watching the perimeter. Between me, him and Crusher, we've got this. That asshole shows up anywhere around here, he's dead. He knows it. He won't chance it. Fuck, I'd lay odds that he's half way to Mexico right now," Ice adds.

"Never underestimate stupid," I warn him. "Let's go if we're going, I need this shit done, and you better not get in my way," I growl to Devil, giving in.

"They warned me you shit sunshine and fart rainbows," Devil mutters, passing me to go outside to his bike.

I grunt in response, I could *almost* like him.

You can bet I'm going to wake Crusher up on my way for sure now. If I can't stay in bed and enjoy Hayden's body, he sure isn't getting to play with Dani.

CHAPTER 89

Beast

IT'S CLOSE TO two in the morning by the time we make it to the Dwellers. Being here makes me sick. Even the air seems to stink in this place, as if Mother Nature knows what kind of filth lived here.

"Damn, this place is a real shithole," Devil says when we pull up to the clubhouse and shut off our bikes.

The parking area is hard-packed earth with stray gravel here and there. You could almost choke on the dust—even with the dew on the ground. The outside of the building is covered in mismatched green and brown tin. It's been slapped up and cut at angles that don't line up with other pieces. They're just butted against each other without care or thought. There are few windows in the building. The ones that are there look like antique, wooden ones. The glass is clouded and foggy in appearance. It's either from weather allowing condensation to slip between the panes, or years of filth. It might be a mixture of both. Trash is littered around the building. Everything from beer cans and liquor bottles to remnants of fast food containers. Clearly, the Dwellers lived up to their filth in all aspects of their lives.

It's harder than hell for me to imagine Hayden here among this shit. Maybe this is why she cleans all the time. Hell, I once caught her sweeping the fucking ground around her front steps—as if she was trying to make the dirt clean. If you were forced to live in this, that would explain the need to be clean now.

I walk from my bike to the front doors. There's two steel doors at the entrance and in front of those are two men almost as big as I am—but dressed in suits. Apparently, even Victor's henchmen have to dress up to his standards. In my peripheral vision, I can see a small building and I know intuitively that it is the place Hayden tried to hide. A fine tremble runs through my body, causing my hand to shake. I clench it into a fist to disguise it.

"Your name?" one of the men asks. He's a fucking giant. I might be taller, but this guy is *definitely* wider. One of his forearms is wider than both of my thighs together. I've never thought twice about taking another man on. I've never actually met a man I couldn't take down. He makes me wonder if it's possible.

"I figure you already know. Victor is expecting me," I grumble, refusing to play the game.

The man looks at his partner, then speaks into a handheld radio. "Yeah, Boss. There's two men out here to see you. One is scarred and about the ugliest bastard I've ever seen in my life."

I shrug off the insult. It's not like I give a fuck. It doesn't bother me and apparently, my scars don't bother Hayden.

"I'd watch who I called ugly. You should look in the mirror," Devil mumbles, I guess offended for me. *I could almost like him.*

The other guy ignores him. He gets the go ahead to let us

inside, and he looks relieved we're leaving. "Go on in," he orders.

"Asshole," Devil tells him, apparently still not over the insult to me. I shake my head at him, trying to tell him to shut the fuck up and let it go—without words. Devil ignores me, continuing to mumble as we pass them. "Dumbass looks like a butt-fuck gone wrong and he wants to talk about someone else. Pathetic."

I find myself smiling despite what's waiting inside. Devil apparently has balls of steel, trying to take on a man who could snap him like a twig. It's either that or he's a stupid motherfucker. We walk into a big room. I have to say the inside of this damn place looks slightly better than the outside—of course it would be hard to look much worse. It's an open space with a bar in the front of the room. A few tables scattered around, some pool tables, poker tables, and big screen televisions. There's some sectional sofas that are worn to Hell and back. Beside one sofa in particular is a fucking metal cage. A big one, like you would house a Great Dane dog inside…or a person.

I know instantly it's the one Hayden talked about, and rage boils through me as I picture her inside that fucking thing for months. Did they allow her clothes? Did they let her out to eat? Did they let her out to use the restroom? Any of that? *Jesus*, what if she didn't care for Blade at all, but had some sort of Stockholm syndrome going with him because he saved her? I'm going to burn this fucking place to the ground. *Tonight.* I don't want a trace of anything left. It will cease to exist, just like the memories I want gone out of Hayden's mind.

I kick the fucking cage with my boot, not feeling better even when it goes back a good five feet. If Devil wonders why, he doesn't say shit. Victor is standing in the corner of the room surrounded by three other men and in front of him is the preacher. He's chained to a stripper pole and naked. From the looks of him it appears that Victor has been having fun interrogating him. He doesn't look so holy now. At least he left him breathing for me. I need something to hit right now. Since Blade isn't around, the *would be* preacher is the next best thing.

Time to get the party started.

CHAPTER 90

Hayden

I TURN OVER, stretching, and immediately know that Michael is gone. I refused to mention it, didn't even ask, but I knew that he would be meeting with Victor about Pastor Sturgill. Part of me wanted to know who the man is and part of me wants to just pretend it never happened. That part obviously won. I have so much more to worry about. My plate is about as full as it can get, and who Pastor Sturgill truly is and what's going to happen to him, are two things that I've decided to ignore. I need to concentrate on other things. Least of all of them, is the fact that I now have no job. Worse, with you-know-who getting whatever is coming to him. I'm pretty sure my side business of selling things to the church is over—or at least cut *very* drastically. Which means I've got to find a way for Maggie and me to survive. A part of me feels guilty for worrying about money after losing Charlie. But, Charlie...she was a realist. She was truly a bottom line kind of girl, so I'm pretty sure she would understand.

Looking over at the clock, it reads five in the morning. Michael's pillow is cold. I have to wonder how long he's been gone.

With a sad, pitiful little sigh, I get out of bed. I jump in the shower after turning on the water and adjusting the temperature. My life has been one emotional crisis after another for so long, I can't remember normal. Still, right now, I have a smile on my face. My body aches in all the right places and I feel...

I stop because only one word comes to mind and it shocks me. It might even *terrify* me. I feel...*loved. Well-loved.*

My heart hammers in my chest, and I have to force myself to breathe. It's too much, with my past life, to imagine that someone as amazing as Michael might love me. *Isn't it?* The most I could hope for is that he might truly care for me...and I think he does. That's enough. It has to be. It's more than I've ever had, and I can be happy with that.

When I get out of the shower, I throw on a pair of jogging pants and t-shirt, and after towel drying my hair, I decide I've wasted enough time. There are two strangers in my house, and Michael is gone. It's okay. He trusts these men and if he does, then I can. Today is the day I let go of the past. That's what Michael wants for me and for Maggie. It's something I want more than I could ever put into words. It's time to stop living in the past, or at least time to stop letting it affect me and everything I do.

I have this delicious ache when I walk. Evidence that what Michael and I did last night worked muscles that have been in hibernation. That thought makes my smile broaden. I never imagined that I would have sex again, that I would ever enjoy it. Enjoy might be too tame of word for what happens when Michael touches me.

I open up the bedroom door to the sound of arguing. I look at my kitchen and there's one of the men from last night, along with a new man I don't remember seeing before along with Crusher and Dani. *Shit.* I know Michael really likes those two, but spending the day with them before wasn't exactly wine and roses.

All talking stops the minute I step through my door. "What's wrong?" I ask.

They look at each other, then back at me. Dani avoids my eyes, and Crusher runs his hand along his five o'clock shadow, and it's clear he's uncomfortable. It's also clear he's lying When he answers, "Nothing. Are you hungry, Hayden? Dani fixed breakfast. It took her a few years, but she's finally learning to cook."

"Kiss my ass, Cowboy."

"I did that last night if I remember correctly." he smiles at her but it doesn't reach his eyes like it should.

"I'm not sure kissing can be used to describe what you did to my ass," Dani smirks.

"What are you guys arguing about?" I interrupt them for two reasons. One and most importantly, I don't want to hear what he did to her ass and secondly, I have a feeling their arguing has a lot to do with Michael.

Crusher lets out a noise that reminds me a lot of Michael's grunts, only his is more drawn out. I look at the other two men and they cross their arms stubbornly. It's clear none of them have any plans of telling me what's going on.

"Okay, Dani. You tell me."

"Why me?" she appears affronted.

"Because, us girls have to stick together."

"We're not exactly best friends," she huffs, but she's smiling.

"We probably never will be," I tell her honestly, which makes her laugh. I wasn't trying to be a bitch; I just don't want people in my life. If I could move to a deserted island and live with Michael and Maggie and no one else. I'd be happy.

"Beast should have been back by now," she admits, and fear

hits me stronger than anything I've ever felt before—and with my history that is saying a lot. On the heels of the fear however, is not panic—at least not right now. It's anger.

"Do you know where he is?" I ask Crusher, and he shrugs which pisses me off. *"Do you know where he is?"* I ask again, stressing the words and so help me if I had my gun right now—*which Michael took somewhere and hid because he said I'd get myself killed*, I'd shoot Crusher!

"Well yeah," he says, uncomfortably.

"Then you're going to go check on him and make sure he's alright then, *right*?"

"I hadn't planned on it," he says calmly, leaning against the counter of my old sink.

"Why the hell not?" I cry.

"Yeah, Cowboy, why the hell not?" Dani adds, rising to stand by me.

"Because this is Beast's business. He told me to watch you and that's what I'm doing. He's probably just taking longer than he planned."

"Taking longer?" I ask, shaking my head.

"Well yeah. It takes a while to get information out of a man when—well, shall we say, they might not be so inclined to give it to you," he says calmly, as if he was discussing what color socks he is wearing today.

"So, he's *torturing* him?"

"More like sternly convincing him to talk," Crusher shrugs.

"But he's a preacher!"

"I don't think he's really a preacher, Hay," Dani interrupts.

"I know that," I grumble, "and my name isn't *Hay*," I add.

"You're very touchy," this comes from one of the men standing close to Crusher.

"I am not," I complain, rubbing the tension between my

eyes, because suddenly I feel a headache coming on.

"You kind of are," Dani says, and I don't turn to look at her. My eyes are on Crusher.

His eyes practically sparkle and he snorts in laughter, but tries to hide it behind his hand with a cough. *He doesn't hide it very well.*

"Are you going to go help Michael?"

"I doubt he needs it. Like I said, he's probably—"

"Convincing him *sternly*, I got it. But, he could need help *convincing*. You need to help him," I urge Crusher.

"You do, Cowboy," Dani tacks on.

"Damn it, Hellcat."

"If something happens to Michael because you didn't help him, I'll make your life hell," I warn him, knowing he probably doesn't care.

"Listen, Beast would—"

"If something happens to Beast and you didn't help him, I'll make your life hell, Cowboy," Dani adds, I turn around and look at her skeptically. She shrugs with a wink. "Girls have to stick together. Besides I owe Beast."

I nod, not knowing what else to say. *Maybe I could like her.*

"Damn it, Hellcat. You know how these things go. We—"

"You know that thing I do with my tongue that you like when I—"

"Woman!" Crusher interrupts her. I make a note to find out later what she does…Michael might like it…

Her mouth creeps into a smile and she shrugs. "I'm just saying, Cowboy, that could be off the table."

"Dani," he warns.

"Permanently," she says calmly.

"So, what's your decision?" I ask Crusher, crossing my arms trying to figure out what my next move is if he says no.

One of the men, I think I heard Michael refer to him as Ice, makes a noise like a whip cracking.

"Fuck you. If you knew what she did, you'd be scared too, asshole."

"Well?" Dani prompts.

"Fine, I'll go check on him," he relents.

"I'm going with you," I tell him relieved, already grabbing my jacket.

"Fuck no you're not! Beast would cut off my dick if I took you to that damn clubhouse and you got hurt," Crusher growls.

"I'm going. Either you take me with you, or I'll sneak away and go to the clubhouse on my own, since you were nice enough to tell me where Michael is," I tell him, leaving no room for argument.

"Son-of-a-bitch!" he growls, but I feel joy inside, because I'm pretty sure I've just won this argument.

"I'm going too!" Dani says, nearly jumping in victory.

"Fuck no!"

"But, Zander, honey, I have to. I need to protect your dick in case Beast tries to cut it off."

"I doubt he will," Ice says.

"Yeah, it's too wrapped around your finger," the other guy mutters.

"I will shoot you," Crusher growls.

"Quit your blustering, Cowboy, think of it this way. If I'm with you, then I can't be hurt. I'll be with you and you can protect me."

"I don't spank your ass enough," he mutters.

"I completely agree," she says with a smirk, winking in my direction, and it amazes me that with everything going on, I can find a smile. I swear I'm starting to feel like I'm part of a crazy family.

"Let's get going. Fuck, I'm going to regret this," Crusher grumbles.

We head out the door and the men walk to their bikes. Dani gets on the back of Crushers. I know a moment of real fear. I've not been on the back of a bike in a long time and there's memories there I don't really want.

"Ice, you can take Hayden in her car," Crusher tells him.

"I don't think my car will make it to the clubhouse," I tell him honestly, pushing back my nerves. *I can do this*. "I'll just ride on the back of his bike."

"The fuck you will," Crusher argues. "Beast will cut off my dick if he sees you on the back of another man's bike."

"There's no other choice. I don't know where Michael's keys to his truck are. I'm sure it will be fine."

"I'm just as sure it won't be," Crusher growls, "and Christ, Hayden, you're pregnant."

"Ice will drive careful. It will be fine."

"Beast is going to kill me. Fine you ride with Ice, but Ice, man you better baby that motherfucker."

"Boss I don't think I should—"

"Neither do I, but you're fucking doing it," Crusher growls.

"Beast is going to kill me," Ice grumbles, as I get on the back of his bike. It's a little awkward at first, but thankfully my stomach isn't huge as it could be.

"We'll take the back roads. No interstates," Crusher grumbles, and his face is tight in anger.

I take a breath of relief as the bike starts up, and I manage to avoid going into a panic attack.

I can do this.

I have to.

I don't have a choice.

CHAPTER 91

Beast

"FUNNY THING, *PREACHER*," I say calmly, looking at the man who is strung up like a side of beef in a packing plant. It's only me and Devil here now. Victor and his men gave up hours ago. It was probably a good call, because I'm starting to think this sack of shit doesn't have any idea where Blade is, and that's the only thing Victor is interested in right now—*revenge for Charlie*. Me? I have a morbid fascination with finding out exactly who this asshole is and what the fuck he fed the Dwellers about Hayden. "Do you know that there's no record of a Pastor Aldin Sturgill? Well, that is up until about six months ago, when he just miraculously appeared out of nowhere."

"Like the second coming? It's probably a damn miracle," Devil jokes. He's on the couch with his legs thrown back as if he doesn't have a care in the world. I really could like the fucker. He reminds me of Torch, but not as crazy. Devil is more sarcastic than certifiable, and strangely, I've only felt the urge to slap him two or three times.

"Go fuck yourselves," the man spits out, having trouble talking. It might be because his mouth and jaw are swollen and bruised. Really, there are bruises coming out all over his body. I haven't really done much to him, sadly. Victor and his men had worked him over pretty good before I ever got here.

"Now, now. Is that anyway for a preacher to talk?" Devil asks. "You don't want a dark spot on your soul, especially when you're so close to meeting your maker."

"End me now! Just fucking do it!" the man growls.

I look over at Devil. I already told him how I wanted this to end. He grabs the two large containers of gas and prepares for work.

"I'm not killing you," I tell the man, calmly. His one eye that's not swelled over looks at me with surprise.

"You're not?"

"No that'd be too good for you. You have a choice—a simple one," I stress.

"What's that?" he asks, doubtfully.

"You tell me your connection to Blade and what his plans are, or…"

"I'm not telling you shit," he growls.

"I have to admit, I was hoping that would be your answer. Tell me, Sturgill," I begin, unable to bring myself to call him preacher. We both know that's a lie at this point. "Have you ever burned your hand or felt the flames wrap around the skin so hot you thought your bones would melt?" He doesn't reply, but then I didn't expect him to. "Because I have. I even watched while the skin peeled away from my body. It's like Hell on Earth. I wouldn't wish it on anyone—"

"What's he doing?" Sturgill calls out, panic thick in his voice now.

The smell of gasoline hits me, and I know that Devil is dousing the tables and things I had him gather up earlier in the center of the room.

"I said I wouldn't wish it on anyone—*except* someone who has messed with what I think of as mine."

"I don't even fucking know you," the guy yells, jerking his bloody hands and legs trying to get free.

"Then let me tell you who I am. I'm Hayden's man, and I'm also the last face you'll see." I take the third container of gas that is sitting beside me on the floor and begin dousing the man with it.

"Don't do this. You don't want to do this."

"Sturgill, if that's even your name, you're dying. The only choice you have is if it goes easy, or…*not so easy*."

"But I don't know where Blade is. I haven't seen him since that day in the hospital," he argues, panic being replaced with utter terror now.

"How do you know, Blade?" I ask making a trail of gas along the wooden floor, leading it back to the pile of refuge that Devil fixed.

"What? Why does that matter. Listen man, you don't have to do this. I have money. I can pay you!"

"How do you know, Blade?" I ask him again, throwing the empty gas can on top of the pile.

"Man, come on. You don't really want to do this."

"You ever play dominos?" I ask, finally deciding to stop playing. He's not going to tell me anything helpful, and I'll eventually hunt Blade down on my own. Maybe he'll give me my answers.

"Dominos?" he asks.

"Yeah," I tell him, picking up the huge cage, lifting it half-way off the floor and stopping to stare straight at him. "A fire can be like that. You give it a place to start, leaving a trail of gas for it to travel, and it will follow, perfectly."

"Fuck. Fuck, man. You have to listen—"

"I'm going to start it at the old shed out front where Hayden was beaten. Then, the trail the fire takes will slowly make its way back to you. You'll be able to see it coming for you. There's a certain amount of justice in that," I tell him, clearing my throat. The more I use my voice lately, the better it's getting. Even so, with Hayden in my life, seems it doesn't bother me nearly the way it used to.

"Don't do this man. Just put a bullet in me if you want me dead. You don't have to do this."

"I could, but where you're going? You might as well get used to the fire. Don't worry. You won't be lonely. I'll send Blade to you before long," I tell him, following Devil back outside, and ignoring the pleadings of the *so-called* preacher.

CHAPTER 92

Beast

I'VE GOT THE cage over my head, and I have to walk at an angle to get through the door and outside. I put it down on the ground and stare at the old shed in front of me.

"Now what?" Devil asks.

I don't answer him. Instead, I walk into the shed. The smell of dirt and musty odors hit me. It's so small in here, I'm almost as broad as the building itself. It's no wonder that Hayden panics at being closed in. There's a light fixture half-ass hanging down off the ceiling. I reach up and yank the pull string and dull light floods the area. There's different tools hanging on the shiplap covered walls—hoes, rakes, pick axes, shovels and even an old axe. The building looks as if it's one stiff wind from falling over. I grab the axe and decide to help it along. I go retrace my steps going to the outside of the building and finding the wall I want—the one that has the small closet on the other side. The closet Hayden tried to hide in. Then I take the axe and begin swinging it into the old wood. With each hit, the rightness of what I'm doing seems to settle into my stomach.

"What are you doing?" Devil asks.

I continue ignoring him, and instead carry on connecting the axe against the wood, determined to bring the small building down.

"Rainbows and sunshine," Devil grumbles, before disappearing. "This might do the job better, Sunshine," he says. I stop mid-swing to look at him. He's carrying a sledgehammer—one in each hand.

I grunt, dropping the axe as he tosses one of them to me. The minute my hand wraps around the handle, it feels better. One large hit against the wall causes it to collapse. Devil joins in and half the damn building has collapsed in no time. I'm about to start on another section when the sound of motorcycles fill the air.

"Fuck," Devil growls, stopping his swing and his hand goes to his gun almost as if by reflex.

We look out over the parking lot and shock fills me when Crusher and Dani pull up, followed closely by Trace and Ice. When I see Hayden on the back of Ice's bike I can't fucking believe it. I'm going to kill Crusher, and then I'm going to tear Ice's head off his body.

"What the fuck?" I roar when the last bike is turned off.

"Hey, man," Crusher calls out.

"Don't hey me, asshole. What the fuck are you doing here? What the fuck is *Hayden* doing here?" I growl, anger vibrating through my system. I stomp over to Ice's bike, ready to rip him off the damn thing and choke the life out of him. One thing stops me.

Hayden jumps off the bike and wraps her arms around me before I get the chance.

"Hayden, what the fuck are you doing on the back of a bike?" I rumble, hugging her with my free arm. I turn to look at Crusher, tempted to take the sledgehammer to his fucking face.

"Why?" I ask him, using just one word, because fuck there's too much pushing in my brain right now to sort through it all.

"You were late. The women wouldn't stop until I agreed to come check on you and…Fuck man, you know what women are like. I figured it was safer to have them with me than it would be for them to sneak out on their own."

"I'm going to fucking kill you later," I warn him. He shrugs like it's what he expected—which it should be.

"Just don't cut his dick off," Dani says, helpfully, over his shoulder.

"I'm not touching his damn dick," I growl.

"Thank God for that," Crusher says and Dani laughs.

"We finishing this or what, Sunshine?" Devil asks.

"I'm going to rip your head off along with his, later," I tell him, motioning over at Crusher.

"You can try. Let's get this shit done, can we? No offense, but I'm getting sick of North Carolina. I'd like to get back to Tennessee."

"He's got a woman he's mooning over there."

"The fuck I do. I don't moon over a woman."

"You do when that woman would rather suck any dick other than yours," Ice jokes, walking toward us.

Devil takes the handle of the hammer and shoves it into Ice's gut. *I think he got off easy.*

"Ow! Motherfucker!" Ice yells.

I pull away from Hayden and move her to stand in front of Crusher's bike. I look down at her, and dare her to move. "Stay here while I finish up," I order. I've barely walked five steps away from her when I hear her following behind me. Crusher and the rest of them are laughing in the background.

"I'm not a dog you can order to stay, Michael. What are you doing?" she asks.

I stop walking, I lean my head back and look up at the sky. In frustration, I let out one long growl.

"Michael!" she demands, trying to get my attention.

"I'm taking out the motherfucking garbage!" I tell her, my voice vibrating in anger. I know it's harsh because she jumps back at my angry reply.

"Michael…"

"This place almost broke you, Hayden. I want it fucking gone!" I remind her, giving her ultimate honesty. Then I spin around and slam the sledgehammer back in that fucking building with all my might.

CHAPTER 93

Hayden

CALL IT ADRENALINE, or stupidity, I'm not sure. But it hadn't occurred to me yet where I'm at. I mean I knew I was headed here. But until this moment, I hadn't allowed myself to consciously register where I am and what I'm doing. When I watch Michael take a swing at the building, that's the moment it actually hits me. I'm back at Blade's home. I'm at the Dwellers. I allow one quick glance, before the sound of Michael's hammer hitting the building jars me. I jerk my head to watch him and realize that it's the garden shed. My body feels flushed. A sick feeling washes over me and my body feels cold and clammy, while at the same time making me feel flushed. *He's tearing down the garden shed.*

"Michael. What are you doing?" I ask, stupidly. I already know. I just…*can't believe it.*

"Stay back, Hayden. I don't want you near this place again," his rough voice demands.

"Give me your hammer," I demand.

"Fuck no. Woman you ain't ever had a real man in your life before, but you need to start listening to me. Now back the hell away from here and let me finish this."

"I want to hit it, Michael."

"You're pregnant," he reminds me, but he doesn't get it.

"I want to know that I helped, Michael. I need that for me and for Maggie," I tell him, my body vibrating with that need.

"I'm doing this for you and for Maggie," he responds.

"They almost killed her here, Michael," I whisper, brokenly, knowing I don't need to. He knows that and I don't doubt that's why he's demolishing it now. What he doesn't understand is I need to look back on this and know I helped. I need it for those days when I'm feeling weak, so that it can be like proof that I'm really not.

"Hayden—"

"They beat me, and I thought I was going to die. I said goodbye to Maggie here," I tell him, my voice and body shaking. I wrap my arms around my stomach as if to protect her. "I want to help," I whisper, and because I'm feeling desperate, I find myself begging. "Please, Michael. Let me help."

"Here you go, darlin'," the other guy that's helping Michael says. I look up and he's bringing me a glass soda bottle with a rag hanging out of it. There's fluid in the bottom that I can only guess is gasoline.

"Damn it, Devil," Beast growls.

"She can throw this and set the fucking shit on fire. It's her right, the way I figure it," he says, and I see compassion in his eyes.

His face is a little blurry, and it's then I realize I'm crying. I use the back of my hand to wipe the tears away and stiffen up my spine. *Today I am strong.*

"Thank you," I tell him.

"My pleasure, darlin'," he says, with a smile.

"Can I do it now?" I ask Michael, taking the lighter that *Devil* hands me.

He huffs, but puts his hammer down and walks over to me. “If you get hurt throwing that, I’m going to kill everyone here and spend the rest of my life in jail,” he mutters, and I could almost smile.

“I’ll be careful.”

“Then do it and get it over with. Fuck, I never realized you were so stubborn,” he says.

“Welcome to my life,” Crusher jokes, as he and Dani come to stand beside us.

“Get it over with,” Michael says.

My hand shakes as I work the lighter. It doesn’t work on the first strike, and not even the second. Michael puts his hand over my shaking one. My eyes go to him.

The dark depths of his eyes are like liquid, reminding me of how he looked when he took my body. “You got this, Hayden. Take a breath, and just do it,” he says in his quiet, gruff voice.

Wetting my lips with my tongue, I do as he suggested and just breathe. I work the lighter, and when the flame shoots up, I put it at the end of the cloth. Once it catches, I take a giant step and throw it on the old building. It’s then I realize that Michael or Devil must have already doused the building with gas, because it explodes into flames. The heat of it is so hot that I start to take a step back. I don’t get the chance though, because Michael comes up behind me, wrapping both his arms around me, practically lifting me from the ground, as he pulls me away from the fire and back into his body.

“Can we do the same to the clubhouse,” I whisper, not sure he can hear me over the roar of the fire, and the crackling of wood. I underestimated Michael again though because he bends down, kisses the side of my face gently, before whispering in my ear.

"Already taken care of, Beauty," he whispers for only me. "Watch."

I'm not sure what he means until I see flames breaking away from the burning building. It's like it follows a path and it's a path that leads straight to the clubhouse and through the open doors. *He made a trail of gas. He's destroying the place of my nightmares.* Those two thoughts ring in my head over and over, until they're drowned out by the one other thought. A thought so huge, so amazing it robs me of breath.

He's doing all of this for me. To avenge…me.

CHAPTER 94

Beast

BEING THIS CLOSE to the flames, isn't fun. It's the only way I could think of to destroy all this shit. I want nothing but ashes left. I know my decision is right, when I feel the way Hayden relaxes into me. I doubt Hayden would be as relaxed if she knew that the fire that just jumped inside the clubhouse is leading to the death of the preacher. I won't tell her that. Some things are better left unsaid. I almost wish I could watch the fucker burn, but it's better this way.

"Hey, Sunshine!" Devil calls out.

I close my eyes. I may have to kill that boy. I rub the back of my neck with a grunt.

"How has Diesel let you live this long?" I grumble.

"It's been a near thing a time or two," Crusher says.

I slap him on the back of the head. "Asshole. You should have kept the women away from here. And I won't even start on how you let Hayden ride on the back of a bike—*on another man's bike.*"

"You try arguing against two stubborn females, man. It's a fucking wonder I'm not mouthing gibberish and rocking back and forth in a corner somewhere."

"You sad-fucks couldn't get along without me. What do you want done with this thing?" Devil asks, bringing my attention back to him.

"With what?" I ask confused.

"This damn dog cage," Devil mutters. "Why you had to bring it out here, I'll never know."

I feel the minute Hayden's body tenses up. I know that she realizes what he's talking about. *Son of a bitch.* I give her arms a squeeze and pull away from her. "I got it," I tell him, picking up the sledgehammer. I make it over to him, before Hayden comes out of her trance and takes off running to me.

"No!" She screams, and it sounds like it's ripped from her very soul. I look up just as she stops beside me. I'm almost ready to swing when her hand grabs hold of my wrist. "No!" she yells again, softer in tone, but still loud.

"Hayden, sweetheart, I want to—"

"Don't you touch it!" she cries. "I don't want you to touch it!"

"Damn it, Beauty," I growl, having no idea how to deal with an irrational woman. This has to be done. It has to be done for my sanity. I don't know why she's opposed to it.

"Don't touch it, Michael!"

"Fuck, I'm glad I'm single," Ice grumbles.

"Can't fucking argue with that," Devil agrees.

"Why's she so fucking crazy over a dog kennel?" Crusher asks, and that's when I realize all of us are standing around the damn cage.

"Because it's not a dog kennel," Dani whispers. She comes up to stand by Hayden, and I watch as she reaches out to hold her hand. Hayden jerks her hand back and takes a couple of steps away from her.

Instead, Hayden puts her hand out and finds mine. Something moves inside of me, and I have to swallow to keep from choking on emotion. Her gray eyes are as round as saucers and panic is shining in their depths.

"Please don't touch it, Michael. I don't want you to touch it. I…I don't want you to touch it," she whispers, her body shaking.

I keep our hands joined, but use my free hand and cup the side of her neck. I let my thumb brush back and forth along the bone of her jawline and chin. "Why don't you want me to touch it, Beauty?" I ask her, my heart physically hurting from seeing the tears falling from her face.

"Michael…"

"Tell me why, Beauty and we'll forget this and move on. Remember my promise? So much good there's no more room for the bad memories. Give this to me."

"I don't want you to touch it because…I don't want you to…" she starts and a violent shudder moves through her body.

"Maybe you should just let it go," Dani whispers, but I ignore her.

All of my focus is on Hayden.

"Tell me, Beauty. Tell me and then we bury it in the past—just like the rest of it. Tell me."

"I was an animal. They joked, and mocked me. Sometimes they'd grab my hair through the metal and pull my head against it. They'd spend time telling me what they were going to do to me, and sometimes, they'd promise me freedom, if I just agreed to whatever they wanted. God help me…sometimes I wanted to give in. Just to be done with it all and say what they wanted to hear, so I could get out. There were times they would leave me in there for days, and when they finally let me out, my legs wouldn't work from being folded up for so long, and I smelled…I…They'd throw food through the holes and I'd grab it up to keep from starving. I should have been brave enough to starve. I should have…Oh God, Michael I was so stupid and weak. It was so bad…I don't want to remember it. I don't, but it's there and if you touch it…if you touch it, Michael that memory will always be there too. *Please*," she begs, the tears falling harder as she pleads, her hand tightening around mine so tight it feels like she stops the blood flow.

"I don't want that. I don't want your memory anywhere near…*that*…Please," she whispers, completely broken.

I pull her deeper into me, shielding her with my body. I kiss the top of her head, wishing I knew magic words to mend the pain she's hiding inside her.

"Motherfucker!" Crusher screams and Hayden and I both jerk up to watch him. He's kicking the cage over and over until it begins to collapse in on itself, a bent mess that is in three separate pieces. "Motherfucking-Son-of-A-Bitch!" he yells out, as he picks up each piece and throws it into the fire.

Once he's done, I pick Hayden up and carry her back to my bike. The others follow us and we only sit there. Ice, Devil, and Trace are quiet, looking straight ahead. Crusher has Dani in his arms. Dani has tears that make sad, silent tracks down her face. Hayden is in my arms, her head resting in the curve of my shoulder. I kiss the top of her head, keeping our joined hands close, as we watch the clubhouse burn to the fucking ground. I'm thankful the roar and heat of the flames, the crackling of the wood and the sounds of the clubhouse crashing in on itself is enough to hide the preacher's screams from Hayden. Maybe the smoke got the fucker before the flames did, but I find myself hoping not. I wanted him to anticipate every second of pain before his eventual death.

CHAPTER 95

"YOU SURE YOU don't want us to stick around for a few more days?" Crusher asks.

"Nah, man you need to get back to your kid."

"I am missing him," Dani says, with a smile.

It's been a week and there's no sign of Blade. I can't keep Diesel's men here forever. More importantly, I want more time alone with Hayden. She hasn't said anything, but I know she's uncomfortable having everyone around. She's also worrying about something, and I need to get her to talk to me about it.

"You need to get back home. We have Victor and his men around here and if something happens, I'll give you a call."

"If you're sure, man," Crusher says. We slap hands together, pull in and pound each other's shoulders, before breaking away.

"I'm sure. Besides if you don't get Devil out of here, I'm liable to kill the son of a bitch." I smirk.

"Oh, Sunshine. You know you fucking love me," Devil says, laughing, and I flip him off—which makes him laugh harder.

"Oh! Here," Hayden calls, running out of the house. "I almost forgot!" she adds, carrying a small cooler and two plastic containers. I had no idea she was doing any of that. It's another sign to her giving nature. A sign that she's unlike any other woman I've ever had in my life.

If things were different she would have fit in good in my old life. The old ladies would have respected her; the men would have treated her as one of the family. Skull has been calling, wanting me to come back, but the more I kick it around, I know I can't. I don't want to go back—even if it meant giving Hayden a better life.

"I made you guys some sandwiches and some other things for the road," she tells Crusher.

I shake off my thoughts and watch as she tentatively hands them to him. Crusher doesn't give Hayden a chance to get away, he pulls her in for a big bear hug. He whispers something to her that I can't hear.

She looks up at him and smiles, but she's got a blush on her cheeks. "I will," she says, and Crusher hugs her again. I barely resist the urge to yank her out of his arms.

"Please, tell me that has those peanut butter cookies in there," Ice says, coming up to get the container out of her hands.

"That's why there are two batches, so you can eat to your heart's content, Ice," Hayden laughs.

"Hayden, if you give me the word, swear to God, I'll claim you, cover you in diamonds and spoil you rotten. All you have to do is bake for me and kick Beast to the curb," he tells her, smoothly getting down on his knees in front of her. That's about all I can stand, joking or not.

"You don't get the fuck away from her, you won't be able to ride that shiny new bike of yours, or eat my woman's food," I growl, pulling her away from him. "I already owe you an ass kicking for letting her on the back of your bike."

"Michael," Hayden chastises, reaching up from her tiptoes to kiss my neck.

"You're a lucky, asshole," Ice whines theatrically, but at least the bastard goes back to his bike—away from Hayden.

"Take care, Beast. And you better fucking watch your back," Crusher growls.

"Always," I tell him, with a nod. Then I lean down and kiss the top of Dani's head. "Take care of yourself, hummingbird."

"I will. You be happy," she says, and I shrug. She thinks Hayden will be my miracle cure-all. She doesn't get that the truth is I'm a fucking bastard who is going to use Hayden to survive. There's no happy for me. "You deserve to be happy you know," she whispers, giving me a hug. "Hayden deserves it too," she adds, and that's one thing we agree on.

"I'll make sure she's happy," I tell her, because I plan on doing my best to make sure that happens. Dani stares at me and I see the sadness in her eyes, I'm not fooling her at all.

"Any other man hugged my woman like that, I'd cut his balls off," Crusher grumbles.

"Any other man tried to hug your woman like that and *she'd* cut his balls off," Dani grumbles. "Take care, Hayden," she adds.

"You can call me Hay…I guess," Hayden tells her, and they smile at each other for a minute, as if silently bonding.

"Women," Crusher laughs with a shake of his head, before starting up his bike.

I watch as they head out with a wave. Once they're gone, Hayden wraps her arm tighter around my back and curls herself into my side.

"Listen to that," she whispers after a bit.

"What's that, Beauty?" I ask her, looking down at her.

"It's silent," she answers, looking completely happy with the idea that we're finally alone.

"Getting tired of all our company?" I ask her, jokingly.

"Yeah, a little. Do you think it's okay though? I mean, Blade is out there…*somewhere.*"

"You don't need to worry about that," I respond, turning her so she stands in front of me, and I let my fingers curl into her hair. "I'll take care of Blade." I meant to reassure her, but I can tell that it doesn't work when she avoids my eyes and looks down the road instead. "What's wrong, Hayden?" I ask her point blank.

"Just getting really tired of old ghosts," she answers, looking a little lost.

"How about I take you inside and remind you of other things?"

"Not sure why you want to, I'm starting to waddle here," she sighs rubbing her stomach. The woman has no idea how beautiful she is. I pick her up and stalk back to the house.

"I can walk," she complains half-heartedly, as her head falls on my shoulder, and her fingers are playing in my hair.

"We'll see if that's the case by the time I finish with you in *our* bed," I grunt, and she gives me that laugh she does sometimes that I've never heard her use with anyone but me. Her laugh rings like bells—almost musical, and the sound makes me feel warm inside.

Damn.

CHAPTER 96

Hayden

"WHAT DO YOU say we go away for a few days?"

"Away?" I question, looking up at Michael. It's been a couple of weeks now since Crusher and the others left to go back home. There's still been no sign of Blade, and though I worry, I'm starting to feel better. There's no reason for him to come here. Michael is probably right, and he's in Mexico or somewhere now. I was never that important to him, and he never truly wanted Maggie. There's no reason to think he would risk his life to get some sort of crazy revenge. It's right after the day at the hospital, I've somehow built Blade up to be even more of a monster in my mind. So, knowing he's out there is always lingering in my thoughts. There's always this...*fear*.

"Yeah. There's a lake in Norman. Let's load up and go up there for a few days, rent a place out by itself and just relax," he answers.

We're on the sofa watching a movie and eating popcorn together. I have my head in Michael's lap, his legs are stretched out, with his bare feet resting on the coffee table. This is something we do almost every evening together. It usually ends with me falling asleep and Michael carrying me to bed. Sometimes we make love, sometimes he simply holds me—either way it's perfect. That's how I would describe my life right now. *Perfect.* I'm happy.

Michael seems happy. We talk, we laugh and we…love. At least it's love for me. I admit that to myself. *I love Michael.* If I had met him earlier, before life went to complete hell, how different would my life have been. I look at our joined hands that are lying over my baby-bump and I know. *Deep down in my soul, I know that life would have been completely different.* I grieve that loss, but I've come to accept what Michael told me the first time we made love together. He is Maggie's father in every way that counts. He's going nowhere. I have no idea how I can trust someone—especially a man, after everything, but I do. *Unconditional Trust.*

"I can't go anywhere, Michael," I tell him, regretfully. I'd actually love to go away with him, but it's not practical.

"Why can't you?" he asks, and he has that tone. The one that says he's mildly upset and determined to get his way. Then again, Michael is always determined to get his way.

"Because, I have things to do here," I reply, not bothering to look up, trying not to engage. I don't want to argue over this, because what usually happens is I give in. I find it hard to concentrate on anything when Michael looks at me with his dark eyes and those beautiful lips of his smile at me like I'm the only woman in the world that matters. Heck, I find it hard to breathe when he does that.

"What kind of things?" he asks, using the remote to pause the movie we're watching. The remote to the brand new sixty-five-inch, ultra HD television he bought last week.

Heck, the coffee table his feet are on, he made. He made it with his own hands, and I love it. It's the most beautiful piece of furniture I've ever had in my life. It's just simple lines, nothing fancy and it's made out of old barn wood that Michael sanded by hand and then stained it with a dark varnish. He even made two matching end tables. I'll keep these tables until the day I die. That's how precious they are to me. When I told Michael that, I was crying in happiness. It's something I do a lot these days. Michael only shook his head and kissed me.

He's always doing things like that. In fact, we're sitting on the new sofa he bought too, and across from the sofa are two matching rocking recliners. *His and Hers recliners.* All these things he bought because he said they were needed, especially the rocking recliners. He told me he wanted to make sure Maggie could be rocked and happy when we have family night. *Family night.* Is there any wonder why I'm not completely in love with him? There's not a woman alive that wouldn't fall head over heels in love with him—it's a physical impossibility.

Still, he has to quit spending money like that. He obviously has money, and I can only assume it's from his time with his club back in Kentucky. But, he's not in *that* life anymore. I don't want him to *waste* his money on me. I'm terrified of him doing that. If he does that and money gets tight, he might go back to Kentucky. He might leave me…or worse. He might expect me to follow him to Kentucky and become part of his life there.

"I know you've been spending money on me like crazy, but Michael, we can't live like *this* forever. We have to think of the future, and for me, that means finding a job. I have the bills paid up for another month, and you've been insisting on buying the groceries, but I need to have a job before long."

"The hell you do. You're not going to work, Hayden. You're pregnant. *Very pregnant.* You have to take care of yourself."

"I have to have a job to support myself."

"Do I look like that kind of guy?" he growls. Pulling me

around so I'm lying on my back, head still in his lap, looking up at him.

From this angle, I can see the scars that run up his neck and I have the strangest urge to reach up and lick them…

"Hayden! Stop ignoring me!"

"I'm not ignoring you," I defend, with a sigh.

"Then what are you doing? I'm trying to have an argument with you here."

"I'm thinking about licking your neck," I tell him, with an annoyed sigh. "And what do you mean, *that kind of guy*? You're the one not making sense."

"You want to lick my neck?" he asks, incredulously.

"All of you really, but I'd start there. If you'd stop being grumpy."

He grunts in reply, and I can't help but giggle.

I also sit up, and turn to the side enough so I can place a kiss against his Adam's apple, then I run my tongue along the groove of the deepest scar there, thankful he let me trim his beard shorter.

"Fuck," he hisses, as I use my teeth to bite along the corded muscle in his neck. His large hand covers my breast, squeezing it. "You're trying to distract me," he grumbles, and he's right, but still…

"I'm feeling needy," I whisper into his ear, my fingers burrowing into his hair.

"You're always needy," he groans, his hands sliding under the nightshirt I'm wearing.

I've given up pajamas lately, opting for Michael's t-shirts, or nightgowns. They give me more freedom with my ever-growing stomach. When his hand reaches underneath and goes straight between my legs, I'm pretty sure I'll never go back to pajamas. There's something to be said about easy access.

"You're bare too," his hoarse voice growls. His fingers dance across the lips of my pussy, before pushing them apart and zeroing in on my clit, teasing it. "Where's your underwear, Beauty?"

"I must have forgotten them." I grin, widening the distance between my legs to give him more access. I'm on my knees now leaning over him to kiss him, while his hand is buried between my legs. His lips devour me, his tongue pushing to own my mouth. *He owns all of me.* "I need you, Michael. I need you to fuck me," I whimper when we break apart.

His fingers glide carefully inside me, and every time, it feels better than the last.

My head goes back in pleasure, my eyes closing, as my body gives a full-on shiver of pleasure.

"Motherfucker. You're already so damned wet, you're covering my hand in that sweet juice of yours."

"Please, Michael," I urge him, already close to orgasming.

"I'll give you what you want, Beauty. I'll make the ache stop, but then you're giving me what I want."

"To suck you?" I gasp.

He jerks his sweatpants down, not even bothering to take them off all the way. He picks me up by his hold on my hips. I cry out in surprise, grabbing hold of his shoulders to steady myself, as he positions me where he wants me. Once I'm steady, he pulls the nightshirt over my head and off my body. I'd be self-conscious about my body right now, because at a little over six months pregnant it's definitely bigger, but Michael never gives me the chance. He always makes me feel beautiful.

"We'll start with that," he agrees, "lower yourself down on my cock slowly, Beauty. Take it only until it's comfortable."

I look at him and his eyes are glued to our bodies. He's watching me slide his cock inside. His face is flushed with hunger, and he's so beautiful in this moment, I can't believe I'm the woman he chose. I never want to give this up—to give him up. I want to tell him, but I don't, I hold back. I'm still not sure what we are—or at least what I am to Michael. I only know one thing. *I love him.*

I lower myself, inch by painstakingly-slow inch, onto his cock, taking all of him in—despite his warning. I settle against him for a minute, letting myself adjust. His hand moves up and down my sides, petting me, giving me the time I need.

"I love the way you feel inside me," I confess, beginning to rock against him. His hands move from my sides to my ass and he squeezes me, hard. My breath catches at the erotic pull it has on me when he tugs the globes of my ass apart, so his fingers can play.

A moment later, I feel his thumb push against the tight ring of muscles. My pussy clenches his cock tightly as I increase the speed of my ride. *I love it when he plays with my ass.* He does it a lot. He seems fascinated with my ass, and I catch him staring at it all the time. There's times I find reasons to bend over in front of him, because I like to watch the look on his face. He keeps talking about me giving him my ass, but we haven't gone there. I've never done anything like that, but the longer I spend time with Michael, the more he talks about it… the more I want it. I get so lost in my thoughts that I slow the way I'm moving on Michael's cock. He puts his hands back on my hips and takes over the rhythm. His mouth captures my tit in his mouth—at least all he can fit of it. He slowly lets it go, but not before seizing the nipple between his teeth and biting hard. My body shakes as the pleasure and pain crash together. I feel more of my desire gather on his cock and run freely down his shaft. *I'm so close.*

"You're going to ride my cock until you come all over it," he says, the words rolling out of him in a way they reverberate on every nerve ending I have.

"If you insist," I tell him, trying to smile but gasping instead as on a downward glide, he rakes his cock against my walls.

"Then you're going to suck my cock clean. Aren't you, Beauty?"

I lick my lips thinking about it. If Michael is obsessed with my ass, then the same can be said about me and his cock. It's beautiful, wide and dark in color, veins throbbing along the underside and so long…I asked him how long once and he looked at me as if I was insane. *"I've never measured. What the fuck does it matter? It's long enough to get the job done."* I grin as I remember that.

"I'm going to suck you clean," I tell him, and get rewarded when he slides his fingers to my clit, giving me that little something extra. "Oh, fuck. Michael, I'm going to come," I warn him, knowing I won't be able to hold back at all now.

"Then do it, Beauty. Take all you want."

So I do…

CHAPTER 97

Beast

"DID VICTOR SAY what he wanted?" Hayden asks again, for maybe the tenth time.

"I told you, he didn't," I remind her, pulling into the diner's parking lot.

"Do you think he's heard from Blade?" she asks, worriedly, wringing her hands together in her lap.

I put my hand over hers, to stop before she manages to pull the skin off her hands. "What did I tell you?"

"Not to worry, you had it all under control," she says, rolling her eyes.

I swear the woman gets sassier and sassier as the days go by. What's amazing is that I like it…*I really like it.*

"Have you got everything you need packed?" I ask, trying to channel her mind elsewhere. It's taken me two weeks to convince her to go to the lake with me for a while. We were packing up and heading out when Victor called. There's been no word from Blade and it's frustrating. I'm busy trying to convince Hayden that Blade is probably on a beach somewhere in Mexico, but in my gut, I know he's not giving up that easily.

Victor feels much the same way I do. I actually do know what this meeting is about, but I don't want to worry Hayden, so I'm not telling her. We both feel that as long as Blade knows Victor is here, he's not going to make a move. It's time to rattle some cages and bring him out of hiding. Victor will be the one in charge of trapping the dog, my only focus is keeping Hayden safe, and I will do that. *Nothing and no one will get the chance to hurt her, ever again.*

"Yeah, it's packed, but right now might not be the best of times to go out of town, Michael."

"It's the perfect time," I argue, and it is—for a lot of reasons unknown to her.

I go around and help her from the truck, keeping her close to me as we walk into the diner. Victor is standing on the inside looking out the window. His two main henchmen are standing close to the door. Hayden is so tense that I rub her back, hoping to calm her.

"Hayden. It's good to see you again. How are you getting along?" Victor asks when he turns around, his weathered face and pale brown eyes almost friendly.

"I…I'm good. How are you Mr. Torasani?" Hayden answers, shyly. She walks over to shake the man's hand as he extends it.

"You seem nervous. There's no need to be, I assure you."

"I'm sorry. It's just…"

"It's okay, I understand," he tells her, not asking her to put her thoughts into words. He has to know how hard it is for her to meet with anyone. "Can we sit? I have a few things to discuss with you and Mr. Jameson."

"Is something going on we should worry about?" Hayden asks, and a deep blush blooms on her face, "I mean you know, besides the obvious and well everything…"

"Not at all my dear. I'm afraid I've been delaying my stay in North Carolina for too long. I have a business and other matters to attend back home."

"Oh…" Hayden whispers, and I know she's worried about Blade. She hasn't said much, but I know that she feels more comfortable with Victor and his men close by.

It should bother me that she doesn't think I can handle that asshole on my own, but it doesn't. Hayden hasn't had many men in her life that she can have faith in. I understand it. I only hope I don't end up letting her down like I have other people in my life who depended on me. For a split second, Annabelle's face flashes through my memories before fading. My hand trembles, the memories of my daughter are getting less and less…*clear*.

Hayden reaches over and grabs my hand. I have no idea if she saw it shake and is comforting me, or if it is to comfort her because of her nerves. Either way works, because her touch centers me, focuses me and keeps me from getting lost in the pain.

"As you know, when Charlotte left me, she wanted to come back here, because it's where she was born. She wanted me to go with her." He looks out the window before saying more. "She didn't understand my business, but now I find myself wishing I had tried things her way then," he says quietly, then he seems to mentally shake himself and continue. "Her sister worked at this diner, and Charlotte asked me for one thing and only one thing when she left. She wanted me to purchase the diner so that her sister would have job security. Sometimes, I think that's the only reason she kept running this place. It didn't make a lot of money, but she enjoyed it and the people that worked for her, became her family. Charlotte and I never had children. In my line of work, children are a weakness you can't afford."

Hayden's hand tightens in mine, and I notice she uses her

free hand to rub her stomach. "I'm sorry," she whispers.

"It is what it is, my dear. I'm an old man and for the most part, I've lived a good life. But, let us get back to the matters at hand. Charlotte left a will and you were named her sole beneficiary."

"Beneficiary? *Me?*"

"Exactly that. I'm afraid she didn't have a lot. She wouldn't take any of my gifts. But the diner and her home are both yours now."

"But…Why? What about her sister?"

"Her sister already has a home, and Charlotte only asked that you make sure her sister always had a job at the diner for as long as she wanted it, or it was in business. Truthfully, I have her sister set up on a trust fund. She doesn't need the money, but like Charlie, she prefers to work instead of doing nothing."

I don't think Hayden is truly listening to Victor at this point she's holding the manila envelope that Victor handed her and tears are falling down her cheeks. "I can't believe she did this," she whispers. "Michael, we have the diner now. I won't need to worry about finding a job!" she cries the last part out louder, as if it just hit her. I want to yell at her, I told her before she didn't have anything to worry about. I would be annoyed except she says *we have the diner*. She's *definitely mine* now—she's claimed *me*, even if she doesn't realize it.

"A job? Doesn't she realize the size of your holdings?" Victor questions, and I shrug. It doesn't surprise me that Victor had me investigated. I have my own folder on him.

"I guess not. Apparently, those things don't matter to some women."

"That's a gift, don't waste it," he says, and I think he gets lost in his memories of Charlie again. I could almost feel sorry for him.

Once all the conversation is done and Victor makes arrangements for Hayden to talk with his attorney, I walk her outside to the truck, and help her in.

"I can't believe that just happened. Just when I think life can't get any better it does," she says, as I click her seatbelt into place. I kiss her lips gently and way too briefly, resting my forehead against hers, taking in her scent, and enjoying it for a moment.

"I told you, Beauty. From here on out, you get nothing but good. So much good that there's no room for the bad."

Her hand comes up and she lets her fingers brush against the side of my jaw where the scars are more evident. The sense of touch there isn't as strong as it once was. There's a deadness now, but I can feel her touch still—soft, whispery, gentle and...*loving*. "You and Maggie are the best of everything, Michael. You're all the good I will ever need," she whispers.

I close my eyes and drink in her words, then I kiss her again. I lose myself in her taste and in the surety that even though she deserves better, I'm never letting her go.

CHAPTER 98

Hayden

"DO WE REALLY have to go back tomorrow?" I sigh. We're lying on the dock out from our rental, letting the sun heat the chill off our bodies, after swimming. We've been here four days, and it's four days that have been the closest to Heaven that I've ever experienced.

Michael captures my hand in his, giving it a squeeze. As is my habit, I find myself tracing the scar on his hand and enjoying the fact that I can touch him. Michael doesn't talk about his past, but I instinctively know that he doesn't let people close to him. The fact that he lets me this close means something—*means everything.*

"You're the one who says we have to go back. I say we move here. Live off the land, become hermits," Michael says.

I move so I can lean over his body and look down at him. "Live off the land? Michael, I am not eating Bambi," I warn him, doing my best to keep my voice and face serious.

"Okay. You can eat Thumper instead," he says, and I see a ghost of smile appear, though he keeps his eyes closed.

"No. Just no. Absolutely not." I shove at him, playfully.

"You'll get awful tired of fish. You'll give in. Besides, rabbit tastes just like chicken," he jokes.

"I'll believe you when I see a chain of Kentucky Fried Rabbit popping up everywhere. I do like fish though. The fish you fixed tonight smelled good," I tell him, still slightly pouting.

"I fixed you a hamburger," he defends, opening his beautiful eyes to look at me. A woman could get lost in those eyes.

"I wanted fish."

"You're pregnant," he says, shaking his head, mostly because he knows I'm only yanking his chain.

"It was mean to eat it in front of me though, Michael," I whine.

"You didn't deserve to eat it anyways," he says, and this time, he is full-on smiling.

"What do you mean by that?"

"*Oh Michael. I can't do that to the poor worm. Oh my God! It's wiggling!*" he says making his voice ridiculously high, or at least as high as he can get it with his injuries. He doesn't talk about it—at all, but I know it limits his voice range and use.

"Well, it was! You're the man. It was your job to bait the hook." I laugh. "My job was to catch the biggest fish, which I might remind you, *I did.*"

Michael surprises me by wrapping his hand in my hair and pulling my face closer to his. "You're one hell of a woman, Hayden Graham," he whispers, giving my lips a light kiss.

I want to stay like this. I never want this moment to end, but for whatever reason, I sense that Michael needs more laughter. It's my job to give it to him. Michael is as damaged as I am. Maybe more. He's only spoken about Annabelle once, but it was clear he loved her. The pain he must be carrying around inside…*I couldn't imagine.* Since we've been here at the lake he's laughed freely; he's laughed often. I want more of that.

Plus...well...*I'm just curious.*

"Hold that thought," I tell him, and I rise slowly to my feet, wrapping one arm protectively over my stomach as I do. I'm wearing a black, one-piece swimsuit. It's a bigger size than I normally wear, and you can definitely see the baby-bump. I was self-conscious at first, but Michael soon showed me that he thought I was beautiful.

"Where are you going?" Michael growls.

"I'll be right back! Don't move!" I order him.

"You get that cute ass back here, or I'll paddle it," he grumbles, and I smile.

My man does have a fascination with my ass. He's getting more and more vocal about all the things he wants to do to it, and I'm starting to wonder if I'm brave enough to let him try. Michael would never hurt me on purpose, but I can't imagine having his dick back...*there.* It would have to hurt...I mean Michael is so big. I make it to the boat we took out earlier, and reach down along the side of my seat. I hid something there earlier. My fingers reach it, and I quickly wrap it in my hand, then head towards Michael.

"Back!" I announce unnecessarily.

"What's that look on your face for, Hayden?"

"What do you mean?"

"You've got something up your sleeve," he answers, appraising me.

"Michael, you're being silly. I don't even have sleeves," I tell him, and like I hoped he laughs—*loudly.*

"You are always surprising me," he says, and there's an emotion on his face I can't read, but I like it. *I like it a lot.*

"That's good, right?" I ponder aloud.

"Yeah, Beauty. That's real, good."

"Then you probably owe me."

"Owe you?" he asks, and I'm pretty sure I see a guarded expression on his face. I want it gone, so I push forward—*quickly*.

"Strip, Michael."

"Strip?"

"Yep. Those trunks, lose 'em."

"Didn't I wear you out enough, earlier?"

"Are you going to whine? Or show me some flesh?"

"Are you going to return the favor?"

"Eventually," I tell him with a smile, relieved when he's back to laughing Michael. *Happy Michael.* I can't help but watch as he slides the trunks from his body. His body is tan, completely. *No tan lines for Michael.* He reminds me of chiseled stone, all perfection like a sculpture in a museum. "You're hard," I whisper, and I'm not embarrassed at all to admit I'm licking my lips.

"I seem to stay that way around you."

"Thank you?" I question, not knowing what else to say. That earns me another laugh. I drop to my knees in front of him, sliding my surprise under my leg. I reach out and use my thumb to stroke across the wetness on the broad, dark, head of his cock. "You're so beautiful."

"You talking to me or my dick?" he asks, and I gaze up at him and he's got this half-smile on his face. He's relaxed and he almost looks happy.

"Well both, but I will admit right now your dick is what is holding my attention."

"Since you're holding my dick and looking like you want to swallow him whole, I'm okay with that," he says softly—*smile still in place*. "Take your clothes off, Beauty," he commands, his voice dropping down to that husky timbre that always makes every feminine part inside of me clench with need.

"Umm…it's daylight," I tell him, without needing to. I mean the sun is shining down on us. *He knows it's daylight.* I stroke his cock once, holding it firmly in my hand. I tell myself I'm only doing it because I want him as hard and as excited as he can get, but truthfully, I can't *not* touch it.

"Does it look like that bothers me?" he asks me, incredulously.

"Well no, but we've already determined that you're beautiful. Me? I've never been that, and it just makes me uncomfortable for you to see me…for you to see my body in broad daylight. You know?"

"Hayden, you're the first woman I've let look at me in over six years," he responds. His answer is stated matter-of-factly. It's as if he is discussing the weather and not rocking my entire world.

"Michael," I start, but then I stop. I have no idea how to respond to that.

"You've seen my scars. Hell, you didn't stop nagging until you trimmed my hair and beard, just so you could see more of them. You know how horrible they look."

"But they don't. Michael, you must know you're beautiful. The scars are bad, but they don't detract from the way you look."

"There was a girl once. She was young, too young for me really, but she was sweet and up until the explosion, she…I could tell she wanted me," he says. He's not looking at me now. He's looking up at the sky. His admission sets off a funny feeling inside of me and if I had to name it, I'd have to say it is jealousy.

"What happened?"

"After the accident, I began to see less and less of her, but then…I wasn't exactly trying to see anyone. My brothers, they all tried to convince me I needed to quit hiding. That nothing had really changed. They were wrong, but I desperately wanted to feel normal again, inside. To be what I once was. So, I tried. I even started seeking the girl out," he tells the story, all without taking his eyes off the sky. He doesn't look at me, and I stay quiet, because I don't want him to stop. I want to hear the story, even as I hate hearing that there's another girl out there he likes. "There was a family picnic one day, and I overheard her and her friends discussing me."

"What did they say?" I ask, unable to stop myself and knowing that it couldn't have been good.

"She called me repulsive. A woman would have to be drunk to want me between her legs. That's when I decided to live up to the animal I had become," he says with a shrug, like what he told me didn't rip my heart to shreds. I wish I had this unknown woman in my reach right now. Pregnant or not, I'd wipe the floor with her. Of all the stupid, fucking bullshit she could utter…

"She's a cow."

"Hayden—"

"A freaking cow who doesn't have a brain in her freaking head. I can't believe that bullshit. If I'm with you and she's ever around Michael, you have to tell me. You have to tell me so I can throat-punch her. You are not repulsive. Jesus, sometimes when I look at you, I get so hot, I feel like I could spontaneously combust. I mean, I thought I'd never want another man for the rest of my life. I was content with that, but I don't know a woman alive who would not jump at the thought of having you in her bed. She's a blue-twat-waffle! And besides…" I stop when Michael's laugher rings out.

"A blue-twat-waffle?" he jokes, as his laughter subsides, but the smile remains.

"Well…*yeah,*" I shrug.

"Besides, what?" he asks and I look at him confused. "What else were you going to say?" he prompts again, and it feels like his eyes are boring into me.

"I mean, your scars, they're bad, I get that. But, I've seen worse and you aren't your scars. You were in the military; I know because I've seen the dog-tags you still wear. I had a friend whose boyfriend came back from Afghanistan and he lost his arm and his scars…*those* were horrific."

"Hayden—"

"But he was still the same man under them. My friend still loved him. They have struggles now they never planned on, but…none of those struggles are over the way he looks, or his body. Those things aren't who makes the person, Michael," I tell him, and he's silent for a bit. I can't tell what he's thinking.

"Then why are you worried, Beauty?"

"Michael—"

"You're not fat, Hayden. You're pregnant and you're fucking gorgeous. I think you know what you do to me, that shit just doesn't happen."

"Men get hard easily, Michael. You guys see a pair of boobs jiggling under a t-shirt and the jack-in-the-box pops out."

"Jack-in-the-box?"

"Those toys that you wind up and then this freaky clown jumps out at you. I used to have nightmares about those things. Who in the world thought that was a good idea is beyond me," I tell him, rattling like a fool. Our conversation has gone places I wasn't expecting and it has left me…*nervous.*

"Are you saying my dick reminds you a clown head waiting to scare you?" he asks, interrupting me.

"Not *yours.* I like *yours.* Your dick can pop out at me anytime," I explain, trying to smile.

"Good to know. Now strip."

"Michael—"

"Do it."

"You're very bossy." I reach behind my neck to let the strings loose and the top part of my bathing suit drops down. I catch it to stop from revealing my breasts.

Michael lets out a grunt, which quickly broadcasts the fact he is unhappy. I frown at him, and he frowns back. *He does it better.* I let it drop down. The warm sun hits my breasts, and the breeze in the air causes my nipples to contract. I bite my lip at the sensation. The further I get in my pregnancy, the more tender they become.

"More," he urges, his voice almost a groan.

Circling my hand around his dick again, it jerks in my hand, and one long stream of pre-cum slides down his shaft, over my fingers. I feel my own wetness gathering in response between my thighs. My clit literally pulsates. *God what this man does to me.* I shift on my knees and that's when I'm reminded of my original plan. It was a joke before, but now it feels like a good plan. I need to lighten Michael's mood, before he realizes how much I think that I might...*love him.*

"In a minute. I need to prove something first," I whisper, unable to stop myself from bending down, flattening my tongue against the head of his cock and licking some of the sweet liquid that has escaped. Then, I only suck the tip of his cock into my mouth, moaning as his pre-cum hits my tongue.

"Hayden, stop teasing me," he growls, when despite his urgings and reaction I don't suck him further in my mouth.

Instead, I pull away and reaching under my knee and grab the rolled up yellow material I've been hiding. A quick glance in Michael's direction reveals his eyes are closed. I unravel the measuring tape with a grin. I found it in a tackle box in the boat. It still had plastic over it and the numbers seemed to call at me.

I've always been a curious kind of girl.

"Oh my," I gasp, as I pull the tape along the hard shaft.

"What the hell are you doing?" Michael asks, but it isn't anger I hear. I look up and see shock written all over his face.

"I was trying to see if I really did catch the biggest fish?" I giggle.

"I...the biggest..." Michael's words are disconnected and his face is still incredulous. His mouth even hangs open for a second. Then he does something *I* didn't expect. He all but pounces on me, taking care to hold my back and head so I fall into his solid hold and he lays me gently on the wooden deck. He grabs each side of my bathing suit and pulls it from my body, so quickly it robs me of the breath I was taking.

"I wasn't finished. You should always double check your measurements," I whisper at the same exact time his fingers push inside of me. I should be embarrassed because of how wet I am. I'm soaked and you can actually hear the way his fingers thrust through my wetness.

"Fuck," Michael groans. "Always so wet for me," he adds.

I whimper as his fingers leave me, though he does skate them across my clit, causing my body to thrust towards him. Then he lowers himself over my frame and braces his weight on one arm. I stretch my legs out so I can cradle his body with my own.

"Hurry, Michael," I urge him, wanting nothing more than his cock inside of me.

"What happened to the shy, scared woman I first met, Hayden?" he asks, as the head of his dick slides against my clit.

I slowly open my eyes to see his head bent down. I look between our bodies to watch the firm hold he has on his dick and the way he's guiding it against my pussy, not entering it. Instead, he's choosing to tease me with his broad head, making me hunger for more. My hand moves down to encircle his, so we hold his shaft together. His eyes find mine, and together we guide him inside me.

"She finally started feeling safe," I tell him, and I know tears are in my eyes. I want to tell him I love him. I don't. Instead, I try to show him with my body.

"You are," he vows, and he proceeds to make love to me. Giving me his body slow and easy. He sinks into me, inch by delicious inch, his eyes never leaving mine. "I promise, you're safe, I'll give everything I can to keep you that way, Hayden."

"I just want you. Give me you, Michael," I tell him, honestly.

"I will. I'm going to give it all to you," he says, and I know realistically we're probably not talking about the same thing. I want more than just his body. But if his body is all I can have, I'll take it. He pulls his dick almost all the way out of me. My fingers bite into his ass, and I demand he comes back. True to his word, he gives it *all* to me.

All eleven, thick, beautiful inches.

CHAPTER 99

Beast

"YOU SURE YOU'RE feeling okay? We didn't overdo it, did we?" I ask Hayden, again.

She's been quiet the whole ride home. Things were a little intense on the dock. I lost myself in her body. Fuck, I always lose myself in her, but something shifted through our talk. Hayden revealed part of her soul to me. She's as beautiful inside as she is out, and even if I don't deserve her, I want her. *I need her.* Still, I'm always mindful of holding back with her, and I didn't this time. At one point, I could feel my cock pushing against her cervix. I know it had to hurt her. *Christ, what was I thinking?*

"Michael," Hayden whispers, putting her hand on mine.

I chance a look at her, before returning my eyes back to the road. I feel her fingers thread through mine, giving me that calm that always happens when we hold hands.

"What we did was perfect. I'm fine," she assures me. She brings our joined hands to her stomach, relaxing her hold on my fingers. "Maggie is fine," she adds. As if to prove it, I feel Maggie shift under our hands and a foot or hand shoves out against us. Hayden laughs. "See? More than fine."

"She's getting strong."

"She is. She's good. You need to stop worrying."

"You're quiet, Beauty."

"I didn't want to leave. I like the world better when it's just you, me, and Maggie," she confesses, and my heart trips in my chest, mostly because I completely agree with her.

"We can go back," I assure her, wishing now I had insisted we stay longer.

"No. There's a lot to do, and I really am looking forward to running the diner. I want to make Charlie proud."

"You will not work yourself to death, Hayden. I forbid it. You delegate that shit out, and you keep your feet up."

"My feet up?"

"Pregnant women's feet swell. It's a medical fact."

"You have to watch the road and can't see me, but just to let you know, I am totally giving you the *'you're crazy'* look right now."

"Whatever," I laugh, turning into our drive. I've done a lot of work on Hayden's home, but there's something we need to talk about. "Hayden, I've been thinking. I know you want a good place for Maggie, and I could fix your place up…but…"

"You think we should move into Charlie's?" she asks, her eyes looking out over the place she's called home.

"I do. It's a nice home. It's big with plenty of room for Maggie to grow. There's a nice yard and it's still private. I think it's what Charlie would have wanted."

"You're right. I've been thinking about it too. Plus, it's not tainted by my brother. It'd be like a fresh start."

"Exactly," I agree, squeezing her hand. I get out of the truck and walk around to let Hayden out. She's finally learned that I like to be the one to unbuckle her seatbelt and let her down, so she waits for me now. I like taking care of her, looking after her, and this is one more thing that helps with that.

"You'd go with me?" she asks, as I unbuckle her seatbelt. My head jerks up at her question. "I mean, I know you have the barn, and I know you just moved in the house while all the stuff with the Dwellers was going on. Plus, I mean Blade is still out there, but even if he wasn't, we haven't discussed things. It's just…I think it would be nice…*Okay not nice*, but—"

I kiss her quickly on the lips to keep her from talking until we're both old and gray. I think she could manage it when she gets nervous.

"Do you want me to live with you?"

"Well…*yeah*," she says, her eyes round and a touch of panic or fear in them.

"Just until Blade is caught?"

"No…I don't care about that. I mean, I want him caught, but…I just really like you, Michael. *A lot*."

"I like you too," I tell her, my chest growing tight at the admission. *Fuck*. I more than like her. I *crave* her. Until Hayden, I had forgotten how to breathe, and with her it feels like I'm learning to breathe all over again. *Fresh, clean air, untainted by the darkness inside of me.*

"So, will you live with me?" she asks shyly, her face blushing so bright it wouldn't surprise me if she glowed in the dark.

"Thought you'd never ask," I tell her, cupping her face in my hand. Our lips touch, and I catch the bottom one between my teeth, pulling on it teasingly and then sucking it back in my mouth before our tongues dance gently with one another. When we break apart her eyes open and her lips spread into a full smile. Her gray-silver eyes sparkle, maybe even brighter than the sun.

We walk hand in hand to the house. Once I have her settled,

I go back outside and collect our suitcases. I'm walking back to the kitchen door when my phone vibrates. I ignore it until I'm inside.

"What would you like for dinner, Michael? If you feel like firing up the grill we could barbeque. I have some chicken breasts in the freezer," Hayden asks, glancing at me over her shoulder.

"Doesn't matter," I answer with a shrug, putting the suitcases down on the floor. My phone vibrates again, and I frown, pulling it out of my pocket. I look down at the screen to see I have a text message from Skull.

"Chicken it is then. Let me go in the pantry and get the charcoal for you," Hayden says in the background, but my eyes are glued on the screen of my phone.

I know yesterday was hard for you, brother. Just remember we're here if you need us.
Skull.

His message confuses the fuck out of me. Yesterday was one of the best days I've had in my life. He's lost it. Beth has finally drove him mad. I start to shut my phone off when I notice it. The date. *The motherfucking date.*

I was sticking my dick in Hayden on my daughter's birthday. I was laughing and happy. I was feeling another child move and making plans. *On Annabelle's birthday.* I scream, clasping my hand so tight I can feel my phone give way. I throw it across the room, watching as it crashes against the window. I can see a crack form in the glass pane, as the phone falls to the floor in two pieces.

"Michael? Oh my God, Michael, are you okay?" Hayden comes running back in, her eyes wide with fright.

I look at her and she disgusts me. *This is her fault.* She made me want to…*Fuck!* Who am I trying to kid? This is me. This is all my fault. Hayden's only another mistake in a long line of mistakes. I spin around, stomping outside without a word. I hear Hayden follow me. "Michael!" she cries.

I ignore her, jumping in my truck, and back out of the driveway, all without looking back. *I need a damn drink.*

CHAPTER 100

Blade

I WATCH AS Beast leaves the bar. It'd be so easy to end him right now. There's no one here watching his back. So easy. Even now, I have him in my gunsights, and his guard is down enough, he has no idea. He's not drunk yet, but if the bottles he's carrying are any indication, he will be soon enough. It'd be so easy... *too easy.*

He needs to suffer for getting into my business. He needs to suffer and bleed. He has a weak spot for Hayden. Somehow, he's even managed to get that fucking Torasani to work with him. They have her place surrounded tonight. I thought I was home free when I saw Beast take off and leave Hayden alone. Then I saw one of the Torasani henchmen, walking the perimeter of her house. I did some digging and there are four men around her house. *Four.* Fucking cunt must have developed some new tricks in bed to get Beast to guard her that well. Shit. Maybe she's spread her legs for old Victor himself. That'd make more sense. I always thought Hayden was as stupid as her brother, but maybe the bitch has more brains than I gave her credit for.

It doesn't matter—none of it. They'll slip up soon and that's when I'll have my opening. At first, it was only to teach Hayden a lesson. She's made a fool of me all these years. Bitch hid the fact she was knocked up and then used my enemies to try and stay out of my reach. The bullshit I got from that, even from my own men. Now, however, it's something *bigger*.

I have revenge to dish out. I've lost my family. I've lost my club. It's all Hayden's fault. I'll make her wish for death. I'll make her beg for it, before I give it. I might keep Beast alive to witness it. His death can hurt Hayden more if she watches. I bet the little cunt will beg for his life. I wonder how Beast will like watching Hayden suck my cock in exchange for letting him breathe? The thought makes my dick hard. I unzip my pants and take my shaft in my hand and stroke myself, watching Beast jump in his truck.

Yeah. I need to take my time and make my revenge perfect…and enjoy every fucking second of it.

CHAPTER 101

Hayden

MICHAEL NEVER SHOWED back up. I waited and waited, but there's been no sign of him. I finally gave up, and went to bed. I tossed and turned, but I must have eventually passed out, because now the bedside clock reads three in the morning. I lay here listening, stupidly getting depressed when I hear nothing. Michael's not here. *I had hoped…*

It's all so frustrating, and I have no idea what happened. I thought everything was good and then…*it just wasn't.* For a minute—right before he left, it looked like he hated me. I've gone over everything, and I have no idea what's going on. It's driving me crazy. I was worried it was me, and my first instinct was to cry. Then, I got worried something else was going on and my nerves were set on end, as panic filled me. Finally, I settled into anger again. He could have at least told me what was going on. Anger is the emotion that I'm keeping with me now. I don't know where he is, I don't know if he's okay and most of all…*I don't know if he'll be back*. It's not like my track record is great with men, but I thought this time Michael was one of the good guys. *Maybe those men don't exist.*

I ease out of bed. I'm still a little sore from the workout that Michael gave me yesterday. Yesterday seems like a lifetime ago. The house feels weird with no one here. It's had so many people in it lately, that's become the new normal. Michael not being here makes it feel really lonely—as empty as I am feeling. I also can't lie; I've been scared to death that Blade will show up when I'm alone. I've kept my mace close by, and I've managed to curse Michael for taking my gun away.

If my mind doesn't change, I'm going to use the mace on him. *If I ever see him again.* I make it into the kitchen to get a glass of water. I can't help but look across the drive at the old barn. The lights are out, but I notice Michael's truck is parked under it and his bike too. *He's back.* He's back and he didn't come here. He didn't even let me know. He went back to the barn. *What does that mean?*

I should probably let it go for the night. That would be the smart thing to do, but then when it comes to men, I've never been that smart. I grab a flashlight off the counter, slip my feet into some flip-flops and walk over there. I hear the frogs in the background, and somewhere in the distance, I can hear a dog barking. I should get a dog. They're more dependable than a man. A mean, junk-yard dog, maybe I could name him Beast and when he would do something I hate, I could put him outside with only dry dogfood.

I point the light up the narrow stairs that lead to the barn loft. My body freezes because I hear a sound from behind me. It sounds like a stick breaking, as if someone stepped on it and it snapped. I whip the light around to look behind me, expecting to see Blade standing there. I know it. I can literally feel him there. *Shit.* I hope I get the chance to tell Michael I hate him. I don't…but I want him to think I do if he gets me killed.

My heart is beating in my chest so hard it feels like a jackhammer. My palms are wet and my nerves are stretched. Even Maggie, who is usually asleep by now, is moving and kicking nervously. Probably feeding off my energy. *"Maggie, girl, your Momma's an idiot,"* I murmur to her. I zig-zag the beam of the light, but thankfully I see nothing out there. I'm only imagining things. It was probably an animal. I've seen quite a few opossums out here. They stir mostly at night. Trying to calm my nerves, I walk up the stairs. I cringe as they squeak underneath me because the sound seems abnormally loud.

"Michael?" I whisper, my voice cracking. I clear my throat again, right as I make it to the top step. "Michael?" I try again, using the beam of my light to look through the room. I am about ready to give up when I see him. He's lying on his stomach, on the couch. His legs are hanging off it a good two foot. One hand is under his chin and the other is holding a bottle that's sitting on the floor. I lower the light to it and the amber color gives way to what the liquid inside is. I swallow, beating down the fear. I don't like men who are drunk. I've seen what can happen when they are. *I've experienced some of it.* I'm about to turn around and leave, when Michael's voice stops me.

"What are you doing here?" he asks, his voice slurring the words, but I still understand them. He doesn't sound mean, maybe drinking doesn't affect him like it can others.

"I was worried about you," I confess, "I wanted to see if you're okay," I add, feeling stupid. I wanted to come over here and yell and scream at him, but after seeing him, I can't. He seems so broken, so lost, lying there like that. Whatever is going on with him, is much bigger than him being upset with me.

"I'll never be okay again," he says, and the sadness in his voice is so thick and heavy it could almost choke me.

Forgetting to be scared, or even angry, I walk to him. I move the bottle out of his hand, putting it out of the way. Then, I kneel down, taking his now empty hand and holding it with both mine. I don't say anything. Honestly, I'm not sure what to say. I'm surprised when he doesn't jerk his hand away.

"What are you doing here, Hayden?" he mumbles, moving his head to the side so he can see me.

I've placed the flashlight on the floor and the beam is shining across the room, so our faces are still mostly hidden in the darkness, and I'm glad. I don't want him to see the pity in my eyes, I know he wouldn't like it. Besides, it's not truly pity for him, as much as I'm hurting inside at the look of pain on his face.

"You shouldn't be here."

"I was worried about you," I whisper, lost on how to deal with this. He promised so much. *Was I stupid in believing his words? What is going on with him*? "Michael, we're…I mean, I've grown to care for you. You had to know you would worry me. I thought we were in a relationship here."

"I'm not a man who can do relationships, Hayden. I'm not him. *I'm not really Michael*," he breathes, his eyes closing.

What do I say to that?

What does he even mean?

"Who are you really?" I dare to ask, afraid of his response.

"I'm no one. Not a person. An animal. That's me. I'm not ever going to be the person I was in my past, Hayden," he says, his eyes still closed, but somehow sounding more alert. "The person I used to be, I'll *never* be that man again."

"If you wanted to be, you could," I encourage him. I don't understand what's going on here, all I really know is the Michael that he's been showing me is the man I love. *He's the man I don't want to lose.*

"All I want now is to be left alone. Why can't you leave me alone? Why won't you let me die in peace?" he questions, and his eyes flutter open to stare at me accusingly.

"I don't know…I just can't seem to stay away," I tell him, truthfully, and because my nerves are increasing, I find my thumb, rubbing back and forth on the largest scar on his hand. It might be my imagination, but it feels like he tightens his hold on me, as if he is welcoming my touch.

"Then I'll destroy you too, Hayden. I destroy everything. Everything I touch, that I care about. I *destroy*."

His words make me hurt. Is he going to tell me about Annabelle now? I want to know. I want to help him. If ever a man needed help, it would be Michael right now. I reach up and kiss his forehead, forgetting my own anger in the face of his despair, and I give him honesty again. *Big honesty. Honesty that could truly destroy me.*

"I wasn't much before you came into my life, Michael. You helped me learn to breathe again. To appreciate life. *I love you.* The only way you could destroy me, is if you leave."

Michael's body stiffens. He growls under his breath and his hand tightens to bruising force. Maybe I said too much, but the words are out there, hanging between us and damning me. I can't call them back. All I can do is hang on and see what Michael does next.

CHAPTER 102

Beast

"SHUT UP," I growl, the alcohol numbing my brain enough to dull some of the pain, but I know what she said. *She has no right to say it.*

"Michael—"

"What we do with each other has nothing to do with *love*, Hayden. I gave you my dick. *It's just fucking*," even as I say the words, I regret them. I regret them because it looks like each sentence wounds her.

Her hand flinches within my hold and still, like an asshole, I don't let go. I want her to hurt. I want her to hurt like I do. *I need someone else to feel the pain I feel inside—to know the agony of your soul being destroyed.*

"Then why did you promise me more? Why did you even bother making me believe in you?" she asks, her voice quiet—*too quiet.*

"I didn't promise anything," I lie, wanting her to leave. Wanting her to just leave me alone to rot. She jerks her hand hard, but for some reason, I still don't let go.

"What was that you were saying? How you'd make sure I

have nothing but good memories? So many good ones there's no room for the bad ones? Wasn't that it, Michael? What was that? Was it all just bullshit?" she cries, and she pulls on her hand again, and when I still don't loosen my hold she screams at me. "Let me go!"

"What is it you want me to say? That I shouldn't have said those things? I shouldn't have! It's your fault! You look at me with those eyes, you make me want things I shouldn't want, need things I have no business needing. You make me forget when I shouldn't! *I can't forget*! Damn you, Hayden you make me want to live again!"

"What's wrong with that? I don't understand! Why are you so mad at me? What did I do? One minute, we're discussing dinner and the next minute, you just walk out the door without a word. *Why, Michael?* What did I do?" she cries again. There are tears gathering in the corner of her eyes, so thick that I can see them, even in the dim light.

"I told you! *You made me forget!*" I growl at her, jumping off the couch and all but pushing her away. When I make it about three or four steps away, I shake my head to try and ward off the dizzy feeling that overcomes me.

Hayden wobbles on her knees, falling on her side, but catching herself with her hands. Even in my drunken state, guilt hits me.

"Forget what?" she asks, her voice shaking, and I don't know if it's from fear of me, or just being upset. Either way, I know I'm to blame and I hate it. It's one more thing to add to my list of failures.

"Just go home, Hayden," I tell her, so tired I feel it in my bones.

"Forget what?" she literally screams, rising up to her feet. She slaps the wall and flips the light switch on. The harsh light causes me to squint as my eyes adjust, and as I focus on Hayden, I realize exactly what emotion she's dealing with—anger and it's directed all at me.

"Annabelle!" I scream back, tired of thinking, tired of hurting, tired of *everything.*

"That's why you're upset?" she asks, and I close my eyes as a wave of dizziness takes over.

"Yes," I mutter weakly, and I think I'm swaying on my feet. I feel Hayden's hands on my stomach and back, and I look to my side and she's standing there trying to guide me to a seat. I stumble, doing my best to remain on my feet. Finally, I give in and throw myself into the chair.

"How do I make you forget Annabelle? I don't understand, Michael," she says, her voice softer. She stands over me, and I look at her and the pain and guilt I feel over Annabelle and for Hayden all collide.

Enough. I've simply had enough. *How much is one man supposed to withstand?*

"Yesterday was my daughter's birthday, Hayden. Yesterday was her birthday, and instead of remembering her, instead of trying to hold onto her, I didn't even think about her. Not one thought. Instead, I was losing myself in you, in your body."

"Your daughter?" she whispers stunned. "Michael—"

"You think you want a life with me, Hayden? You don't even know me. I'm no better than, Blade."

"Bullshit, you can never make me believe that, Michael. I…Oh God, honey, I didn't realize you lost a child, but you can't stop living. You're here. You have to live."

"I don't. I don't deserve to live."

"Of course you do. Annabelle would want you to live," she says, and in this moment, I could truly despise her.

"Live? What for, Hayden? So I can pretend to be happy? To

make a life using you and your daughter to fill up the emptiness that is slowly eating me up inside? Because that's all I've been doing, and I think it's clear that's not working."

"You…You…are you saying you're using me and Maggie? I won't believe that, Michael. What we shared together…it's not a lie. It can't be. You're not *that* kind of man. You wouldn't do that," she argues—defending me. *It's time to show her everything.*

I shake my head and the room spins. "You think you know so much about me, don't you, Hayden?"

"I know you're a good man," she tells me, and the belief in her words is so strong it resonates in her voice.

It hurts me to hear her faith in me, and I feel the need to lash out. To unleash the darkness so she sees the real me—the Beast.

"A good man?" I scoff. "You're lying to yourself, Hayden. I dealt in death as a member of the Blaze. I didn't even blink dealing out our form of justice."

"Michael, I know enough about the club life to know what goes on. I also know that you're nothing like Blade and his men. You aren't evil. You wouldn't murd—"

I cut her off, not wanting to listen to her defend me any longer. "I killed my own daughter, Hayden. No one else. I'm the reason my daughter isn't alive. *Me.* Do you understand now? Do you finally see it? Do you realize the *monster* you let between your legs? I'm worse than Blade, I'm your worst fucking nightmare," I tell her, then I lay my head back, close my eyes, and wait for the sound of her footsteps taking her away from me. Footsteps that will leave me alone.

Just like I deserve.

CHAPTER 103

THE SOUND OF the footsteps never come. I open my eyes slowly and see her standing in front of me, her arms crossed at her chest, staring down.

"I told you to leave," I growl like a spoiled child. *Why is she still here? Why won't she leave?*

"There's nothing you can say, Michael, that will make me believe that you killed your child. Nothing," she answers, and I hate her. She looks so absolute in her stance, standing there, speaking down to me. *I hate her.*

"Because I'm such a good person," I half-laugh, keeping contempt so thick in my voice she flinches.

"You are. You can say whatever you want, but I know it in my heart. You wouldn't use me or my daughter. You care about us," she whispers so innocently.

It's time for the monster to make an appearance. "Was I such a good moral person when I grabbed the arms of your dead brother and pulled him out of the basement he'd been chained up in like a dog?" I ask, as if I am discussing the weather. I look at her with all the self-hate I have boiling inside of me.

Her gasp tells me that my aim was true. She trembles as she deals with the body blow I just delivered.

I allow a smile to contort to my face, one full of cynicism. "He'd been chained up in that fucking basement for a year. *Fuck*, a lot longer, really. I only knew about it for a year, and I did nothing to stop his torture, nothing to help him. I used to lay awake at night, and I'd get hard imagining the pain he was enduring."

"Michael—"

"When Skull finally cut him down and fucking let him draw his last breath, I was disappointed. Your brother was such a sick, bloody mess, he was unrecognizable. He was a bag of fucking bones and most of those were broken."

"You're lying! Why are you saying this stuff?" What is wrong with you? *Stop it!*"

"Stop? But don't you want to know where your brother is buried?" I rub my beard.

"You…you know?"

"Know? Who do you think put him there?"

"Michael," she cries, and she looks so small and innocent standing there, her arms hugging her body as if to ward off more pain.

I should let it go, but I don't. I need to make sure I drive her away. "There's no cemetery for you to visit though. There's not a bench in sight that you could sit on and feel the breeze in your hair, while you talk with your brother. You'll never have that, Hayden, and do you want to know why?"

"No," she whispers, pleadingly. "Michael, stop this. You're not this man, please…*Don't do this*," she begs, her breath and tears both coming harder and faster.

I should listen, but I don't. "Because I threw him in the ground, in a hole big enough to bury two of him. I poured in chemical after chemical on his body. Then I watched as he literally rotted before my eyes. Want to know what I did then, Hayden?"

"No..."

"But you need to know, since you think I'm such a *good* person. When it was all done, I spit on him."

"Michael..."

"And because that still wasn't enough, I took a piss on him before we finally covered him up."

"I can't. I can't hear this anymore," she whispers, turning to leave.

"It still didn't help, not until Skull and I decided to build an outhouse over his damn grave. I can't tell you the times I literally took a shit on your brother, Hayden, and I loved every fucking second of it. Hell, Skull still does it. *Every. Fucking. Day.*"

That does it.

I hear her literally run down the stairs, the door below slamming behind her.

She's gone.

It's finished.

That should make me feel better.

It doesn't.

The Conclusion Will Be Coming Next Month.

Be on the lookout for Book 2: Beauty.

A NOTE FROM THE AUTHOR

Dear Readers:

I hope you aren't cursing me too loudly. I really didn't want to make this book into a cliffhanger. I didn't! I fought it. There were several spots I could have stopped, but I kept going. This is the largest book I've written to date. But after that last meeting with Hayden and Beast, there was just no easy way to reconcile the gulf between them. These characters are emotionally damaged. They had to take their time getting together and they have hurdles that realistically can't be made into a happily ever after, easily. I hope you'll stick around for part two. Pre-Orders should already be up, and if not will be shortly. Thank you for your continued support. Thank you for letting me tell the stories that grow in my heart.

Xoxo
J

OTHER AVAILABLE TITLES BY JORDAN

Savage Brothers MC:

Breaking Dragon

Saving Dancer

Loving Nicole

Claiming Crusher

Trusting Bull

Devil's Blaze MC

Captured

Burned

Released

Shafted

Beast

Beauty (Coming Soon)

Lucas Brothers Series

Perfect Stroke

Raging Heart On

Happy Trail (Coming Soon)

Works Written Under the Pen Name

Baylee Rose

Unlawful Seizure

Unjustified Demands

LINKS

Want to keep up on all the latest happenings? Here's my social media links! Make sure you sign up for my newsletter. I give things away there and you get to see things before others! I also have a blog on my webpage you can subscribe to and besides my strange ramblings I'll update you on my work in progress and other nifty things there! (She said nifty—she might be old).

Newsletter:
www.jordanmarieromance.com/subscribe

Facebook Page:
www.facebook.com/JordanMarieAuthor

Twitter:
twitter.com/Author_JordanM

Webpage:
jordanmarieromance.com